MURCHESTON

The Wolf's Tale

MURCHESTON

The Wolf's Tale

DAVID HOLLAND

A TOM DOHERTY ASSOCIATES BOOK
NEW YORK

This is a work of fiction. All the characters and events portrayed in this novel are either fictitious or are used fictitiously.

MURCHESTON: THE WOLF'S TALE

Copyright © 2000 by David Holland

This book is printed on acid-free paper.

A Forge Book
Published by Tom Doherty Associates, LLC
175 Fifth Avenue
New York, NY 10010

www.tor.com

Forge® is a registered trademark of Tom Doherty Associates, LLC.

Design by Lisa Pifher

Library of Congress Cataloging-in-Publication Data

Holland, David.
     Murcheston : the wolf's tale / David Holland.
         p.   cm.
     "A Tom Doherty Associates book."
     ISBN 0-312-87213-5 (alk. paper)
     1. Werewolves—England—London—Fiction. 2. London
(England)—Fiction. I. Title.
     PS3558.O3482 M87 2000
     813'.54—dc21   99-055052

First Edition: February 2000

Printed in the United States of America

0 9 8 7 6 5 4 3 2 1

To Gwendolyn, my wife,
who makes me want to be good.
And to Mary Kate, my daughter,
who makes me want to be great.

Preface

There once was a custom among novelists, a sort of gentle address, a polite bow before the raising of the curtain. Though much honored still, its practice is sadly neglected. The curtain has hardened this past century into a wall. The human voice of the storyteller is supplanted by a call for greater Realism, as though some Reality exists to be measured outside of ourselves. Measured by whom? According to what yardstick?

And so this custom has faded from the pages of novels. I think it a custom worth reviving. It is a civil custom, and these are uncivil times. A patient custom for a hurried age. A warm hearth and a welcoming hand extended on a cold, cheerless night.

Allow me, therefore, my conceit, Gentle Reader, to proffer you these words of welcome. The hearth is blazing. There is a kettle on the fire, and the story waits upon your good company. Without, the wind howls and passions rage. It may be, before we are finished, you and I, that passions will rage within as well. But for now, relax, sip your cup of tea and listen to my tale. And when I am through, we may go our separate ways into the world. Perhaps to meet again sometime, before another hearth, over another tale.

—D. Holland
February 2000

Book One

1

The Legacy

I have a tale."

Standing in a lofty corner of the city of London, past a lofty park, down a lofty lane, at a truly estimable and lofty address, a building, proud and disdainful, cast the shadow of its cold face across the common paths of men. A capacious, ancient, crafty-looking old monument, it possessed the very air of a structure which, if it could have said anything it liked to every soul who walked beneath its unwelcoming facade, would have said nothing at all. So contemptuous an attitude was not merely an expression of satisfied complacence with its own imposing architecture, but a concrete reflection of the bland superiority affected by such powerful lords and titled industrialists as passed in and out of its portals throughout the year. This haughty pile suffered the comings and goings of these eminent figures as something unrelated to its own purpose, confirmed in the belief that mankind existed for the building and not the building for men.

A character of general disaffection was equally apparent in the peculiar atmosphere surrounding the place, which was always colder and heavier than the prevailing air, as if the building were some infernal machine wholly capable of manufacturing its own climate. This singular property was proof against the sultriest of summer days, and on a blustery winter's evening (of which the present was an example), there is little doubt but that the Supreme Intelligence of the Weather found his work in this part of the city made easier by the presence of such a Palace of Ice as this.

While it might be argued that the primary purpose of this building was to numb the blood of humanity to insensitivity, it was generally agreed that its secondary work was to accommodate the Gabriel Club. For the better part of two centuries, since the glorious days of the second Charles, the Gabriel had beckoned the pride and wealth of British society to its spaciousness: to dance in its tall and icy ballroom, to dine in its high and frigid halls, to seek warmth at its impressive (though largely ornamental) hearths, and generally to cultivate that frosty attitude toward the rest of the human race that the building itself affected.

"I have a tale." The words hung frozen in the air.

On this particular evening, the drifting snows and sharp winds had deposited a weblike rime across the face of the Gabriel, blurring and obscuring the old building so that it seemed to be covered with a veil of its own cold nature. The only feature of the place that could be recognized through this shroud was the figure of Gabriel himself, a stony, hard-cut angel hovering, wings outspread but still, above the entrance. He held a long and stately horn just inches from his lips and seemed about to lay such a note upon the world as men had been waiting to hear for some time. He was frozen in the very act, however, so that the music which might have emanated from that celestial instrument to shake the ice from the bleakest corners of this realm was silenced.

Notwithstanding the lateness of the hour and the inclemency of the weather (which the members might have been excused from noticing, acclimated as they were to the Club's own chilling demeanor), the ceaseless activity of men of the highest standing—up halls and down halls, in doors and out doors—created a general impression of busyness throughout the Gabriel. In the study, the conservatory, the smoking room, even in the library, the sound of discourse played throughout the Club like the music of the spheres, creating a single hum of noise. Had there been but half so much listening as there was talking going on, a great deal might have been learned this night.

"I have a tale." The last echoes reverberated weakly about the room and died.

The harmonic center of this oratorio was the Trophy Room, a smoky, darkly paneled chamber whose walls were decorated in funereal fashion with the grinning heads of a menagerie of wild animals. Here, among the physical proof of so many battles waged and won by man over beast, the young gallants of the Club adjourned after dinner to tell again their tales of hunt and chase, conquest and adventure. One tale in particular, a current favorite of the present company, involved a ferocious Bengal tiger who only in the past year had taken up residence at the Gabriel, and was snarling now from his perch above the fireplace, glaring down at the very fellow who had sponsored his membership. This courageous young gentleman had just finished narrating, for perhaps the third time in the past month, the details of the animal's demise, much to the delight of the enthusiastic crowd.

Yet the delight of a mere instant before had already passed away, and an unexpected hush settled over the merry proceedings of the Trophy Room. Some dozen or so young blades, until recently draped about the furniture with a languid ease, were now all upright attention. They stared, some in amusement, some in surprise, some in actual disbelief with eyes wide and mouths agape, at a large though unprepossessing figure standing slightly apart from the rest in what might have been considered dangerous proximity to the fire burning in the hearth. The silence, as ponderous as the stillness following a thunder clap, lasted for but a moment, when a dapper fellow, a thin, pale young man with limp whiskers and a decidedly mouselike appearance (he, in fact, who had killed the tiger), addressed the large man by the fire. "What was that?" he asked disinterestedly.

"I have a tale." The voice was deep and clear, filling the room easily. The voice's owner was the senior of every man there by at least three decades, giving him a paternal aspect offensive to some present.

"Sir Charles, is it not? Sir Charles Meredith?" the mouselike man continued, looking not at the fellow he was addressing but about him at the larger audience, in response to which several heads bent down to several other heads and inquired, "Meredith?" while the latter answered with the words, "Wine merchant."

"At your service, Lord Whitby." The old gentleman bowed.

"Indeed," Whitby joked easily, "if the damnable claret they serve here gets any cloudier, I hope you might be," at which the company laughed heartily, regaining that composure which was so sorely tried by this interruption.

When the laughter had subsided, Whitby returned his drowsy eyes to Meredith. "So you have some adventure to share with us, for the amusement of the company?" he asked. "Very good of you, I daresay."

"An adventure?" Meredith repeated, pulling himself up as one finally embarked on a journey long anticipated. "No, I shouldn't call it an adventure. It is more of a confession."

"Better still!" Whitby smiled, small pointed teeth peeking out from between his mustache and his thin lower lip. "But really now, what could you possibly have to confess, a man of your humble, I mean to say, your irreproachable character? Have you been pricing your wine more dearly than you ought?" and a chuckle passed across the room.

Meredith looked sharply at the young company about him. "Every man has a confession to make, humble though his life may be. Each brilliant day has its shadow. As for the amusement of the company, that's a charge for which I cannot be held responsible. My tale is not designed to amuse."

"You intrigue me, Sir Charles," Whitby admitted. "You shock us all into silence by announcing your intention to tell a story, and immediately state that your story will not amuse us. A suspiciously doomed tale, I think."

"Not doomed, Your Lordship. Let us say fated. After all, it cannot help seeming dull following your own amazing exploit. To stand above the prostrate body of your wounded porter and unload both barrels into the tiger's breast as it rushed you, giving no thought at all to your own peril, it's more than most men can comprehend. Such coolness in the face of a horrible end almost defies belief."

"But really, Sir Charles," Whitby said, ignoring the remarks, which made him feel somehow uncomfortable, "you shouldn't begin in this manner. You've offered us a tale yet begun with an apology. Charge manfully into the thing, old fellow, and be damned to these prologues." He glanced about him at the smiling faces ready to pounce upon this homely story, prepared to derive their own cruel amusement from it. "Begin now with, 'Once upon a time.'"

The laughter died down as Meredith stood coolly before them. "No, that won't do," he said matter-of-factly, as though to himself. "This tale is not for the ears of the company. It's for you alone."

A hush embraced the room. "For me?" Whitby exclaimed. "You wish to make your confession to me?" and he felt more uncomfortable yet, and decidedly put out at this strange fellow who had invaded their domain.

"Yes," was all the old man replied.

This was too much, Whitby considered, and he determined to put a stop to it at once. Yet when he searched for some cutting remark he might make to reduce Meredith in the face of the others, some off-handed insult to send the old wine seller on his way, he found that his wits failed him. He looked into the eyes of the fellow standing there beneath the tiger, but the words would not come. "I don't see why I should be so singularly graced with your attentions?" was all he could manage, with a sharp and petulant air. "Who am I to you, or you to me for that matter?"

"Who are you?" Meredith answered. "You are Lord Whitby, only son of the fourteenth Duke of Darnley, heir to a vast estate and, if my information is accurate, very soon to come into your title and inheritance. As we speak, your father lies upon his deathbed."

"Yes, well," Whitby stammered, "anyone might learn as much from the daily press."

"And you are here, with your friends."

A wave of disaffection passed slowly over the gentlemen, and several eyes turned to Whitby in anticipation of some riposte. They had, in fact, been toasting the ill health of the old duke not half an hour before, though whether Meredith had been present among their company then, no one could be certain, least of all Whitby. The young lord and duke-to-be glared at the old man, but found his anger checked, like a recusant schoolboy before the headmaster, stifled by the honest silence of his accuser.

"I can see you are reluctant to give me a hearing," Meredith went on. "Very wise of you, of course. 'Who am I?' you wish to know." The old fellow shrugged his shoulders. "I am not at liberty to tell you all of who I am, not yet. But I will tell you this much. I am in possession of something that is yours," and Meredith's eyes clouded over as he spoke, and his voice dropped to a whisper. "A legacy, if you will, a part of your history that you do not know." Reaching into his waist-coat pocket, he pulled out a length of ribbon from which hung a small key.

"What the hell is that?" Whitby uttered, trying a laugh but managing only a cough.

"It goes with a box—a box that has been in my possession these thirty years and more." Meredith dangled the key before him as though it were a child's plaything. "The box goes with the tale, and both of them I would give to you tomorrow. In private."

Whitby glanced nervously about. All eyes were upon him, waiting impatiently for his decision. To refuse would be to lose an ounce of that command he held over his companions. Yet to accept the bargain laid before him by this old devil, who was even then winding him about in some dark trap—the thought of it touched a cold, empty place deep within Whitby, and he shuddered.

"Very well, sir," he answered at last, with an icy precision. "I accept your conditions. And gentlemen," he said, addressing the company, "I invite you all on the evening following to hear me relate this wonderful confession. I daresay it will amuse us no end, and for quite a long time to come," and he looked meaningfully at Meredith.

The two men agreed to meet the next afternoon at the Club, and it was time passed anxiously by Whitby. He felt grave misgivings at this appointment, though he could not say why he should be so doubtful about the business. It was in all likelihood some senile folly of the old man's, he kept telling himself. He passed most of the next day making casual inquiries about Meredith, yet no one seemed to know anything concerning the man, outside of his professional character. He was a highly reputable tradesman, having taken a modest wine firm left him by his father and turned it into one of the largest interests in the nation. Most of the bottles in most of the cellars throughout the city had passed through his hands, and yet very few people knew anything about the man. Even at the Club, where he had been a member for over twenty years, he was known for his quiet ways, keeping always to himself, eating his meals in solitude. It was generally believed that he had been married, that he had no children, and that his wife had passed away some time ago. Other than this, no personal details of his life seemed to exist, at least, none that had attracted anyone's interest.

And yet there must be more to the man than this. Whitby prided himself on being up to any gambit, but this walking cipher, this nonentity, less than a shadow drifting through the halls of the Club, had played him for a simpleton, and quite skillfully at that, baited and lured him along as a fish might be until there was no choice left but to accept the hook or lose face among his companions. Was it the man's advanced years, or something else that made Whitby feel like a babe in his presence, a green youth unable to command his own destiny? As the hour of their assignation approached, therefore, Whitby was keenly aware of a nervous agitation rising within him, a sense of being carried along on a rushing current he could not control, and he secretly harbored the sincerest wish that Meredith might fall prey to some calamity before their appointment arrived.

Arrive it did, however. When Whitby stepped through the doors of the Club at just past five, a full three-quarters of an hour before their rendezvous, he found Meredith waiting for him. The old man wore a heavy, black topcoat against which he clasped what appeared to be a parcel tied up in brown paper and twine. As Whitby approached, Meredith smiled that sly smile of his and offered his hand. "I can see we are both anxious for this to begin," he admitted.

Whitby shook hands with a stiff formality, looking conspicuously at the parcel, which was about the size of a book, or perhaps several books. "I must say, I am rather more anxious for it to be over," he said.

Meredith bowed slightly, acknowledging Whitby's awkward position with a graciousness that startled the younger man. "Follow me, then," Meredith bid him. "It's not far, but the way can be difficult if you're not familiar with it," and they were off.

Since their previous interview, the weather had turned even frostier and more formidable, and snow was again falling over the city in great, lazy flakes that adhered to everything, masking all under a soft, white coverlet. Notwithstanding this arctic landscape, the traffic of men and women hurrying home from their days' businesses was little affected by the weather, and the crush of the crowd was so great that it forced the two travelers to thread their way in single file, the larger man creating a path with his more massive bulk while the smaller came up wearily behind. To a casual observer they looked like nothing so much as a mummer's version of Good King Wenceslaus and his page.

The streetlamps now resembled bright smudges in the dark, wintry night, offering slight illumination to the pedestrians scurrying past with heads pressed down and collars pulled up. The carpet of snow and mud coating the streets from building to building and block after block made walking even a short distance as strenuous as trudging over an Alpine pass. Whitby, who despite his slender frame was quite athletic, soon found himself puffing great clouds of steam under the exertion. He was about to suggest that they hire a cab when Meredith vanished into a dank, narrow lane whose entrance Whitby had not even noticed.

This side street was mercifully vacant, for had they come upon anyone traveling in the opposite direction through that close passage, the encounter would have resulted in the most profound intimacy. Not even the snow could find its way between the nearness of those walls without difficulty, but had to slip in forcibly with every gust of wind. Even so, it filled the air thickly enough to afford Whitby an eerie sense of isolation as he looked out from the folds of his coat. The snow and cold not only stung his eyes and blurred his vision, but numbed his fingers, muffled his hearing, and even seemed to deaden his power of scent. With just a moderate amount of imagination, he could suppose himself to be a disembodied phantom detached from the physical realities of the world about him. Yet, as he was not by nature a fanciful man, the thought did not linger with him.

They soon passed out of this alley and into another broad thoroughfare, not so busy nor so well-to-do as the first, but pleasant enough. Whitby did not have the opportunity to observe it closely, however, for no sooner had they marched fifty paces than they turned again into a little byway, and after another short passage emerged into yet another bustling street. So they wove their way through the city, turning first left and then right and then right again and then left, until Whitby had no notion of where they were or how far they had gone. Indeed, if before he had felt baited and hooked, now he had the uncomfortable sensation of being reeled in. The only general impression he had of their journey was that, the longer they walked, the more desolate and abandoned the streets appeared.

At last they came to a lane that was completely deserted and of a wholly disreputable character. Whitby had just considered to himself that it was unlikely for a man as unassuming as Meredith to have any business in such a quarter, and he was convinced that they were, in fact, hopelessly lost, when he watched with astonishment as his host and guide turned boldly in at the door of a dangerous-looking public house. Whitby could do nothing but follow in mute amazement and even though he scarcely admitted as much, slight trepidation.

Inside, a thick, damp atmosphere struck Whitby full in the face, causing him to catch his breath and blink from the blast of heat. He blew twice to compose himself and then looked about. A steamy mist hung over a large, crowded den weakly lit by the sick, yellow flames of several sputtering gaslights. To the right, a large mob was milling about at long, heavy wooden tables packed closely together for commerce's sake rather than comfort's. To the left a bar, plain, dark, and ornamented only with the scratches and scars evocative of a long history of abuse, jutted out into the room, while behind this a large, whiskered man in a dirty apron, himself as plain and dark as his furnishings and similarly adorned, leered unpleasantly over the whole scene. Everywhere men in filthy coats and crumpled hats, and women in garish, threadbare finery flaunted their familiarity as they raised a din of mindless chatter and tuneless singing.

In one corner of the room Whitby's notice was drawn to a large party attempting the refrain of a vulgar song in a variety of keys and times. As they swayed drunkenly and beat tempi upon the tables and each other, the unhealthy light threw their silhouettes against the bare brick walls creating an animated shadow-dance. Removing his hat and coat, Whitby became absorbed in observing these specters as they cavorted wildly about on every side. He was briefly seized with the fantasy that, in the chaos of the moment, these shadows were dancing independently of their masters, like infernal spirits reveling over their human prey. He blinked his watery eyes and in an instant the conceit passed, and he turned his attention once again to Meredith as to a familiar and now welcome sight.

The old gentleman, his face a ruddy glow from the exertion of their walk, had already approached the barman, and the two were conversing with an easy intimacy that Whitby found hard to reconcile with what he knew of his companion, although it was gradually dawning upon him that what he knew was precious little indeed, and most of it wrong. It appeared that their arrival was anticipated, for Meredith now motioned Whitby to accompany him through a door behind the bar, which the young lord did eagerly, grateful to escape the mayhem of the public room. They were led by the barman down a dark hall with several doors along the right-hand wall. This fellow took out from under his grimy apron a massive, jangling collection of metal, and with a particularly large key he unlocked and opened one of these doors and stepped aside to allow his guests to pass through.

The room they entered offered yet another surprise for Whitby, who by now was almost beyond the ability to be surprised. It was as cozy, as elegant, and as charming a sitting room as could be found at the finest address in Mayfair. Two large, comfortable chairs stood before a modest but attractive hearth in which roared a blazing fire. Between them was a small table laid out with brandy, port and cigars. Against the left wall was a larger table with two smaller chairs, and on it a cold roast had been set with bread, cheese and boiled potatoes in gravy. A bookcase stood opposite to this, overflowing with volumes lying about the shelves and on top as though they were made good and regular use of, and next to this was a small writing desk cluttered with papers and pens in a sort of organized disarray. A delicately carved coat tree hid in a corner near the door, and from its branches hung a red smoking jacket. To complete the image of casual domesticity, a veritable gallery of paintings and sketches was displayed along the walls, works of every imaginable size and style, yet all of them handsome.

When the barman had left, Meredith placed the mysterious parcel on the writing desk. He then took Whitby's coat and hat from him. "Allow me," he offered, and hung these, along with his own, upon the coat tree. "The furnishings are modest, I admit," he continued. "Still, I don't think the place is too frightfully inhospitable," and he removed his suitcoat and waistcoat and put on the smoking jacket.

"My own study isn't half so comfortable," Whitby confessed, in spite of himself. "How did you ever come across such a place in this vile little hole?"

"I am cursed with a restless nature and am used to spending my odd hours moving about the city. I've become well acquainted with many a vile little hole," he answered, the least note of reproach in his voice. "Of course, the furnishings are my own. I consider this place my personal and most exclusive club."

Just then there was a knock at the door, and a pretty young girl with a pronounced limp came hobbling in with a tray on which rested an open bottle of claret and two glasses. She placed this on the table next to the roast, and then quietly asked if there might be anything else the gentlemen required.

"Not now, Alice," she was told. "I'll ring if we want anything," and Alice went out as she had come in. "My own private stock," Meredith announced as he poured the wine. "I must apologize for the modest fare, but there are limits to what can be accomplished under the circumstances. Alice does her best."

"I'm certain she does," Whitby replied, with more meaning than goodwill.

The two sat to dinner as a necessary though unhappy prelude to the evening. Whitby especially felt that they were like a pair of adversaries in the ring, probing each other nervously in the first rounds, searching for a weakness that might be exploited later.

"May I ask you a question, Meredith?" Whitby tried while his companion was carving the meat.

"Please," Meredith offered.

"How long have you been contemplating this madness? From what I can gather, you've been a gentleman of the Club for onto twenty years now, while I have been a member for six, and in all that time you have held this . . . this thing of mine, this legacy. How did it come into your hands? And why do you choose this time to reveal yourself to me?"

Meredith passed a slab of roast beef over to the younger man and responded without looking up. "My life has been intimately tied to the House of Darnley, or was many years ago. But that tale must wait a little longer." He coughed, a deep, rasping cough. "Now, Whitby, you answer a question for me. That tale of the tiger. It's a lie, isn't it?"

Whitby blinked, but otherwise stayed calm. Such an impertinent suggestion was surely designed to elicit some kind of emotion from him, and he had no intention of providing one.

"I thought so," Meredith continued. "You've never stared death in the face, or smelled its hot breath against your cheek."

"The story is true in its essential points," insisted Whitby.

"Minor truths hiding a greater fiction. You are not the man you present yourself to be."

"And how could you know such a thing?" he demanded.

"I see it in your eyes. For I have faced death, and know what it is to whisper one's last prayer. I know how it affects a man, changes him."

Whitby struggled to contain his rising outrage. For the accusation was true. The story was false, embellished and augmented until what there was of the truth about it had been left far behind. A porter was injured. Whitby had in fact shot the beast. So had two other porters as the thing mauled its victim. And now he was found out, by this simpleton, this merchant! It was beyond humiliating. "So you drag me along with you to chide me like an old woman?"

Meredith hemmed a bit. "No," he answered. "No, not that. I have no strong desire to expose you to your friends, if that's your fear." And the two men continued their meal in an awkward truce.

As the minutes passed, Meredith appeared to grow disturbed and anxious, a sense of profound anticipation overspreading his earlier ease, signs of discomfort that were pleasing to his young companion. Suddenly, after draining the last dregs from his glass, he grasped the carving knife from the table and walked across to the writing desk. He stood silently for a moment, almost in contemplation, before adroitly cutting open the parcel which lay there and removing a large, intricately carved box. It possessed elegant brass fittings decorated in a vaguely Eastern fashion, and an ornate lock that shone in the glow from the fire. Meredith placed the box on the small table by the hearth, removed the ribbon and key from a shirt pocket and motioned for Whitby to join him. Whitby did so, noticing with some satisfaction the excited way in which Meredith played with the key.

"I appreciate your patience in putting up with my unusual arrangements," the old man began.

"Sir Charles," Whitby interrupted, feeling at last a sense of command in these remarkable proceedings, "you have an annoying penchant for prologues. Might we get on with it?"

A cold flame of anger erupted from the old man's stare, a spark of violent emotion that Whitby was unprepared for, and it shocked him into immediate remorse at his gibing comment. The flame passed away in an instant, however, and was replaced by a firm resolve and a renewed confidence. Meredith inserted the key into the lock and opened the box. He removed a stack of papers, yellow and crackling with age.

"You are to be the fifteenth Duke of Darnley, young man," he began. "And yet I have no doubt that you are unfamiliar with the tale of the thirteenth duke, your cousin, and his mysterious disappearance so many years ago. At the time, it crowded the pages of the most respectable periodicals and caused a general uproar among the authorities. It may still occupy an honored place in the unsolved files at Scotland Yard. But such scandals are easily silenced in the best families, and I know your father exerted some effort to send this one to oblivion. Darnley, the Darnley I knew, was a dear and trusted friend. We'd been companions from the moment we met at university, though a more dissimilar pair you couldn't imagine. We shared only a passion for hunting and a love for the same woman, my dear Elizabeth.

"Darnley was a notorious rascal and was subsequently invited everywhere and approved of by everyone. I followed along because he would have it so. Yet somehow, even in his shadow, I caught Elizabeth's eye. She and Darnley had been bound together for a time in a relationship as stormy as their natures, by turns intimate and estranged." Meredith paused for a moment and coughed. "But this was before I knew her, you see, so it meant nothing. There is no telling why a creature so vibrant and vital as she, so filled with life and its joys should have preferred me to Darnley. That she did surprised all of our acquaintances, me more than the rest. She was a magnificent creature, with a soul and a mind that sparkled beneath her ethereal beauty. In many ways, she was more like Darnley than I was, volatile and passionate, and perhaps that is why she bestowed her love upon me in the end, just as he gave me his friendship. Darnley took this solitary defeat with the grace society demanded. His affection for me never waned, grew stronger, in fact. His feelings for Elizabeth turned dark, however. He could not forgive her, though I know that he always loved her in his terrible way, until in the end his love . . . but I tell the tale badly.

"When I had taken full control of the family business, after Elizabeth and I were married and settled into a suitably conservative address by the Park, become upright and uninteresting, we continued to be admitted into society, part of that dull circle that is always invited because they have always been invited. Through it all Darnley and I remained close. I was his nearest and truest friend, finally his only friend."

Here Meredith paused for a moment and looked into the fire as though he might find there the answer to some unasked question. In this he must have been disappointed, for he only shook his head and continued. "These papers are the last testament of the thirteenth Duke of Darnley. I have held them in my possession these many years. Now I am ready to return them, for good or ill. Are you prepared to accept his legacy?"

Whitby hesitated for the slightest instant, only enough to unsettle his companion. Yet he had to admit silently to himself that he had been drawn in by all this mystery, and was far more interested in this business than he cared to be. "Go on," he murmured, at last.

"Very well then," sighed Meredith, and he began his tale.

2

The Contest

I shall begin," Meredith said, "where it began for Darnley, with his personal account of a journey to the Carpathian Mountains," and he took the top page from the stack of papers before him.

4 November

The train pulled into Cluj two hours late. Punctual for these continental railways. I'm only thankful we didn't come in later. Why can't European trains run with the efficiency of our British ones? Damned annoying. One of my fellow pilgrims couldn't get used to it, this "I-don't-care-a-shit-for-your-timetables" attitude. From the moment we left Vienna until we pulled into Cluj, the pompous ass kept pulling out his watch to complain about our schedule. As though the passengers could make the train go faster. I last saw him berating the poor conductor at the platform as I was seeing to my things. Thank God, I'm used to the whole business and took it all with better grace than that.

The station was a crush of people. Not so crowded as Buda-Pest, but infinitely more hectic. The place reeked of humanity and garlic. (God, they must eat nothing but that noisome little bud here.) The authorities aren't as ubiquitous in this backward district as they are at the borders of the Empire and in the capital, and the people's Magyar spirit takes advantage of their liberty. I was practically molested wading through the throng, accosted by ambitious devils hoping to turn a profit from my comparative innocence. It was all I could do to keep from trampling some poor beggar. Of course, I might have arranged to be met at the platform, but I'm damned if I'll resort to such nervous hand-holding. Where's the adventure of being in a strange new land if one is constantly chaperoned? It was enough that I should meet the coach to Borsec at a nearby inn. Truth is, I couldn't begin to spell the name of the place much less pronounce it, but I'd been assured it lay within sight of the station.

Damn it all, Cluj is larger than one would think. And the streets are that narrow, medieval kind so typical on the continent. Kind of Prague-ish, only more so. The lanes wind about each other like vipers in a pit, through alleys and past grotesque little piazzas. Yet they never lead anyplace. At least, not anyplace I cared to go. They only circle round and round about themselves. I must have looked a bloody lunatic wandering the halls of Bedlam. Marched about stubbornly in my ignorance, the proper British fool, peering around corners as though I might recognize anything, trying to read signs whose alphabet was so much squiggling nonsense. I carried on like this for three-quarters of an hour before seeking help.

Even then, it was twenty minutes before I could make myself understood to anyone. I'd been told my German would prove invaluable, but I found that tongue useless so far from the Austrian border. I finally managed a sort of sign language with a boy of seven or so. Gave him a coin which might have been worth a penny and might have been worth a guinea, but whatever it was worth it was money well spent, for he took only five minutes to lead me to my destination. The place was back the way I'd come, less than fifty yards from the station. Damn.

The Borsec coach sat idle in a picture-book courtyard. No horse, no post, no coachman in sight. The entire place abandoned. I hallooed a bit and caught the attention of a thin young girl carrying a vast bundle of linens. By pointing meaningfully to the coach, and then to myself, and then shrugging my shoulders a few times and waving my arms, I made her understand my problem and was directed to a dining room where my livery was resting on his ass, drinking freely while I'd been tottering about the town like an idiot. I let the fellow know who I was with enough violence to impress on him my desire to leave for Borsec at once.

This coachman, a slight, active little man called Ladislav, or something like Ladislav, with a colorful complexion made all the more livid by the draughts he'd just drunk, set about his work with a passion. Dispatched the postboy to retrieve my baggage, harnessed the horses, saw that all was trim and neat within the coach, and in less than an hour we set off for Borsec. The resort lies higher in the Carpathians than I'd thought, and closer to the Russian border, so that the journey took five hours at a pace I considered lunacy. Seemed leisurely enough to my driver, though. Ladislav is an artist in the box, a veritable Michael Angelo. Maneuvered us through the most treacherous mountain passes with the ease of a strong wind. At first I couldn't appreciate his talents, being occupied with a series of prayers I'd forgotten since childhood. But my confidence improved at every harrowing turn and non-existent strip of road, and I started to relax and admire the scenery.

Admire? That isn't the word. Absorb? Devour? The mountains cut a jagged swath against the sky like rows of serrated teeth. Dark, hard peaks rising and falling abruptly. Clouds moving over and about and even through them. Sometimes these are mere wisps of vapor, lending an air of ethereal mystery to the wildness.

Or they might be pale gray streaks against the forbidding landscape, like looking through a smudged glass at some dark beast.
Or again they might be thick and wet, obliterating everything
they cover, but always there, hovering about the top of the world
like an elemental power. Curiously, for all the sense of danger and
human frailty these mountains evoke, they're not that tall. Truth
is, the Alps would dwarf them. Yet the Alps are only beautiful in
a conventional way that anyone can recognize. The Carpathians
move one to the very core, touch the dark places of one's soul.
The Alps are pretty, the Carpathians fascinate. The Alps offer
majesty, the Carpathians—madness.

The path finally turned from its upward course, and coming
out between two close peaks, we started to descend into a valley.
At the bottom lay Borsec. Rustic collection of buildings huddled
about what was likely the single habitable spot in the district. We
soon swooped into the courtyard of the lodge where I was embraced by a fat, solicitous elf with feathery whiskers and a wheez-
ing voice. This is Bela, my host, and if I can overlook an intimacy
that borders on the intrusive, he's companionable enough. I'm
surprised to discover he has little English, though our correspondence was conducted in that language. Lucky for me, his German
is good if colloquial, and we communicate with enough fluency
to get by. A tall, dour-looking woman in a severe black dress, with
raven hair pulled back on her thin head, was introduced to me as
Madame Bela. She uttered nothing more than a curt, "Willkomen,
Herr Herzog," as she saw to my luggage, and her husband ushered
me about the place.

Damned grateful to find things as comfortable and modern
here as at Grossende or Mandelberg. The public rooms are large
and well furnished, and there's a sort of parlor or study or something that's especially snug, with airy windows and a small piano
Madame plays (less likely Muse there never was). Hanging from
the walls wherever I turn is an impressive display of heads and
trophies that my host takes particular pride in. When he speaks
of them he tugs at his whiskers, a gesture he makes only when his

feelings are more than his German can express. Taxidermy is one of the personal services of the lodge, it seems, and Bela is always honored when a guest can spare a head or two for his private collection.

5 November

Today for preparation! All my equipment has been checked, guns cleaned and a general reconnaissance made of the valley. Bela was pleased to act as my guide, and a very real asset he proved, too. Pointed out the best spots from which to survey the countryside, described the habits of the local game, told me where the easiest trails and surest passes lay. He was at his most ebullient discussing a recent spoor we came across. Assured me it was left not two hours previously by a ram of colossal size. I had some grave doubts about this, though I didn't voice them. Only complimented Bela on his mastery of woodlore.

After three hours touring the heavily forested peaks immediately to the south of Borsec, I spied a wisp of smoke rising from among the trees far to our north. I asked Bela about this and he seemed at first as ignorant as I. Offered only an evasive response, mentioning local goatherds or poor travelers unable to afford a room at the lodge. These answers weren't particularly convincing, however, especially as his entire manner became less effusive. He proceeded to qualify his earlier enthusiasm with a litany of precautions and warnings. I should confine my hunting to the southern half of the valley. The north had been all but played out the month before by a trio of Russian aristocrats. Indeed, I was to limit my activities to the valley proper and never stray beyond the mountains, for the weather could be very changeable, even dangerous this time of year.

I listened politely and assured Bela that I'd keep one eye on the skies at all times and return promptly to the lodge if conditions warranted. As to his other concerns, however, I had to beg his indulgence. I reminded him in all good humor that I'll be spend-

ing but a single week here and have no intention of confining my
sport to so small an area. I mean, the valley's a mere three or four
miles long, after all. He made an effort to undermine my resolve.
Cited my inexperience with what he termed "the temperament of
our mountains." But I laughed off his warnings as best I could. He
was becoming tiresome, and upon our return to the lodge I
pleaded fatigue and the morrow's business and retired to my
rooms.

This sudden, I'd even say this petulant attitude Bela has
adopted is a puzzle, produced, it would appear, by the rising col-
umn of smoke we saw to the north. Intruders upon the sanctuary
of his petty kingdom, no doubt. I suppose I should show greater
respect for his opinion in this matter. He's a genuinely good-
hearted fellow. Still, I'm paying dearly for my time in this obscure
little valley, and I'll be damned if I let half its meager length be
closed to me.

11 November

I have suffered the most harrowing encounter and only just escaped with my life! For some time I was feverish, drifting back
and forth, into consciousness and out again at intervals, racked
with delirium and infirmity. Even now, after five days, I'm only
just able to hold a pen and record at last the details of this adventure.

Following my last entry I fell straight off to sleep and was
roused the next morning by Bela, punctual as death, tapping gently at my door as the clock in my bedroom chimed the three hours.
I called for him to enter and he scurried in, all cherubic smiles
and hearty solicitude, carrying a tray with a pot of the thick, bitter
coffee they drink here, along with a brioche and a warmed lamb
chop. Barren fare, but a light meal is always best before a cold
hunt. His importunate manner of the day before was still with
him, though he tried to mask it under a cover of casual discourse.
He let me know, as I sat down to eat in my dressing gown, that

a fog had drifted into the valley overnight. "A great fog," he put it in his peasant's German. "Such fogs are not unheard of this time of year, and we people of the mountains, we get through them well. But you, Herr Herzog, you are new to this place. A great fog such as this, it could make your way most treacherous," and he shook his head gravely to punctuate his concern. Still, he reassured me, I was not to abandon all hope, for he, Bela, the finest guide to be found in the entire stretch of the Carpathians, would accompany me personally on this first day of hunting. Gallant gesture, certainly, yet I suspected it wasn't without an unspoken motive. I let him know, therefore, that his worries about my safety, though gratifying, were unnecessary. I'd tracked game across three continents, through conditions more formidable than a fog bank, over terrain equally demanding. With a compass to guide me, it was unlikely I should lose my direction, though in deference to his kind attentions, I'd keep to the valley until the skies cleared.

"To the southern valley," Bela added with some urgency, and I acquiesced. That is, I told him I would heed his advice, although I hadn't entirely made up my mind that I would, and I think honestly that's the most he should have expected from me. My words had a conciliatory effect, easing his mind and producing a return of that loquacious charm so natural to him. While I finished my meal and dressed, he busied himself with arranging the gear, keeping up a running commentary all the while on the excellence of my equipment, the certainty of my success, and his own philosophy of the hunt as an act of near religious devotion. Indeed, Bela's spirits rose to such a degree that I felt a sudden desire to dash them a bit. Just a spot of fun with the old bird. Had he discovered, I inquired, the source of that smoke we'd seen the day before?

His face darkened the moment I mentioned it. At first I had difficulty understanding him, for he used a word with which I was unfamiliar, some Slavic epithet. I begged him speak more to the point, and he told me plainly that there were Gypsies in the valley. Here was welcome news! I'd never met any of that ancient and much-maligned race, and I expressed a desire to make their acquaintance. Unwise request, it turned out, for it sent Bela into a paroxysm of anxiety. Such pulled whiskers and florid cheeks, that I at once regretted having pronounced the wish. He called them "children of the devil" and "accursed" and "witches" and several things in Hungarian which sounded perfectly libelous, until I was forced to be cross with him and accuse him of being superstitious and unkind. He remained unbending in his hatred of these nomads, however, and I could only conclude that such venom from one so gregarious stemmed from a personal injury of which I had a great desire to remain ignorant. So, as I was forced to choose between seven days' peace with Bela and a few hours' entertainment with the Gypsies, I chose peace and let him know that I would forego their company.

I left the poor man at the door of his lodge, still indignantly pulling his whiskers and even more insistent that I stay clear of the north. What a relief when he finally disappeared behind me!

A damned heavy fog had indeed settled over the valley, though it didn't hinder me inordinately as I made my way toward the southeast, shotgun in my arms and rifle slung across my back. I could as yet see some eighty yards about me. So I hiked blithely on, confident that the rising sun would dispel the mist. There was a spot high up on the mountainside that Bela had pointed out to me, a rocky outcropping from which I could command the entire region and so better chart my course. It was to this place that I climbed with the intention of reaching it by dawn.

Yet the fog grew thicker as I progressed, and before long my vision was limited to sixty yards, then forty. A half an hour passed as I continued to ascend. I supposed by then that I must be quite near my destination, but the fog had become so dense that I could see only thirty yards ahead. I decided to stop and take my ease under a tree until it should lift, certain that I was just a short walk from my goal. The sun would burn away the

fog before long, and I'd resume my climb better rested and read-
ier for the day's rigors. So, propping my weapons up next to me,
I closed my eyes. Only for a moment, I told myself, only for a
moment.

I have no way of knowing how long I slumbered on that hard,
damp cushion of earth, for when I awoke the sun was still invisible, hidden behind a bank of fog that had grown thicker in the
time I was asleep. My vision was now limited to a scant fifteen or
twenty yards. Everything beyond that spare circle was held behind
an impenetrable curtain, lost in a sea of milky, unyielding whiteness. Nor was I able to say what caused me to awaken. Perhaps it
was the soft padding of feet upon the rough, stony ground, or the
whisper of subdued breaths carrying through the heavy air. But
something had disturbed my rest. I was struck with a premonition,
as if I were trapped in a dream that wasn't dispelled by my waking.
Reaching for my gun and cradling it lightly, I rose to my feet.
Stood motionless, my head tilted to hear what lay beyond that
blank wall enshrouding me. But the quiet proved as adamant as
the fog.

Silence. A silence so thick it made me dizzy, as unnatural in
these mountains as the sound of a locomotive engine would have
been. Some presence in the fog had stilled the multitude of animals doubtless huddling in the trees all about me. I considered
that I myself might be the cause of this tense silence, but as I
twisted my head back and forth, trying desperately to perceive
anything, my instincts said something was indeed out there, not
watching me, for nothing could have pierced that mist, but aware
of me as I was aware of it.

Then I remembered the Gypsies. All of Bela's cautionary
advice suddenly rushed back upon me and I was almost embarrassed by the thought that his concern, which I'd taken so
lightly before, might prove my salvation now. Truth is, the idea
that I was being stalked by some damned rascally vagabond
made brave by the fog seemed a touch romantic, but if that
were indeed the case, the remedy was near at hand. I brought

the gun up to my shoulder and pulled back both hammers. The click as they locked into place split the eerie calm, serving notice to my mysterious companion of the cost involved in his criminal enterprise.

The sound that answered me shattered all thought of Gypsies. My muscles contracted and a sweat broke instantly upon my brow. Back through the fog, softly, as though whispering to me, came a throaty rumble, like rasping thunder heard vaguely in the distance. It was the low growl of a predator hungering for prey.

The sound came from my left, directly up the slope. I spun instinctively, fingers tensing against the twin triggers, but the fog was all I could see. What a thrill rushed through my every vein now, as if my blood had been chilled and then heated to the point of boiling! Senses sprang to life, reached out beyond me to grasp the slightest detail, every muted color and stir in the air, every smell and even every sound, for the silence became something alive to me. I didn't allow myself to be carried away by the rapture of the moment, though, for I knew that a single thoughtless second, the briefest lapse in discipline, one innocent action rashly taken could very well prove fatal. So, keeping my gun at the ready and my sights clear, I gradually lowered myself to one knee and assessed my position.

No matter what the creature was, if it were a predator it possessed the patience of Job. Yet it would be quick to pounce once it saw the game was all on its side, especially as it was unlikely to be aware of its own danger, treating me as just another victim, some helpless, vulnerable thing. When it came at me, it would do so quickly and fearlessly, and, I hoped, recklessly. My sole charge was to remain calm, to wait for the thing to act, knowing that it couldn't do so without exposing itself. Then, I need only trust to my own powers as a hunter and a marksman.

Time passed. Though fear has its cure in preparedness, uncertainty is the stuff on which it thrives, and as the minutes lapsed and the creature failed to attack, I found myself battling a more dangerous foe than the one in the fog. Five minutes went by in that deceptive calm. Ten minutes. A quarter of an hour and nothing more. Surely the beast realized its mastery of the situation, sensed my natural defenselessness. Why did it hesitate? Was there some detail I'd ignored, a contingency I'd missed? Perhaps my scent was familiar to it. Having experience of man, it might have suspected the threat I posed and stalked quietly away. As the thought occurred to me, I felt a sudden pang of disappointment and sighed with regret that the adventure should have ended so pitifully.

In that instant a twig snapped, hard by me and on my right. I spun and the muscles of my back and legs strained against the effort. I peered feverishly into the whiteness, but nothing emerged and I controlled the urge to fire. Damn! The patience of this beast had almost bested me. I'd slipped into myself, indulged in idle reflection when my every faculty was needed to sustain my readiness. Damn it, concentrate! Yet it had hesitated when the advantage was so clearly won. Why? I refused the temptation to consider. Determined to wait. Wait indefinitely. Be calm. Be ready. Have no thought. Wait.

By now perhaps half an hour had elapsed and the weight of my gun began to tell on my arm. I crouched lower and rested an elbow upon my knee to ease the strain, but this slight shift in position made me conscious of the price my body paid for such intense mental excitement. A dull soreness grew steadily in my back and shoulders. Eyes burned from the effort of staring into the fog. I was forced to blink often, a dangerous practice when my sight was already so severely handicapped. Fingers felt stiff, but I feared removing my hand from the triggers for even an instant. Worst of all, my legs began to ache. I swayed slowly, backward and forward, trying to relieve the pain, but the motion did little good and I could sense the blood throbbing through my thighs and calves with every pulse.

The fog thickened. I could see perhaps ten yards before me.

The passage of time was less certain now as my perceptions became more rarefied, stripped of every extraneous thought, focused exclusively on the small bit of earth around me. Nothing existed but the moment. In this state of elevated sensitivity, I began to detect shadows gliding by in the fog, always on the edge of awareness. Tried to follow these phantoms with my weapon, but I dared not fire. I waited. Heard sounds from out of the mist, low, barely audible, as though the fog itself were gently caressing the trees. Still I forced myself to remain calm in the face of these delusions. My bravado fled, and more than once I found myself wondering whether I hadn't imagined the thing all along, and that I was a great fool sitting alone on the side of a mountain held in dread by a cloud. Yet the fog couldn't last forever. It had to lift eventually. And when it did, the contest would be decided.

Slightly behind me and to my left! A noise breaking the quiet! Something sliding, tripping down the mountainside! I twisted round and every aching fiber in my body screamed and resisted the motion. A spasm of pain shot through my right side and I winced. Convulsively, my finger squeezed one of the triggers and an explosion ripped through the stillness of the mountain, echoing and re-echoing like a clap of thunder across the valley. My senses were confounded by the violence of the report. I tumbled backward to the ground.

Immediately, through the roar and flash of the shot, something on my right, from up the slope. A movement or a sound, I can't say what. I turned towards it with an almost exaggerated calm. Slowly, gracefully, from out of the mist, a dark shape materialized. At first just a shadow against the whiteness, but it quickly grew and became more definite, until it stood out clearly from the surrounding void. Slathering jaws and teeth glistening with hunger, a tongue lolling inside a red maw, paws outstretched with claws like scythes ready to rip whatever they first contacted. A wolf.

I saw it all in less time than it takes to imagine I see it again. The moment created its own time, stretching a single second of life into an elegant and deadly dance. From my prone position I took aim down the barrel of the gun, and my eyes met those of the wolf. That look alone was almost my doom. The sharpness and cunning in its stare froze me. For how brief an instant did my life lie forfeit, yet what an eternity it might have proved. The beast sailed into me as I emptied the second barrel. How could I defend myself? I can't remember. I recall only the impact as we rolled and tumbled down the side of the mountain, more a single thing than two creatures pitted against each other. A tree or rock brought our descent to a sudden, shocking halt, and I slipped into darkness.

Luckily, I didn't die. When I opened my eyes again, it was to see the anxious face of Bela looking down upon me and pulling his whiskers. My return to consciousness relieved him greatly, and he smiled and said something I couldn't understand. I closed my eyes and drifted off once more.

I've since learned that, once the fog lifted at last, Madame Bela sent her husband out after me with a small party of servants. They carried me back, and she has tended to me through the days of my recovery. My injuries consist of a cut along the back of my head, various bruises and lacerations distributed generally about my person and, most serious, a deep wound to my left forearm. This last caused the loss of a great deal of blood, and I fell into a severe fever upon my return. For many hours I was quite delirious. Madame Bela remained at my bedside through the entire ordeal, I'm told. Indeed, for a woman of such dour countenance, she's an admirable nurse. Compassionate, gentle and wonderfully knowledgeable about folk remedies. Takes every care for the least of my needs, and now that I've recovered from my initial delirium and begun to mend in earnest, she's expressed a deep interest in the details of my adventure. (I'm surprised to discover that her English is impeccable.) I now have ample opportunity to converse with her, for needless to say, my hunting here is over.

The days pass in restful though solitary ease, and I'm staying on an extra week to regain my strength, though this is returning to me with remarkable swiftness. Aside from a tingling about my arm I feel in perfect fit, and no doubt this latent numbness will disappear in time.

16 November

Farewell to Borsec! My parting came, I confess, not a moment too soon. Such damnable peace tires a man worse than enforced labor. Bid adieu to Bela and his wife with grateful pleasure, and while he affected the sort of pained remorse at my going that one expects from an innkeeper, Madame Bela seemed genuinely moved. She isn't entirely satisfied with the progress of my recovery, I believe, although my health has returned with an almost miraculous rapidity.

She came up to me as I was supervising the loading of my baggage, which now includes a very large and cumbersome crate, the trophy of my kill. The monster was enormous, some thirteen stone in weight and just short of seven feet from tip to tail. Bela's pride in it was unconfined. He insisted that no wolf that size, or even approaching it, had ever been seen in those parts before, and he was honored to mount the head for me. As I directed Ladislav in securing it to the top of the coach, Madame Bela looked on.

"It makes an impressive trophy," she stated as the final rope was pulled taut and made fast.

"Yes," I answered. "I'm looking forward to showing it off a bit when I return home. You know, host a sort of triumphal procession, a party in honor of the vanquished. Such a huge monster, it really takes one's breath away when seen for the first time."

She looked at me with a disquieting intensity, the sort of look that's like being scolded in a language one doesn't comprehend. "But perhaps it is you who has yet to see it for the first time," she suggested cryptically, "or has Your Grace not looked closely enough to discover that the thing is not a wolf at all?"

I was amused at this and admitted as much to her. I did know something of big game and had hunted wolf before, I observed. And had I not actually grappled with the creature? Besides, her own husband had stuffed and mounted the head, and he'd never intimated that it was other than a wolf. A monstrous big wolf, yes, but a wolf nonetheless.

"Not all men see what they see, nor do they admit what they know, even to themselves," she said. "Bela is a good man, but he is also a fool, and he will not always believe what his eyes tell him to believe."

"Then if this isn't a wolf," I asked incredulously, "what is it?"

She didn't answer me, however. Only turned away and began walking back into the lodge. I followed, curious as to the meaning of this strange concern of hers.

"Your arm is not yet healed," she commented. "Will you see to it?"

I told her that I planned on visiting a physician as soon as I returned to London, but that she needn't worry. No doubt the stiffness will work itself out on the journey home, I said. I didn't mention that it actually seems to be growing worse.

"But you will not remain in London. You have a country place, no doubt. That is where you must go. To recuperate in solitude." She made this comment, not as an inquiry, but with an imperative tone that I did not take kindly. Still, I owe her a great debt, and I admit the advice is sound. Perhaps a week at Murcheston after all this excitement would be wise.

I was happy to let the topic alone after this. For a woman of her intelligence and sensitivity, living at that far remove from society must be trying. I suppose she's susceptible to such odd humors. Yet it was most unusual behavior. I didn't see her again before I left. Bela informed me that she was ill, and perhaps the explanation lies in that. Poor woman.

And now it's back to London. I suppose the ordeal is past. E. must be over her time by now, must be delivered of the child. Boy or girl, I wonder? Blessed ignorance, I'd actually forgotten for a time why I left all that behind.

3

Darnley and Meredith

most gratifying narrative," Whitby acknowledged, only partly in mockery.

Meredith lay the pages aside for a moment, then turned and poured himself a glass of port, drinking it straight off. "I had it originally from Darnley upon the morning of his return," he continued. "I can recall the meeting with unusual clarity, etched in my mind forever. It was upon the week following the birth of my child, my daughter. Elizabeth had experienced a very trying delivery, and indeed, I believe the doctor had despaired for a time of her recovery, though he would not tell me so much. That's why Darnley was traveling, to escape all the bother and fuss associated with such a time." He put the glass down again. "That's neither here nor there, at present," he murmured, and went on with the tale.

"I met Darnley at the station, full of my own news, of course. But he expressed little interest in such domestic affairs. Some signs of alarm escaped him when I spoke of Elizabeth and my misgivings that the physician had withheld the truth, but I reassured him that all was well at last, and he recovered himself quickly, congratulating me in a cursory manner before launching into his own adventure. I confess, after the rigors of my wife's lying in, a time when no man ever felt more useless or out of place, the details of Darnley's extraordinary story soon carried me away from my own concerns. I begged to see the wolf for myself, and he invited me to dine with him the next day. As we parted, I took his hand warmly in my own and only then noticed the weakness of his grip. I looked at him, perhaps with more concern than was quite warranted, and Darnley laughed off my 'womanly cares' in the ridiculous way he had. He was always chiding me for having turned soft and rather matronly after my marriage, for having gone over to the enemy, as it were.

" 'Don't fret your gray hairs away, Merry,' he told me. 'I'll have it looked to this very afternoon.' Yet I could tell, through the laughter in his voice, that he was not entirely easy in his mind about the numbness creeping along his arm, that nagging reminder of the peril he had only just escaped.

"When I called upon Darnley the following evening, I was surprised to learn that he had left London, had gone off to Murcheston. Of course, it was very like him to make an appointment and then forget to keep it, but to leave the City after only just arriving from the most backward haunts of the continent, to forgo society and retire to the wastes of his northern estate, that was unheard of. I learned from his servant that Darnley had been visited by a physician, and I considered that perhaps the injury to his arm were more serious than he had allowed, but soon events in my own household overshadowed any qualms I had for him. The child took a sudden turn for the worse, and what with doctors flowing in and out of the nursery and females reigning over me like an army of Amazons, I had little time to worry about anything else. The crisis was managed, however, and life went on as it always does go on.

"Some weeks later I was traveling through the City, my mind divided between the *Times* before me and the parade of humanity passing outside my chaise, when whom should I spy darting along the pavement but Darnley. He seemed overflowing with vigor and vitality, moving at an extraordinary pace, weaving his busy way through the throng. I ordered my coachman to halt and immediately leapt to the street, calling out his name. He was delighted to see me, apologized for not calling on me sooner, and as he was carrying a great bundle of books in his right hand, he grasped mine in his left. The grip almost crushed my fingers. The hand had simply healed itself, he informed me. No residual numbness, no pain, no weakness. Of course, the doctor had felt that amputation was the only cure, and so Darnley had bolted to Murcheston to be safely away from the charlatan's saws. That explained his mysterious disappearance. Indeed, Darnley appeared stronger than ever, and I was beside myself with joy for him, invited him at once to come to dinner with Elizabeth and me. He demurred, begging some important work he was involved in, but that was quite like him. Domestic scenes always made Darnley uncomfortable.

"So my life settled into a completely usual and easy routine. I had my family and I had my friend. My business prospered, my wealth increased, I possessed all the trappings of a happy life, except for happiness itself. Eugenie was not a healthy child, though she was beautiful like her mother, a radiant light that flickered and dimmed, yet did not go out. The doctor was a common visitor to our home in those days. The strain of it all wore terribly upon Elizabeth, especially as we had been advised not to attempt another child. She had barely survived her first labor, the doctor told us finally, and another birth would likely prove fatal.

"Darnley also was a great trial at this time. His modern views, his inconstant manner of living, the scientific bent he placed on everything, inquiring into the nature of things best left unexamined, such behavior had always made him an oddity in society, an entertaining rascal whose idiosyncrasies were balanced neatly against his remarkable wealth and position. Now, however, rumors began to swirl about him that were really too damaging to be endured. It was known that he traveled regularly to Murcheston, and it was believed that he was conducting some dreadful experiments in the seclusion of his estate. As the weeks turned into months, these tales became more incredible. Word started to circulate that he had dismissed his entire staff, expelled every living soul from the grounds and lived there in total solitude. When he returned to town, which was quite often, he seemed to drift between extremes of conviviality and misanthropy, either attending every function in a whirl of activity or barricading himself against intrusion. Some of the more imaginative social wits devised elaborate explanations for Darnley's behavior, and nothing short of a contract with the devil was ruled out.

"For my part, I was too involved in my own affairs at first to notice any change in his mercurial nature. When I met him at parties or in the street, as I did occasionally, he seemed his usual infuriating self, always moved by some new experience, filled with the ebb and flow of life, his spirits either too full or too empty. Yet after many months had passed, even I noted how his darker self began to predominate, and I could not ignore the gossip. So I determined to speak with him about these matters, if only to make him aware of what people were saying. By this time, however, Darnley had become such a hermit that getting a message to him was a mission in itself, and it was some weeks before I managed to arrange a quiet evening together at my home, just Darnley and me for drinks, for I knew how agitated Elizabeth made him, and she was rather against the whole idea herself.

"Darnley was as punctual as ever, flying through our door a good hour and a quarter late, and from the moment he exploded over the threshold I saw that I was in for a blow. He was all mad energy and excitement, like a man possessed. I was familiar with this attitude of his, a stance of defiance in the face of absolute benevolence, a swagger and a posture of worldliness that wouldn't allow any man's soul to be completely innocent. Still, at first, I thought he might be managed.

"Elizabeth came out to greet him, and as the three of us paused in the foyer, I remarked that we had not stood together like this since university. The observation was ill-received, however. Darnley made only a stiff bow to Elizabeth, then shot past her into the library before she could utter a word.

"She did not take this slight well. 'Insufferable, arrogant ass,' Elizabeth muttered, somewhat too loudly for my comfort, and I pulled her away into the parlor.

" 'My dear,' I said, soothingly, 'please try to remember why he is here. Darnley requires our help, I feel sure of it.'

" 'Then you help him, Charles, for he can rot in hell as far as I'm concerned.' Such strong emotion between the two was not unusual. They were twin spirits, too like to suffer each other's company for long, and must either be lovers or enemies. There was no middle ground for them. I sighed, and said that I regretted she should feel so about an old and dear friend in his need.

" 'He's no friend of yours, Charles,' she insisted. 'Those days are over.'

" 'I suppose they are,' I told her. 'Still, I feel that I'm a friend of his. I can't help it. And he does need a friend right now. It might as well be me.'

"Her look softened, and she reached up a tender hand to smooth my worried brow. 'You are too generous, Charles, do you know that? Too generous by half.'

"I looked at her, somewhat startled at this exclamation. 'How can one be too generous?' I asked, but she only gave me a pat on the arm and a kiss on the cheek and retired to her sitting room.

"I hurried to join Darnley. His lean, lithe figure stood by the fire blazing warmly in the hearth, and he began fingering through a humidor upon the mantle while I poured drinks. 'You know, I should be outraged at you for insulting my wife in this cavalier manner,' I chided him, fired by the afterglow of Elizabeth's anger.

" 'Was I insulting?' he exclaimed too easily, removing cigar after cigar, rolling each about in his fingers with a crackling sound.

" 'Don't be simple,' I said, handing over the brandy with a stern look as I seated myself in a chair by the fire.

" 'What would you have me do, Merry? Kiss the mistress' hand like the dear family friend I am not?' Having finally identified a cigar that met his superior tastes, he dipped a taper into the flames and lit it.

"I observed him closely as he did so. The idle, preoccupied attitude he had affected for the evening wasn't merely an excess of energy. He had something on his mind, something that excited him and made him—did I believe it?—a little bashful. While no one else might have noted the marks of nervousness in Darnley, they were unmistakable to me. It was clear that he wished to unburden himself of some news but didn't quite know how.

"Notwithstanding this uncharacteristic, and I might add humanizing reticence, I can't say I was perfectly satisfied with him. There was yet a misanthropic posture about the man, some undercurrent of disaffection and disdain, a loathing for all things common and homely. I felt it in the way he glanced about at the symbols of domestic housekeeping scattered throughout the room, that part of Elizabeth which expressed itself in the very scent of the air. Darnley hated such touches of feminine delicacy. Why he had ever decided to place his confidence in me, I can't even begin to conjecture, but it certainly didn't extend to any of my family or acquaintances. After a few awkward minutes of mere prattle, therefore, I launched into the topic of the rumors circulating about him.

" 'Asses and fools, Merry,' he prated, 'fools and asses everywhere,' and he laughed, resting his arm upon the mantle and looking idly at the red glow of his cigar. 'Do you gather what they're trying to do? Do you follow their game? They can't stand seeing a man who's free of their ugly little sphere. Really free. Want to keep me tucked up close and safe where my independence doesn't threaten them. So they devise these fictions to explain away my freedom.'

" 'Freedom from what?' I ventured.

" 'From weakness. From the prison of their civilized society, their fatuous morality, mere gilt shackles. I refuse their invitations, and so what's the reason? I'm a monster, of course, a social aberration, despondent, depraved and dissolute.' And he laughed again, a chilling sort of laugh. 'Don't bother yourself with them, Merry. They aim their puny darts at me like Lilliputians firing arrows at Gulliver.'

" 'Yes, but even Gulliver had to protect himself against such assaults.'

" 'Only because he was weak, too, like them. Unwilling to make use of his natural advantages,' and with a sweep of his hand Darnley demonstrated plainly what he would have done in Gulliver's position. 'Away with all the asses and fools, eh?'

"I rose to take a cigar of my own, and also to collect my thoughts.

These rantings didn't sound like Darnley, not the fellow I had known at university, had traipsed about the continent with. Or rather, it was Darnley, but too much of him. He had always been a callous sort of fellow, the kind who was either at once your dearest friend or your most infuriating nemesis, but this talk of 'weakness' and 'natural advantages' went beyond anything I had heard him speak of before.

" 'Can't I make you understand?' I tried again. 'This is more than the idle chatter of bored gossips. You have been implicated in every sort of foul deed short of murder. You can't just ignore that.'

" 'Can, do and will,' he exclaimed. 'I tell you, it's less than nothing to me.'

" 'But if you allow this to continue without any effort to refute these tales . . .'

" ' . . . they'll be forgotten by next Season. I understand this mob as well as you do. They can't keep it up. Not one of them with the mental powers to sustain a single idea beyond a gnat's lifetime. You watch. Inside of a month I'll be old news again. Sooner, if we have a war.'

"I cannot recall ever feeling more vexed. Everything he said sounded quite true, even admirable. Yet such superior detachment never works out in practice the way you expect it to do. 'Be careful,' I warned, returning to my chair and affecting his mood of nonchalance. 'In forgetting about the rumors, these fools and asses might just forget all about you as well.'

" 'Would that they did, Meredith.' He sighed. 'But don't fret. I've not given up on them completely. They'll be hearing from me again.'

"I told him I was glad to know it, although there was something in his eye, a look of rapacious intent that made me dread the day when he would return to society. Still, our wrangling proceeded, as it always would when he was in one of his tempers, with Darnley taking the position that society is a false constraint upon human nature, and I asserting that our very nature is social, that we require the company of our fellows to exist. He spouted natural laws to me, the dictates of desire as superior to our limpid morality, while I accused him of being nothing more than an apologist for Rousseau and his ilk.

" 'Rousseau?' He laughed. 'That coward? A perverse pedant who could think of nothing better with which to replace your noble society than his noble savagery. But it's the nobility that's the lie, Merry! What is there noble in man? I ask you. What's nobility but the sheerest veil draped over the strength and power of our truer nature? Strip away these clothes and conventions, and you'll discover the animal that you are and always have been. Phantoms like nobility and morality—right and wrong—they have nothing to do with the truth of it! The truth of us!'

" 'Which is why society with all its sins is superior to your anarchy,' I shot back, rather warmly myself, 'a lawlessness that leaves each man free to exercise his every depraved whim. Allow that, and soon there will be no one left to enjoy your superior nature. These conventions you are so quick to strip away are the only security we have against a very bloodthirsty world.'

" 'Precisely!' he crowed. 'For where's that blood beat if not in ourselves, in our true selves as we're meant to be? You can't disguise it. Try as you might, it will poke its way through the veil. Our claws bare themselves in spite of your weak efforts to deny them. Look at history, for God's sake! Every generation more murderous than the last, each century hungrier for slaughter. Every war of every age bringing greater destruction, more killing from greater distances, fewer soldiers capable of destroying greater numbers. What was Marathon next to Waterloo, or an entire legion of Romans against a single well-manned cannon? And what glorious horrors will tomorrow bring with it? It's the red dawn of a new age, Merry! Not an age of reason or morality, but an age of blood!'

"I was truly frightened now, frightened for Darnley and, I admit, frightened for myself. 'Of course, you make it all sound very true,' I ventured, 'but that doesn't make it right. There is, after all, a great gulf between what we are and what we ought to be.'

"He laughed. 'Always hoping to find yourself an angel instead of a man? But you are a man, and that means you're an animal. The only angels exist in the dreams of the weak and the frightened.' Darnley's eyes filled with passion and his voice shivered with intense excitement as he spoke. 'The real world, the world of nature, it offers no sanctified path to follow. No golden road through a vale of tears to a happier time after death. Death is final, absolute! Nature's example shows us the only true way to live before death devours us. Power triumphant, that's the way! Right and wrong judged by strength alone! Honor, morality, duty, mercy, forbearance, benevolence, charity—they're myths, tales told by the weak to propagate their weakness. There's one truth, a single gospel! Strength! The strength to grasp life in your hands and rip from its fabric what you will! Think of it, Merry, the freedom!' Darnley went on, his voice becoming sharper, more cruel. 'If but a single man accepted that challenge, acknowledged the truth about himself, if just one man would act with all the cunning and power that nature has endowed him with, do you know what such a man might become?'

" 'Lonely, I should think.'

"I didn't expect my answer to satisfy Darnley. He was almost mesmerized by his own wild thoughts. Yet my response acted upon him with a violence I could not have anticipated. He stared at me first with that same inhuman cruelty that had characterized this entire harangue, the look of a man intent upon himself alone, seeing in everything mere fodder for his mad imaginings. Then, slowly, a degree of humane softness began to displace the almost leonine ferocity of Darnley's countenance. He looked away with a hesitancy that I can only describe as embarrassment, as though he'd said more than he wished, exposed something intimate, something he desired to keep within the privacy of his silent, secret breast. He turned to the fire, busying himself momentarily with relighting his cigar. Then he faced me, and he appeared to have recovered from his shock. Yet wasn't there some hint of the depth of his feelings left behind, some residue of pain in his glance that showed how my words had touched him?

" 'Merry,' he continued, in a voice that was perhaps a touch too easy, 'I have a request to make. A favor.' I don't think in all our acquaintance Darnley had ever condescended to ask a favor of anyone. Was this the opportunity I'd been so anxious to see present itself, the chance to offer some palpable assistance, some way out of whatever troubles had been afflicting him? I stated at once, before hearing what the favor might be, that whatever was mine that might be of the least service to him was at his complete disposal.

"He chuckled, and the tensions that had pervaded the room just moments before were dispelled as by a friendly breeze. 'No, no,' he told me, 'it's only you I want. I'm going up to Murcheston in three days. Come with me. There's something there I want you to see. Something that I think will explain what I'm trying to say.' His eyes glimmered with excitement. 'It's so wonderful, Merry. You've no idea. Say you'll come with me.'

"Go with him? What force on earth could have kept me away? We made plans in an instant. I was to meet him at Waterloo Station. Together we would journey, as we had journeyed so often years before, and we sat there and remembered those travels as the first warm glow of our friendship seemed to leap up again like a smoldering ember in the fire. The evening was late by the time we finished our drinks, and we made our good-byes in a renewed spirit of understanding that left me so light-headed and expectant that I almost laughed for joy. Before turning away at the door, Darnley grasped my hand, and giving such a squeeze that I winced in pain, he looked fast upon me and said, 'Never, through the rest of your days, will you regret this. We'll be great companions from now on, Merry, great companions. You'll see.'

"I was practically dizzy as I closed the door and returned to my chair in the library. The whole evening spread out before me, and I was filled, not with misgivings, but with a certain confusion as to what precisely had caused this change in Darnley, in our relations, in the whole world it seemed. I'd desired it, of course, could almost be said to have willed it to happen, yet I wasn't entirely comfortable with this sudden rapprochement. There was too much of Darnley about the thing. Was it too mercurial to be real, too perfect to be lasting? Or was I merely too cautious where he was concerned?

"The noise of a violent crash shook me from my thoughts, followed by screams and the sounds of riot in the street. I rose and crossed to the window. The yellow light of the lamps revealed a scene of surprising calm, people standing about in the middle of the street, staring at a great black box that had somehow planted itself in that unlikely spot. It was a hansom, overturned in the road. Just beyond it I could make out the dark mass of a horse, still hitched and fighting against its traces to get up.

"I left the library and went quickly to the front door. My man Prowell was there before me, and I sent him off at once for a physician. As he ran down the street, I walked over to survey things and see if I might be useful to anyone. A crush of people was concentrated at the front of the cab, but as no one was doing anything particularly productive, I pushed my way through to get a better look at the damage. At the center of the throng, shrouded by the shadow of the crowd, a figure lay twisted in the mud of the street. Even in the darkness I could see it was Darnley. He was insensible, his arms extended above his head, still trying vainly to ward off the oncoming carriage. His face was a patchwork of cuts and scrapes, but at a glance he didn't appear to have suffered any severe injury to the head. His left leg, however, was trapped beneath the cab, and it was obvious from what little I could see that the injury was extensive. The upper thigh was only so much ripped clothing and torn flesh, and by the faint moonlight that filtered down through the crowd, I detected the soft glistening of blood seeping over everything, soaking into the mud, insinuating itself into the street.

"With a monstrous rattling the cab gave a great jolt and Darnley uttered an unearthly moan as the weight of the thing ground against his wound and the pain tore through the cloud enveloping his mind. The horse was still fighting to free itself. Grasping the man next to me by the shirt front, I demanded that he produce a knife at once. This proved to be all the impetus necessary to stir the mob into activity, for on the instant some dozen blades were held out to me. I took the largest and proceeded to cut the horse away from its harness, calling for the distraught cabby to make every effort to calm the animal. That done, the beast lurched awkwardly to its feet and immediately galloped away in fright. Next I organized the six largest men to lift the cab off of Darnley. In a single, explosive burst of strength, they pushed the thing upright onto its wheels.

"Soon thereafter, the doctor arrived, and after a quick examination he directed Prowell and another man to carry Darnley with the greatest possible care into the house and onto the nearest bed. Prowell volunteered his own, on the ground floor at the back, where there might be a modicum of privacy. I remained outside for a time determining precisely what had happened, which was simple enough. Darnley, with his impetuous nature, had simply darted out into the street without thinking to look, and the poor cabby, in trying to avoid a collision, had toppled the cab onto him. I concluded my inquiry quickly, which ended with the dispersal of some quantity of money to the witnesses and especially to the cabby, and rushed back inside.

"I entered to find my wife busily arranging the household, moving Prowell into the guest room on the floor above, discovering which of the servants had any experience tending the sick. Then, we waited for the doctor's report. It was not long in coming. The wizened old physician, a neighbor of ours who lived in comparative retirement and thus had little of the delicacy one expects from a healer, stated bluntly that Darnley's leg was shattered, and that the likelihood of his ever using it again was negligible. What was worse, Darnley was registering a high fever, indicating the possibility of internal trauma. Yet, he advised, in Darnley's weakened state it was unwise to venture any dramatic remedies. Time and patience were the only physicians he required, along with a good dose of laudanum now and then.

"So we were left, Elizabeth and I, with my wounded friend lying feverish in our midst. It was a trying time, the days that followed, spent worrying, wondering, wrestling with the dread possibilities. I kept returning to our conversation in the library, Darnley's wild philosophy, his grand pronouncements about natural morality, or immorality, or unmorality, and it seemed to me that his superior nature was useless to him, after all, that the violence he seemed to be justifying in the name of nature had been visited upon himself in the end. It was a smug irony to consider, and I came to regret it.

"Some five days later I was sitting quietly at my writing desk when I was startled by howls of anguish and agony coming from the rear of the house. I knew at once the meaning of these harrowing cries and raced with all speed through the kitchen to the room in which Darnley was convalescing, where I arrived at the same instant as Elizabeth. We burst in and there found our girl Miriam forcibly restraining Darnley from rising out of his bed. The man's appearance was ghastly, wraithlike. His face and neck glistened with perspiration and the nightshirt he wore clung wretchedly to his body. His hair was plastered in thick, lifeless strands across his scalp. His skin was pale to the point of translucence, so white that it actually appeared mottled and red like marble, with every throbbing, striated muscle and pulsating vein marking its clear path beneath the surface. And his eyes—wild, bloodshot orbs—eyes that have looked upon something terrible, some dreadful reality that branded itself fiery hot and glowing on the innermost reaches of his memory. All of his strength, his mad passion and insane energies seemed to gather themselves there in his dark, savage eyes.

"These were all the observations of an instant. Darnley struggled against Miriam frantically, screaming in misery and frustration, in his weakness still managing to exert considerable force. Miriam was a good, powerful girl, however, though had I not arrived Darnley might nevertheless have succeeded in throwing her off and doing himself further injury. I moved quickly to her aid, and our combined strengths were enough to overcome him at last, so that he fell back onto his pillow in exhaustion.

"Elizabeth had already gone to send for the doctor, and I instructed Miriam to prepare a dose of laudanum at once, to drug Darnley back into a state of comparative comfort, but suddenly a hand grasped my collar and pulled me violently down. Darnley, with his wild, frantic eyes, stared at me and said in a feeble though emphatic voice, 'Send her away!' I hesitated, unsure what to do, wondering that this might be some derangement on his part, some delirium it were best to ignore. I felt his grip tighten about my collar. 'Send her away now!'

"I motioned for Miriam to leave us and turned to Darnley, who loosened his grasp upon me. 'That girl,' and he pointed to the door after Miriam, 'she said it's Friday! But that's impossible, isn't it? I came here . . .' and his mind stumbled, searching for the date. 'It was Sunday, so it can't be Friday! Please God, tell me it isn't true!'

"The loss of five entire days from a man's life, the realization that time itself has been stolen, must be a terrible revelation to someone returning to consciousness, so I tried as delicately as I could to reassure Darnley that he was alive, that he had been in a dreadful accident, and that it was indeed Friday, the twenty-sixth of November.

" 'The time? What time of day is it?'

" 'It's only just gone eleven,' I informed him, and the bells began to ring out the hour about the City as I spoke.

"He stared at me, pierced me through my very soul with his mad eyes, and then his glance darted about the room as though he were looking for something. I placed a tender hand upon his shoulder, but he only brushed it aside angrily.

" 'There's no time,' he muttered to the far walls of the room. 'No God-damn time! Look, Meredith,' and his stare returned to me. 'You must go to Murcheston! Do you understand me! Murcheston! Leave now! This minute! Dear God, I didn't mean for it to be like this! But there's no time to do any good! You must at least learn the truth!'

" 'What truth, old man?' I asked, trying to calm him.

" 'You won't believe, not yet! Even you aren't so credulous, not now, not without the whole of it, not without proof!'

" 'Of course I'll believe you. I'll believe anything you tell me,' but I was shocked to hear Darnley utter a sickly laugh at my reassurance.

" 'Very good,' he said, and I could see that he was severely taxed by his efforts to go on speaking. 'All I must do is open my breast, is that it? And you'll accept whatever I tell you. No questions. You'd never doubt my sanity. You'd never pass it off as the mad ravings of a weak and injured man. Wouldn't call it delirium, hallucinations, the sick fantasies of a mind left in darkness these past days. Good God, Merry,' and his voice turned wild and frantic once more, 'if I were to tell you only half of it, you'd have me shipped off to Bedlam within the hour.'

"I protested my constancy.

" 'Shut up!' he commanded, gripping my arm, and I could see Darnley gather his strength as the pain became more intense and his mind longed again for the soothing void of oblivion. A forced calm descended upon him as he struggled to control his physical suffering and this strange mental agitation. 'If you're so ready to believe me, then believe this,' he began. 'You must go to Murcheston without delay! In the study, the large study, there's a sideboard with three drawers in it. Open the middle drawer. Under the lip is a lever. Throw it, and the wall in front of you will swing open. The chamber beyond is an aberration of the architecture, an irregular space left between two rooms. Inside is a desk with papers spread about, a journal of these past months. Take it with you. Don't wait at Murcheston to read it. Don't stay a moment, but come back here. Even then you won't be convinced, I know it, not until you return.'

" 'If you wish me to go, then go I shall,' I assured him, though my only thought at the time was to relieve his anxiety.

" 'Go then,' he murmured, weakening. 'Go.'

" 'Should you want anything,' I added, 'all you must do is call for Elizabeth. She'll be close by.'

"A sudden look of panic gripped him again. 'No,' he whispered, 'no, she should go, too.' But his eyes raced back and forth, trying to capture some point in the air, some idea that flitted about his troubled mind. 'All right,' he said finally. 'Yes, she will stay. She will be here. Elizabeth.' His voice trailed off into silence as these exertions caught up with his broken health, and soon the doctor arrived and ordered me out of the room.

"What was I to do? I spoke briefly with Elizabeth, waited for the doctor to assure us that Darnley was well, though heavily sedated against the pain and a bit the worse for this wild demonstration. Elizabeth did not relish the idea of being left with Darnley in his present state of confusion, but there was nothing to be done for it. I had made my promise, so I must journey alone to Murcheston. In less than an hour I was on a train traveling north. To discover what, though? That was the question haunting me as the miles raced by.

"The train pulled into Brixton Station toward dusk, and as the urgency of my departure had left no time to wire ahead, I proceeded to the pub to procure a conveyance for the final leg of my travels. It was a more daunting task than I could have anticipated. I found a group of miners standing idly about with mugs in their fists. Their conversation stopped the moment I entered the room. I approached the barman and expressed my desire for a cart and driver to take me to Murcheston. The fellow, a rough and battered character, gave me a queer look, part suspicion and part disbelief, and said, 'You'll be welcome to try your luck, squire. Here's nary a man to stop you. But I'll tell you this and maybe save you the trouble. I'll not go with you, not though you offer me a guinea for the journey and a pound for my pains.' He was answered with nods of approval from about the room, and I was startled to discover that not a man there was willing to accept the task. At last, I was able to hire a cart to take myself out to Murcheston, and that alone cost me dearly.

"The solitary ride through weather that was biting cold only made my sour temper more miserable yet, and the trip out to Murcheston seemed to take twice as long holding the reins myself as it ever took when I was a mere passenger. Luckily, the night was exceedingly bright and I was able to move along at a respectable pace.

"The windows all were empty and lifeless as I pulled up the long drive of the hall and stopped before the front entrance. The place was dark, thoroughly abandoned. Of course, I knew the rumors current about London, that Darnley had given the sack to his entire staff, but I'd never taken such talk seriously, not until that moment. I secured my horse to a post, leaving her twitching nervously, for even she felt the strangeness of the place. Walking up to the massive oak doors, I first knocked loudly, more from form than any expectation of an answer. I next tried the latch and was surprised when the door swung open easily. I reflected, however, that Murcheston's reputation among the miners was a far better security than iron bars, and so I marched bravely in, as though my heart were not pounding violently against my breast, nor the sweat beginning to stand out upon my brow.

"It wasn't a place to stand idly about in. Once I had a light I went directly to Darnley's study, found the sideboard and located the lever precisely where he said it would be. I threw it, and a sharp crack echoed through the empty halls as the wall before me, sideboard and all, swayed subtly forward. Beyond was a dark hole, and even my desire to finish with this macabre business couldn't keep me from hesitating before such a terrible sanctuary.

"The room was as Darnley described it, the result of an obvious miscalculation. Paneled walls danced in and out at awkward, insane angles, made more maddening by the shadows they threw recklessly about, twisting and writhing in a gay tarantella as my candle flickered a mute melody that left me disoriented, as though my mind had been spun around until I couldn't tell which way my thoughts were facing. Still, I pushed forward.

"The far end of this mad cell, perhaps some thirty feet in front of me, was yet enveloped in blackness. I took two cautious steps in that direction, and the shadows parted like a cloth being rent. In an instant, from out of the dark a creature leapt forward, looming high above me, fangs like spikes in a cavernous maw, eyes cold and sharp, a vision of pure, malevolent horror. I fell backwards to escape its fearful attack, stumbled and crashed to the floor only just managing to keep my candle lit. The flame swayed and twisted and set the whole world awhirl. In a moment the thing would be upon me. But the moment passed. Darkness reclaimed the beast.

"Had I screamed? The echo of a cry wandered through the halls of Murcheston, though I didn't recall uttering it. What had I seen? A pair of bestial eyes, ravenous jaws gaping hungrily, a fierce and terrible expression, the parts all played before my imagination, but the whole eluded my memory. I rose and, holding my breath within my lungs, stepped forward.

"At the end of the room squatted a desk, cluttered with papers, a lamp, and all the paraphernalia of writing scattered about with no apparent order. Hanging above this glared the head of the beast. A trophy, of course, some animal of repugnant carnality staring like the evil genius of this secret, tainted world. The flame flickered again in sympathy with my own failing nerve and gave the disquieting illusion of life to this monster. I steeled myself and approached the thing.

"The initial impression it gave was of a wolf. The ears were pointed and set wide apart on a thickly-furred head, but it was far too large to be a wolf, at least twice the size of any I'd ever come across. And the snout wasn't as elongated as a wolf's, but more compact, like a bear's. I thought it might be a cat, for the forehead was capacious and the eyes vaguely feline, yet this also failed adequately to describe the thing. It was then that I recalled the creature Darnley had killed, that had almost killed him, in the Carpathian Mountains so many months before.

"I felt the madness such a beast could inspire, felt it as surely as if I had been trapped there with the thing alive. The brow was furrowed, only slightly, but enough to project a sort of rudimentary intelligence, not merely a sense of animal cunning, but actual awareness, threatening my person, my very soul. It was as though the monster were looking down on me, saying, 'I know you. Your superior intellect is not superior to mine. Your exclusive claim to Nature's throne is a fraud. You share your place with me, for we are brethren, you and I. We understand. We know.'

"I tore myself from this apparition and turned to the flotsam of papers on the desk. From this I hurriedly assembled a manuscript, and having no desire to remain in that place any longer than was necessary, I bundled my prize and departed, leaving the room and its single occupant behind."

Meredith paused in his tale, and his fingers played lightly over the stack of yellowing papers that rested on his knee.

"This is the manuscript," he continued. "Here is the tale as Darnley alone can tell it, in his own hand. It begins where it all began, shortly after his return from the Carpathians."

Book Two

4

The Tale Begins

5 January

I am a werewolf.

There it is. The first time I've actually expressed it, put it down in so many words. I'm a werewolf. God, I must be mad, but to see it there at last, spelled out. It's so exhilarating and insanely wonderful. A werewolf! I'm a werewolf!

The more precise name for my condition is lycanthropy, and for myself, a lycanthrope, but who can abide the pretense of that Latin rubbish? Like saying, "I'm a Homo Sapiens." I'm a werewolf, good Anglo-Saxon word, and that's what I'll call myself.

This state of affairs is still relatively new to me. I've only done it twice. Been a werewolf, that is. Undergone my physical transformation. Last month and again last night. I admit that, until the recurrence of my metamorphosis, I was afraid to fully acknowledge the truth to myself. I didn't quite know what to make of my initial change and half suspected, despite certain evidence to the contrary, that I'd developed some insidious brain fever. Was fast on my way to being a howling lunatic, actually. So my second change has understandably been a great relief to me. It's confirmed me in my new nature and freed my mind of the fear that I'd lost my senses. I now feel quite at peace with myself. Not merely resigned to being a werewolf, but genuinely revitalized by the knowledge. After all, where's the wisdom in being at odds with yourself? Be natural, that's my philosophy. Don't affect to tamper with the nature that's been handed to you. Cultivate it. Learn to understand and appreciate it. Only a fool attempts to grow spinach where potatoes have already been planted. If nature has seen fit to make me a werewolf, don't struggle against the bit. Be a werewolf, that's the modern view.

Of course, others might be filled with revulsion at the knowledge that I've been—what's the word for it? Altered? Infected? In a way, it *is* like a disease, but one that, so far as I can tell, produces no harmful effects and several quite agreeable ones. Affected, perhaps? Yes, I've been affected, and most people will be horrified by the very fact of my existence. Would even be horrified at themselves were they to be similarly affected. There's insanity for you. Popular prejudice, unscientific, superstitious crap. Practically medieval, really. People used to burn alive scientists as witches and demons. Knowledge is a curse to the common man. As for me, what's there to be afraid of? I ask. If I'm a werewolf, that's fine. But how have I really changed otherwise? The fact is, I haven't. I'm still what I was. I'm only now more than that. Not something else, but something in addition. I must get to know what that something is.

Such, I believe, is a modern attitude, and it's with a modern attitude that I hope to study, develop and redefine my new self. What benefit to mankind might there not be in a discovery of this nature? The first acknowledged werewolf. What good may not come of it? I won't pass the rest of my life in dread, that's certain. Muttering *Ave Marias* and draping myself in garlic and rosaries. (Is it garlic that's supposed to hold a special potency for werewolves? I must test this.) A century of advancement in science, of progress and enlightenment, has taught the world a single truth, if men would only open their clouded minds and learn it: Nothing that is, is bad. How healthy would it be for me to hate myself for the thing that I am? Not very, I think. As sane to hate myself for my humanity. That would be a damned sight easier, to my mind, than coming to loathe myself for being a werewolf.

So, here I am. Not afflicted, not blessed. Simply possessed of a singular and thrilling nature. One whose discovery and close examination will be felt to the very bedrock of the scientific world. I've therefore begun this journal to record my observations during these early months of my newfound state. It's not a confession, but an apologia. I'll learn all that's possible to learn in solitude before addressing myself to the world, and I'll require this record if I'm to overcome the antiquated prejudices sure to rise against me when I appear at last as I truly am, upon the larger stage of popular opinion.

Let me begin, then, with first things. My essential transformation, as opposed to my monthly metamorphoses, occurred on a hunting expedition in Transylvania. I was affected, in what I assume to be the only method of passing on the germ, or whatever it is that causes this condition, by surviving an attack from a fellow werewolf. I can only guess that the essence of the werewolf is somehow carried over to another through a break in the skin, a mingling of bloods, though it's impossible to even theorize on the actual operations that produce the effect. As well to admit, too, that on many questions of physiology and the material nature of my transformations, I'll be unable to provide any adequate answers, no more than a man can tell you precisely how he goes about digesting his dinner. Such discoveries can wait until I'm dead, thank you, and beyond the power to object to a more thorough examination than I currently feel comfortable with.

At the time that this fellow werewolf made me like himself (and I should mention that wasn't his intent), I was unaware of the change that had occurred within me. I know I suffered from a mysterious fever for several days, but whether because of my lycanthropy or merely owing to the wounds inflicted upon me, I can't say. The only lasting effect I was sure of was a growing numbness in my arm, which proved to be degenerative nerve and muscle damage. The news that I was gradually to lose the use of my hand touched me deeply. Truth is, I fled to Murcheston and sulked about the estate like an invalid already. Locked myself in the study all day, proof against any effort to reclaim me. Infantile response to misfortune, I know. I offer no excuse. Still, it provided the accidental benefit of making certain I was alone when I first transformed, so it turned out to be a lucky sulk, after all.

Here's how it happened. On the evening of 6 December, after the servants had retired, as I was sitting by a small fire in the study immersed in my usual hobby of contemplating suicide, I became aware of an uncomfortable warmth growing about me. It seemed out of all proportion to the size of the flames in the grate, sputtering weakly, crackling and popping. I roused myself to prod the few logs that were there, trying to extinguish them completely.

My efforts proved futile, however, for while the fire smoldered and died the heat grew steadily more intense. I looked about me. The room was dark, yet I found I could see every detail quite clearly. Nothing there could be giving off such heat. I felt its burning on all sides of me, close and stifling, like being smothered under a weight of bodies. The air grew thick. My breathing labored. By now I knew the heat couldn't be coming from any external source. I must be generating it myself. I'd always viewed with contempt reports of spontaneous combustion, but at that moment, as I began to roast from the inside out, I recalled every such tale that I'd ever heard.

I was soon awash in sweat. My clothing stuck to my flesh and pulled in a way that was maddening. I grasped my shirt and ripped it from my body. Darting about the room now, I began to breathe in sharp, explosive pants while the burning grew within me. I could almost believe that I might soon ignite the house if I continued like this much longer. Was I afraid? I can't recall. I think I was far too agitated to be afraid. No, I couldn't have felt a personal sense of fear, for I'd lost all sense of myself, of my being at its most basic level. How can I relate what I felt? A sensation that almost defies description. Words only cheapen it, impose a logic that's alien to it, totally alien, like telling a story through music or painting in poetry. All I can do is describe my impression of the phenomenon: I ceased to be Darnley and became instead the embodiment of a desire, a desire for relief from the heat primarily. But more than this, simply desire as a perpetual state of being. A longing and fulfillment that became one. I didn't think about my need for relief and so tear off my shirt as a means to that end. I needed to tear off my shirt, that's all. But no, even that's too involved. I didn't *need* anything. I merely acted. Not in response to outside influences but acted in perfect simplicity, pure volition, with a surety that made desire and gratification as natural as inhaling and exhaling. Two inseparable parts of the same life-giving process. Damn, but there just aren't any words for it, this feeling.

And yet I now understand that incessant pacing of the caged beast. For soon this purity of desire crystallized within me, refined itself to the single, overriding passion to be free, to escape the confinement of my room, my body, my very being. To find my reward, not in any result this freedom could produce, but in the freedom itself. I ran madly from side to side of the study, until by chance, for I knew no design, I brushed against the curtains. Took them in my hands and tore them down, my strength ripping them from their rings with ease. They fell heavily to the ground. Before me, through the glass of the French doors, was the moon. I saw it rising full and white above the trees of Murcheston Wood. The moon filling the landscape with its luminous beauty. Milky light suffusing the entire scene with a spectral brilliance. Here was my desire! Here was my freedom! I pushed through the doors to embrace it, to make it mine.

What a wonder I'd become! I raced towards the woods, towards the moon. Leaping and bounding as though by sheer delight I could cover the distance between the earth and this pearl, this goddess of the twilight sky. I can't say when my metamorphosis began or when it ended. By the time I'd reached the trees I was racing on four legs, my transformation complete, my true nature fulfilled. I became possessed of an exuberance and energy unconfined, my every movement an expression of vitality that flowed through my muscles, spilled forth into the world of night surrounding me. Strength enough to realize any urge I could imagine. Or perhaps my animal nature was so true that I couldn't desire anything beyond my grasp. Complete sympathy between soul and body. No, there was no sympathy, for there was no distinction. My body was a mere extension of my soul. My soul an expression of my body.

In this euphoric state I darted about, running for the blissful pleasure to be had in running. Sailing across the stream, over fallen trees. Feeling the strength build in my hind legs, released like a coil let suddenly loose, sending me flying through the air. No longer part of the earth-bound world, lighter than a thought, freer than a dream. I rolled about in the dead autumn leaves out of the most perfect sense of joy I've ever known. Every emotion, every mood that took me did so as for the first time, with an intensity drawn from my physical strength. There are some moments that I can recall, as I sit here recording my impressions, some fantasies almost, of childhood, times spent bounding through that same wooded landscape, supremely happy in the simple rightness of the moment. Multiply that boyish happiness by the fullness of experience, and you can approach an understanding of my ecstasy.

I finally rested, panting as I lay on the carpet of the forest, tired but not spent. Enjoying even the feeling of exhaustion. Put my head down on my forelegs and closed my eyes. The woods were silent. A wind gently pushed the branches of the trees and, close by, the stream sang its eternal melody. All else was still. Soon the sounds of the night creatures returned. Birds and small animals, shocked into quiet by my revels, now went about their business, taking no greater notice of me than of the stars. I was no more foreign to their world than were the grass and the stream.

I became witness to the round of their nocturnal life as I could never be privy to it as a man, when my very scent was enough to fill them with mute fear. I opened my eyes and looked about. In the brightness of the moonlight, I made out birds fluttering from branch to branch in the treetops, a ballet of ceaseless activity. In the distance, at the edge of the woods, a family of rabbits sat lazily munching on weeds. Suddenly, to my left and hard by, an owl swooped down from its perch and carried off a hapless mouse in its talons. Some few yards before me a snake moved soundlessly out of its home in a dead tree.

This entire drama played itself out with a total disregard for my presence. I was not an observer of this world but a participant. For a long time I lay there in the grass, attentive, serene, satisfied just to be where I was and what I was. A contentment filled with possibilities. At last I rose and trotted off silently to the stream. Lapped up the cool water and was refreshed.

The taste of the water after my exertions made me hungry, so I turned, raised my snout into the air, sniffed. A thousand different smells I'd been oblivious to before rushed upon me, almost moved me physically with their intensity and complexity, their very numbers a sensual riot. Quite surprisingly, I knew many of them. Caught the fragrance of every flower and leaf of course, but above this I recognized the slightly oily scent of the rabbits, the mustiness of the owl and the sharp pungency of the fish in the stream. And then there was the rich, sweet smell of venison. My muscles went taut at the aroma. For an instant I sat in stillness, lapping up the smell, tasting it, feeding off of it. Then I was away, moving quickly but noiselessly in the direction of the scent. The deer was nearby, I could tell, and I followed its invisible trail stealthily, keeping myself downwind and staying within the shadows as much as possible.

I picked up its scent in the leaves and knew where and how long ago it had passed and where it was heading. My nerves were attuned to every change in the breeze and to every presence in the air. I moved smoothly and surely, not with the tentative step of the human hunter afraid to make a sound, but with a swift, silent tread imperceptible amid the life of the night. As I closed in on my prey, my eyes cut through the dark and penetrated the shadows, perceiving all, leaving no smallest detail unnoticed, not the graceful swaying of the leaves in the trees and the birds in the branches, not the rolling bustle of a hedgehog attacking an anthill, not even, I think, the low rumbling beneath my feet of a badger stirring himself for his night's activity. Yet, in spite of my heightened sensibilities, I was oddly relaxed. My breathing slow and calm. My heart beating evenly. My muscles possessed of a peculiar ease, as though preserving themselves for the contest ahead.

The scent became stronger with each step, and I knew where the deer was even before I saw it. A doe with her fawn grazing among the trees, unconcerned for their safety, unaware of their danger. I could see, actually see the slackness of her muscles, the easy confidence of her motions. I crouched low to the earth and slowly circled about them, instinctively cautious not to allow my own scent to give me away. They stood in a close growth of poplars affording some slight protection, but also limiting their opportunities of escape. I was in no hurry, for I was downwind and the breeze was strong to hide my presence, and the night was yet new. I edged about until I discovered a clear path through the trees, one that gave me the advantage of movement while trap-ping the pair in the closeness of their natural cage. I lay still for several minutes, not from indecision, but gauging the moment within myself, tensing my muscles and waiting for the instant when the force of my spring and their own easy attitude were in perfect concert.

At the last second, I growled. The fawn's head shot up. I launched myself through the trees. The doe stamped frantically for a moment. Tried to find a path among the thickness around her. Then shot off through a narrow space no larger than a crack. The fawn couldn't follow in time. I was on top of it, crushed it to the earth and killed it in the same instant. I felt no exhilaration in this, no sense of triumph like I have known when hunting as a man. The fawn was prey. I was hungry. No other thought entered my mind. When I had killed it, I fed. Its flesh was tender and sweet, wild and delicate at the same time, and I devoured it languidly. Not savoring the flavor so much as the moment, the experience of eating so freely, tearing flesh from bone with my teeth, drinking the blood, nourishing my life with the life of another. Sated, I trotted off again, this time to rest by the stream. The mud of the bank felt soothing as I lay down under a tree at the water's edge. And soon I was asleep.

When I awoke, it was dawn. The sunlight melted through the branches like amber and, in the distance, birds sang their good mornings. I knew before I opened my eyes that I was a man again, but I found that fact neither troubling nor a relief, as I suppose I should have been expected to do. After my nocturnal adventures everything seemed right to me, and I felt the most delicious sense of renewal. As though that morose, self-pitying fool I'd been was devoured by the werewolf I'd become. I felt healthy and whole, complete somehow, fulfilled. It didn't for a second occur to me at the time to question the reality of what I'd experienced. My every atom attested to the change I'd undergone. I stretched as I lay there on the bank and rolled over toward the stream to splash some water in my face.

No sooner had I done so than, lifting my eyes to the opposite side, I saw that I wasn't alone. Three men, staring at me in what I must admit was a perfectly understandable attitude of astonishment, stood at the edge of the stream. Sterling, my butler, looking more concerned than confused, frowned with knitted brow, causing his bushy silver eyebrows to join in the center of his forehead. My man Branford looked away the instant I glanced at him, obviously humiliated by the spectacle I presented. And the stable hand, Cabrini, his massive jaw hanging limply open, screwed up his face into a vulgar expression that made him appear almost to be laughing silently. I rose at once to my feet, and only then realized that I was absolutely naked and bespattered with mud and gore. It was a delicate moment. I didn't know at first what to say, so all I got out was a weak, "Good morning," which was answered by Sterling with a nod and a barely audible, "Your Grace."

Although I hadn't been aware of it before, the chill in the autumn air now sliced through me to the bone and I began to shiver. This proved to be the catalyst the situation needed. Sterling and Branford immediately waded across the stream, draping a coat around my shoulders, helping me cross over to the other side. (Branford had, I learned later, discovered my abandoned clothing, some of it strewn out across the lawn, and Sterling had organized this impromptu party to come rescue me from whatever peril I'd fallen into.) My contented state of the minute before temporarily deserted me. Truth is, I was feeling rather compromised by the situation. Once we'd reached the far bank and Cabrini succeeded in helping us all out of the stream, I stopped to rest against a large oak. I needed time to consider how to deal with this awkward business. What excuses could I plausibly make? What reason was there for sleeping in the woods in autumn, naked, covered in mud and blood and filth? Nothing came to mind.

It was Sterling who demonstrated his good sense and loyalty by paving the way to a solution. "Gentlemen," he said, turning to his companions, "I don't believe that it will be necessary to mention any details surrounding this matter once we return to the manor. It's enough that we have located His Grace and he is well. 'Least said, soonest mended,' I think an appropriate guide by which to govern our behavior, under the circumstances."

Branford merely nodded his assent. (He wasted little time later that very day in serving notice, however.) But Cabrini, who's a large, brash Italian with an insolent manner and the natural arrogance of his race, couldn't contain his amusement at my predicament. He laughed mockingly under his breath and said, "As well it is to keep this a secret. Talk about this and we'd every one of us be taken for a loony."

His mirth had only just passed his lips when I flung the coat aside and threw myself upon him. In a single leap I covered the yards separating us. Took him forcibly by the collar, striking him twice across the face, knocking him soundly to the earth with the second blow. It all happened more quickly than can be spoken. Even before Cabrini came to rest on the ground, I regretted the rashness of the act, but the man's presumption had goaded me into an unthinking rage. The violence of my response caught everyone by surprise, and we all stood in mute amazement. Cabrini lay in the dirt with his mouth open, rubbing his jaw and staring up at me with a mixture of disbelief and anger.

Once more Sterling salvaged the moment. "Mr. Branford, see to that scoundrel, if you would," he ordered calmly, picking up the coat and replacing it across my shoulders. "Cabrini," he continued when the stable hand had been lifted to his feet, "when we have returned to the manor, you will please collect your wages and go."

"No," I interposed. "Just let this be a lesson to temper his rudeness with a little good sense." Sterling nodded his approval of my generosity, prompted more by contrition than mercy, and we all started back.

The blow I'd struck stung my right hand. As I walked behind the sullen Cabrini, with Sterling and Branford at my side, I stroked the hand beneath the folds of my coat, soothing the ache vigorously, rubbing, rubbing. With a gasp, as though I'd been physically stung, I realized that the hand I was using to minister to my hurt, my left hand, the hand that had the night before been doomed to slow death and decay, this hand was now quite strong and whole! I lifted it before my face. There was no doubt. The scars that had been left by the wound were all but gone, and the feeling had returned even down to my fingertips! Of course, the reason for this remarkable recovery is still obscure to me, but that it's a direct result of my metamorphosis seems indisputable. I thought about this for a good while upon my return. The transformation from man to wolf and back again almost certainly causes a general restructuring of my physical form, and one of the happier effects of this is that it produces a miraculous healing property. The tissue, which had been previously severed, must have been knitted together by the very act of my becoming a wolf, the alteration effecting the repairs.

I didn't leap to this conclusion at once. I arrived at it during the month following. Of course, there was precious little about which I could theorize after only a single transformation, and my first idea, that I'd be similarly affected the next evening, proved mistaken. I waited impatiently for the moon to rise, and even thought that I felt again that growing warmth that heralds the change, but the evening passed uneventfully. If it weren't for my hand, I'd have lost all faith that I'd ever experienced any of it. My restored health was compelling proof that I hadn't gone totally mad and imagined everything, however, and the time until the next full moon passed for me in an almost unendurable fog of anxiety and anticipation.

The days progressed in a sort of frantic stasis. Everything seemed to be standing still to me. I tried any number of senseless activities to take my mind off my questions and hopes. One of my chief occupations was rummaging through the library for information. The Old Governor, the twelfth duke, was a voracious reader, and his collection reflects not just an appetite for books but eclectic tastes as well. I pored over everything I could find, which wasn't much. Some half dozen volumes on supernatural phenomena, a classification which annoys me no end. What is there *super*natural about it? What is in greater sympathy with nature than a werewolf? What more perfectly illustrates the union between man and animal? Be that as it may, the volumes possessed limited interest for me. Still, I found them entertaining, if not particularly instructive.

Most of what I uncovered was complete rubbish; fairy stories and fables of ravenous monsters terrorizing the countryside. Damned senseless tales told out of ignorance. Still, some of it's useful. Werewolves, it seems, are as old as man's own history, and shape-changing is considered by some races to be a sign of celestial favor. Primitive religions place great faith in an individual's power to become an animal, acquiring the attributes of the beast, as strength from a lion, cunning from a fox, swiftness from a deer and so forth. In the East especially, these beliefs bear all the authority of common wisdom. Truth is, few of these legends agree with each other in the details. Such a fundamental matter as the species itself is rarely uniform from one culture to the next. The Chinese, for example, join myth with myth by making the dragon the preferred object of shape-changing, while the leopard and the lion are favored in Africa. The method of transformation is likewise problematic, and the moon is no more likely to be mentioned than is the eating of certain herbs and roots, or even the simple volition of the shape-changer himself.

To learn so much was the work of four afternoons, leaving me with about three and one-half weeks until the next full moon. I tried to ignore my own eagerness. To pass the time in quiet simplicity. To control my thoughts, my fancies, my dreams and hopes. These studies into the phenomenon rekindled a fascination with the library that I've always held, though rarely had the time or inclination to act upon, and I determined to keep myself busy with a regular diet of reading. Breakfast at eight, at the books by nine, throw myself into any volumes that caught my eye until one, luncheon for two hours, with more reading until dinner and an evening spent jotting down odd thoughts that had come to me during my studies, then an early bed. A monk would have envied my regularity and discipline. But, as a means of taking my mind off my concerns, the whole program was a failure. Like a traveler through a distant country who sees in every foreign landscape some reminder of home, so everything I read held some reference to my condition. Indeed, some of the allusions were startling. Naturally, my mind was remarkably receptive to the vaguest mention of anything approaching lycanthropy. But there was still enough specific information, in what's generally considered serious literature, to support my theory that werewolves have existed beside men throughout the centuries.

Of course, every schoolboy is familiar with the tale of Lucan, how he reveled and mocked the gods until Zeus, enraged and vengeful at such jolly atheism, transformed that contemptuous king into a wolf. Ovid chose this story above all others to launch his *Metamorphosis*. But fewer recognize the shape-changing details in Homer's *Odyssey*, when Circe transforms Odysseus' crew into swine. And fewer still recall the werewolves mentioned in two of the most highly regarded works of antiquity. First, the *History* of Herodotus, that well-spring of classical knowledge, makes a direct reference to werewolves in describing the customs of the Neurian race. These people, who lived as a tribe near the Scythians, are reported by the historian to have changed into wolves, every one of them, for a few days out of each year. That such was the case was sworn to by both the Scythians and the Greeks living in Scythia, and Herodotus seems to place some credence in the rumor. A similar, though somewhat grislier reference, occurs in *The Republic*. There, Plato makes note in passing of the tradition of the temple of the Lycaean Zeus in Arcadia, and the belief held by the devotees of that place that any man who tastes of the entrails of a human victim when mixed up with the entrails of other victims, though but once, that man is destined to change into a wolf.

The authority of these references enthralled me and I leapt into my studies with renewed vigor, but with no great result, and the time passed more slowly still. The calendar seemed as immovable as Gibraltar, and from dawn to dusk I lived a whole life in nervous anxiety, waiting for the full moon.

Last night it occurred again. I gave the entire staff the evening off and instructed Sterling to see to it that everyone remained close by their quarters while I retired to the study. There, in spite of the severely cold weather, I opened the French doors, removed all of my clothing, and waited for the rising of the moon. The warmth that precedes the metamorphosis wasn't so uncomfortable this time. Soothing, actually. It began in the region just above my groin and gradually enveloped me until I was filled with a flow of vitality, every muscle awake, every sense alert. The agitation I displayed last month was also gone, replaced by a sense of comfortable certainty, a rightness about the changes happening to me. Still, I paced about from the very excess of energy. Strength doubling and redoubling in my shoulders, back, and legs. The sharpening of my sight, smell, and hearing, all intensely receptive to the world of nature surrounding me. Power growing within me, which I felt most keenly at the very pit of my stomach and followed as it spread itself out to my extremities. All part of a larger fullness that pervaded my entire being, reshaping and redefining not merely my form, but my self. What satisfaction, what bliss I felt at that moment! The suffusion of life embracing me as my true nature was manifested. I returned to the woods I'd left a month before.

No need to go into the details of last night. I'd only be repeating sensations I've already described. Yet the event was no less exciting for me than it had been. Once again I lost myself in the moment, in the everlasting now of my wolf-life. It's as though I live with a separate notion of time when I'm a wolf, in a perpetual present renewing itself constantly, and I have no concept of tomorrow or yesterday, no sense of a time other than the very night of my transformation. My whole memory is tied to the physical, the tangible objects of my desire. My only future is the hunger I feel that causes me to stalk. My past is but instinct. My greatest pleasure comes from my most immediate experience of life, the simple exertion of the powers that possess me, my strength and agility, speed and animal cunning.

I didn't feed last night, for the opportunity never showed itself. I did sleep, but only briefly, and yet that short slumber might have ended in a repetition of the last month's humiliation and is worth considering. I'd determined that I should remain awake for the entirety of my transformation, and hoped by preparedness to avoid another embarrassing discovery. I hadn't counted on the fact that, once in my animal state, such plans are of absolutely no importance to me. Indeed, are quite literally unthinkable to me. I was therefore roused in my human form only by the merest chance, a chipmunk rustling the dry leaves. The sun was already climbing into the blue of the daytime sky, and with a yelp I bounded out of the woods and ran naked over the lawn toward the manor. I didn't even slow down as I neared the haha but threw myself across it and came down on the other side without breaking my stride.

The life of Murcheston had already begun. Through the windows of the kitchen I could see the cook readying breakfast. Above, on the first floor, someone was opening the curtains of my bedroom. Soon they would come looking for me in the study. With a final great burst of energy I flew over the remaining yards and only just managed to make it back through the French doors before there was a knock and Sterling's voice asked if I were well. Breathlessly, panting and gasping like a drowning man, I assured him that I was perfectly fine. Gathering my clothes up and throwing them on, I asked that he draw me a bath. I was once more covered in filth from my nocturnal games.

On reflection, I realize the peril of discovery I placed myself in last night. The danger will only become more acute as the nights grow shorter and the moon remains in the sky well into the daylight hours. I've therefore started on a course of action that will almost certainly create some talk about Brixton and Darnley Well. But I think a little gossip infinitely more acceptable than the alternative. I'm releasing the entire staff, letting them all go. Sounds drastic, I know. But damn it all, what else can I do? Can't keep a reliable track of twenty-seven people. Can't expect them to stay locked up in their rooms one night out of the month and not have them wonder why. To allow so many about me during my transformation is to court disaster. It's really for their safety that I'm doing this. Naturally, I'll leave on a few servants to keep the place in my absence. But for all its size, how many are truly necessary to run the manor? No more than two or three, I should guess. These I'll send to Brixton every month, and that way I'll have the freedom I need without risking an untimely encounter.

I've already consulted Sterling about this new arrangement.

He was at first deeply troubled. Convinced himself in an instant that his management of the estate somehow is the cause for these measures of economy. I told him he wasn't to blame, that I had no need for so large a staff as I would be using Murcheston only as a retreat from the city in the future, but his guilt wouldn't be assuaged. Still, he recovered himself sufficiently to recommend how I might decide whom should be retained. Of course, I'll keep him and his wife. She'll serve as cook and housekeeper while he attends to what few duties remain pertaining to the operations of the manor. I don't know why he should be so grief-stricken. This is practically a retirement on pension for him. I plan to replace Branford upon my return to London, and the new man need never come up with me. Sterling convinced me that I might keep Grey and his boys easily enough to handle the immediate grounds, especially as their cottage is on the edge of the estate, making them less likely to prove a nuisance. It looks as though I'll be forced to keep on Cabrini as well. Sterling is getting on and will require someone to tend the horses and do the heavy work, and Cabrini is well-suited to hard labor. The rest I'll send off with references and some coins.

As to my own schedule, I've already acquired a reliable almanac from Old Grey, and using this I hope to compile a lunar table, allowing me to arrive with certainty no less than twenty-four hours before the full moon. I'll doubtless be a topic of great speculation in Brixton, but it's better to be considered a hermit and an eccentric than to be known for a werewolf. I'm equally certain that my domestic arrangements will have to be altered in other ways as I accustom myself to my new life, but I shouldn't have to plan for that yet. Whatever bridges of that sort I have to cross can wait.

And so it's off to London with me, and the vast scholarly resources of the metropolis. I'm filled with the task that lies before me, to research this condition, this lycanthropy of mine. To make myself an authority on the topic, just as nature has made me its practitioner. I mustn't raise my hopes too far, of course. Much of the available literature will be of highly questionable value. Still, whatever is out there, I'll find it. It can't escape me. Once I have the scent, there's nothing can shake me in my purpose. I am indomitable. I must learn everything, everything there is to know about this novel life I'm living, this miraculous existence that's so suddenly mine. Mine to explore and enjoy. And eventually, mine to share with all the world.

5

Discoveries

18 January

Nothing. Not a shred, not a scrap of information can I find. For a week now I've haunted the book stalls looking for anything that might contain reliable information on werewolves and their habits. I never hoped to discover serious scholarship, of course. No Parliamentary reports or university tracts. But, damn it, I expected to find something! The faintest glimmer of a tale to shed some light on what I am. A legend, a rumor, a bit of country gossip, anything!

And what's worse than my complete failure is that I'm constantly being teased with success, as though the gods of my fate are deliberately toying with me. More than once I've deceived myself into believing I found the very thing I'm searching for. Just this afternoon I was rummaging through an obscure corner of a depressingly dark and dusty shop, scanning titles in a stupor, hypnotized by the dull repetition of my toil. Suddenly, my eye lit on a book high above me, on the topmost shelf of a veritable Gargantua of a bookcase, fourteen feet high and at least six feet broad.

A massive volume, too, elaborately bound, all leather and gilding. With the enticing title of *Santerre the Wolf* embroidered along its spine. My heart flew up to it in an instant, spirited away on the wings of desire while my poor, wretched body struggled painfully behind, moving from shelf to shelf, more than once in danger of bringing the whole thing down upon me. Like Moses daring the heights of Mount Sinai, I went my tortured way up the side of the bookcase. And no sooner had I reached my prize and grasped it in my fist than I lost hold of the bookcase altogether and fell crashing back to the floor. Suffering these indignities to acquire the cursed thing, I skimmed feverishly through its pages only to discover that it's a damned sickly romance about a French high-wayman. I cursed so violently I fear I scandalized the old witch who ran the place. No less than I deserve for daring to hope.

20 January

Ashamed to record that my frustrations got the better of me today. It occurred while I was walking about the stalls down a dark, narrow lane in Camden Town. The air was cold and thick, saturated with the sort of nasty January rain that doesn't so much fall from the skies as lace the air like a spider's web, waiting for you to step into it. My spirits hung about me, heavy and limp like my overcoat, drenched through with the chill of my temper. I'd just been fooled by another volume with the word "wolf" in the title, another trap set by a sadistic destiny to play with me. I can't even recall what the title was except that it was typically sensational and turned out to be another damned romance. The disappointment was too great, and in spite of the fact that it was still early, I pulled my collar up about my ears and turned toward home. A dark cloud hovered above my head as I pushed through the crowd, only mechanically aware of the people closing me in on every side.

All of a sudden, and seemingly from out of the very substance of the weather, a coach, a juggernaut, resplendent and terrible, came rumbling down the lane at full gallop, flinging mud and confusion upon the passersby in its wake. All was noise, chaos, a tumult of bodies as the solid mass of men and women split asunder, dodging the horses and the filth. A crush of humanity along the narrow pavement, pressing against the windows of the surrounding shops, with umbrellas turned to stilettos and heels transformed into millstones. It was a situation to sour the sweetest temper and send mine into a blind rage. As soon as I felt this press of flesh closing in on me from all sides, grinding me down, smothering me, stifling me with its weight and odor, I instinctively pressed back hard, and three working-class men trying innocently to avoid the muck of the street ended up sprawled at my feet, wallowing in it.

What had I done? For an instant I stood dumbfounded, appalled with myself, with this fit of childish pique. I've never been a man of violent actions, but the situation was so suffocating and my mood so black that I reacted without thinking. Of course, I remained to help the poor souls up from the ground, and offered my card to each of them so they might charge me with any repairs they required. But I confess, at the moment that I exerted myself and sent them splashing, I felt the most marvelous sense of justice. As if they were the true causes of my larger troubles, not merely the victims of my despondency. And I left the scene feeling—I don't really want to admit it, but I felt easier in my mind for having asserted myself in this demonstrative fashion. I went whistling on my way in fitter mettle than I've been in these many days.

I thought little of this at the time. But I've been sitting here this evening with nothing else to occupy my mind and the questions keep popping up over and over again. What prompted me to push those fellows into the mud? Why did I enjoy it so? I've noticed, ever since returning from Murcheston, that I've felt differently about people. I'm detached from them. Kept apart by the secret knowledge that I hold. Do I fear discovery? I don't see how that's possible. But if I have no cause to fear, why haven't I ventured out into society since being affected? I've had several attractive invitations. This very day, a card came from Lady Shippley demanding that I attend her at her salon, and I'm sure to run into E. if I go. Perhaps that's why I stay away, to keep my distance from her. The truth is, the very thought of sharing my time with others frightens me somehow, makes me deeply uneasy. And this incident today has only focused my mind on these fears.

Yet all these questions, these doubts, what do they amount to? Not a bloody thing. Why do I feel so oppressed by what's obviously a very natural reaction to my unique situation? I alone in the whole world carry about the knowledge of my true nature. It's a momentous secret. Doubtless the burden of possessing it, the weight of it on my consciousness, is enough to make me feel this way. It's still so very new to me. I mustn't make too much of this sense of isolation. It will pass before long, I'm sure of it. I'll become more comfortable with myself, with my nature. And as I do so, I'll feel more at home in the world again. It takes only patience. That, and a bit more luck with my studies.

4 February

Despite my best planning, I can see now that allowing even a small staff to remain at Murcheston while I conduct my researches is too dangerous. Dangerous for me and dangerous for others. I must continue alone. I've suffered through a little domestic comedy here, and I can't let such a thing ever happen again. Already exposed myself to too much talk, too much speculation. There must be an end to it.

I arrived two days ago at Brixton, meeting Cabrini at the station. He brought me out in the cabriolet, for it was unseasonably bright and warm through the afternoon, and the fragrant air was a delightful change from the stench of London. He delivered me to the door, where Sterling and his missus stood dutifully to receive me, as though they were the usual army of servants and not just themselves. I was amazed at how settled and well-kept everything appeared, and at first my arrangements seemed to be working ideally. The larger rooms were left in a state of storage. Windows shuttered, carpets rolled up, sheets draped over everything, a museum of ghostly figures. Only the foyer, the dining hall, the study, the parlor, and the library on the ground floor, and the master bedroom on the first floor were left uncovered. All else was shrouded and abandoned.

I spent my first day busy with the mundane chores of the estate. Listened to Sterling report on how he'd managed the manor. Spent a tedious three hours with Pike as he explained his plans to convert another few acres from pasturage to agriculture this spring. Awful, dry stuff. And Pike is just the sort of fellow you don't want to hear it all from. His chief recommendation as a steward is that he's a bloody bore with no imagination. Now he tells me he's afraid of losing more boys from Darnley Well to the coal mines at Brixton, and he'll have that many fewer hands this year for the planting. I needn't have reminded him that it's the mines that pay for the farming lately. Still, I told him he could prohibit any further migrations to Brixton with my authority. Stupid business, really, keeping the fields going when there's so much more to be had beneath them. The tenants are the only ones now to make anything out of the soil, and that's precious little for them as it is.

All of these problems put me in a nasty mood by nightfall, and the next morning I gratefully packed Sterling and his wife into the cart, along with Cabrini, and told them not to return for two days. No questions, at least none were asked, but dear Mrs. Sterling was loathe to abandon me at the last. Said it was an insult to her industry that I should survive for two days without her services, and she knew I would suffer for it. She left such a buffet of cold meats, cheeses, breads and cakes on the sideboard, however, that I told her I doubted I should miss her attentions overly much, and so shipped her off with a clear conscience. Dear God, what liberty at last! I took a deep breath, and then another, filling my body with the air of freedom. Finally escaping the throng of the City, its foulness and noise, the crush of its millions, I felt the pressure of my secret fall away from me, and I could relax, truly relax for the first time in a month.

The metamorphosis itself came as an intense relief and has absolutely transformed my damaged soul. To take pleasure in the immediacy of existence, to revel in the *now* of life, without a worry for the future or a thought about the past. This is the only real panacea that I know of. I can't imagine an ailment it shouldn't cure, and even as I sit here and recall my last night's pursuits, I'm filled with a sustaining contentment. All would be perfect if it weren't for a single development that's complicated matters.

It happened toward dawn, when the color is drained from the sky and the only sign of the approaching sun is a graying of the horizon. I rose from my place by the stream and, still in my wolf-state, began to trot carelessly about the edge of the woods facing the manor. I don't know what held me so close to the house, why I didn't venture deeper into the forest, but there was something about the place that captured my attention. It was late. I hadn't eaten all night. The long rest I'd taken had sharpened my appetite, and I put my nose to the air to see what might be about. The breeze blew across the lawn, carrying with it a single strong scent, musty and full, a scent I knew quite well, even as a man. I wouldn't have thought a horse particularly appetizing, but no sooner did I catch the whiff of a mare on the wind than my stomach took a hot grip of me, and I dropped down and peered intently toward the house.

I couldn't see my prey, but I could smell the turned earth and manure of Mrs. Sterling's garden just outside the kitchen door, and my instincts told me that the creature was there, with the corner of the manor safely between us. I didn't hesitate, not for an instant. Leapt from the woods and darted across the expanse of the lawn, flying over the haha and pulling myself up alongside the house. Crouched low and close to the wall, moving in rapid starts from shadow to shadow, the whole while keeping my nose up and feeling the air for my prey. Finally, I came to the corner of a wall and, lying deep in the grass, stretched my neck out slowly, an inch at a time, to peer around the edge. She was an old mare, sway-backed, well past the years of her greatest usefulness. Her head hung down like a great weight as she grazed on Mrs. Sterling's carrots. She was facing slightly away from the house, just angled toward me. My eyes danced about for the merest moment, looking for any available cover, a shrub or a wall that might disguise my approach, give me the advantage I required to move nearer. Nothing presented itself, and I knew I must rely on strength more than cunning if I were to feed that night.

The moment is alive to me as I sit here. I pull my head back, gradually tense and relax my muscles and tense them again. Shift my paws in the dirt, rapidly, tearing up clods of earth, not from nerves or agitation, but only to bring my energy to the very pitch of an explosion. This time, I make not the slightest sound when I spring. With the stealth of a dream I move, light and airy through the night, nothing more than a shade floating amid shadows and darkness. A quarter of the distance to her and I see her every sinew convulse, transforming her to granite. I devour the space between us with each bound. She raises her head and stares at me. Our eyes meet. Her panic, her fear, even her death are all writ there, writ large and awful, stoking the hunger within me, making me mad for her, to possess her. At the last moment she turns to flee. Too late. I pounce. Flying through the air, soaring, sailing at her, landing squarely on her withers. Desperation and fright and agony are all her cry as I sink my claws and teeth into her tough, aged flesh. She bolts, throws herself about in a vain attempt to dislodge me. But my hold is sure and she soon stumbles and falls under my weight. I leap away before she hits the ground and bound lightly back to finish her. Rake my claws across her throat, six, seven, eight times in less than half as many seconds. At last I tear away at her with my teeth. I taste that she is dead. The moon doesn't set for another hour, and I feed contentedly until then.

The sun was already up and the moon long gone when I found myself lying amid the viscera of the mare. Her throat was torn open and blood seeped across the terrace where she'd fallen. Her belly and haunches were also shredded and offal spilled out from the wound and splayed over the paving stones. All in all, I'd have to say I made a bloody mess of her. As I looked down upon the beast and the grisly picture she presented, I confess a sharp pang of remorse pierced my soul, only for a moment. The mare was an old, placid creature used by Mrs. Sterling on Sundays for going to church in Darnley Well and for the infrequent trip to Brixton. A gentler animal was hard to find, and her loss will be a blow to the old woman. But what can be done for it? Who's really culpable for this death? Am I to blame? I was merely responding to my hunger, which bade me kill to sustain my own life. In my wolf-state I can't defer my meals for a more propitious time. When hungry, I eat. To eat, I kill. What's more obvious, more natural than that? If anyone is to answer for this affair, it's Cabrini. I gave him explicit instructions to leave the horses in the stable with sufficient food and water to see them through until his return. If the mare escaped from her stall, then he's the one who must be held accountable. For the moment I brushed these thoughts aside and set about cleaning up.

It soon became apparent, however, that while a brisk scrub would do for me, the mare was a more difficult problem. The morning was rapidly growing late as I stood out on the terrace before her, looking at that vast lump of flesh. To move her even an inch was impossible, at least as she was. But I thought, if I could cut her up into more manageable bits, perhaps just the shanks and the head, then quarter the remainder, I might be able to get her out into the woods where I could bury her with no great trouble. The idea seemed perfectly plausible at the time. I was honestly willing to try anything rather than have to explain this to Sterling. So I went foraging about the kitchen without delay, looking for Mrs. Sterling's butchering tools. Found a large cleaver, a knife that was almost a machete, and a handful of smaller blades for the more delicate work.

I started off to decapitate the beast. The cleaver was sharp enough for the task, but had never been meant for anything near the size of the mare's neck. I soon found myself hacking away madly at the thing, severing meat and bone in short segments with wild strikes of the blade. I'm lucky I didn't cut off my own hand. It took me almost three-quarters of an hour to work my way through and finally free the head from the body. Even so, I found that I could barely lift it much less carry it across the lawn to the woods, and so I set about reluctantly to dissect it even further. It took me another hour to separate the bony snout from the rest of the head, but at least by then I could pick up and transport the two halves with comparative ease. Next, the haunches. These were even tougher going than the neck had been, requiring slow sawing instead of hacking. My shoulders, back, and arms tired quickly, and I was almost spent by the time I'd cut away the right hind leg. Thank God, I was able to make quicker work of the right foreleg, but then I was confronted with the prospect of turning the carcass over so as to reach the left side. I couldn't do it. It was just impossible. What's worse, I'd lost all sense of time. After huffing and puffing with the body for a good hour trying vainly to roll it over, I noticed with sudden dismay that the sun had begun to dip under the horizon and I knew there was no chance of disposing of this damned monster before the morning when the servants would return. There was nothing to be done for it. I left the scattered remains where they were and dragged myself into the study to clean up.

And so again I'm thwarted. Once more circumstances conspire to mock my careful preparations. After reducing my entire staff to a skeleton in the hopes of avoiding any more embarrassing incidents and explanations, I immediately suffer a damned worse catastrophe than I've yet known. I can't allow this to happen again. I must take whatever steps are needed to ensure, to positively guarantee my privacy in the future.

What's more, the day has been warm and the stench of the mare is becoming intolerable. I've splashed some water over the various parts of her and washed the blood away, but it's done little good. As it is, that wing of the house which contains the kitchen and the dining hall has become uninhabitable. I've taken my supper and am sleeping in the study. God, what a miserable, frightful business this all has gotten to be.

5 February

My life becomes more complicated with each dawn. Sterling and the others returned today. No sense in trying to hide the mare's death. The evidence hung palpably in the air. I was surprised at how Mrs. Sterling took it. She really was a brick about the whole thing, for when the men were confronted with the sight of the mare, partially devoured and sloppily butchered and already bloated with decay, they blanched and turned away with sick expressions on their faces. Not Mrs. Sterling. She's handled enough carcasses in her day, I should think, to last her through a month of such sights. She started in to rail against the creature at once, damning it in her modest way for getting where it had no good cause to be. She next confronted me and gave me a good hiding for trying to manage the business of disposal myself and doing such a wretched job of it. Finally, she turned brusquely to Cabrini and sent him off for spades and a wagon, and for the remainder of the day Sterling, Cabrini and I (for I felt a substantial degree of responsibility and so took my share in the labor) set to work burying the thing.

Of course, Mrs. Sterling's sole concern was cleaning up the terrace and removing every trace of the sorry affair, but her husband had other worries on his mind. He understood the larger significance of what had happened, its portent for the estate. Once the thing was loaded on the wagon and we three men proceeded with it down the drive and away from the house, Sterling voiced these silent fears. "Forgive me for asking, Your Grace," he inquired, respectfully, of course, always respectfully, "but have you any idea what could have slain Riga? One can't help noticing that she has been fed upon, and I was just wondering if you saw anything during your time alone that might explain that fact. My interest is more than curiosity, I assure you."

"I really can't say," I told him. "I awoke yesterday morning and found her dead and devoured this way. Possibly she died of natural causes and some wild scavenger about the place took advantage of the situation."

"Scavengers, is it?" Cabrini cried incredulously. "Do you suppose a fox did this? Or maybe it were a badger, for that's the fiercest thing I've seen in these woods. This'd be a good piece of work for a bear, I should think, or a whole pack of wolves. But whatever's done it, I don't suppose it'll be quitting the neighborhood anytime soon."

"I'm afraid Mr. Cabrini is correct, sir," Sterling added with cold precision. "You need only glance at the condition of her throat. This is not the work of scavengers. With Your Grace's permission, I think we should organize a hunting party at once to look into this matter more thoroughly."

I felt myself falling into the depths of this dilemma as into a well of deceit. Was there any way to divert attention from the incident? I had no time to think. I felt as crowded now by Cabrini and Sterling as ever I felt in the suffocating atmosphere of the City. "For now the job is to dispose of this rotting carcass before it becomes entirely corrupt," I informed them. "We can worry ourselves about what caused this later." I succeeded in neither silencing them completely nor allaying their fears, however.

We set to the task with an ill will. Cabrini kept muttering about the unlikely cause of the mare's demise, though I felt it wiser to let him suppose what he would than to appear too cavalier. The fool's opinions were slight cause for concern regardless. What I found disturbing was Sterling's gloominess. He was too well-bred to air his thoughts outright after I'd dismissed the topic, yet I could tell that his mind was turning the problem over every which way, and he wasn't satisfied with what he saw. If his suspicions could be aroused over this, I thought, he whose very nature is discretion, then what chance did I have of passing over the incident lightly as the idle marauding of some passing beast now gone from the premises? Absurd that anyone should accept such an outrageous lie. But damn it, I had nothing else to offer at the time.

After a bit Grey showed up with his two sons to see what we were about. What an odd trio we must have made, too, digging away in this secluded corner of the woods. Old Grey's response to the ragged corpse was slightly less dramatic than my companions' had been, but he was more openly inquisitive. I got tired very soon of his unwelcome company. Still, what could I say to silence him that wouldn't arouse suspicion? Even on my own estate, I was held prisoner by my secret. Sterling took the opportunity to interrogate the caretaker, ask whether he were aware of any large predators in the vicinity. But Grey could give no good answer. He only said that he and his boys would look about for signs of anything and let me know what they found. I was damned grateful to leave the matter in his hands, and so appear to be pursuing a solution to a problem I knew didn't exist.

Grey's older boy remained to lend his strong back to the work, but it still took most of the day to accomplish. By the time we were finished and poor Riga lay beneath the sod, *requiescat in pace*, it was nearly dusk, and the shadows of the trees were reaching out across the lawn toward the manor. I told Sterling to supervise whatever little details remained, and then to see me in the study after he'd dined. I had a great deal to consider, and I strolled through the woods back to the house, thinking, "What the hell can I do? How can I ensure my privacy, my safety?" But it was all a pretense, this mooning and worrying over the situation. There was no doubt about what I had to do. I'd already decided on the course to take. I only had to do it, that was all.

I ate a little something and then prepared myself for the disagreeable task that lay ahead. Sterling appeared promptly and

stood before me while I sat behind my desk in my most serious
ducal manner. I hate these administrative duties. I always pass
such work on to Sterling or Pike. But this was obviously something
I had to do myself. I informed him that, although it had been my
intention to leave a small staff on hand while I was away, I could
see now that even this was an unnecessary extravagance. As I
would be coming up to the estate but once a month or so, and
then only for a few days, I needn't keep him, his wife, or Cabrini
any longer. Grey could see to the basic upkeep of the place, and
I could supply my meager needs from Brixton. I commended
Sterling on his work and offered him a letter of recommendation
I'd already prepared, as well as something more than the usual
remuneration. I also let it be known that, should he wish to retire
on a pension, that was perfectly acceptable to me as well, and I'd
have my solicitor see to the details at once.

The old fellow stood looking at me for a few seconds—a dull,
lifeless look. He appeared to age before my eyes. His shoulders
stooped and his head bowed down heavily under the sudden
weight of his years. I turned away. Took up some obscure papers
on my desk, not wishing to confront that gaze, so reproachful
because it failed to reproach me. I was more than fair, I think,
but there's no denying the justice of the man's dismay. His whole
existence has been service, and to be told abruptly that those
services are no longer required must be very deflating. Truth is,
there was nothing he could do but accept my conditions on behalf
of himself and his wife, and he'll inform me later by post whether
he prefers the pension or will seek employment elsewhere. I let
him know his work has always been satisfactory, exemplary even,
for myself as well as for the Old Governor. But there you have it.
Nothing else to be done. Not a damned thing. I assured him of
that. I wouldn't be doing this if there were any alternative at all.

It was a painful scene, but one I'm relieved I got through. Now
I can continue my pursuits in the perfection of solitude that I need.
Still, I wish there might have been some other way.

I had a more colorful time with Cabrini, and I confess, I

looked forward to giving him the sack. Told him only so much as I'd told Sterling and made him the same offer of assistance, with the exception of the pension. Instead, I pressed upon him an envelope containing a letter of recommendation (suitable lies for whatever poor chap hires him next) and a pair of banknotes. All of this he listened to in sullen silence, and when I'd finished and put the envelope down on the desk before him, he took it up with a dogged air.

"I suppose that's as suits me, then," he said after a lengthy pause, and he laughed softly to himself, adding, "It's a queer idea of housekeeping you've got, Your Grace, and no denying that. Up here all to yourself with who knows what creatures lurking around about you, devouring the horses and terrorizing the country. And you go and bid a fond fare-thee-well to the whole staff. To do what, as a fellow might ask? To set yourself up in a butcher's shop? Why, there's some might call that behavior unnatural. There's some, and I'm not saying who or what or why, mind you, but there's some might talk under their breath, and wonder what a fine, healthy young peer like yourself would want to be doing up here all alone."

"Doubtless," I responded coolly, and said no more.

"Ah, but that's it, you see. Of course, to a gentleman such as yourself, the tongues of gossips is little things, but a fellow like me, now I can hardly afford to be the subject of talk. You just take poor Riga this morning. If word of that gets out to Brixton, it might prove a disparagement, as it were, to my reputation. And besides, you'd have people running all about this place in no time at all, looking to destroy the beast what done it. Now ain't that a fair and lovely picture for you. An army of fools running about here with not even a 'by your leave.' "

"Your point, Cabrini?" I asked impatiently, taking up a stack of papers that lay before me, attempting to appear preoccupied.

"Only this, Your Grace," and the great idiot took two steps closer to me and leaned his big, meaty hands on the desk with an air of familiarity that caused my gall to rise. "Think if you had a fellow in town, a clever fellow, an agent you might say, whose only job were to keep the peace, to look after your best interests among the mob. Well then, you'd have all the peace in the world that you wanted, wouldn't you? No one come sneaking about to see what they might see. Only yourself and the security of knowing your agent is at work in Brixton and in Darnley Well, keeping folks quiet."

I couldn't decide. Was the fellow seriously offering his services, or threatening me with discovery? I chose to take him at his word, however, and politely declined the offer. Informed him that Pike and Grey were sufficient protection for my peace of mind.

"If you don't think ill of my brass, Your Grace," he continued, pulling himself up in mock pride to the fullness of his stature, "that would be a mistake."

But I cut him short. "Your services aren't required, Cabrini. Can you understand that? Not in the stables. Not in Brixton. Not in Darnley Well. There is nowhere that I can use you. Now if you'd like a job in the mines," and I was perfectly aware of the insult I gave him with that offer, "if that's what you're after, I can arrange it. Otherwise, you're dismissed." And I turned away from him and back to the papers in my fist. He strode out with a pronounced attitude of defiance. Impertinent ass. I suspect I gave him credit for more honesty than he deserves.

That nasty business taken care of, I relaxed for an hour with a brandy and a book, was just getting ready to retire when there came a knock at the study door and Sterling announced Old Grey. Considering that my every act to this point was designed to provide me with the privacy I lacked, I'd rarely entertained such a steady flow of callers. I allowed the man to enter, and he shuffled past Sterling with a careworn look. I offered him a seat and a glass. He declined them both, only stood nervously before me, cap in hand, and wasted no time getting down to his business. "The truth is, Your Grace," he started, "I've just heard from Mr. Sterling that you've decided to let the whole house go. Now, I'm not one to offer advice where none's asked."

"Thank you, Grey, I appreciate that," I interrupted, hoping to stave off the inevitable. But he continued, twisting his cap about into all manner of elaborate knots.

"I say I'm not the kind to offer my advice where I think it's not valued, but I'll tell you, settling the whole of the business on me and my boys is a might thick, if you'll pardon an old man his rash temper." If this were the old man's temper, I could freely pardon it.

I asked him why he was so displeased, as I thought he'd be the last to complain of a little extra work. "It ain't the work, so much," he confided, "it ain't that at all. Only, well, it is the work, but not the way you're meaning. Now me and the boys is already operating the whole of affairs about the grounds," and he swept his hands expansively before himself for emphasis, giving the countryside a quick dusting with his cap. "We keep up the lawn and the gardens, and've always done about the manor with little repairs and things what need doing. And we've helped out Mr. Pike with the tenants on more than one occasion, and I'm obliged, Your Grace, obliged I am at the good opinion it all bespeaks. But now to have to deal with the housekeeping on top of all. It ain't proper work for men, sir, not a bit."

I assured Grey that I was not asking him to take on any of Mrs. Sterling's duties. I would supply my own wants in that regard. He need only add a few of Sterling's old chores to his own, such as walking about the place to see that all is well, and some few of Cabrini's lesser duties. This news relieved his mind considerably, but he still harbored reservations, misgivings that I'd been precipitate in my planning. "There's always things what gets left unthought of in such matters," he assured me, and asked if I might not reconsider my design. I told him I was quite determined, and that satisfied him. Old Grey's is the sort of pliant will that need only be shown how a certain course of action is unavoidable, and he'll set himself to it with a firm resolve.

Before dismissing him, I went on and settled my new schedule. Gave him a list of the days and times I'd be arriving for the coming six months and told him to have one of his sons meet me at the station in Brixton with enough food and drink to keep me comfortable for a few days. I required absolute solitude, I let him know, and while I was in residence I was not to be disturbed, not for any reason. I impressed upon him that this rule was absolute, and if he violated it in any way I would send him packing on the spot. If he or Pike had any business they needed to conduct with me, they could do so the evening before my departure. I'd ring the bell that hung beside the kitchen door to let them know they might approach. Most importantly, I said, neither Grey nor either of his sons should venture into the woods at night while I was in residence. I told him I was involved in some studies of the nocturnal wildlife of the area, and I would not be troubled by any interference. As implausible as this sounded, Grey's credulity accepted it without any further explanation.

Before leaving, he offered his report on the mare's death. There'd indeed been an animal in the woods, he said, and from the size of it he let me know that, if I had been out at all that night, I was luckier than a man had a right to be. "It's a monster, Your Grace, whatever it is. Paws like this," and he spread out his hands before me impressively. "I should say it's a wolf, but I've never heard of one coming this far south, especially with the weather so pleasant. And the good Lord knows I've never known one that size. The boys have set up some traps about the place, in case it returns."

I commended him on his diligence and advised that the traps were in all likelihood an unnecessary precaution, as I doubted the beast should come back. Still, he could keep them out for a few days, provided none were left in the woods on my return. I also told Grey that, since I'd need only so many horses as he might require to run the place, he should tell Pike from me to sell off the majority of the stock at once. Grey assured me he would see to it and left.

I have every confidence in my new arrangements. Now I must steel myself for the return to London and the frustration of again attempting to find any information on the nature of my lycan-thropy. I can feel my spirits sag as I think of it. My earliest hope had been to discover an authoritative text, but now I'd settle for even the most casual reference to werewolves, so long as it contains no obvious falsehoods. But I mustn't despair completely, not yet. It took me a few tries here at Murcheston before I arrived at a solution to my problems, but a solution I've found and a damned good one it is, I'll guarantee it. It will be the same in London. I'll discover the books I seek. It's incomprehensible that, in all the history of man, no curious and insightful mind has ever stumbled across the phenomenon. Someone must have done so, someone like me who understands the importance of this discovery, its sig-nificance to all mankind. Although centuries of prejudice may have relegated such a work to the annals of the fabulous and fantastic, I know it's out there somewhere. Damn it all, I have only to find it.

6

The Bookseller

20 February

An ecstasy of triumph! Not merely one book, but a dozen, a hundred! An entire shop! A library of the occult! Works of ancient and dusty knowledge, arcane studies made at a time when men were willing to believe the incredible. There's one book in particular, one on which I base all my hopes. Even with a cursory glance I can tell it's authentic, unquestionably authentic. Any fool could see it. And where one exists, more must surely follow. I've tapped the mother source of all lycanthropic literature at last, a treasure of inestimable riches! After so many vain, fruitless weeks, I can't begin to believe my sudden good fortune!

I started out this morning with even fewer hopes of success than are usual with me lately, which is to say no hopes at all. Only went searching through the most mechanical routine. The day was suited for such work, cold and cheerless, failure betokened from every damp corner. The dismal spirit of the weather gripped me fiercely and I soon found myself drifting through the streets, my mind empty, my will untouched by desire, the object of my

search all but forgotten in the prevailing gloom. A persistent drizzle began to fall, driven hard by the stiff wind, like icy pinpricks
blown into my face. At least it helped to clear the streets. Soon,
only a few umbrellas and bundled overcoats were left to sail those
dark waters with me.

Guided more by instinct than design, I found myself at last
in a quiet lane hard by the Temple that I'd been down many
times before. Don't know how I got there. I only recall the rain
and the cold and my own relentless stride when a small, stout
little cannonball of a man, wrapped in a dark cloak with a fur
collar and a ridiculous beaver hat, suddenly shot out from a wall
of solid brick and almost knocked me down into the muddy street.
Before I could think I reached out and grasped his arm, wrenching
him violently about to confront me. He squealed in dismay and
dropped a parcel at my feet. Fat, flaccid cheeks that puffed in
shock and surprise. Round glasses with thick lenses that magnified
his eyes. Queer sort of chap to be fate's tool.

"Pardon. Beg pardon," the fellow stammered at once, attempting weakly to free his arm. I could see now that he was somewhat
advanced in age, the picture of benign docility. I felt rather bad
for having treated him so roughly. "Sorry. Most very," he continued by way of a confused apology, squirming in my grasp. "The
rain, you see. And these blasted spectacles. Clouding over. As a
bat."

"If your vision is so obscured, I think less haste is called for,
not more," I admonished him, releasing my grip and reaching
down to pick up his fallen package. Though wrapped in brown
paper and now soiled and damp, it obviously contained several
books. In an instant and involuntarily, every dead hope harbored
in my soul coursed through me with new life. I handed the parcel
back to him, asked whether he'd purchased these in the neighborhood.

"What? Oh, yes. Wattles," was all he got out, and motioned
with a jerk of his head backwards as he hurried off in the opposite
direction through the obscuring rain. I looked about at the wall

from which he'd materialized. There it was. Damn me, I'd never noticed it before. An aperture, a nearly invisible threshold hidden in a corner leading past an iron gate, through a short passage and down two ancient and uneven steps into a quiet court. I approached and peered inside. A sign posted just within read *Black Abbots Yard.* How many times had I wandered past this very spot, rushed by in my hurry to locate some new and undiscovered bookstall, and never once paused to observe this wall or to consider what riches might lie beyond? I hurried through and entered into a small court, ringed round by buildings of no inconsiderable height, so that the wind and slanting rain were held at bay, incapable of finding an easy way in. From the humble modesty of the offices and piles of flats lining that homely well, it's apparent that commercial traffic has an equally hard time locating the place.

Strangely, there were no signs or placards about to indicate which door might be the bookshop's, so I set off methodically to my right, darting along from awning to awning, peering in at successive windows. The square looked to be a little colony of financiers, hopeless, withered clerks and pettifogging old men fishing after large sacks of gold using small sacks of gold as bait. My inquisitive gaze was universally ignored, and I continued my circuit of the place.

Finally I came to a dark shop with a single candle burning within, just enough light to show a desk and a row of bookcases all lined up neatly against the back wall. There were other dark shapes, too, and shadows that I could not so readily identify, baubles hanging from the ceiling and odd artifacts interspersed among the books. I tried to press my face closer to the window, but my breath only fogged the glass. I wasn't even positive that the place was open, for I could make out no sign of human life within. But I tried the door and, finding that it swung freely on well-oiled hinges, assumed that business hours were being observed and so entered.

The air inside was cool yet dry, surprising in light of the

weather. An exotic odor permeated the place, a smell of spices and woodsmoke not in keeping with the propriety one usually finds among bookstalls. I'm so accustomed to that air of dust and old paper that I found the present aroma practically scandalous. The shop was exactly as it appeared from the street, a small room bounded by several shelves of books along the back wall and a large desk off to one side. The odd shadows I saw from without were indeed mysterious artifacts, magical objects of heathenish design, clay pots descending from the rafters, masks and weird implements on the shelves, some with a truly horrible aspect, ghastly and evil, and many others just as fascinating. Pagan beauty, brightly colored and intricately painted with primitive art-istry. The lone candle burned on the desk, sufficient light to go blind by. In front of the desk stood a severe, straight-backed chair, while behind it a plush armchair rested and beyond that, against the wall, a small stove gave off a comforting warmth with a kettle set snugly atop like a cat curled up on a fat pillow.

I turned to the books and scanned the titles quickly. There seemed to be no method of cataloguing about the place. Volumes were tossed here and there on the shelves with gay abandon, standing up and lying down, back-to-front and front-to-back. A few were even open, as though someone had been reading them but were suddenly called away. Yet, in spite of all, I wouldn't say the shop was disordered. Something about it seemed quite tidy, really, as though it answered to a higher logic that I couldn't fathom. I continued to glance about at the various volumes, amazed at the range of books resting together. Histories and ro-mances, works of philosophy and science, poetry and religion, po-litical economy and industrial mechanics. I was about to give up this little stall as another dead end when a soft, firm voice, deep and musical, startled me from my investigation. I spun around and beheld an individual no less singular and mysterious than the shop itself.

Sitting behind the desk, where but a moment before there had been no one, was a woman, a figure of such expansive size that it was incomprehensible for her to have entered the room, much less settled herself in the chair, without my being aware of it. I couldn't be certain, but I guessed that she weighed over twenty stone. What's more remarkable, she was a Negress. Her skin was black, inky black, so black as to seem almost blue against the flatter black of her plain black dress. Yet her face emitted a dark glow, an ebon light that illumined her features amid the shadows of the shop. The only relief from the pure blackness she presented was her hair, white and cropped close to her scalp. It was otherwise impossible to tell how old she might be. Large, hard-looking hands sat clasped on top of the desk. Bright, clever eyes peered at me from behind tiny spectacles that were almost lost against the black background of her broad face. Her eyes took in every inch of me in a second. Assessed me, sized me up, and deposited me in some little compartment in her mind, some pigeon hole likely labeled *Wealthy Dilettante* or *Wayward Financier*. When she was satisfied with this rapid valuation, she smiled a tight-lipped smile. Or perhaps I should more properly say winced, for there was something distinctly pained in her expression.

"May I help you locate something? A book, perhaps?" This question I found rather odd, and I answered that yes, I was looking for a work on a very special subject and would like to speak to the proprietor. I don't know why I made this request. I've always relied on my own resources before. But this little shop was practically a world unto itself, and I suppose I felt the need of a guide.

The Negress continued to stare at me unblinkingly. Again the pained glance, the wincing smile. "Oh, my dear," she sighed softly. "Are you surprised then to hear that you are addressing the proprietress?" She spoke these words quite precisely, so as to leave no doubt as to the truth of the matter. "Mrs. Wattles, by name," she continued after a moment's pause, motioning to the straight-backed chair before her desk.

And why should I not have been surprised? The fact is I was struck dumb. I've only occasionally had cause to speak with any person of her race, and this was always some fellow in service.

Never have I met a Negro in a position of independence, although I know such things aren't unheard of. And I've most assuredly never known of a Negress in such a condition. I was genuinely taken aback, and for a moment I actually forgot what it was I was looking for. The thought came to me eventually, however, and I told her as I sat down that I was searching for anything she might have that dealt with the supernatural.

She stared at me that same inscrutable stare one moment longer, then reached behind her desk, opened a drawer and extracted a very delicate, blue porcelain tea service. This she arranged in front of her, service for two, simple as that, without a word, as if I were some poor, benighted uncle come round for my weekly visit. "The supernatural, you say. An expansive topic," she mused knowingly, "filled with any number of fascinating avenues for study. Now, my dear, if you could only be the slightest whit more precise as to where your own peculiar interest lies?"

"Werewolves, specifically."

"Ah, lycanthropes," she announced with a confidential air, nodding.

Had I heard right? Had she said "lycanthropes"? I couldn't believe it at first. "Do you know the subject?" I exclaimed in spite of myself.

"Oh, my dear," she cooed, and her eyes flashed merrily with the first genuine feeling I'd seen in them. She continued her business calmly, however, readying the teapot and setting out the cups and saucers. "I am familiar with the subject, indeed. With few other subjects, it is true, but with the supernatural and all that it entails, yes, I am familiar." The kettle on the stove behind her began to sing, and turning gracefully in her chair, she lifted it to the desk and poured its boiling contents into the teapot. "Call it my speciality. A rare word in these modern days. We live in a time of generalists, do we not? A great many men know a very little about very much." And she swirled the hot water about in the teapot once, twice, and emptied it into a container at her feet. "Political economy. Art. Religion. Natural History. Philosophy.

Mathematics and the sciences. They are all of them widely studied. Widely though not deeply. The spirit of the age, my dear, that is what it is. Would you agree?" She stopped pointedly in her preparations, looking up at me, waiting for my acquiescence.

"Yes, quite," was all I could stammer.

She winced again and, measuring out the tea, continued. "But what are the superficial fruits of such general accomplishments? How can they sustain the spirit of inquiry that hungers for a more profound knowledge, that thirsts for the fundamental mysteries, the deepest secrets of that goddess we hight Nature? If you will forgive me the poetical conceit, I find the shallow waters covering a vast expanse unhealthy, fetid and stagnant." A look of disgust crossed her brow as she refilled the teapot. "But the refreshing spring, which seems little more than a puddle at the surface, reaches deep into the heart of the earth, its sweetness drawn from the very core of knowledge. Am I clear?"

I nodded.

"Wonderful. And so I cater to the trade of specialists such as yourself, gentlemen and ladies with a passion for—how shall we put it?" Her eyes darted about, searching for the right word in the air. "A passion for the profound, my dear, a desire for things out of the common track. My little shop contains a great deal of information on a truly select handful of topics, all of which," and here she made a sweeping motion toward the back wall of the room, "fall under the single rubric of the Occult."

She paused, and it occurred to me that I'd just witnessed, not so much a dissertation as a ceremony. A very polished performance, too. "But forgive an old woman her prattling," she went on while the tea steeped. "As I said, my name is Wattles. Mrs. Wattles. There was once a Mr. Wattles, more than one, I think, but only one who really counts. A fine man, my dear, a Christian man whom I met in Haiti when I was but a child, an orphan living off the streets. He took me in, raised me, educated me, and when I had reached an age, he married me. He is no more, I fear, and this surrounding you is his legacy." She poured the tea and placed a cup in front of me. "And your name is?"

Good Lord, what an extraordinary person! Her voice melodious yet strong. Her figure imposing and exotic. In perfect harmony with my quest, but somehow detached. I looked upon her with an almost magnetic intensity, entranced by her words, her eyes, her every fluid movement. Still, despite all my hopes, I wasn't prepared to believe from the evidence I had about me that she could offer much I didn't already possess. "It doesn't seem to me that your little spring can hold much water," I remarked as I took up the cup of tea in front of me, dodging her question for the time and looking about at the close walls and the few bookcases. "Your selection is hardly substantial."

I can't be sure, but I believe her eyes twinkled when I said this. "We shall see if it is substantial enough for the task at hand, my dear. I am off to hunt lycanthropes!" And with that she rose from her chair (and I saw that she was quite as tall as she was large), and moving with an easy, rapid grace, she disappeared, positively vanished behind one of the bookcases as though walking through a wall. Left me sitting there alone, like a fool with the cup at my lips and my mouth hanging open at this magician's trick. I recovered myself and, setting down the cup, moved to the other side of the desk to peer around the bookcase. What did I see? Yet another shock in what had become a rather tedious display of novelty. What I'd thought was the back wall was, in fact, a single row of bookcases pushed together. Behind this I now discovered another, similar row, and another row past that, and yet another past that and a long aisle receding into the darkness with row upon row following exactly like the others, layer upon layer of books.

It became clear at once that Mrs. Wattles was a woman of far greater resources than I'd realized. Turning to the desk, I took up the candle and ventured into this Forest Primeval of bookcases. Apt description, for although the first few rows were quite neat and orderly (and I counted no less than eight of these), there soon began a space where each bookcase stood some few inches from its neighbor, and eventually I found that they were no longer even grouped in rows, but stood entirely apart from each other, as though they had grown about the place like trees. I glanced at some of the titles as I wandered, and indeed they all dealt with topics of the supernatural. Witchcraft and haunts and voodoo and the like. Many quite old, some written in languages whose very alphabets were a riddle to me. Given the nature of the literature and the singular arrangement of the bookshelves, it's small wonder that I soon began to feel a trifle disoriented and uneasy. I'm not usually a sensitive person, but this was no usual bookshop. I continued relentlessly nonetheless, pushing on like some African explorer, but there was as yet no telling how large this wonderful library was. I expected at any moment to meet with either the back wall or Mrs. Wattles herself, but never seemed to get close to either. I'd gone some fifty feet straight back (or rather, I believe it was straight back, and I think it was fifty feet), when that clear, resonant voice came to me as if from a great distance and above me.

"I shouldn't go any farther with that candle, my dear," the voice intoned. "My little shop can be an elusive place, a labyrinth, and books, after all, are flammable things, are they not?" What could I do when confronted with such omniscience? I retraced my steps, getting lost only once, and returned to the front room. There I sat impatiently, sipping my tea.

She was not much longer about her business and soon returned, seating herself silently in her chair. And what a treasure she brought back with her! Not one, but half a dozen volumes she carried, cradling them like children in her vast arms. I caught my breath in expectation. "I believe we can find something worthwhile in one of these," she informed me, trying to appear as cool as you please. But wasn't I mistaken or did there sound a touch of boastful pride in her voice? "Not quite the definitive word on the subject," she told me as she set the books gently down upon her desk. "That great work still waits to be written, as doubtless you are aware, but each one interesting in its own right, and they should profit you the time you spend with them. Shall we have a look?" I joined her at the desk, and together we glanced through her discoveries.

I was disappointed to find that the first two of these were works with which I'm already familiar. Popular, sensational studies of the occult which treat of werewolves in just a few pages, but nonetheless pack an astonishing amount of erroneous detail and prejudice into that small space. These I handed back to Mrs. Wattles without a word. The next three volumes were nominally more intriguing insofar as they carried the authority of age and I didn't already own them. The newest of them was at least half a century old. They had the appearance of easy scholarship, however, the sort of superstitious anthologies that I already know better than I care to. Still, I set them by as likely purchases, although my enthusiasm suffered noticeably.

"You display an admirable discrimination in the literature of your field, my dear. Now don't be disheartened. Forward, my love. Push bravely on."

The sixth volume was a large, leather-bound book, scores of years old, written in Latin by a Bavarian scholar who called himself Gustavus Albapetrus Germanicus. The book was entitled (and I offer my own poor translation), A Compendium of Illuminating and Instructive Observations, with Illustrations by the Author, Concerning the Beasts and Monsters of Fantasy and Their Various Derivations in Fact, Including Such Tales as May convince the Reader of Their True Existence.

I flipped through the pages quickly, almost idly. They were profusely illustrated and the drawings showed a commendable attention to detail, griffins and dragons and some things the like of which I've never come across before. Suddenly a picture appeared that made my heart flutter in my breast. A marginal sketch, rough but executed with some proficiency: a werewolf leaping through the air at a terrified wayfarer. I've discovered much the same image in other books. But this time, there appeared a telling difference. For this wasn't just a picture of a wolf with a caption identifying the sometimes human, sometimes animal monster. No, there before me, on the desk of that weird shop, I saw the shortened snout, the catlike ears, the great size of the true werewolf! The werewolf as I know it to be from my adventure in the Carpathians. If the artist had been at my side when the beast lunged at me, the picture couldn't have been more right! I tried to read the text, but my mind was too agitated to translate it properly. I purchased the book on the spot. I'm not even certain what I paid for the thing, but it's invaluable to me and I would have given any price for it.

"The good Gustavus," cooed Mrs. Wattles approvingly. "One of the few genuine authorities the world has known. It is said of him, my dear, that he only reported what he had experienced himself. He traveled widely throughout Europe and Asia, and I believe into Africa as well, recording sights that would hardly stand up today to the harsh glare of modern science. No doubt his wish to believe often led him to be less skeptical than a man of scholarship by rights ought to be. But still, a charming collection of local myths and fables. If your speciality runs along broader lines than mere lycanthropy, you might find his chapter on sprites and fairies most enlightening. Of course, if you require a translator to render the book into English, I can recommend a most accomplished gentleman, elderly but with a sharp eye and lucid understanding. A veritable Roman."

I thanked her for the recommendation but informed her that I'd taken firsts in Latin at university and had kept my hand in since. After squaring my account I gathered up my prize, along with the other books I'd set aside, and was about to leave when a clap of thunder startled me back to reality. The rain. I'd forgotten all about it in my excitement, and while I'd passed my time in the shop it had begun to fall in earnest, was coming down now with a vigor and a vengeance. I found myself torn between my desire to rush home with the book and my fear lest the weather damage it. It was far too large to fit beneath my overcoat and too ancient to survive a thorough damping.

I stood for a moment in indecision when Mrs. Wattles again came to my aid. "Allow me to have the book delivered to your door, my dear, once the rain abates." My initial instinct was to decline. After so long a time searching I didn't want to relinquish my treasure to anyone so readily. But there seemed no alternative. I accepted her offer. She asked for my name and address and I handed her a card which she read without the least indication of surprise. She merely entered my name in a large ledger and said, "Your patronage is most appreciated, my dear. If I may be so bold as to offer my services further? Several of my customers with special interests, such as yourself, permit me to inform them whenever anything comes across my notice that I feel they might value. As yours must be a particularly challenging field for the casual browser, could I perform a similar office for Your Grace?"

It seems that this woman is destined to become a partner in my studies, and her offer overcame any further reluctance on my part. Nothing could be more to my purpose. For the first time in months I feel that I can relax from the trials of my labor. At last I'm no longer aimless and alone, wandering through the confusing morass of questionable scholarship to be found on the bookshelves out there. I now have a guide, and from all appearances, an eminently resourceful and highly qualified one.

The rain has just ceased, and I hope to hear a knock at my door any minute. God, how anxious I am! Like a schoolboy! I'm full of such nervous anticipation waiting for my book to arrive. I shall doubtless spend the entire night poring over its pages.

2 March

On the train to Murcheston with Gustavus tucked away in my portmanteau. It seems I was an ass with Mrs. Wattles. A shade too boastful concerning my Latin, I fear, and now I'm paying dearly for such hubris. The going has been damnably slow and my frustration just terrible at times. Still, I'd rather persevere on my own than give over to a translator, so I slog through with the old school textbooks close at hand and the old school obstinacy in my heart.

Mrs. Wattles' estimate of Gustavus proves to be very accurate, I think. He's a scholar of rare abilities, a mind quick and lithe, yet perhaps too powerful for all that. He pursues the defense of his thesis with greater enthusiasm than wisdom and is prone to accept lore as law. Just take, for an example, his description of the rapacious behavior of the werewolf: "The lycanthrope possesses a hunger for man-flesh so powerful within the beast, that it shall willingly forego other, surer meat for the delicacy of a plump parson, and has been known to ignore an entire flock of sheep in its relentless desire for the shepherd." What humbug! Positive rot! Naturally he offers no firsthand evidence to support this outrageous claim. Just all the same ridiculous, prejudicial, unfounded crap I've discovered at every juncture. To consider that a soul with no serious ill will towards anyone, without the least propensity for violence, can be transformed into a death-dealing monster solely as the result of a physical transformation? It defies reason.

Notwithstanding such occasional credulity, there are passages in Gustavus of the greatest interest, especially his physical descriptions of the werewolf. He's a mirror I can hold up to myself. His detailed account of the actual metamorphosis is a marvel. It's a question that's taxed my imagination, but I've thought any objective observation impossible. According to him, the process of change begins when the first rays of the moon break over the horizon. Initially, any alteration in appearance is imperceptible, and yet it would seem to me that the warmth I've felt (and which Gustavus fails to mention; proof, I think, that his information comes by observation and not experience), that this might be a signal of internal changes, some subcutaneous alterations, as for example would allow my system to tolerate raw meat for food. But that's just supposition. The first external indication of a metamorphosis is the rapid growth of hair about the entire body, with the exception of the palms of the hands and the soles of the feet, the skin of which thickens, taking on an almost leathery toughness. Next, the muscles of the legs and back, especially those of the shoulders, expand and, as Gustavus puts it, inflate, gaining in both length and breadth. The transformation progresses rapidly at this point, the tail developing from the base of the spine and the fingers and toes "drawing in." The final change is the metamorphosis of the features. The snout protrudes, the brow recedes, the ears adopt their characteristic shape.

Something I've just written has put an idea into my head, an experiment that might allow me to observe my own transformation. The answer is a mirror, of course. I have a large dressing glass in my rooms, six feet tall with a carved wooden frame. I should be able to get it downstairs easily. Only set this up in the study and, when the moon rises, I can watch myself transform. A personal account of the comparative morphologies of man and werewolf, made by the subject himself. What a thing that will be! The very sort of empirical observation I'd hoped all along to perform. To go Gustavus one better! To bring the werewolf out of the fairy stories and into the realm of science. Expose the medieval mindlessness surrounding his lore with a modern light. My lycanthropy may have been merely an accident, but I'll turn it to use. Damn me if I don't.

5 March

A refreshingly uneventful time at Murcheston this month. I think I've finally settled upon a system that will suit me well. Grey's younger boy met me at the station with a full load of food and drink in the cart (for Grey wisely saw no need to bring out the coach). After a leisurely journey he deposited me at the door of the estate, where I reminded him that his family were not to disturb me, or to venture out into the woods, until they should hear me ring the bell by the kitchen door some three days hence.

Left alone, I started out at once to put my experiment into effect. Getting the mirror to the study was more difficult than I'd imagined. The thing was prodigiously heavy. I managed well enough getting it to the top of the staircase, but maneuvering the steps was another matter, and I stumbled against the balustrade and inflicted a great crack in the glass from top to bottom. By the time I had it set up in the study it was already quite dark out, so I retired in some anticipation of the discoveries I might make the following night.

All of yesterday I spent in idleness. Took a long walk about the manor to see if it were the worse for a month of inattention. Everything seemed musty but in reasonable order, and I was well satisfied until I reached the servants' quarters. There I learned that Cabrini had thoroughly cleaned out his lodgings. Spirited everything away, furniture, curtains, bed and bedding. No less than I might have expected from him, and I cursed myself for not having sacked him the first go-round.

I'd intended to perform a similar inspection of the grounds, but as the weather was bitingly cold, I decided to remain before a large fire and have a go at Gustavus. Despite my almost conscious effort to make the time crawl along interminably, dusk finally came, and I began to put my experiment into practice. I disrobed, being careful to unlatch the French doors when I was done so as not to break the lock when I rushed out into the night, and positioned myself in front of the mirror. The crack I'd caused in the glass made it impossible to achieve a perfect image, for it split my reflection and offset the two sides of my body so that, try as I might, they could not be aligned. But my eyes soon accustomed themselves to the defect, and I waited patiently for the moon to rise.

What followed can only be acknowledged as a crushing disappointment, for no sooner did I feel the warmth beginning to build in my belly than I found my glance wandering excitedly about the room. The more I tried to concentrate my attention on the image in the mirror, the more impossible that task became. I can recall a tightening of the muscles in my chest and abdomen, and the appearance of dark, thick hair over my person, but at the time all my preparations and hopes for making some useful discovery became as irrelevant to me as the clothes I'd left neatly folded by the fire.

Needless to say, it wasn't long before I was racing toward the woods again. Dear God, what freedom! A revelation to me every month! I can hardly make myself believe how wonderful is the time I spend as a wolf. The moon, though obviously full, was hidden from view all night by a blanket of dark clouds, and for the first time I became aware of the remarkable power I have to see at night. This nocturnal vision is unlike anything I've ever experienced as a man, and is difficult even to describe. If it's possible to imagine a full spectrum of light made up, not of color, but of shades and shadows, an infinite variety of blacks and grays allowing a clarity of perception every bit as sharp and well-defined as that available in daylight, then one can approach an understanding of the sensation. But even that fails to grasp the key feature of the phenomenon, for just as daylight vision derives its powers from the intensity of light, so night vision depends upon the depth of darkness. It's not that my optic nerves simply increase their capacity for receiving light, allowing me to adapt to whatever source is available. It's more that darkness itself becomes a source of illumination for me. I absorb the void of night, as another creature might absorb rays of sunshine. I see blacks beyond the blackest pitch any man can detect, shadows within shadows creating subtle layers of obscurity. In the murkiest corner of the woods I see a tree, and in the tree I see a hole, and in the hole I see a moth, and on its wings I see intricate patterns of black design. And I see it all the more clearly for the total absence of any light.

But even this depth of perception is as nothing compared to my olfactory abilities. If I were suddenly struck blind, I'm convinced it wouldn't impede my activities one bit, for the air carries with it all I need to know about the world around me. In the same way that vision operates spatially, so scent provides me with a temporal landscape. I quite literally perceive the past. From a single trail I determine what sort of creatures were in a given spot before I arrived, how many they were, how long they remained, which direction they went and how long ago they've been gone. And what's most remarkable is that I didn't have to learn to read the signs. From my very first transformation I could distinguish between a rabbit and a squirrel, and at times I'm convinced I can tell apart two rabbits. Every creature has its own scent, as unique and unmistakable as its form, and I seem to have carried a record of these about with me in some forgotten corner of my brain, a certain reckoning based upon observations I didn't require but couldn't help but make.

These heightened sensibilities of sight and smell proved their worth last night, saving me from what could have been a very dangerous encounter. As I was trotting along the banks of the stream, leaping easily from side to side and trying unsuccessfully to land the occasional fish, a scent caught my attention that I hadn't smelled before and that I had great trouble recognizing. I put my nose to the ground and soon discovered a trail of very peculiar odors, all mixed together in a jumble. Of these, the most prominent was a salty, fragrant scent that I knew at once to be man. But there was another odor I couldn't quite identify, and I set off immediately to investigate. The scent moved away from the stream into the deepest part of the woods. The path was clearly marked by the man's lumbering, reckless gait, and even without the aid of my nose I'd have had no difficulty following the trail of broken twigs, heavy footprints and trampled shrubs.

After perhaps a mile the scent became stronger, as though the man had stopped for a long time considering which way to go. I could tell the trail was old, however, and I knew there was little chance of seeing who'd left it. Still, my curiosity impelled me forward, for the strange odor was more pronounced now, and fresher than the man-scent. I moved cautiously through the leaves on the ground, making no more noise than the wind, for some-thing told me I was in some danger, of what sort or from what cause I couldn't say, but danger true enough, and close by. I stopped. Ahead of me some twenty or so paces I could see a dark shape under the brush. This was the source of the scent, and it had obviously been placed there as an awkward attempt at concealment. I approached slowly, keeping my body low and ready to spring, but the thing remained still.

I didn't come close enough to disturb it, only so near as to identify it. It was a trap, not a little snare for rabbits and squirrels, but a large contraption with metal jaws used for grabbing and holding an animal by the leg until the trapper comes to place a bullet in its brain.

I awoke this morning by the stream, and for the first time walked freely across the open field to the manor, unconcerned about discovery. I washed myself at the pump, got dressed and, going out behind the kitchen, rang the bell. Returning to the study I built a fire, for it was frightfully cold still about the place. I settled down with a brandy and had only to wait half an hour before there was a knock on the door and Old Grey entered with his elder boy.

I got to the point at once. Truth is, I had quite a time controlling my temper. "I was wondering, Grey," I began in a very measured tone, "whether you ever discovered what killed that mare last month."

"No, Your Grace," the old man answered. "Me and the boys, we set up enough traps to catch the thing if he was still scampering about, but we come up with naught to speak of but hares and foxes."

"I see, I see. And so I suppose you followed my instructions and collected all the traps before I arrived?"

"Aye, Your Grace, that we did, every one. Days ago that was, weren't it, Jemmy?" he asked, turning to his son.

"A week Sunday, sir," the boy answered, addressing me.

"Then," I demanded, hotly now, "how would you explain the fact that I almost tripped over one of your traps last night as I was walking through the woods?"

"Couldn't have been," Grey started to respond, but I cut him off at once.

"Don't dare to contradict me, old man! I'll take you to the thing this very moment! I'll thrust your head into it if that's what it takes to convince you!"

My words were harsher than I'd intended, but who wouldn't be enraged at this lapse? More than just my leg might have been trapped in that snare, and more than my life was endangered by it. If my anger seems excessive now, I have but to imagine myself sprawled naked in the woods, covered in my own blood and filth, the metal jaws of the trap clamped hard against the bone of my leg, splintering it, leaving me open to suspicion, detection, discovery. Only imagine so much and my anger seems more reasonable. Of course, Grey's boy came to his father's defense, shouting a vivid denial of all my accusations. This impudence was more than I was willing to stand for, and I had a strong desire to throttle the lad, but with an effort I managed my temper and only replied, in a voice thick with rage, "Control your son, sir."

Grey held out a hand before his boy and said, "There now, Jemmy." Then he looked at me and his eyes narrowed in indignation. He spoke calmly, but it was apparent that he was struggling with his emotions. "I'd not dare to contradict Your Grace," he began. "I don't doubt you've found what you say you've found. God's truth, I'd be amazed and astounded if you hadn't found such a thing, and I think you can count yourself lucky you found only one and didn't stumble onto others."

"What do you mean by that?" I demanded.

"I mean, Your Grace," the old man went on with some energy, "that when the lord of the manor all of a sudden, and without any reason or warning, takes it into his head to abandon the estate, to strip it of its staff, to take away its life and its dignity, when the lord of the manor does as much as he can to cheapen the place in the eyes of regular folk, who would have thought twice about trespassing on the property before, then them folks won't bother to think twice again. I mean, sir, that if you had raised a sign at the gates saying *Poachers welcome. Refreshments provided*, you wouldn't have done a better job of bringing the rascals in here. Me and my boys've had our hands full keeping them off, and if you only found the one trap, then I think you have Jemmy here to thank for it. And I'm right sorry for my tone, but that's the truth of it, plain as I can put it."

To say that I wasn't entirely deflated by this rather polite tirade would be understating the case. It never occurred to me that my absence would be carte blanche for poachers, and it was now my turn to apologize, which I did with I hope a proper air of contrition. I explained to Grey that while I understood his concern at what must seem to him my most precipitate and eccentric actions of the past few months, I was determined to continue in the course I'd set. I allowed, however, that his position must be seriously compromised by the changes on the estate, and I gave him all necessary authority to hire any extra hands from Brixton or among the tenants that he might require to do his job. My only stipulation was that the rules I'd set down are to remain in full effect for anyone he brings on. The grounds are to be left for my exclusive use whenever I should come up from London, and no one is to venture near until I leave.

We parted, I feel, with a better understanding than we had shared before, and I took young Grey's hand as he left, a gesture not wasted on the fellow, for he almost dislodged my shoulder in his eagerness. I also told Grey that he might send his younger son around with the cart this afternoon, as I'm leaving as soon as I've spoken with Pike.

As I sit here now waiting for Pike to arrive, I confess I almost look forward to seeing the man, as tedious as his company always is to me. Truth is, since I awoke in the woods this morning, and especially since entering the manor, I've suffered the most profound melancholy. I can't explain it. I feel oppressed by a deep sense of loss, but of what? Aside from my misunderstanding with Grey, all has gone smoothly. I might even say perfectly. Why then should I be so downcast? Likely just a passing mood, and I shouldn't concern myself with it. I wish I had some interest about here to help me take my mind off myself. When I return to London I might make the social rounds a bit. I've been quite the hermit lately, and now that I have Mrs. Wattles' assistance with my studies, I can afford the odd amusement. Yes, that's precisely the cure I need. I shall take a few idle hours to dispel this dreary mood.

I am back in London. It is night, and I am restless. The moon peers down through the window at me, yet she seems deformed somehow, awkward, imperfect in her less-than-fullness. My thoughts are troubled by feelings from the past. E. haunts me, as she hasn't done for some time, and I feel alone, very much alone.

Liam Grey

7 March

Such a black mood I've fallen into. What can have set it off? Cabrini? This news in Brixton? I enjoyed an enlightening conversation with young Liam Grey the other day as we drove there, and he opened my eyes to a business I might need to look into. Perceptive lad. One of that quiet sort who sees all but speaks little. And surprisingly quick-witted, considering the station he holds. Such qualities are generally so little valued among simple folk that they're rarely allowed to develop, are regularly discouraged among the ruder set.

It was the perfect day for a chat. Warming, with the first signs of emergent spring giving everything a lazy, luxuriant feel. We moved slowly down the lane, in no hurry, letting the horse set our pace for us. Liam kept an easy hand on the reins, giving them an occasional flick, just so the horse didn't come to a complete stop. "Tell me, Liam," I began, "do you make the journey to Brixton often? When you're not collecting me, I mean."

"No sir, Your Grace," he answered nervously, clucking at the horse. "That is, not often enough, sir."

"I see," I replied with a conspiratorial air, hoping to put him at his ease. "And why this desire to get to Brixton more often than you do? Some special reason for wanting to get away to town?"

He heaved a sigh and looked about him. "No, sir. Not so special, I mean. But, yes sir, I guess you could say there's something makes me want to go there more than Jemmy or father do."

"Of course there is. I knew it," I crowed. "And what might this special something be, I wonder? I don't suppose a fellow might guess at it? I don't suppose it's a something with long, soft hair and beautiful, dark eyes, is it?"

"No, sir!" Liam exclaimed, and I thought I saw his youthful face redden beneath the loose folds of his woolen scarf.

"Come now, boy," I went on. "You can confide in me. I'm not going to tell your father, not that I suspect he has many doubts on the subject. What else should attract a handsome young fellow like you to Brixton?"

"Well, it's not a girl, sir," he replied spiritedly, encouraging the horse on to a quicker pace. "I'd have to be a rare fool indeed to beg the privilege of bouncing back and forth over this rotten road till my teeth are practically jarred from my head just to spend half an hour with some girl."

What was this? Was I dealing with something more than the usual country lout here? "And you're not a fool, are you, Liam?"

"Well, you wouldn't say so if you heard Old Dad tell it. But no, Your Grace. I'm not that kind of fool. If it were a girl I wanted, there'd be plenty of that sort among the tenants at Darnley Well, and I think they'd be a deal less trouble than Brixton girls."

"Oh? And why less trouble?"

"Because my father sometimes helps Mr. Pike collect the rents, sir. One thing you can say for girls, they always know a better than they've got when it comes their way. You take the tenant girls. Now to them," and he turned and looked at me for the first time, "I'm the son of an important man, and that makes me important. Why, just last harvest, when I was helping out in the fields, there's one or another of them was constantly bumping into me, saying things it just isn't proper for a girl to say to a fellow."

"Things like?"

"It wouldn't be right to repeat them, sir," he announced in a shocked voice that chided me for knowing as much.

"Perfectly correct," I demurred. "And the girls in Brixton?"

"Oh, they don't give me any notice at all. Because to them, a fellow from the estate isn't . . ." And he looked down the lane for a word. "Well, he doesn't come from the right direction to suit them."

"Right direction?"

"Yes, sir. Now a boy from York, or even from Edinburgh, he'd be in the right direction, and they'd probably commit murder to cozy up to him. But me? I'm just the caretaker's son from Murcheston to them."

The lad possessed a remarkable intuition into the geography of romance. "How old are you, Liam?" I asked.

"Fifteen last Christmas Day, Your Grace." I was surprised, for he looked some years older.

"Well, if I'm not being too inquisitive, would you please tell me what's in Brixton that could attract a lad of fifteen if not girls?"

He hesitated, and I could see that he's been made to feel that, whatever desire impels him to town, it's misdirected. After staring about expectantly for a time, however, as though he were afraid to see his father standing by the side of the road, he answered in a hushed voice, "Books."

"Books?" I repeated, startled.

"I know it sounds shameful, sir," he cried, turning to me imploringly. "That's why Old Dad objects so. He's never had much use for books. None but the Good Book, I mean, and he doesn't see why I should, either. But he's willing to let me go up to town once in a while all the same to borrow books of the schoolmaster there. He says he only allows it to keep me from sneaking away and lying to him. I know he means that as a rebuke, but I'm afraid that's what I'd probably do if I couldn't get them any other way. The schoolmaster, he's a fine gentleman and lets me borrow one book at a time, and he helps me pick them out, too. I'm far too stupid myself to know what to read."

I was frankly amazed at the lad. I asked him whether he were presently returning a book to the schoolmaster, and he produced a small sack from under the bench. Some popular novel, I thought, a romantic adventure of foreign lands or some high seas escapades. I laughed aloud when he handed out a translation of the *Meditations of Marcus Aurelius.*

"And you say you make regular visits to Brixton to borrow such books as this?" I asked.

"Not so often in the past as I've liked. But now that you're coming to Murcheston so regular, I mean, now that *Your Grace* is coming, and there's no one else to go fetch you and take you back, I'll be able to get to town every month."

"Glad to be of service," I told him, laughing again. The boy was a genuine delight to converse with. But there were other matters I wanted to learn from him, so I finally brought the discussion around to the public opinion of my visits and whether this recent change in my habits had caused any comment in Brixton.

"I'm afraid I couldn't say, Your Grace. I don't speak to many people while I'm in town. Of course, Mr. Cabrini . . ." and the boy hesitated, as though unwilling to go on.

"What is it, lad? You can tell me," I reassured him. "I won't be cross."

"I'd hate to say anything mean, sir," Liam admitted, shaking the reins nervously again, "but Mr. Cabrini was nosing it about town that you were up to no good at all. He spread the story all over that poor Riga'd been found so horribly slaughtered, but that you didn't seem any more concerned than if you'd had a hand in the work yourself. It didn't come to anything, though, as all this was after you'd sacked him and no one put much stock in the word of a man like that anyway. And once Old Dad got wind of it, he went right up to town himself and told Mr. Cabrini to hold his tongue or others would hold it for him. Mr. Cabrini left soon after, and nothing's come of it at all, I swear to you, sir."

Cabrini again, damn the oaf! Still, he's gone at last. But the seed has been planted, and there's no digging it up again to destroy it. I wondered how Cabrini's speculations might have been received, so I turned once again to Liam. "And tell me, since your father must have told you about the incident, what do you think happened to the mare?"

The lad laughed a light, charming laugh and shook his head. "Lord, sir, I don't bother myself with such things. Old Dad and Jemmy, now they've been worrying over that question for a month now. But I figure it was done by whatever did it. And if it's still about then it's around somewhere, and if it's gone away, then it's somewhere else. Either way, it's not the sort of thing I'll trouble myself over."

"But aren't you afraid, boy?" I cautioned him. "That thing might find you as tender a morsel as it found the mare. And doubtless you'd be a good deal tastier. Don't you worry that it might take you unawares some night as you wander about the woods?"

"What? Leap upon me and gobble me up like the wolf in the fairy stories?" he said with a natural contempt, looking into the trees. "Forgive me, sir, but I can't work up a second's bother over something I've no control over. Something I haven't even seen and don't know for certain whether it even exists. I can't fear what's invisible, sir. I've got to know a thing for myself before I let it concern me that way."

I laughed heartily at this natural skepticism and clapped him on the shoulder. An astonishing philosopher, this country lad. To think such a young Epicurean has been growing up just under my nose, and I never aware of it. We passed the remainder of our journey in pleasant talk about books he'd read and hoped to read. The schoolmaster at Brixton certainly knows his business, and I daresay the only thing distinguishing Liam from the best scholars at Eton is his lack of languages and mathematics. In philosophy, history and letters, however, he's equal to any of them. I'd do well to take an interest in the boy. A quick mind, coupled with a handsome figure and pleasing countenance, is a formidable asset, and with guidance, plus a little encouragement, and patronage, he could do very well for himself. At any rate, he could prove a pleasant diversion. And I need some diversion from my growing disaffection, this black, foul mood.

16 March

I've completed my translation of Gustavus. Lord, what a chore. I never thought I'd be done with the thing. I remember having enjoyed Latin at one time, too, young fool that I was. In spite of the good man's obvious knowledge of werewolves, I have to admit that much of his information is tainted by prejudice and myth. Still, he's the most reliable source I've come across, and the histories he relates are a cut above the norm for such literature. One of these tales is especially noteworthy, but not for the reasons that led Gustavus to include it in his collection. There's a right way to understand such things, after all, and when viewed correctly this tale is an excellent example of how the unnatural bias of humanity against my kind can lead to tragedy. I offer it in my own rather free translation, poor as it is.

> "There lived, in a small yet wealthy principality on the eastern shore of the Rhine many decades ago, a powerful abbot, a man no better and no worse than most others of his type in those days, which is to say venal, lecherous, corrupt and profane, abusing the secular and spiritual powers of his office and ruling both abbey and town with a ruthless will and an eye for profit. His monk's cell was more richly appointed than

many a king's chambers, with gilded furnishings and brilliant tapestries by the finest Florentine artisans, a downy mattress and pillows filled with the hair of young virgins. His robes were all velvet and silk and soft furs, and his rosary was set with precious gems on a golden chain. His table was the finest in the land, overflowing with the rarest delicacies and sweetest wines and the most glowing conversation, for he entertained more often than he heard confession, although to his credit he administered penance with the same enthusiasm he displayed when collecting alms. In sum, he was a successful cleric, and his name was Brother Pius.

"As part of his service to the town it was his duty to say the mass on Sundays, a practice which he held to diligently owing to the marvelous effect his homilies had on the collection plate. For it takes a man of worldly tastes to understand the passions that drive his fellows to sin, and it could easily be argued in his favor that Brother Pius' mortal ways gave him a more than passing knowledge of the true terrors of hell. Be that as it may, it is a fact that his descriptions of that place were a wonderful expedient for opening purses.

"It was while distributing the communion, that holiest of offices, that Brother Pius first laid eyes on his desire. Her name was Gabriella, a lovely creature of sixteen, delicate and pale, with large, dark eyes that peered out from under her pretty veil, eyes that were quick to look away from a longing glance, and a modest charm as yet ignorant of the world. She was not so perfectly free from experience but that she noted the attention Brother Pius afforded her that day, and it was she who sought him out to be her confessor the following Sunday. So can modesty be turned to good use in the world.

"Gabriella visited Brother Pius often, and it would have been a subject of gossip among the people that such a sweet child could have so much cause for confession, if any had been brave enough to talk of it. But as Brother Pius' character was so well known, no one offered the least comment about the frequency of Gabriella's visits to his cell. Nor was it considered necessary to express oneself on the occasion of young Gabriella being removed from the rigors of the mundane sphere and admitted as a novice to a cloister whose walls were hard by the abbey, and whose sisters were often given to worshiping privately with the monks. Certainly her parents profited from their daughter's piety, both spiritually and materially, and who would dare object, if they did not?

"But for all her simplicity, Gabriella was a lively girl, gay and free, and the walls of the cloister were not always capable of containing her spirit. Which is why, when summer arrived and the countryside was grown green and lush, Brother Pius suggested that she spend some time in a retreat he had in the mountains, a cottage, less rude than rustic, with a stable and a few servants. It was here, while she was out riding one fine morning, when the moon hung full and low on the horizon, that she was attacked by a werewolf. The creature leapt upon her as she rode through a narrow pass, throwing her to the ground and sending her horse fleeing in mad panic. Why the werewolf failed to kill her is a mystery. Did it favor the horse over the girl and so abandon the one in pursuit of the other?"

(So much for the notion that werewolves favor human prey!)

"Or did the moon set before the monster had a chance to complete its work? No sign of man or beast lay near Gabriella when she was finally discovered, and she had no memory of anything after the attack. The servants found her, severely hurt but alive, and so carried her back to the cottage while a doctor and Brother Pius were sent for.

"Both appeared at Gabriella's bedside within hours, and although the wounds were not deep, the poor girl suffered greatly from a fever, and the doctor could offer no guarantees that she would recover. Brother Pius genuinely loved Gabriella, and the doctor's opinion moved his heart, perhaps more sincerely than it had been moved in many years. Still, he was a worldly man, and with a strong will he proceeded to administer the rites of his office, paving the way for Gabriella to enter her eternal home in the full purity of her great good spirit.

"Such preparedness was premature, however, for Gabriella was herself possessed of a strong will, and slowly the fever abated so that, within a week, the doctor proclaimed her beyond the worst and announced that she could rise from her satin pallet, although he insisted that she continue her recuperation in the easy confinement of the mountain cottage. So she remained while her benefactor returned. Under the close supervision of the doctor she quickly regained her strength, though it was noticed that she displayed less improvement in her humor. Indeed, in a girl renowned for mildness, Gabriella's temper became remarkably fierce, and the doctor was forced on two separate occasions to apply leeches in an attempt to eliminate the foul blood left from her wounds.

"It was a month after her accident that she first disappeared from her retreat at night. She was discovered the next day sleeping high up on the mountain, with no clothing and a foully mutilated goat in her embrace. Again, Brother Pius was called. When he heard the conditions under which Gabriella had been found, he blanched and fell into a chair, for he knew that the beast which attacked her could have been none other than a demon, sent to possess her soul. He ordered a servant to the town to retrieve some books from the abbey, as well as some other volumes from his private library, works of secret and terrible teachings, hideous caballa proscribed by most sober men as more dangerous in their cures than the spiritual maladies they were supposed to remedy. But Brother Pius was not a sober man in this business, and the only rule he obeyed was the rule of his own passions.

"He dismissed the servants and set about his work in solitude. No one can say what went on in that cottage over those days. Nearby goatherds reported strange lights floating from window to window in the house, and heard screams and other devilish noises emitted from the confines of those walls. But none of them had the courage to investigate, and after many days the noises became less weird, and the lights less frequent, until on a clear, bright afternoon some two weeks after his ministrations had begun, Brother Pius emerged from the cottage, called the servants back, and announced that Gabriella was saved. And so he believed."

(Saved? Saved from her natural self, her new and deeply affected being? This is the pale, pathetic weakness of mankind's ignorance, soothing its fears with the magical incantations of an inadequate faith. Science tries to fathom the depths of nature, as I am doing for myself. But religion battles against profound forces with empty prayers and wishes. And by this the man hopes the girl is saved! Saved!)

"Some two weeks later the devil again took hold of the poor girl's soul. When her maid came to awaken Gabriella in the morning, she found the room abandoned, bed and bedclothes strewn about like so much straw before a whirlwind, and the window shattered as by a great weight hurtling through it. Gabriella was found over a mile distant, resting by a mountain stream. All around her, fouling her naked flesh and scattered about a clearing for a hundred yards, were the remains of a peasant child.

"Who can describe the pains of Brother Pius at this latest discovery? What humiliations did he not suffer? What fears were not his? Did he rail against the Satanic powers that took delight in tormenting him through his beloved? Or did he save his curses for even greater powers that were silent? Whatever his thoughts, his actions were sure and determined. Again he sent the servants away. Again he held dark counsel with his books through long nights of mysterious ceremony.

And again the goatherds were plagued by weird sights and weirder sounds emanating from the cottage. For days and weeks Brother Pius battled for the soul of Gabriella. He kept her in close confinement, strapping her to her bed when necessary so that he could scourge her flesh and break the devil's grip upon her. He recited lengthy charms over her, sometimes prayers, sometimes incantations. He did not stop this time at apparent success, but continued his ministrations over the tearful protests of his subject, ignoring the pitiful cries for a cessation to her tortures. He sealed his ears against the demon and carried on with his work.

"One evening, as he knelt by the bedside invoking powers of darkness and light to come deliver the girl from the throes of evil, Brother Pius noticed a strange agitation in Gabriella. She wore only a shift and was tied securely to her bed with silken cords, but though she had stopped long ago to fight against her velvet bonds, something at the window was causing her to pull at them with renewed strength. Her eyes were turned with yearning toward the casement, and her struggles grew in energy and violence until they produced a great sweat about her. Brother Pius turned from Gabriella and glanced up at the window where the moonlight was just beginning to stream into the room. He felt a sudden dread, as if the confrontation he had so longed for and feared were finally arrived. He rose from his place and went to look outside.

"He did not know what he might see that would cause such a reaction in the girl. He more than half thought that the demon was returned to claim his victim, and Brother Pius would not have been surprised to see the monster walking toward the cottage in all his horror. Whatever he had expected, however, he was not prepared to see nothing. The night was perfectly still. No breeze stirred the slumber of the leaves. Not a single cloud moved across the starlit sky. Even the birds were silent and unmoving. But for the slow rising of the moon as it cleared the peaks of the mountain and shone in the fullness of its brilliance, the scene might have been a painted landscape of sublime tranquillity.

"A sound behind him attracted Brother Pius' attention from this reverie. It was a low growl, almost like the purring of a great cat. He turned and saw, lying in the place where Gabriella had been, the beast. It presented itself in the aspect of a wolf, still wrapped in the rags and shreds of Gabriella's nightclothes. With ease it snapped the cords that tied it to the bed and rolled awkwardly onto its legs to confront the monk, tormentor of the girl it had been. For the barest moment Brother Pius stood frozen, not in terror, but in fascination. The calm that touched his spirit at this instant was a credit to his preparations. Kneeling down and holding up his crucifix before him, he removed a small vial from the folds of his robe and, reciting a Latin formula, sprayed the contents over the monster.

"Perhaps it was the placid demeanor of the abbot as he performed this act, or perhaps it was the beast's longing to escape the scene of so many trials and so much pain, but however one explains it, the fact is that the creature ran past the form of the kneeling monk, knocking him violently down in the process, and in one bound soared through the open window and raced across the mountainside toward the moon slowly climbing upwards in the night sky. When Brother Pius related the story later, he acknowledged that his only protection lay in the vial he had sprinkled over the demon, an ancient concoction of rainwater caught in a silver vessel mixed with a virgin's first blood. Be that as it may, the potion proved even more efficacious than Brother Pius had expected, for that was the last anyone saw of Gabriella.

"The ordeal took a dire toll on the abbot, and for several days he suffered from a fever, the cause of which the doctor attributed to exhaustion, for Brother Pius received nothing more serious from his adventure than a scratch on the forehead. He soon recovered his strength, and the tale of how he had fought against the devil increased his renown, so that there was not a pew left open in the cathedral when he once more said the mass there. The young boys were hanging irreverently from the very arms of the saints along the aisles, and in a single morning Brother Pius collected more than he had ever done in an entire month previously. True, he felt pangs at the loss of his Gabriella, but these passed, somewhat sooner than he had expected them to, and it appeared that his life would be even more blessed by profit and good fortune than before.

"But at the next full moon, a strange figure moved through the halls of the abbey, and the following morning Brother Pius was discovered in the courtyard, naked and bloodied, the ravaged corpse of a novitiate by his side. His brother monks assisted him back to his cell and wiped away the stains from his person. What was there else for them to do? They dared not consider the worst, not openly. Their comfort depended too much upon the leadership of Brother Pius. A tale formulated itself among them that a demon had breached the walls of their abbey, had fallen upon the novitiate, but had been frightened away by Brother Pius in a terrible battle before it could claim the poor lad's soul. This, they told themselves about the common table, was what happened. But what they harbored in their breasts was another matter. They swore terrible oaths of silence, bonds that were a sacrilege to hold. But the strictest vows could not keep the truth from overreaching the walls of the abbey, and that same day the entire town was speaking of it, covering Brother Pius in stains that could not be washed clean.

"For three days the abbot spoke not a word to the monks. He kept to his cell in perfect silence, and only his muttered prayers could be heard through the door. On the fourth day a venerable old brother of the order ventured in and found the body of Brother Pius, stiff and cold, lying prostrate before an image of the Virgin Mother, still clasping a black bottle in his hand. The exact nature of his death was never discussed, not by anyone, and Brother Pius was laid in the abbey's cemetery with every rite and honor that the order could bestow. The mourning in the town went on for a month."

What folly! Could I have come across a more evident condemnation of the destructive power of superstition? After all, what evil did Gabriella commit that wasn't forced upon her by Brother Pius? Hadn't she been subjected to all sorts of mad rites and incantations in his efforts to subvert her true nature? What accusation can be brought against a girl so abused, so tormented that she must have been driven to frenzy? Yet if the abbot's knowledge had gone beyond the absurdities of magic and alchemy and religion into a genuine understanding of lycanthropy, the tragedy could have been averted. Such simple precautions as I've implemented at Murcheston would have been all that were necessary to ensure that the tale ended differently, far differently. Indeed, the fact that Gabriella failed to attack Brother Pius belies the reputation held against werewolves. All she desired was her freedom, and that was all she took away with her.

So much for commentary. It's with the purpose of inspiring this sort of understanding that I record my observations and findings, to combat the evils of superstition with the truth. Someday, when I'm able to address the world openly, these horror stories will be recognized as the bloodthirsty products, not of the werewolf, but of the human mind that hates and fears us.

20 March

I've done it at last. Just closed my eyes and leapt in with both feet to get a good, thorough soaking. I've returned to the world of the living, reentered society. In the end it seems that I had to. There was simply no other way for me to go. I found myself this evening slouching deeply in my same chair before the same comfortless fire, sipping the same drink and flipping idly through the same books, when I suddenly became sick of this hermit's existence. What affectation to build a solitary, nervous, mirthless life amid the most vital city in the world. Without really thinking what I was doing, I shut the book in front of me, called out for my evening clothes, and before my purpose could fail me I was bolting out into the night and back into the world.

I felt as giddy as a young bride as I rode through the crowded streets, like some foreigner lost in a strange land. Of course I went to the opera. They were performing Wagner, for one thing, *Der fliegende Hollander*, and I knew that, at the very least, I could spend the evening enjoying the music. But there was no place else for me to go, really. I'd completely lost touch with who was in residence and who was not, with how the Season was faring and which balls had already been held and which were still to come. All of these trivia had been second nature to me before, and I was surprised at how lost I'd actually become. Ridiculous, I know, and once I arrived at the Opera I must have cut a perfectly absurd figure darting among the crowd in the grand lobby, a single gentleman unattached to any group, drifting about the edges of parties large and small like an empty boat tossed upon the ocean's waves through some vast archipelago, rolling from one little island to another, never landing on any friendly beach. I worried over whom I might meet first and what I would say about my months of self-exile. I don't know what would have been worse: to discover that I'd become notorious for my solitary ways, or to learn that no one had even noticed my absence. Yet it all turned out right in the end. I fell in with Shelburne and his set. A perfectly tedious crew, but they asked no embarrassing questions and only took my appearance there as a matter of course. It really was a fine evening.

4 April

My visits to Murcheston are becoming almost routine, and I must confess I'm a little disappointed. I'm not courting incident, of course, but this month I was practically bored by my transformation. It was all too nice somehow. I can't really explain why I feel that way. Just disappointed, that's all. Trotted about the woods as usual, slept by the stream as usual, hunted a bit as usual. The only notable occurrence was my discovery of a fox in a poacher's trap, and the fact that, despite my hunger at the time, I didn't eat the thing. Just sniffed at it and walked away. It was already dead, and as I'm not a scavenger I left it undisturbed. It's worth considering, this delicacy of taste. Such indifference on my part wasn't a conscious decision as men understand such things. No, it was nothing more than a natural response to the situation. The creature was already dead so I didn't eat it, in spite of my hunger. Perfectly natural. And yet, I know there's something significant to this, an indication of something. What is it?

Is it morality? God, I detest that word and all its religious baggage. But could my actions be governed by some source other than my desire, some controlling knowledge of what is right and what is wrong? A natural ethic? A primal law? Are my instincts based on something more than immediate need?

What seems inescapably true is that, as a werewolf, I'm not confused by the same ethical paradoxes that plague men. The moral precepts humans are forever codifying and debating, imposing on a recalcitrant nature, these are matters of course for me. I behave as I do out of the very essence of my being, because I can't do otherwise, and no amount of reasoning is necessary to force ethical behavior from me. In this regard, it would seem, the popular view of progress as the inevitable way of human development is mistaken. Nature provides her children with a surer grasp of right and wrong than man possesses, for all his vaunted reason, and the beasts of the field act upon this understanding as easily and freely as breathing.

This was the only incident of note during my fifth transformation. Indeed, I was actually more concerned with certain developments in the management of the estate this month than I was with any lycanthropic business. On my arrival from Brixton

I was further entertained by the conversation of young Liam Grey. The boy owns a truly remarkable mind considering the conditions of his upbringing. We talked at length about the books he'd read. He was currently struggling over Plato, whose *Apology* he was just finishing. In his boyish naiveté, he had trouble comprehending why the citizens of so enlightened a community as Athens wanted to destroy a man of Socrates' wisdom.

"Because," I explained to him, "Socrates' chief talent was to show other men that they are fools. This isn't a popular occupation, and most municipalities are little inclined to subsidize it, no matter how genuine the need for it might be."

"But you can't condemn a man just for calling you a fool," he observed with charming earnestness. "The Greeks couldn't have been that petty, could they?"

"They were human. How much more petty must you be than that? Besides, they didn't accuse him of holding the mirror up to their own folly, but of corrupting their sons."

"How could he do that?" Liam wondered.

"By showing them the truth about their fool fathers," I told him.

Our discussion went on for many miles in the same vein of inquiry and explication. I'd forgotten how a simple conversation can be so stimulating, and I was taken back to the days of my own ingenuousness at Magdalen and the fine company I kept there. Madness to remember it all now, old loves grown bitter with time, hurts that never heal. But this boy's eager attentions act like a salve upon the wound. It seems to be the rite of youth to make brilliant discoveries of very tired truths, to probe daringly along much-traveled paths. The experience of seeing someone wander darkly down lanes that have long been illuminated is gratifying and stirred in me some former, better longing.

When we arrived at the manor, Liam unloaded my supplies and carried them to the pantry while I looked quickly about the rooms. Satisfied that nothing had been disturbed in my absence, I was just about to bid him farewell when I was struck with an inspiration. I called the boy to me and, placing my arm around him, led him through the main hall. He appeared to be surprised at my familiarity, but I soon put him at his ease.

"Have you ever seen the rooms along the east wing?" I asked.

"No, Your Grace. I've seen the hallway and the kitchen and the pantry, and that's all I've seen."

"Well, I'd like you to be free with the place between my visits, Liam," I told him, leading him along the hallway. "I need someone to take a special interest in the manor, and I think you'd be choicely suited to the job."

He looked at me with large, startled eyes and asked, "Why me so much, sir?"

"Because of this," I said, throwing open the doors of the library just as we reached them.

The look on Liam's face was one I hope never to forget. At first, he merely glanced about the room as I ushered him into it. Slowly, however, the purport of my offer dawned upon him, and his mouth dropped open until I'm convinced his chin was resting squarely on his breast. Walls covered with the Old Governor's books, shelf upon shelf and case upon case of volumes, most of which haven't been touched in decades. Liam took it all in with a slow, measured glance, and then he asked me if I meant for him to peek into the room from time to time and see that the books were all right.

I laughed and said, "No, Liam, I mean for you to sit in this room frequently while I'm away and see that the books are well read. Believe it or not, the slight value placed upon such things is all the protection a good library needs. But you love books, really love them, and that's a rare sort of affection these days. I want you to requite your love as freely as you'd like. Indulge your passions, Liam. Indulgence is the secret road to understanding that no one tells you about. If your passions are right, then drown yourself in them."

Over and over he thanked me for my thoughtfulness, and I confess I found the lad's sense of gratitude not only commendable but pleasing. It gave me a feeling of great warmth to be able to do something meaningful for him, and to do it so easily, for he really shall be performing a valuable service by looking into the house occasionally.

I mustn't allow myself to be carried away in good works, however. I recall the last time I experienced so much pleasure at doing a good turn for someone. And how she left me for another, chose the dreary, mundane existence of a merchant's wife to the passion I offered her, a wedding of souls unbounded by convention, a conflagration of love that would feed upon itself for good or ill, damning tomorrow and damning society but living, truly living! Curse her for choosing so safely and so foolishly.

And even now, with Liam, I'm in immediate danger of losing my stake in the boy. I hadn't counted on the suspicious nature of his father. When I rang the bell this morning, it was the old man who showed up.

"I hope I'll not be taking liberties, Your Grace," Grey began the moment I showed him into the study, "if I was to ask you a question of a personal nature."

"By no means," I assured him.

"It's just that I need to look after my boys, sir," he began, worrying his cap in his hands, as he usually does when he feels himself out of his element. "I watch them carefully, for they've never known a mother since they was babies, and I've had to be all their parents to them at once. I only say as much so you won't think I'm ungrateful, but my youngest tells me that you've given him the freedom of the house while you're away, and I need to know first if what he says is true."

"It's true, Grey," I told him, sitting down at my desk to give myself an added aspect of authority. I began to suspect that there might be trouble ahead. "I told Liam when I arrived that he could use the library anytime he wished, so long as I wasn't in residence."

"Aye, I thought it must be so, for Liam's never been one to lie. But if I may ask Your Grace, why did you make him the offer?"

This question struck me as a little odd and somewhat impertinent, but I suppressed my feelings and inquired of Grey whether he had any cause for asking.

"Cause enough, I believe, where my boy's involved," he retorted politely. "It ain't that I don't appreciate the kind attention you're showing him, but Liam is still a young lad. Younger than his years, truth be told. I've naught against education itself, you see, but a man should be ready to live the life that God gives him, and neither of my boys is ever going to make a life for himself as a scholar. I've been at pains to get the lad to see as much in the past," he confessed, shaking his head, "and I'm feared this new position will fill his head with ideas it's best he never got."

"I suspect you're not giving the boy enough credit," I observed. "He already has the makings of a first-rate scholar about him."

"The makings, yes sir. No doubt of that. But has he the means, Your Grace, that's my question." The old man began to pace about in front of me, and I could see the conflict at work within him: the desire to give his son what he most wants battling against the harshness of the only life he has to offer. It was, in its homely way, a moving vision. "Reading won't earn a man his bread, you know. Now, I've let him go to town on occasion to borrow a book or two off the schoolmaster, and I see nothing wrong with getting a little innocent enjoyment from books. But Liam, he'd spend all his days and all his nights reading, and I'm afraid the temptation of having a whole library of books about will lead him down a road he just can't travel, not in this life."

"Is it really so awful, Grey," I asked, leaning forward in sympathy with the father, "allowing the boy his freedom so he can read what he wants? Many great men began with no better advantage in life than a thirst for knowledge and a roomful of books."

"But we're not great men, me and the boys, nor like to be. You and me, we know something of the world, Your Grace," the old man said, approaching the desk again, and truth is I found this acknowledgment of shared experience amusing. "Now you tell me, what chance have my boys ever got to move among educated people? The learning you'd have for Liam won't do him a stitch of good in the world he's got to be a part of. I don't want it to be that way, but that's how it is. And it's my fear that all these books'll just give him a taste for a life he can't have."

The father's plea was simple, yet eloquent, and I hadn't considered the implications of my offer in this way. Still, I felt that any advantage I could give the boy would be beneficial to him in the long term, so I made a deal with Grey. Liam might have the use of my library, but only on two days a week, to be chosen by his father, and then only after all of his work is done. He was at first reluctant to accept even this small kindness, but I pointed out to him that, now with the idea planted in Liam's head, and as the house is so much closer than the schoolmaster, Grey would have the devil's own time keeping the lad away. And besides, Liam's prospects needn't be so bleak as his father paints them, now that I've taken an interest in him. Only let him value my patronage as it should be valued, not betray my trust, and I'll guarantee the lad's future.

8

An Intrusion

9 April

Such a marvel is Mrs. Wattles! Returned from Brixton this past week, and what do I find waiting at my door? A bundle of six volumes, all trussed up neatly for my approval. She writes that she'd attempted to contact me, but I was away from town, and she knew I'd want the advantage of a first inspection before she put them out on her shelves. "Where they might be snatched up by any lycanthropist," as she puts it.

Little here of interest, though. An alchemist's text, two books on magic and witchcraft, two children's books, and a bestiary of fantastic animals. The usual sort of rot, silver bullets and the like, no evidence of even the most incidental knowledge of werewolves as they really are. Still, I sent back only the children's books. I seem to have developed into a collector of all manner of lycan-thropic literature, with a more than academic interest in the myths and legends surrounding my kind. Even a work with no scientific value is instructive of mankind's attitudes towards us and the hateful poison I must overcome. Why does this fear grip humanity, so unwarranted and yet so pervasive? All my work will be useless, a complete waste, if upon revealing myself to the world, I only succeed in evoking universal revulsion. I must find a way to dispel these prejudices. And so my library keeps growing, despite the dearth of authoritative material.

15 April

A note from Mrs. Wattles this morning at breakfast. She's stumbled upon a work of genuine value. "Truly inestimable worth," she wrote. Such a singular find indeed that she dares not trust it to be delivered but insists that I come to her shop at my soonest convenience to inspect it before her personally. What a thrill of delight shot through me at the news! It was the fire of the hunt, when the hounds cry out through the woods that the quarry is at bay and you feel your breath bolt on ahead of you in quick anticipation. I left my meal half eaten and hurried to get dressed. Almost broke my neck in the rush to put on my trousers. In less time than it takes to imagine, I was racing out into the street.

It was just before ten when I marched breathless and sweating into Black Abbots Yard. I was amazed to find a boiling pitch of activity within its narrow confines. My own memory of the place was so full of damp weather and desertion that I hadn't considered how, under more pleasant conditions, it might accommodate a healthy commerce. But the warmth of the day and the brightness of the sky peeking down between the close rooftops gave to the yard an undeniable cheer that seemed quite natural to it. Of course, it was still buried in shadows. I don't suppose the light of the sun finds its way down that wellshaft until quite late in the morning, and then only for a few meager hours. I only paused for a moment to note the general transformation of the place and then directed my steps towards Mrs. Wattles'. Entering, I found that shop unaltered from my first visit. The same exotic smells and weird displays, the same orderly disorderliness, and still deserted in spite of the activity outside. Indeed, the same candle that had been the only source of illumination before still burned on the desk to faint purpose.

No sooner had I stepped over the threshold than I was greeted by the disembodied voice of the lady herself, softly penetrating, coming from deep within her forest of bookcases, a whimsical fairy tempting passersby off the beaten path of scholarship. "My goodness, how prompt you are, Your Grace. A clockwork man. Give me just a moment, will you be so kind, and I shall retrieve the volume and attend to you post haste."

I waited—what else could I do?—bouncing anxiously on my heels. I felt certain that Mrs. Wattles wouldn't have summoned me with such urgency for just any text. I could tell, even from our brief commerce, that she was not so frivolous as that, nor so readily impressed. I stood about looking over the shelves in her front room, paying damned slight attention to what I saw there, listening for the merest sound that might herald her approach. Naturally there wasn't any. She simply materialized from behind her desk, an immensely large, ancient book clutched to the blackness of her swelling bosom.

"Behold the Grail!" she exclaimed, eyes alight with the triumphant fire of discovery. She extended the book out to me at arm's length, offered it up, whether for inspection or sacrifice I couldn't tell. I didn't even ask what it might be but snatched it from her greedily, casting it down upon the neatness of her desk, throwing it open. What a crushing disappointment! The thing was penned in some heathenish scrawl! I couldn't begin to decipher it. Rude lines writhing across the page like so many hungry worms. I looked up at Mrs. Wattles in confusion, my pain written so palpably on my face that she apologized at once.

"But I was unthinking not to have told you, my dear," she said, sitting down, her voice redolent with sympathy. "Arabic is not one of your languages, I suppose? You are not familiar with it? No, of course not. Who is these days, really, except the odd Arab? And few enough of those loitering about." She grinned a sly grin, though I thought her humor misplaced. "Well, do not be discouraged. Do not be cast down, Your Grace. Luckily, I know a young scholar who has made the study of Arabian texts his *métier*, and I don't suppose he would object too strongly to a bit of work in the evenings. It wouldn't take him long, I think. He's quite accomplished, a veritable Muhammadan." And she opened a paperbound notebook that rested on a corner of her desk and began writing.

"That's all very well, I'm sure," I said, irritated and feeling forgotten in her plans. I closed the book with a crashing report. "But do you think I could know what this bloody mess is before I go to the trouble of having it translated? I can't say for a fact that I want to commission any work in the first place."

Mrs. Wattles put her pen down gently and clasped her hands before her. "But have I not told you? My dear, you must think me the idiot's own child. To call you here so precipitately and then forget to explain myself. I am going mad, my love, I know it," she exclaimed, grasping her skull with both hands and shaking it, as though this action would cure her addled brain. "Quite the lunatic I am. Well then, I'll put it to you in a nutshell, and the tastiest nut it is. The book before Your Grace is none other than the *Medical Oddities and Notable Cases of Muhammad al-Azimi*. This famed Muhammad was court physician to the great Caliph Harun al-Rashid, who, you will recall I am sure, ruled the vastness of Islam in the late eighth century. A noble patron of letters was Harun, an oriental Charlemagne, as famous for his cultured and gentle manner as for his ruthless and warlike policies. He had a special fondness for the sciences, in those grand days when art and science were not split by the modern gulf that separates them in our own time. So, in the interests of the ages and the furtherance of knowledge, Harun ordered Muhammad to record some of the more enchanting medical histories he had come across in his long career, a career which saw him rise from a humble doctor in the streets of Tarsus to be hailed as the most renowned medical man of his day. The resultant work you hold in your hands, my dear. Luckily for subsequent generations, the good doctor was an excellent judge of his caliph, and instead of relating the sort of dry pedantry that he found enlightening himself, included only those tales of sensational aspect that were sure to please Harun. The most famous of these is 'The Celebrated Story of the Man in the Cage.' It is a tale of lycanthropy, Your Grace, and its authenticity is incontestable, endorsed as it is by al-Azimi himself, who was its chief witness. It is, beyond the least doubt, the truest thing ever writ on the subject."

My pique of the moment before was lost in this intriguing history, and I asked Mrs. Wattles how soon her Arab scholar could have the thing translated for me. She muttered to herself, calculating. "It is a medieval dialect that is rather out of use these days. That should add a degree of challenge. And then this is a handwritten manuscript. Always more difficult that way. I should think two weeks would suffice to complete the task," she speculated, picking up her pen again. "Shall we say by the first of next month? If you will be so good as to return then, I think I can guarantee a most acceptable piece of work for you."

"But surely he can be persuaded to work faster," I insisted.

"He can work as fast as you like, Your Grace, but I still believe the first is the soonest anything productive can be expected from him."

"I'll pay handsomely for the extra effort, of course," I pursued.

"Doubtless you will," she replied. "But how could I possibly deceive you by presuming that he might finish the translation prior to the first? Of course, I will contact you at once if we should prove fortunate. Still, I think we might just keep the first as our appointed time."

"I won't be available the first," I admitted at last. "I'll be out of the city."

"Unavailable?" Mrs. Wattles asked, her voice bright with interest. "A trip to Brixton, I suppose. Brixton is your country, isn't it?"

"Yes," I acknowledged, surprised at what from another I might have considered impertinence. "How did you know that?"

"Oh, it behooves me to remain current on all the military and aristocratic rolls. Let me see," and she began to recite as though she had a copy of the *Peerage* in front of her. "The Dukes of Darnley. Family came over with William the Conqueror. A charmed and charming lineage. The eighth Earl of Darnley I believe stood valiantly with Lancaster against York, while the first duke held a less successful position with Charles' cavaliers at Marston Moor. Other members of the clan have been renowned less for military bearing than financial acumen. As to matters of economy—ancestral estate at Murcheston, with a personal manor covering some three thousand acres and complete holdings in the vicinity of thirty-five thousand acres. Grounds include an active agricultural tenantry of roughly one hundred fifty yeomen. Also included is the village of Brixton with its eight thousand souls, all involved directly or indirectly in the mining of coal along a corner of the estate. The whole augmented nicely with some substantial properties in London . . ."

"Thank you," I interrupted, feeling uneasy. "You seem to be as well informed of my affairs as I am myself. Certainly this is more than idle curiosity."

Mrs. Wattles shrugged her massive shoulders and spread her hands out wide in a show of resignation. "Aye, such is the pitiable truth. I fear it is just that. Curiosity. Mine is a life devoted to study, my dear, and when a topic captures my attention, it is only natural for me to hunt out every detail surrounding it. I do it almost without thinking, and I extend a sincere apology if I have insulted you in any way. But my research often results in pleasant dividends. For example, I have acquaintances in your county, and if you ever anticipate an extended stay, I could have them call on you from time to time with news of any discoveries I might come across. Sometimes it is advisable to act quickly if a valuable text is not to be lost."

"Thank you for the offer," I responded, a shade icily, I think. This unwanted interest cast the first pall over my burgeoning relationship with Mrs. Wattles, and I was unsure how to respond.

"But my visits to Murcheston are never longer than two or three days. And as I prefer to pass my time there in solitude, even such good news as you would no doubt bring wouldn't be welcome. If I'm out of the city, you may, however, always leave a note with my man in town."

"And doesn't your valet accompany you to your estate?"

"As I said, Mrs. Wattles, I prefer solitude." I understand her heightened sense of inquisitiveness, but this was uncomfortably intrusive. I turned the conversation to the topic of my accounts with her. These I settled quickly. Then, arranging that she should notify me as soon as the translation was completed (and with her final tiresome insistence that it should not be finished before the first of the month trailing close behind me), I left.

Truth is, I'm still disturbed by this attention to my private life. And yet, Mrs. Wattles has been such a help. I'm beginning to rely so completely on her abilities and discrimination that she's become indispensable to me, even after such a brief time. If it weren't for her inexhaustible resources, I'm convinced I'd have given up the struggle long before now and resigned from my studies. Just led a useless, mundane life between here and Murcheston, with nothing worthwhile to show for my lycanthropy but the monthly romp through the woods. And what harm can come of her curiosity, after all? I mustn't be so nervous, so quick to discover danger. I'm getting to be a dreadful old woman.

21 April

Cabrini! Damn the man to hell, he's back! What is it that keeps him forever at my heels, yapping like a mongrel? I'd thought to be rid of him when I sent him packing three months ago. Then I hear from Liam Grey of the trouble he tried to cause for me in Brixton. Now he turns up as if by design at Epsom. By God, the man is hounding me, for what purpose I'm beginning to understand.

I was enjoying an afternoon at the races, really enjoying myself. The freedom I felt, the pleasure of simply being out in the world was revitalizing. I was drunk with the excitement of the track, the colors, the sounds, the smells, the people crowding and jostling and laughing and screaming. I threw myself into it gaily until it all became too delightful and I retired to the stables. Something about strolling among the horses, something calming that soothes my too-full spirits. I wandered in and out and about the place, talking to the hands and jockeys, listening to the trainers as they gave their instructions before mounting. The earnestness of these fellows as they went about their work refreshed me after the merry artifice of society, and I'd almost forgotten myself when I was intruded upon by Cabrini.

His clothes were threadbare. Dirty red waistcoat over a tattered yellow shirt with open cuffs, and brown checkered trousers worn almost through at the knees. His face sports whiskers now, untrimmed and unkempt, and his general appearance is debased. His manner is as bold as ever, though, and immediately shattered my carefree mood. He spoke with a familiarity that galled me, but as he asked for the chance to have a private word, and I saw this as the best opportunity to be rid of him, I consented. We walked to a corner of the stables, and when he turned to me with an insolent grin, it was all I could do to keep from striking him.

"Your Grace is looking wondrous fit for a man what keeps to himself so much," he began. "Your being so secret and solitary, it makes it hard for a chap to see you. Bless me, but I've had the worst time of it to get even so much as a word with you, and here I run into you quite without meaning to."

"State your business," I returned curtly, knowing this meeting was no accident.

He chuckled and I seethed. "Now there's a right proper way to handle things," he remarked, reaching down for a piece of straw on the ground and placing it between his grinning teeth. "Get business cleared away up front, as you might say, and then a fellow has the rest of his time for enjoyment. All right then, to put it to you straight, as I know you'd like to hear it," and he leered at me with what I suppose was meant to be a friendly glance, "I was just curious as to how you was faring all alone at the old manor. What a big, empty bucket of a place it must be for a lone fellow to rattle about in. Many's the time I thought of Your Grace like that, it's true, pictured you to myself all surrounded by so much of nobody. Still, I guess a man has the right to make his own life for himself. Especially a man like you, with all the resources you've got at hand, eh?"

Infuriating! "Enough of your idle games, man. What is it you want?"

"Aye, there I am, not being businesslike," clucked Cabrini, shaking his head with a grin. "You've got to forgive me my clumsy manner, Your Grace. I'm a bit out of practice. Haven't had much to do in the way of business these many weeks. Sweet Jesus, but I've had a miserable time of it, hunting about for a position as suited my singular abilities, and can't say I've found anything near as nice as the situation I had under Your Grace."

"If times are bad, then I suggest you busy yourself about this place," I told him, taking in all the bustle of the stables with a sweeping gesture, "and stop bothering me. I have nothing for you, and doubtless someone here could use a man with your experience."

"Aye sir, that they could," he went on, nodding and grinning like an ape. "Take good care of myself about this place. Truth it is. But there's the rub. As the fellow said, it ain't so much the work, as the labor."

"If you're too lazy for honest employment, I daresay you know other ways to earn your bread."

He laughed at this, and gave me another repulsive leer. "There you've hit on it, Your Grace. God, but you're a sharp one. A man would prick himself on your wit, he would. A fellow's got to earn his bread, just as you say, and whether he does it one way or another is all one to him. Now, let's suppose," and the smile dropped away from his lips, "that a man such as me was to know something about a man such as you."

I'd begun to suspect as much, that this game was something of the kind. I wish I could say I felt no fear at the thought of Cabrini's scheming. Still, I put on a cool face. "What do you know that I might possibly care about?"

He positioned the smile back on his lips. "That's the peculiar thing, you see," he went on, twisting the straw in his mouth. "What I might know ain't nothing. A fellow sees a horse butchered on the master's lawn. He notices signs that some great monster of a beast is making free with the old estate right up to the very walls. And the master, he don't seem any more concerned than if he was to hear of a stray dog wandering about. What's a fellow to make of that, I ask you? Or why should a fellow want to make anything of it? You couldn't turn a ha'penny from such a flimsy bit of news."

"Is that all?" I asked, surprised that the fool had nothing more than this.

"Not all, Your Grace, not all by half. For that's the whole point of it, you see. It ain't information that matters. It's suspicion the master fears. People nosing about, asking questions, that's what he ain't too keen on, and what maybe he'd be willing to cough up a little scratch to avoid." He leaned back against the stable wall and stretched languidly, sure of himself and his position. "Think of it. All a fellow's got to do is plant the idea in people's heads. That shouldn't be too hard. After all, you're a fair mysterious character these days. People are longing to think the worst of you, and that's naught but the wicked truth. Oh, if I knew something, something genuine that could really make the kettle boil, then we'd have a lot to talk over, you and me. Hundreds of things. But, you see, I'm a simple man with no real harm in me. Just looking for the easiest way to a few quid. Say twenty. Now, is it worth that tiny bit to be rid of the likes of me for good? Ain't that worth a bit of the stuff? What do you think?"

So he was swinging wildly in the dark, trying to score a hit. For a moment I was amazed. The arrogance of this buffoon! I knew he was a lazy bastard, but actually trying to extort money on speculation! I turned a smile upon him, confident now that he had nothing, not a shred of anything against me. Taking two steps forward, I backed him physically against the wall and, snatching the straw from his mouth with one hand, I planted a finger in the middle of his chest with the other. "I'll tell you what I think," I said in a voice calm with suppressed rage. "I think you've overplayed your hand a bit, my man. I think that if you ever approach me again, anywhere, at any time, for any purpose, I'll flog you myself, flay you with my own hand until you're not fit to be called human, and then I'll have you brought up on charges before the magistrate. And if you dare to come within a hundred miles of my lands, I'll have you transported to Australia for life. Now you take your ludicrous proposition and be damned with it." And so saying, I took him by the waistcoat and sent him forcibly on his way.

The impossible cheek of Cabrini, attempting to wrench money from me on such inconsequential grounds as this. I knew he was a rank opportunist, but this exceeds even my low opinion of him. The entire episode left me out of sorts with the world, and I left the races soon after. Damn the man!

8 May

Dear God, what's happening to me? A terrible accident has occurred at Murcheston. My metamorphosis has gone wrong, horribly wrong. It was an accident. I know it was. Except that—no, not an accident, but not purposeful either. I didn't mean for it to happen! It just unfolded naturally, inevitably. There's something— I'm almost afraid to think it, but there's something right about the whole thing. I can hardly convince myself that I've done anything so terrible. But it *is* terrible! It's monstrous! Am I going mad? What fears and joys I've known in the last twenty-four hours. How can I convey any impression of the conflicts at work within me even now? Revulsion and shame—yes, true—but ecstasy as well. How can I feel such freedom, such release?

Last night was unusually bright with a moon like a burning wheel glowing white hot in the black sky. I trotted easily, unhurriedly across the field to the woods, absorbing all the noises and scents that made a pageant of activity in the air. A soft breeze blew through the trees and the new green leaves whispered of primal spring and the promise of summer. Along the forest floor it seemed as though every creature had some work to be doing and the scurrying from all about me played a rhythmic counterpoint to the rustling above. The burst of energy with which I usually begin my nocturnal adventures, running and leaping in the heady enjoyment of my strength, I deferred for more vernal pleasures. Found at once my favorite spot by the stream, an old, mossy oak for my companion and the aroma of the night air for my food.

As is usual with me in my wolf-state, I had no conception of the passage of time, so I can't say when I became aware of something different in the woods. I know what first aroused my curiosity: the distinct sound of silence coming from upwind of me. It must be difficult for a man to imagine how piercing a silence can be in the woods, for silence follows men everywhere. No man has ever experienced the full chorus of life that the forest sings only to itself. But to an ear attuned to such music, a quiet corner of the woods is as unmistakable as a cry in an abandoned house. No sooner was I aware of this stitch in the fabric of the night than I rose and trotted off in the direction of the silence, or rather circled round toward it, for being upwind it presented a genuine mystery to me, as though I were walking into a darkened room.

At the time I only acted, keenly aware of my desire, even though I didn't know yet what the object of my desire was. Yet while I was attempting to place myself downwind of the silence, the silence itself was moving into the breeze, so that I didn't so much circle it as trade places with it, and the first hint of a scent came upon me very quickly. There was no mistaking it. The salty, sweet odor was a beam of light illuminating the shadows. It was man. I'd encountered the scent before, of course, but only as traces upon the trees and the ground and the poacher's trap that I'd uncovered. Never had I known it like this, the fullness of it, the rich variety of the smell. Man's sweat mingles with the odor of his clothing, cotton and leather, the metal of his weapons and tools. Even the smell of beer and grease accompany him wherever he wanders. It's no wonder that even a man with stealthy tread will cause the animals to be still, for there's no masking it, this man-scent.

And how did I respond to it, I who am incapable of anticipation or design, whose every desire becomes an action? I at once began to stalk. Not with animosity. No wicked intent. There was no conscious decision in it at all. I was as indifferent to the man as I would be to a stag. I felt no hostility, no great passion for him. Only, perhaps, his smell urged me on, drove me forward with greater hunger than I'd known before. Yes, my appetite was more acute for him, this man. And yet he was still simply prey, no more than a prize for my irresistible longing.

With the wind ahead of me now and his scent clear and unequivocal in the night air, I proceeded to move cautiously forward. I held my body close to the ground, stepping delicately among the debris of the forest floor, making no more sound than the breeze. I was in no hurry, was suffering from no anxiety that might impel me to divulge myself too soon. It's man who lives this way, upon expectations of the future. But I act, and in acting either win or fail with the moment. What comes after is nothing to me. My all is engrossed in the now.

Such is the consciousness with which I stalk my prey. I felt every nuance of behavior that the wind disclosed, telling me of the creature I hadn't even seen but knew with a knowledge more certain than if I'd been walking by his side. A sudden change in the intensity of the scent and I stopped. He'd halted and was busying himself with some work. I moved now with a slowness no human could have matched. It would have strained his nerves beyond endurance to display such patience, to show such complete awareness of every muscle as I edged closer to my prey in the dark. Indeed, to race the wind is nothing to a werewolf. But stealth can be damned exhausting.

In the brightness of the night I held close to the shadows. The light limited my vision, and I was dangerously close to the man before I saw him on his knees, his back to me as he struggled with something on the ground, completely absorbed in his work, making noises to himself under his breath. For a mere moment, I watched him at his labors. Then I growled. It wasn't his back I wanted, and so I caused him to hear me, to turn in sudden fear, to confront me. I left the ground as he raised up, my pounce timed so perfectly that my jaws met his throat at the exact moment that it presented itself in the moonlight. My fangs sank deep into his flesh, and the warm, wet sweetness of his blood was delicious to me. The force of my attack carried us several yards through the air, and for a time we were one indivisible thing, a single being flying through space, life and death entangled inextricably. Or rather, his existence was subsumed to my own, his essence reduced to my desire. We landed hard upon the earth. He didn't struggle, was almost assuredly dead before I tore away his throat. I doubt that he felt more than a sudden jolt.

The meat of him was fat and luscious, and I fed with a relish I haven't known before. In all my other kills there was not this sense of—what is it?—not triumph, but fulfillment. I ate until I was satisfied, and then I lay beside the carcass and slept. When I awoke it was daylight, but the moon was still in the sky, and so I returned to the banks of the stream till it set and I became a man again. With the transformation accomplished, I went back into the house, naked and smeared with gore.

I remembered every detail of the night, and for the first time I felt shame at what I'd become. Blind shame, hot inside me, inside my stomach where the flesh of my victim still filled me. I wept, sobbed long and loud, howled in disgust with myself. What had I become? I thought I'd known, but now every fear came welling up like gorge inside me, sickening me. I washed myself clean of the blood caked to my face and hair, and after dressing

I took a spade from the stables and set out to dispose of the proof of my savagery, tears of confusion flowing down my face.

And then, as I passed back into the woods, into that special place so much my own every month, a remarkable change occurred. I found it impossible to sustain my sense of horror, for equally insistent within me, just lying under the surface of my grief, I discovered a feeling of sublime joy, as though I had at last consummated my new self. Till now I've denied the rapacity attributed to werewolves. Every author I've read treats us as blood-thirsty monsters with a special, diabolical design against humanity. I know this to be absurd, yet I've carried the knowledge silently with me, the fear that at some point I would take a human life.

How can I now record these events so calmly? Is that how much I've lost touch with my humanity, that I'm no longer even moved by the memory of what's happened? But if I am that far removed from my former self, what have I really lost? My sense of guilt? My fears and suspicions? These things are nothing to me, the baggage of reason, useless weights men carry about with them, keeping them fit for society, not nature. But my freedom, my exuberance in the face of what's happened, that's natural, that's true and real. Isn't it? I know—no, I feel that it's so. Why must I try to deny it, to cover my strength in remorse and a fool's misgivings? I did what I did. What more justification is there than that?

And now that I've done it, what's the result? What now? What's changed in my situation now that I've murdered a human being? Perfectly absurd to call it "murder." What I've done is no murder, no more than a tiger can be said to murder when it kills a man. The beast behaves as it does from the deepest stirrings of its being, kills not with malice but out of the justness of its nature. Might as well accuse the ocean of murder when it drowns sailors, or the earth when she traps miners. Indeed, isn't God the greatest murderer of all, who kills with pestilence and famine and by simply wearing down his victims until they can no longer bear to live? The way of nature is the way of death in the service of a stronger life. That which is weak feeds the strength of another. If this is true of a deer or an old mare, why should it be any less true of a man at the height of his vigor, taken by superior cunning and power? Where lies the shame in this?

Yet there was still a taint upon me as I searched for the remains of my victim, for I hadn't merely taken a life, but had fed upon that life, had feasted on human flesh. Wasn't this cause for the most profound repugnance? The more my mind tried to revive in me some loathing at the enormity of my actions, however, the more I came to feel that no such aversion stirred my breast any longer. I'd killed and that was that. I felt no blame, no remorse, only the nagging belief, the residue of a morality instilled in me since childhood, that I *should* be blamed, *should* be remorseful.

And then I discovered what there was left of the man, and this internal debate was ended in a rush of satisfaction. Staring up at me from the ground, his features untouched by any reflection of his violent end, was Cabrini. No sign of terror lay upon his brow, no mark of pain or anguish, not even any sign of peace, but the dumb, blank stare of death in all its dull and arbitrary certainty. Only here death was perhaps less capricious than usual, for there was in this some quality of justice. Cabrini's own insolence had been the cause of his destruction. Several feet away lay a poacher's metal trap. Resting against a tree was a gun foolishly placed beyond his reach. An empty sack showed that he had only just begun his night's work. And it wasn't the simple lure of illicit game that had brought him back to Murcheston, for doubtless he could have practiced such arts at any large estate between here and London. Poaching was only his means of turning some profit while engaged in other pursuits. At once his threats became clear to me. He'd hoped to spy on my solitary activities, to discover something that might give his blackmailing scheme greater force. But in wagering on his luck he had lost his life.

No one will pity such a fool. The fact of his death is nothing. Indeed, had he been apprehended, his life would have been no less forfeit, and though as magistrate I may have felt constrained to sentence him to death, the man would certainly have been transported, closing out his days in Australia. So where at last is the tragedy in what I've done?

I set about the task of concealing this episode. The work was hard, and as the morning drew on into afternoon, a bank of clouds, thick and gray and heavy with wet, crept sluggishly across the sky, obscuring the sun and dropping a soft rain upon everything. Still, I didn't mind the work. After the spiritual ordeal of the past few hours, the monotony of lifting the earth in heavy spadefuls was a relief. The most extreme rites of the church are nothing compared to the efficacy of a day's honest work. By the time I'd laid what there was of Cabrini under the sod and patted down the earth beneath a blanket of leaves, I'd nearly forgotten my troubled thoughts.

I feel more at peace with myself now. This very act of recording the event has brought it into a clearer light for me, and I see at last the justice in what's happened. Cabrini's folly killed him, not I. I was merely the vehicle of nature. Now, in the calmness of the night again, I can see how wrong my earlier fears were. If I've killed a man, that's nothing blameworthy. Yet this doesn't change the fact that I must never allow a recurrence of this business. It won't do, not in my delicate, my precarious, situation.

4 May

No sooner had I finished my last night's entry than I was interrupted by a timid rapping. I almost didn't hear the noise it was so weak, and I had a hard time at first identifying where it came from. After a quick search, however, I found the cause at the back kitchen door. Liam Grey. And fiercely angry I was to see him.

"What the hell are you doing here?" I began in my strictest tones. "I thought you understood, I am never to be intruded upon while in residence. Damn it all, boy, I ought to have you whipped for this. How long have you been standing here?"

"I got here with . . . with the storm, sir," he stammered, his hands held right under his arms and the teeth in his head chattering like a senorita's castanets. I hadn't noticed how wet it had gotten until he mentioned it. The soft drizzle had turned into a regular tempest. "This is your third day," he went on, "and you usually ring the bell in the morning. When we didn't hear anything, I convinced Old Dad to let me come over here. Just to look in and see that you were all right, sir. The Lord only knows what might have happened with you here all alone."

The boy presented such a pathetic sight, shivering in the rain, hair matted flat against his scalp, his concern so sincere and so touching, that I had no heart to scold him. I merely put my arm about him and led him into the house. Once I had him situated in the study, however, with a fire glowing and a cup of tea warming his hands, I let him know that he had done a very foolish thing. "You must never disobey any of my standing orders again, Liam. I haven't placed them in effect out of caprice. They're designed to give me the freedom I need to carry on my work in privacy, a privacy that must be absolute and beyond recall. To do what you've done is very dangerous."

"Dangerous, sir?" he asked.

"Yes, dangerous to my work," I explained, cloaking the truth in a convenient half-truth. "I'll not have my studies ruined by an inquisitive boy. I'm sorry if it hurts you to hear it, but that's my command."

He apologized again for his presumption, and I believe he was afraid my displeasure might lead me to revoke his privileges in the library. I set his mind at rest on that matter by asking how he'd been passing his time among the books. His eyes lit up at once, and for the next hours we discussed what he had read, what he hoped to read, what I thought he ought to read, what I had read when I was young, what I had always wanted to read but never got around to, and a thousand other delightful subjects all centered around books. It's a rare fraternity, that of the bibliophile, and Liam's passion roused within me the memory of all the forgotten hours I'd spent exploring grandfather's volumes like Ali Baba amid the thieves' treasure. It was the most exhilarating evening I have spent in many months, and we were not finished until well toward midnight.

When the clock chimed the witching time of night, Liam wanted to return to his cottage, insisting that his father would be worried about him. But the rain was still falling and I wouldn't hear of his going back out into it. So we set up a little camp there in the study, he upon the floor by the fire, me on the sofa where I was used to spending the night. We continued our idle conversation intermittently until sleep finally sent us our separate ways.

I awoke this morning alone and wandered about looking for Liam. What I found was a large breakfast in the kitchen, cold beef, coddled eggs, toasted bread, and a note saying that he'd risen at his usual time and, as he didn't want to disturb me, had made my breakfast and sneaked back home.

I'm now waiting for Liam to bring the cart around and take me to the station. As I sit here recalling the events of the past few days, I'm overcome with an odd feeling, a gnawing sense that things have altered for me, that the unknown lies before me not black and inscrutable, but roaring like a conflagration, burning me with tongues of flame. I can't make out what's being consumed there in the fire, but I know it must in some way be me, a part of me I don't yet know. I've uncovered things about myself, things I'd feared to know. But now I see it was only the idea of them that frightened me. In a way, I've been released from the bondage of my fear. I've killed a man, a man well worth the killing, and in this I find the greatest sense of freedom. My werewolf's nature is now fully realized and can race forward beyond the restraints of my human weakness.

Yet here I go, setting off to London again, a city swarming with human weakness, feeding off of it, consuming men by the hundreds of thousands. And there I must confess I find some part of me that I keep thinking I've lost. Some small corner of my being that longs for the crowds, the souls all huddled and wretched with their humanity. I need to feel a part of something, anything, and only in society do I find that place where I can be less than myself. What a comfort it is, to reduce oneself to a mere element in a vast machine. It's the sole pleasure nature denies me, this sense of escape from myself, of belonging to something grander. Or lesser.

9

An Arabian Tale

5 May

Bad news upon my return to London. Mrs. Wattles reports that the translation hasn't gone well. Something to do with the antiquity of the material. Her young Arab friend is being taxed to the limits of his resources. There's even some concern as to whether he's up to the task at all. No doubt a dearth of archaic Arabic lexicons in England. So I must wait another two weeks at least for the text of Muhammad's tale to be ready. The unpleasantness with Cabrini had already put me out of humor, and now this new disappointment comes along to keep my nerves on a fine edge. I must get out tonight, even if it's but to prowl about the streets, and see if I can dispel my black temper.

6 May

The life of the city! There's a cure for any ill! The panoply of life, undiluted! I had the most fascinating time last night. Went out with no destination, no intent except to be about. Just walked.

Opened myself up and let my inclinations lead me. Gave the old brain a holiday. There really isn't any difference between the woods at Murcheston and some of the seedier haunts of London. Down by the river, that's where I eventually found myself. Can't recall how I got there, except that I just set out following any sign that looked promising. First this fat chap with a limp, then some young boys scurrying around the shadows, a whore casting about the streets. I even took off after a carriage, just because of the way the lights behind danced in the dark of the night. Before I knew it, the sound of the waves lapping at the piers caught my ear and reeled me in.

What life there is to be found there! The real stuff, not genteel and suffocating, but sharp and true. I nosed about the edges of this world, hovered here and there, seeing what there is to be seen. It was late, but the society I discovered by the river knows no distinctions of night or day. Men and women and even little children running around, darting about, crying and yelling and panting for life. I don't think a single creature among them had any notion of purpose, knew where they were going or why they were there. Or maybe I was too dizzied by it all to see any pattern in these comings and goings. I allowed myself to be wrapped up in it all, the very breath of it, jogging through the streets and alleys, aimlessly, artlessly, flying with my coat behind me, brushing by others who seemed just as merry and meaningless as I, bumping into them, cursing them as they cursed me, laughing with them in turn, until, exhausted and delirious, I collapsed in a doorway, an old abandoned entry to an old decaying building, right on the very edge of the Thames.

I sat there for a bit, alone and not alone, silently rejoicing. I don't know why. After a bit the hysteria left me and I raised myself, tired but happy, and wandered back here. I can't explain why I felt better about things, about my life. But I did, infinitely better. I should have stopped there, with that feeling, but like an ass I couldn't leave it alone. I had to try again tonight, and of course I couldn't recapture that rapturous sense of abandon. Still, some afterglow remains with me, an ember burning in the pit of my soul. I must be careful to keep it there, and not blow it out with too much fanning.

15 May

Another night in society. It's been my third engagement this week. There was a day when I would have considered such a schedule a hermit's existence. I'd have attended as many parties in an evening as I now squeeze into a week. Am I getting old? Or is it the other thing? Truth is, when I'm in London I find myself loathe to even write about my lycanthropy. It's come to be so inextricably associated with Murcheston and the woods. Perhaps that's why I feel uneasy of late, unsure of myself, as though I'm keeping watch over something.

Who was it the other night? Wilberforce, I think, at Admiral Prescott's. Turned to me as I was sitting at table and said he'd never seen me so serious. "Like some wretched philosopher," that's what he said. I thought I'd been having a marvelous time. The rest of the evening was hell. I felt as though everyone were observing me for some sign, an indication of what I am, what my secret is. I know I've become a topic of conversation. Still, they need someone to gossip about, don't they?

I draw some life from the grand parade, I admit. To emerge from the darkness of the night into the blaze of gold and glitter of jewels is a shock that thrills my senses. Ballrooms dripping with elegant display, so many pounds sterling hanging from the columns and chandeliers. Crystal and ivory everywhere, and liveried servants standing like statues against the walls, in every corner, ready to spring to life in attendance, and then dissolve again to lifeless decoration. The movement of so many miles of silk and satin, creating a rush of delicate sound and shimmering deluge of color. Voices rise and fall in an operatic fury of social graces, the studied insincerity of man played out with a zeal that no dervish could match in his dizzying whirl. And I, amid all, only I am aware of what deep shadows are cast by such grandeur, the darkness permeating the world made only darker by this show of light. Such is the social sphere I have found myself in of late, a maddening confusion of disparate tunes, played in a darkened theater, before a silent, starving crowd.

E. was there. I hadn't seen her in God knows how long. The sight of her sitting beside her husband, like Hephaestus and Aphrodite, the comic couple. It was enough to wring howls of laughter from a stone. I decided to have some fun, but it all went wrong in the end.

I followed her out onto the terrace after supper. She always wearied of the inane discourse enjoyed by the ladies and could be counted on to retire from the sitting room early, while the rest were still having their coffee.

"Admiring the moon?" I asked.

She jumped and spun about. "Good God, Darnley," she laughed, turning back to the night. "How you do creep up on a person! Advertise yourself with a polite cough next time."

"I would," I told her, stepping up to the railing and looking into the sky, "if I wanted my presence known."

From the corner of my eye I saw her dart me a glance, but she said nothing. Always cautious, my girl.

"It's ages since Charles and I have seen you. Do you remember the nights we three used to spend like this, under the stars while some party raged behind us?" Polite, impersonal, and she mentioned the husband. Very cautious. "The days seemed greener then," she went on, "and the skies more golden. Everything brighter."

"Not everything," I said, hardly hearing myself speak. "You could never have been more brilliant than you are tonight."

A strand of hair escaped its proper place and blew gently on the wind, across her face. She pulled it away with a soft, white hand. "You're a sweet liar. What on earth have you been doing with yourself?"

"I spend most of my time with my studies," I informed her.

She laughed. Even her mockery was beautiful. "What could you be studying?"

"Dark matters." And she looked at me and laughed again.

My God, what a spell that laugh cast upon me. Her eyes dancing with fire in the moonlight. Her voice like the wind brushing the leaves of the trees. The pale gleam of her throat as she threw her head back. My desire surged within me, memories overwhelming me, the thought of her flooding me. I wanted her. More than anything in the world, I wanted her. "Come with me," I found myself saying, in spite of all. "Come with me and see what I am studying."

"Accompany you to your laboratory, you mean?" she gaily replied. "I think not." And she turned back to the railing.

For the first time my nature acted against me, and I grasped her and spun her about, suddenly frantic that she, she of all people, should understand me. "Come with me now, Elizabeth! To Murcheston! Come away with me and we shall share a life more glorious than you have ever imagined!"

She tried to wrench herself from my grasp, but when she saw she could not, she relaxed, and I found my grip weakening under her pitying gaze. My arms dropped limp at my side. "Darnley," she began, her voice thick with charity and forbearance, "don't talk madness."

"Is it madness to always love you?"

"Yes. Yes it is. All that's done with. You and I are too much alike for love. We were never more than a bad joke together. Charles. . . ."

"That cipher! That pleasant nothing! You can't prefer that to me!" I shouted, unveiling the thoughts that had slept within me for so long, yet shocked at my own harsh cruelty.

Her eyes grew dark at once. "I won't have that," she said with steel in her voice. "Say what you like about me, but I won't have you berate Charles."

"What would you have me to do, then?" I demanded with more malice than care. "Shall I die at your feet, the spurned lover?

Or does it arouse your feminine pride to know that I still live and love you? How long will you be able to put up with this domestic charade, the cool love of a well-meaning merchant? Or was the child designed to prolong your weak affection, the second act of the farce?"

Her eyes devoured me with scorn, yet I relished their sting. "How can you know what I feel for Charles?" she asked coldly. "What have you ever known of real love that can outlast a life-time and not just a few minutes' cheap exercise?"

It was more than I could stomach. To stand by while she spoke of love. I raced away, fled the house, and wandered for hours amid the soothing dark of the streets. Why did I do it? To suddenly lay myself open before her like that. What was I looking to do? Introduce her to my secret life? Make her know that I am a werewolf? Impossible! No one can share this with me! What then? I can't say, can't even imagine. I only know that I love her and want her and always will. Yet how shall a man gain what he cannot have? How?

19 May

At last, a note from Mrs. Wattles that the translation is completed. I've wired her to have it delivered, but I won't be able to read it until tomorrow, for I'm already committed to attend a banquet at Sir Reginald Paten's. The Prime Minister is to be there and that means apologies are out of the question. It's time I curtail this socializing. It's all gone sour for me. Mrs. Wattles assures me that I'll be greatly rewarded for my patience, so I suppose demonstrating a little more fortitude can only work to my credit. She also informs me to expect word of a shipment of rare alchemy texts in which she has hopes of discovering more treasures. Requests my presence on the first of June when they arrive, but I told her plainly that I was going to be indisposed that day, and that it was unclear to me how my presence at the opening of a crate of books might improve her already formidable luck. Why is it the case that those for whom we have the greatest need are invariably the greatest bother? Still, she must be endured, especially now when I have so little time to spare in searching for books.

21 May

I've read Muhammad's tale and am deeply troubled by it. It relates the most deplorable cruelty I have yet encountered in my researches. This al-Azimi was a learned man, a physician in the trading city of Tarsus, whose success in treating cases thought hopeless and his relentlessly scientific approach to medicine, substituting reason and observation for superstitious lore, soon brought him to the attention of the Caliph Harun al-Rashid. Summoned to Baghdad, al-Azimi was escorted along the way by a detachment of the palace guard led by an ambitious warrior named Fallah. What follows are the salient points of this lengthy and rather wandering narrative.

"The journey was hard, for it was made at the hottest time of the year. But the will of the great Caliph, may Allah favor his line forever, was not to be denied by sun or wind. And so Fallah saw to my every conceivable comfort, but pushed on notwithstanding, setting the heavens at naught. I fear I did not make his task easier, for, not being a widely traveled man, I was everywhere entreating the captain to halt our progress that I might investigate some interesting case or other, and we more than once were compelled to abandon a direct route so as to accommodate my professional curiosity. As I explained to the worthy Fallah, insofar as it was my medical knowledge that had brought me to the attention of the Caliph, it would be prudent to indulge me in my practice of it.

"It was while we were traversing a mountain pass that I first heard of the caged man. Our way had been repeatedly crossed by small groups of simple folk, children of the soil and the blessed of Allah, going up into the hills. When I stopped one of these bands and inquired where they all were traveling, and with what purpose, I was informed of a great oddity in a mountain village, a man held in captivity in the town square. The fellow had not committed any crime to deserve this imprisonment, but was suffering from a curse, a word which I have always known to be employed in the service of ignorance to indicate a disease that the local authorities cannot treat. I immediately let Fallah know that I must look into this matter, and he, with greater resignation than enthusiasm, ordered a half dozen of his men to accompany us while the remainder he sent on to pitch camp and await our return.

"Guided by the party I had spoken to, we made our way up the mountain and along the range. It was an easy climb, and yet Fallah's soldiers, with their heavy gear and cumbersome weapons, were no match for the natural endurance and speed of the mountain people, and the captain's temper was not improved by the difficulties his guard experienced in keeping up. We continued for some three-quarters of an hour, the sun creeping closer to the horizon every moment, a fact which seemed of the greatest interest to our companions, who encouraged us to quicken our pace if we were not to be late. We arrived at a village settled snugly in a shallow valley, little more than a collection of rough huts about a central market, but evidently the chief city of the region.

"The market was filled to overflowing with people, and more were coming in from all directions, creating the usual excitement one would expect at a local holiday. Stalls were opened around the perimeter of the square and merchants with lungs of leather were attempting to out-shout each other in the full spirit of commerce. Even the poorest peasant was attired in the gayest colors he could find. There was a general milling about as of people waiting for some entertainment to begin, and the noise and shuffling of the crowd added to the impression of confused expectancy.

"Our own appearance caused some stir. Entering the little market square, we were greeted by the headman of the village, an ancient relic of the mountains named Ouda, may his head at last be cradled in the breasts of the houri, asking who we were and what business we had in his humble town. Fallah answered only that we were travelers through the mountains who had heard of a great wonder to be seen and so had left our path that we might be amazed. Ouda beamed with pride at this report, and informing us that we should not be disappointed, he invited us to occupy the place of honor at the festival, a small covered dais at the very center of the square. Fallah, always the cautious soldier, wished to remain on the outskirts of the crowd, but I insisted, and we followed Ouda to the front, pushing our way through the multicolored field of people.

"When we reached the dais, the sight for which we had journeyed stood not forty feet before us. It was a rude wooden cage some ten feet square, rough hewn but sturdy, sitting on four wheels like a wagon. My first thought was that it must be empty, for as twilight set in I could see nothing more than a bundle or rags lying within. Soon, however, four large torches were set at the corners of the cage, and when these were lit I saw that the bundle was a man. He was emaciated and bereft of any semblance of health, evidently supplied with only so much food as could be expected to keep breath within him. Never had I been confronted with such human degradation in all my experience, and I asked our host if this person were actually alive. He responded by motioning to one of his attendants, who approached the cage with a long pole and thrust it in at the man. The fellow stirred and raised himself up enough for me to see that, in spite of his humiliated aspect, he was indeed living.

"The man in the cage now pulled himself upright and proceeded to move about weakly in his portable cell. I had treated criminals before in the Tarsus prisons, and so recog-

nized the look of one who has been reduced by long confinement to the state of an animal."

(Rubbish! We *are* animals! How can a man be reduced to his
own nature? Reduced to the state of a man, you might say. For
this poor wretch's misery stems from those about him, not himself—their stupidity and ignorance and greed gnawing away at
him, degrading him, like a foul beggar gnaws a bone. He suffers,
as I suffer, from too much humanity.)

"His head he held down at all times, keeping his eyes on the
ground before him, oblivious to anything beyond the bars that
defined his world. He was not young, but his age was impossible to estimate, and could have been anywhere from twenty
to fifty. His muscles showed the taut wiriness of the inmate
and he moved with sporadic, furtive gestures. I asked Ouda
how long he had been imprisoned, and guessed that it was
over five years, for the man demonstrated the debased attitude
of one who has abandoned all hope and given himself up
completely to his fate. I was told, however, that it was only
six months since the cage had been built especially for its
occupant.

"I had other questions, naturally. Who was he? What had
been his crime? Why was he the object of such intense interest? But before I could utter them, a drum began to sound
somewhere in the village, and immediately the noise and activity of the festival came to a halt, the crowd settled to the
ground, and all eyes turned to the cage. I leaned toward Ouda
and asked what was happening, but he merely pointed off to
the edge of the horizon and said cryptically, 'The moon.'

"Indeed, the moon was just beginning to show itself over
the low shoulder of a nearby mountain, but what this signaled
I could not tell. At first I found nothing unusual in the man
as he paced about the cell. He seemed filled with greater ur-

gency as he moved from one side to the other, almost as if he were gathering strength, yet this was understandable with so many eyes turned suddenly upon him. He began to clutch at his torn and ragged clothing, and eventually flung it off, but I had at times witnessed similar behavior in inmates when they became agitated by too much attention. These signs of distress did not abate, however. They only continued and intensified. He began to move faster and faster, back and forth inside his cell, and as it was too small for him to run, he leapt from side to side against the bars, shaking the entire vehicle. The man was clearly healthier than I had thought. His muscles were larger, his motions more fluid and less convulsive. Indeed, his back and shoulders seemed to become more expansive as I watched.

"It was not long before I knew this was no illusion, that he was indeed changing before my eyes. The darkness might have obscured the fact at first, but the man in the cage was altering, his shape transforming itself into something not human. The process was too gradual to be observed, but the results were unmistakable. His torso gained strength and size, as did his arms. He sank to all fours now, and his abdomen lengthened and became more taut. A thick fur appeared covering his entire body. A tail extruded and grew from his lower back, and his buttocks became smaller. Owing to the violence of his motions it was difficult to observe the more minute details of his transformation, but I could see that his face was now elongated, resolving itself in a blunt snout, and his ears became pointed and tufted with hair. Finally, as the moon fully cleared the ridge, I saw that the entire orientation of his body had changed from the vertical to the horizontal. His head thrust, not up from his shoulders, but forward, and indeed there was no way of telling that the beast pacing within the cage before me had ever been human. It was a sight to wring tears from the devil."

(Or cries of approval from every corner of nature! What does the devil know of freedom, of a will unconfined? Let him save his tears for those trapped like himself, bound by chains of their own making, wrought by religion, forged in the furnaces of society!)

"This marvel had taken no more time to be accomplished than for the moon to rise into the sky, and the two occurrences seemed inextricably wed. Once the event was over, the assembled crowd rose to its feet cheering its enthusiasm, and quickly the activity of the festival recommenced with even greater energy than before. I walked forward to the cage and stood about six feet from its bars gazing intently at the pacing beast inside. It was clear to anyone who bothered to notice that this was no wolf. The snout was shorter, the ears longer, and of course it was far larger than any wolf I had ever heard of. Indeed, it seemed to be the same general size and weight as the man it had previously been, though its length was enhanced by the addition of a snout and tail. As I watched, it became less agitated in its behavior, and lay down upon the floor of its cage with its eyes upon the moon. This fascination for the planet I also found interesting, and would have eagerly welcomed the opportunity to perform a thorough examination of the beast. I have known, of course, that some behavior is attributable to the waxing and waning of the moon, but never had I encountered such a singular demonstration of this power, and I wanted desperately to learn all that I could in the brief time I had.

"As it lay there, several villagers came up with long poles and began tormenting the creature, causing it to snarl and snap and leap violently against its restraints, much to the delight of the crowd, which laughed all the more insanely the more vicious the beast became."

(Is this the future in store for me? Where can I possibly find understanding in a world of men? Such taunting cruelty is unknown in the woods. One must seek out the haunts of humanity to discover it. So what kind of existence can I expect when I finally reveal myself to the world? Shall I be made an object of sport? I cannot change my nature, but can I hope to change the nature of mankind? Al-Azimi, for all his pity, does nothing to stop the torturing of this poor man. He only walks away to avoid the sight. He and his escort spend the night in the village and he continues his story with the following dawn.)

"I arose the next morning to a great uproar erupting outside. It sounded as though the entire village were shouting and screaming denunciations at someone, and I immediately rushed out to see what the trouble was. I was met by a contingent of our guard, not those who had accompanied Fallah and myself the night before, but a party of those we had left behind. These accompanied me to the village square where I discovered, not the small handful of soldiers that Fallah had brought with us, but our entire force, surrounding and apparently protecting the beast in the cage from the hostile intentions of the villagers threatening it from all sides. I was taken directly to Fallah and soon came to understand that it was not the creature but ourselves who were the target of hostility among the mountain-folk. Ouda was standing before the captain screaming curses and oaths at him, and it was a long time before I could tell what was going on.

"What had happened was this. Fallah had been favorably impressed by the previous night's entertainment, so impressed, in fact, that he determined on the spot to purchase this phenomenon for the Caliph's menagerie. Naturally he understood the effect of such a proposal on Ouda and his people, so he secretly dispatched one of our number to retrieve the full escort, thus providing himself with an advantage when it came time to bargain for a price. Fallah now accomplished this transaction by dropping a few gold coins in the dust at Ouda's feet and positioning the troops in preparation of a massacre, if one were deemed necessary. By the time I arrived Ouda had nearly exhausted his wealth of oaths, and it was the captain's turn to explain his position.

"Fallah spoke in the measured tones of one who is not arguing, merely informing. He told Ouda that the old chief could receive the coins at his feet in payment for the beast. Once this marvel had reached Baghdad, he continued, and won the admiration of the court, Ouda could expect even greater favors from the generous purse of the all-powerful Caliph, and so would prosper all the days of his life. If, on the other hand, either he or any member of his tribe offered the least resistance to this plan, then Fallah would reduce the village to cinders and extinguish the fire with Ouda's blood.

"The old man was struck dumb with rage, and could only sputter and gasp for several minutes. When he finally regained the power of speech, he shrieked that he would never agree to such thievery, and that his people would trample Fallah's soldiers underfoot and grind their bones into meal for their bread if they so much as cast a covetous eye upon the beast. Fallah only smiled at this threat, and then very casually lifted a hand and issued a silent order to the guard. On the instant, metal flashed against the blue of the morning sky and three village men lay dead in the market square."

(What greater evidence of man's rapacity is required than this? Why is the werewolf left caged and these monsters allowed to roam freely about the face of the world?)

"This display had a remarkably pacifying effect upon the gathered throng, and before another hour had passed we were well out of the village and on our way again, our cargo rumbling along in our midst. During the excitement of the morning, and while all eyes were directed elsewhere, the beast had reverted to his human form. This was a disappointment to me, for I had hoped to make a closer observation of the metamorphosis, presumably when the moon set. Now I had to content myself with riding beside the cage and keeping an eye on the man within.

"While we were stopped to rest during the hottest part of the day, I was surprised to hear a question come from the man. In almost a whisper he asked me where we were taking him. It had not occurred to me that the fellow might be curious about his fate, and I confess that I had supposed him to be little more than a beast in human shape, or at best some benighted imbecile. It now dawned upon me that this was indeed a man we were transporting, and I began to converse with him, asking him freely about his life and the odd fate that had led him to this point. He told me that he had been a shepherd in those same mountains, indeed, was a member of Ouda's tribe, until one night while watching the flocks he had fought off the attack of a huge wolf. The creature had injured him before escaping, and it was on the night of the next full moon, as this pitiful fellow told it, that he had become the very creature he had battled. I was going to ask about his transformations, his experiences as an animal, the influence that the moon exerted on him, and a hundred other questions, when a guard approached and informed me that Fallah wished to see me at once. I innocently complied, believing I would have all the time I required to interrogate the fellow during the long journey ahead.

"Fallah disabused me of this conceit. He told me frankly that I would not be allowed to associate with the monster, as he called the man in the cage. It was the property of the mighty Caliph, bought and paid for, and if it pleased His Eminence when we arrived in Baghdad, I might talk with it all I cared to then, but not before. I protested vehemently. This was no monster but a man, a medical oddity to which my profession gave me undeniable rights. Fallah had no authority to interfere. But authority is a luxury of which power need not avail itself. Fallah had no trouble keeping me from the cage. So I continued our journey in ignorance of this remarkable novelty, to my great consternation and the boot-less pleas of future ages.

"I was not even given the chance to observe the trans-formation of man into beast at the next full moon, and this fact proved the tragic end of the adventure. On the very night, Fallah, concerned about the effect the sight might have on his soldiers, ordered a great sheet be placed over the cage. I knew by then that it would be useless to object. I held my tongue and in a fit of vexation retired to my tent early. I could not sleep, however, and found myself stirred by the approaching moon. I ventured out into the night and stood in the dark at a distance from the covered cage, just so I could be nearby when the event took place. It was heralded by a great cry from the recesses of the sheet, and the sentries that had been stationed about were filled with apprehension at the sound.

"Perhaps it was because of his new situation, or from an inability to see the moon, that brilliant orb which cast such a spell upon him, but the man in the cage seemed to be possessed of greater energy and violence than he was the month before. The entire contraption began to rock back and forth, and Fallah was summoned from his tent by the anxious guards. The cries from within were now markedly bestial, and the bars could be heard to crack and groan under the strain being exerted upon them. The crude vehicle was never de-signed for such a journey, and the rumbling of our way along uneven roads had weakened it. Fallah came running only to see the covered cage tumble over into the dirt with a crash and splinter against the ground. For a moment the sheet jerked and flew as if alive, and then the beast emerged, roaring with ferocity, free and defiant.

"It glared about, baring its horrible fangs and snarling at the men surrounding it. They would have fled had not Fallah's voice, strong and sure, ordered them to hold their positions. The beast looked at the captain as he uttered the command, and for a second the two adversaries sized each other. I cannot say who moved first. All I recall is that, with no warning, Fallah was racing directly at the creature with blade held aloft, and the thing was leaping into the air at him, the one shouting the glory of Allah, the other roaring hungrily. They appeared about to explode upon each other, and I felt a sudden pang that the captain could not possibly resist the power of the animal as it launched itself at his throat, when Fallah dropped down, sliding beneath the flight of the beast, and with a deft flick of his blade opened its belly in a single pass. The creature flew above him and crashed to the ground beyond, already dead.

"For a moment, when it was finished, no one moved, too stunned were we all by the suddenness of it. Then Fallah rose from the dust and his men let out a cheer of triumph and rushed to his side. I alone walked over to the beast. It lay in the dirt, its blood flowing freely from the gaping wound. I had considered that, upon dying, it might revert to its true, human form, but no further transformation occurred. It retained the shape in which it had died. As there was nothing to be done for anyone, I returned to my tent unobserved and slept fitfully until morning.

"When I arose, I at once asked Fallah if we might put off our departure long enough for me to perform a thorough examination of the beast. He informed me that it had already been attended to, that the monster had been skinned and its skeleton removed and packed away. It was to be delivered to the royal taxidermist, who would make of it a suitable trophy for the Caliph. I did not even bother to feel outraged at this desecration. The creature stands to this day in the halls of the Caliph's palace in Baghdad, where it is known only as the Great Wolf."

So ends the tale of Muhammad al-Azimi. Now, even in the calmness of reflection, I can't suppress my indignation at this pathetic story. Tortured, abused, reviled, imprisoned and finally executed! And for what? What was the man's crime that he deserved such treatment? And is this the future fate is weaving for me, my brilliant life's thread made into a tale of misery?

It is, more than anything, the solitude of this poor victim that troubles me. For am I not like him now? Imprisoned in my own world? Held captive within the confines of my estate, not freed when I walk the streets of London! Alone and bereft of any companion to share these wonders with! I write these thoughts down, but for whom? What future reader will ever find these pages? For whom do I exist? For myself alone? Always alone?

Silence my only answer. Perseverance my one commandment. "Thou shalt not despair." Enough to comment now that, as a clear indictment of humanity, it's a damning document. To any man who will read it in the future, I would simply ask, "Where lies the cruelty here? Who is the victim?"

2 June

Nothing. Nothing to report. Nothing has occurred of interest, and glad I am of it. My life has been somewhat too eventful of late, too filled with incident and sensational developments. A respite from my studies has been just the prescription I've needed to refresh me. So I passed this transformation as easily as I could.

I was pleased that Liam Grey was waiting for me at the station as usual. He said that he'd convinced his father not to worry over his scholarly pursuits. "It's after all the nineteenth century, isn't it," said Liam, "and if a man has the available stuff at hand to improve his position in life, then he should be free to make use of it without interference. Shouldn't he? Well, it's just the old notion that a son must follow his father's calling, which is fine for a world that offers no other paths. But when I could get on that train right now and be in London before dark, what opportunities aren't open to a man with initiative in a world such as that?"

My God, the boy was bloody eloquent, and pleased I was to hear him defend himself against his father's way of thinking. It was very gratifying to see him take some of the responsibility for his future upon himself. As we drove slowly along in the warmth of the afternoon, I questioned him about everything he'd read since our last discussion, and the informal ease we'd shared in our previous meeting was quickly reestablished. He told me that he so enjoyed *Gulliver's Travels* that he'd gone on to read *The Battle of the Books* and *The Tale of a Tub* as well, with both of which he'd struggled. (I didn't think it worth mentioning that my familiarity with these works is purely by reputation, for I've never even opened them.) He did admit to feeling some qualms of moral horror when he read the "Modest Proposal" with its satirical descriptions of cannibalism and the sale of Irish children to supply the tables of British aristocracy.

This politeness I couldn't let pass without comment, and I told Liam that a scholar has little room to scruple at unpleasantness. All ideas are necessary if only to illuminate the road of error so others might avoid its pitfalls. And the more disturbing ideas are the most necessary of all, for those are the only ideas that cause the unenlightened mob to think. Any fool can object to Swift's scheme on the standard of public decency, but it takes a man of genuine perception to recognize that society as a whole is just one vast meal, each class devouring the strength and resources of the class below. If he's troubled by the notion, I said, then perhaps he'd best abandon my library with its morass of dangerous ideas and entertain himself with the romances and penny-dreadfuls he could purchase easily in Brixton.

Liam was startled by my reprimand, but it did him good, I think, to understand that the notions of right and wrong on which he's been raised will serve him poorly in the path he's chosen. They might even make that path more difficult to travel. At any rate, he seemed to take my words to heart, for he apologized for his ignorance and promised to read the essay again and try better to understand it.

My transformation was a matter of course this month, and I won't say much about it. I enjoyed the warmth of the season and sported about in the stream, terrifying the fish and making, I'm sure, quite a row with my splashing. A stray cat had wandered into the woods and I made a quick meal of it. Beyond this, there's nothing worth mentioning that occurred.

I've attempted this morning to settle my affairs with Pike very quickly, as I'm expected again at the opera this evening, and would actually have taken the morning train if the vicar hadn't wanted to have a few words with me. I asked Pike if the interview might be avoided, but he thought that it were best I saw the man, so I had him shown in.

The Reverend Mr. Kirkland entered in his usual deferential fashion. He was appointed to his post while I was yet a boy, and I think the Old Governor showed a very sound judgment in the case, for I've only been troubled with meeting the fellow on five or six other occasions my entire life. He is a man of few professions beyond the simplicity of his faith, made equally uncomfortable, I think, with High Church and Low. His is a middling way that suits me nicely, for it leaves me alone.

"I am very, very sorry to have to bother Your Grace like this," he whispered, and I had to ask him to speak loud.

"I am sorry," he repeated. "I hope you have not been ill, Your Grace. I have not seen Your Grace at service in over a year, not even at Christmas, and Easter having just passed, I hope you are well." The fellow's way of stringing together a pair of thoughts in this way is rather frustrating. It's one of the reasons I always feel unbalanced when I speak with him.

"I'm fit, Mr. Kirkland. And yourself?"

"Thank you for asking, Your Grace," was the only answer he gave to my question, and went right on with his rambling. "I am sorry to have to bear bad news, but this past winter was particularly mild, don't you think? I cannot remember when we have enjoyed such, well, a mild winter. Though wet, of course. I am sorry to say it, but it was wet."

"I am aware that the weather was rather damp, Mr. Kirkland, but as winter has been over these months now, I don't think we should be troubled by it any further. You had business with me, I believe?"

"Ah yes, down to business." He rubbed his hands together in a nervous way that reminded me of a man washing himself. "The winter, as you observe, has been over some time now, and as it was mild, and is generally an idle season for our youth, as there is no planting, of course, and many evenings to be spent in, uh, idleness."

"Yes, but your business, Mr. Kirkland?" I was trying to be patient with the man, I truly was, but he has such a damned meandering way that it makes me want to grasp him by the throat and squeeze the point out of him.

"Oh dear," he muttered to himself. "Well, just say it, I suppose." And he looked me in the eye and blurted out forcefully, "The girls, Your Grace," and then settled back as if he had just delivered an oration before Parliament.

"The girls," I repeated.

"Ah, good, then you understand," he said triumphantly, and heaved a relieved sigh.

"Mr. Kirkland—" I began, greatly put out by this bewildering conversation. Thankfully Pike was standing behind me, and took it upon himself to lean down and whisper in my ear, "Family matters, sir."

I saw at once the trouble. Healthy young people during a long and pleasant winter (though wet), and it wasn't until spring that the fruits of their activities became apparent to the good vicar. Some half dozen young ladies have been so affected, and now Mr. Kirkland wants my help in discovering the fathers. He's been unable to match the appropriate pairs, it seems, for the boys aren't quite as honorable as the girls by nature are forced to be. I thanked Mr. Kirkland for his report, and told him I'd have Pike look into the matter fully, although I don't think it's really so important to match these couples too nicely, so long as the numbers come out right.

As I sit here now, I'm struck by the comparison between Liam and his peers. Here he is, this boy of genuine intellect and more than modest potential, plagued by an outmoded sense of propriety, so that he can't so much as read a book without his conscience stepping forward to interfere. And here are his fellows, the same age, raised in the same country, every one of them as little bothered by conscience as a rock. Religion and morality are shrewd and dreadful millstones hanging about the throat of humanity. As I see it, their only profitable use would be as checks on the promiscuity of the lower classes, yet that's where they invariably fail to have any effect. Wholly inadequate to silence the superior urgings of nature. But let a fellow just once attempt to pull himself beyond his state, to climb out of the condition in which the accident of fate has placed him, and watch tyrannical morality exert itself.

That's why Liam needs a sponsor in his ambitions. To champion his cause against the assaults of common morality. To show him that there is a better way, a path that leads up from the homely life he's led and into a brighter sphere.

10

Darnley at Bay

14 — June

At present I'm sitting alone in the darkened halls of Murcheston. Pike tells me that by tomorrow evening at the latest he can pull together a skeleton crew from the tenants. Just ample enough to see to my few needs, at least until a really proper staff can be assembled. I've left London behind me with its parties and its dinners, the galas and balls and nights at the opera and the theater. Such a life as I've known in the past, and which I dreamed I might be fit for again, I've left. I'm through with it, with all of it. Nothing has occurred to lead me to this course of action. Nothing of any great moment. Even now I can't say with any certainty why I've abandoned society. Can it be that my werewolf's nature has left me unsuited for the fellowship of men? Yet why was I ever tempted back into that whirl of lights and life?

I'm no more a part of their world than a real wolf is. I belong only here, in Murcheston, near the woods that are my true home now. The same home I had as a child, playing beneath their canopy. It feels like a loss, of course it does, putting aside all the trappings of my success and station, but I must be able to place it all behind me finally. At least until I can confront it without having to disguise the truth about myself.

The impossibility of my position was made apparent two nights ago at the Duke of Weltenham's ball. I was, for what reason I can't recall, out of temper that evening, and circumstances hardly conspired to put me in a better frame of mind. I saw E. as soon as I arrived, and that by itself would be enough to infuriate me. Looking angelic and too God-damned pleased with her life for my comfort. I tried to duck away, but all through the first round of dancing Lady de Couvrecort made me her personal project, attempting to light the fire of affection within me for her young niece. As though any woman could have interest for me now. All I could learn from the girl in a quarter-hour's conversation was that she has the most obscure sense of humor and considers herself to be a complete ninny. Not wishing to influence this rather sound valuation, I took the first opportunity to offer my apologies and sought more stimulating company.

As I left the ballroom, she found me. I could mark the signs of nervousness in her, the strained smile and watery eyes. Yet even that could not mask her loveliness.

"Darnley," she began, all innocence and compassion. "I'm glad I caught you. Might we have a word?" I let her pull me aside into a quiet corner, affecting as much disinterest as I could. "Some weeks ago, we said things it would be best to forget. Come, can't we be friends?" she asked simply.

"That episode is of no matter to me," I responded, "just as you are no matter to me, madam."

"No, please," she implored, her eyes sparkling now with moisture, and I felt my heart ache and my resolve grow firm and terrible.

"Yes," I continued, "I think that we've said all we need to each other. You made it perfectly clear that you prefer your husband and that brat to me." Anger flared up within her now, and I determined to fan its flame. "A pretty trio you will make, I hope.

You know, Elizabeth, I had never thought to be over you, but the image of your domestic drudgery, the thought of you three together—the simpleton, the bitch, and their mewling whelp . . ." But I did not complete the picture.

"You bastard!" she muttered with a vicious gasp of breath. "You insufferable, arrogant bastard!" And she turned and stormed away, leaving me alone with my ill temper compounding itself. It needed some release, and I went off for fresh game.

My search soon led me to the gallery, where a crowd had assembled about Bishop Ealing and Viscount Montrose as they engaged in an animated debate. I positioned myself on the outskirts of the throng, hoping to hear something other than idle gossip. I'm not familiar with Montrose, but I knew the bishop to be a fellow of serious, if parochial, intelligence. The topic they batted about was some new reform legislation. I really am behind in such matters and know very little about the bill, other than the fact that it's the sort of thing always cropping up in Commons. The bishop, a committed Tory, simply repeated the usual arguments against any extension of the franchise. His chief weapon was fear, and he wielded this clumsy instrument with some grace, painting a picture of the government entirely in the hands of the merchant classes, "whose Benthamite leanings will soon become apparent and reduce the running of the nation to a simple matter of profit and loss, with no room for compassion and no sense of a higher calling to which the state may aspire. No, far rather for the good of the working classes that the government rest in the hands of those with the power to stand up to these industrialists and carry the people's interests for them."

"By which I presume you mean the aristocracy," Montrose clarified.

Ealing conceded. "Yes, if you like, the nobility."

Against this, Montrose offered the typical populist reply, that the right to vote was merely the right of each man to govern himself, a right which couldn't be denied purely on the basis of property. "Besides," this lukewarm firebrand argued, "the franchise was extended previously with no great damage to the government, and it might be extended again without apprehension, except perhaps to the Tory seats in Commons."

"Not merely extended this time, Viscount," the bishop corrected, his cadaverous face smiling grimly, "doubled. And as for the question of property, I think that you underestimate its power to demonstrate the true nature of a man. For what is the right to vote but the right to rule, and who is better able to rule with justice and wisdom than he who owns and manages property. Taken all in all, I should say that the successful landowner, from whatever class, is better qualified to govern than the shrewdest merchant. For land is nothing other than the people who inhabit it. Learn to manage them and you have learned all. But the merchant knows only how to manage figures in a counting book."

The tenor of the conversation was temperate, as befitted the casual arena, and I was quickly bored with these gentle combatants. So I decided to play the part of Discord and see what I might stir up.

"Forgive me, sir" I barged ahead, directing my comments to the bishop as the more capable of the two, "but your arguments sound familiar. Do you take them from the Gospel according to Darwin?"

"Who said that?" Ealing asked, looking about the crowd. "Ah, Darnley! Yes, I suppose you would find that fellow's taint in everything. But tell me, how have I embraced that pernicious doctrine?"

"Isn't it apparent? Your idea of rule by the gentry, governance by those who've proven themselves fittest to govern. What more clearly bears the stamp of Mr. Darwin's natural selection than such rule by the strongest?"

Ealing chuckled and looked about at the assembled faces. "You surprise me, Darnley," he said in his sophist's style, as though he were speaking from a popular pulpit. "I hadn't thought you interested in natural philosophy. Yes, I suppose my remarks might be misconstrued in that fashion."

"I think they must be," I answered. "I don't know what other fashion fits them so well. The strong must govern the weak. The weak must be governed whether it suits them or not. That seems to be your position concisely put, yet accurately."

And he laughed again, that patristic laugh. "Oh, I dress my opinions in an ancient fashion, my boy, one I'm certain you're not familiar with, but one that still wears well. 'And God said, Let us make men in Our image, after Our likeness; and let them have dominion over the fish of the sea, and over the fowl of the air, and over the cattle, and over all the earth, and over every creeping thing that creepeth upon the earth.' There is your Darwinism, Darnley."

"Darwinism in Genesis," I gasped. "You scandalize me, Ealing."

"No doubt, but I believe you'll recover. As to your Mr. Darwin, he puts a backward interpretation on things by asserting strength as the final arbiter in nature. But as Genesis illustrates, no right or strength exists that does not come from God, and therefore only through His grace are men able to govern justly."

"Divine dispensation to govern over caterpillars." I laughed in my turn, and a few brave souls joined me in my mirth.

Ealing was unmoved by the gibe. "Might I inquire," he ventured, "what interest you have in the Reform Bill? I hadn't thought political science to be one of your passions. Indeed, I cannot say that I'm familiar with a single subject toward which you have applied your talents with any regularity."

"I'm a student of nature, sir, that's all," I told him, "and as such my interest is academic. Whether men govern themselves as Montrose here would have it, or they allow you to govern them, I find that their behavior is the same in the end."

"And how would you judge that behavior?"

"Judge it?" I returned. "I leave judgment to you and your fraternity. I don't judge. I only observe."

"Very well, then," the cleric chortled, "what do you observe?"

"What I observe in man," and I addressed the company at large now, "is that in spite of his vaunted civilization, his belief in a cosmic design and a humane purpose, his governments and his luxuries and his undeniable supremacy over the animals, as your scripture so rightly states," and I nodded to the bishop, who smiled in answer, "that in spite of these trappings, man is to the end motivated by self-interest, the same self-interest that motivates all creatures, whether they creep or fly or swim or crawl."

"But surely common decency and morality dictate that men must act more forthrightly with each other than animals are wont to do."

"It's religion and morality that force man to be other than he is. You'd have us believe, Ealing, that we aren't animals at all, but are touched with some divine spark that raises us above the muck and mire of earth. And yet man is no angel. No matter how you try to gild him, he's still an animal for all of that. History is filled with cases of man's barbarity to man. Whenever men are threatened with an encroachment upon their slightest comfort, be they ever so civilized, they'll fight with the ferocity of savages to preserve their interests. And this occurs, you'll forgive me, with the full sanction of that forthright morality and common decency you place such faith in. I'll leave it to you, Ealing, to denounce such behavior as profane, but you can't call it unnatural."

What a tidy little dissertation. I confess, once I'd gotten underway, with the wind behind me and my sails full, I was surprised at how I flew. I'd rather hoped to have sent the bishop into a paroxysm of moralistic outrage. At the very least I expected a little polite indignation for all the trouble I put myself to in baiting the old bear. But the only response I received was a mildly intrigued pause, just long enough to allow my last words to reverberate among the company, and then a rather measured retort.

"A reasonable assessment of the human condition, I should say, at least on the surface," he remarked at last. "But I hardly think that you've carried your arguments to their ultimate conclusions, or else you would not be so quick to accept the innate superiority of what you would term a natural existence over one tempered by the civilizing influence of morality. For it's the very morality that you hope to refute that belies your argument. It's precisely because you are correct in your observations that morality is so necessary. To protect the weak, to deny the power of self-interest, this is the necessary role of morality. I won't even mention religion," he added for the benefit of the listeners, "as I'm afraid that word might send you into another sermon." And the crowd laughed.

"Use any word you like," I told him, barely able to conceal my growing contempt for this country parson. "Religion or morality, they're equally inventions of the weak to subjugate the strong, to keep the animal buried deep within the man, disguising his real strength. And I assure you, I'm fully aware of the ends my arguments anticipate, and I repeat that self-interest alone is the proper standard of natural action."

I was gratified that this statement had an effect on the bishop after all. His wizened countenance darkened perceptibly and he stared at me with a more piercing gaze than he had used before. His voice, when he spoke next, was incredulous, and I think even distressed. "And to what lengths, if I may ask, are you willing to pursue this philosophy of self-interest? How far is one allowed to impose his will upon that of another?"

"As far as nature allows," I answered easily. "Does the lion honor any limitations beyond those of his own strength? Is the eagle checked in its flight by the sparrow? Throughout nature, the only universal law is that one is free to do what one is capable of doing. What authority can supersede this most basic right of the strong to make use of the strength they possess?"

Here, I thought to myself, I have him. I expected at any moment to see his pale features turn crimson in biblical rage, a tempest of wrathful ire that would have done the severest prophet proud. It was all I required, to be able to throw his own anger before him as proof of the justice of my arguments. Let him rail against me to show them all how right I was, that every man, even this stalwart bishop, was a beast at heart. But no such storm ensued. Ealing's only response was to nod slowly and say, almost to himself, "It is a great shame that you should think so, and admit it openly." And then he turned to the crowd and said, "I believe the gentleman has left little room for debate, so if you will all excuse me," and he made as if to leave.

I was outraged. His leaving the field so abruptly looked like cowardice, but there was something in this sudden departure that smacked of arrogance as well, of one not bested but repulsed. I therefore demanded that the bishop respond to my statements.

"Respond, sir?" he said sadly, turning about. "No sir, I shall not respond. I feel that your statements are clear enough to be understood without the aid of a response." And he gave his back to me again and proceeded through the crowd, which made way for him like he was Jesus Christ himself.

Damn the old God-monger! I couldn't let him go in this way, reeking of ancient wisdom and holiness, leaving me to look like a hot-blooded villain. No Pyrrhic victory for me! Damn me to hell if I'd allow it!

"You admit, then, that my arguments are irrefutable?" I shouted as he retired.

He stopped, and spinning about briskly, walked back, walked right up to me, and placed his withered hand upon my shoulder. "No, young man, I won't be prodded and led into any such admission," and he spoke softly, for my ears alone, with a sincerity that left me even more furious than before. "But I will tell you this, Darnley, purely for your own sake. A man who believes as you do invariably finds the proof of his arguments within himself. You see the worst in your own soul, and accepting it as your proper condition, you apply the same standard to others. But don't do it, my boy. For God's sake, for your own sake if for no other, deny it. Men are not to be reduced to the lowest commonality. Don't forget that we have the one power that no animal possesses, the power to aspire to something greater than we are. Discover the truth of that, and stick to it, my boy. Stick to it!" And so saying, he turned his back to me again and retreated into the crowd.

God, I was hot! The insufferable cheek of this saintly relic.

To lecture me like I was some erring schoolboy. I couldn't contain my anger, and heaped upon the back of this dottering ass such a load of abusive language, such vituperation and venom, that I had to be led away from the scene almost by force. I only wish the weight of my attack might have broken the spine of that sanctified bastard. It certainly was sufficient to break the hold that these civilized theatricals have exercised over me, and I soon left the ball and decided in the carriage home that I must absent myself from society completely.

And so I find that I am now at Murcheston. The serenity of these gentle surroundings has already worked a charm on my troubled spirits, helped me see clearly the choice I must make. To deny my nature is impossible, of course. A werewolf I am and a werewolf I shall be. But I'm not a hermit, either, in spite of my efforts to make myself one. What sort of fellowship am I fit for? In whom can I place my entire trust? I must find the answer to these questions or I may go mad, living in two worlds so hostile to each other.

16 June

Pike has outdone himself, assembling a thoroughly acceptable staff from the tenants. In a single day this army of women and young boys has got the estate in as tidy a shape as it was ever in before. Just turned the place inside out and given it a good shake. The darkness and gloom that had settled over everything during my months of isolation are so scattered that if I wanted to entertain Her Majesty and the entire court, I'm confident they couldn't find a pleasanter spot to pass their time in.

Pike assures me that he can have a more professional staff here in a fortnight, but I've considered the inconvenience of live-in servants, especially to my unorthodox way of life, and have decided against it, with a single exception. I've told Pike to find where Sterling and his wife have got to and to offer them their old positions back. My idea is to give them a place in the village, with a cart and a little pony to help them go to and from the estate, and so allow them to return to the service they've spent their lives in.

The tenants arrive for work from the village in the morning and depart again at dusk, leaving me in that privacy I so desperately require. Pike has already told the new staff the rules, but I daresay no one will complain of the monthly holiday they'll all receive. It's a very happy arrangement, I think, and one that shall profit me greatly in the future. I've even instructed Pike to stock the stables again, and by riding out frequently I hope to make myself a familiar sight in this country of mine. For the first time since I was a boy I believe I could actually live at Murcheston in peace.

As soon as I was well established, I sent for Liam Grey and told him of my plans to pass an indefinite period of time here, and let him know that I hoped my presence would in no way deter him from his studies, that he should continue to enjoy the freedom of the house and might even be accommodated in one of the guest rooms if he ever desired to stay the night. This will be one of my chief occupations while I'm here, to attend to Liam's education personally. Of course, his father might object to such attentions, but I have a plan that will beard that old lion in his den. Truth is, even if he should protest, I think I can instill enough spirit into Liam to stand up to Old Grey. Besides, if I can't do that much for the boy, then he's probably not worth my efforts in the first place. Liam can't be a slave to old thinking if he's to make anything of himself in the modern world. Perhaps his father's anger would be just the test he needs to prove himself.

22 June

Everything is perfect. My life has never been so neatly ordered, nor so satisfying. Pike took me on a tour of the entire estate today. That is, of the agricultural portions, the fields and pastures. The coal operation is no real concern of ours, as it's operated by Messrs.

Smithson, Wellerby and Dodge, Ltd. We merely accept rent on the land. This is a great relief to me, for the romance of a pastoral life as lord of the estate would be severely damaged if I had to bother myself in that nasty business. But I'm assured that I'm quite free of Brixton, which appears, from my limited understanding, to produce the majority of my income with the least possible interference from me.

The same can't be said for my agricultural concerns. I've been just barely able to keep up a profit in that quarter, and the tenants are only sustaining themselves. I detected the slightest reproach from Pike in my negligent behavior towards these people, and yet he was pleased to demonstrate that despite their failing fortunes they don't live in any great discomfort. Pike is rightly proud of the condition of Darnley Well. The cottages are neat and the roofs in good repair. Of course, they're rather small, and the families who occupy them more than usually large, but taken altogether, it seems a generally happy community. Pike has some fascinating ideas of how we might make the farms productive again, certain experimental techniques that until now he's lacked the funds to implement. I've asked him to give me a list of the expenditures needed to put his plans into operation, and he tells me that within three or four years, with luck and the proper equipment, we might turn things about. It's all incomprehensible to me now. Doubtless I'll come to understand it by and by. Pike has promised me pamphlets that detail the techniques and machinery that would be best suited to our situation, and I've promised that I'll study them closely.

I've also entertained a visit from the vicar, Mr. Kirkland, or perhaps I should say *been* entertained by a visit from that muddled gentleman. He took only three-quarters of an hour to tell me that he was pleased to see me well and hoped I would enjoy a prolonged stay in the parish. A not too subtle request, I think, that I find the time to attend Sunday service. He went into a lengthy disquisition upon the importance of the lord of the manor setting the right example to the tenantry, and delivered it in such a circuitous fashion that it left me breathless. Indeed, if his sermons are only a little like his conversation, he must keep the congregation perfectly giddy.

As for Liam Grey (so many things to keep track of amid the "simplicity" of this pastoral life), I'm pleased to report that he's at present residing with me at Murcheston.

His father wasn't what I'd call supportive of this move, but when I explained the conditions to him he was a little mollified. I've hired Liam at a quite reasonable salary to be my personal secretary. I was unaware when I did so that the boy writes with a very pretty hand, and he's taken to his duties with the utmost enthusiasm. He occupies the large guest room just off the main wing of the manor, some two doors down from my own, and every morning we breakfast together and review the schedule for the day's work. Liam handles most of my correspondence and is learning the books from Pike, who will now be freed from the drudgery of that chore and able to spend more time in the field. The lad is also proving to be an invaluable help in managing the staff until Sterling can be brought back, for in the absence of a butler he's made himself seneschal of the manor and commands the respect of the servants despite his years.

Of the troubles that drew me here, I confess I haven't given them much thought. I devote some time each night to a few books that I brought along with me, but there's little in them of substance. For the time being I think that I won't force my attention upon the issue, but instead enjoy the productive life I'm creating. I'll take my lycanthropy as it comes. I've instructed Mrs. Wattles to forward any works she uncovers directly to Murcheston, and so I'll still be able to pursue my studies quite comfortably.

1 July

I'd looked forward to this month's transformation with the greatest anticipation, and more than a little anxiety. It was nothing to dispose of the servants. They've long been accustomed to my eccentric habits. The only difficulty was Liam, who wasn't eager to leave. Whether this was owing to his affection for me or his growing independence from the severe authority of his father I can't say, but I was insistent that if he wished to remain in my employ he must be obedient in this. I did offer to set him up with his own flat in Brixton if he'd rather, but in the end he returned to his father's cottage, and if I'm not mistaken was even glad to be able to report on his new life and responsibilities.

And so I was left to myself again, and it was as if for the first time, so nervous was I. The moon rose in the late afternoon, although both it and the sun were quite invisible behind a solid blanket of clouds threatening rain. The night promised to be as black as the devil, perfect weather for my revels. When I felt the first stirrings within me of the metamorphosis, the warmth that grew inside and signaled the change about to occur, I felt the same rush of happiness that one experiences when spying a dear friend after a lengthy separation. All of my concerns, all of my worries and fears vanished as I became the physical manifestation of my innermost nature, the animal I know I am. No doubts or riddles plague me in this form. All seems marvelously clear, like the night vision that allows me to perceive the impenetrable soul of darkness and see what, in my other shape, is only blackness and confusion. I bolted across the lawn and toward the woods, stretching my muscles as I have so often before, renewing my spirit with every bound. I didn't stop when I reached the trees, but darted about in a rapture of strength and agility. My power and the celebration of my power were one and the same, and the faster I ran and the farther I leapt, the more joyously my heart pounded in my breast, the very life coursing through my veins. I don't know when I've felt more deliriously happy.

After a time I settled down to a more leisurely pace and found myself in a part of the woods that I'd never frequented before, at least not in my animal state. I was hardly lost, however, for every sound and every scent told me where I was as clearly as any map could. And so I set about to explore the countryside, not from any sense of curiosity, but simply to know what was there, and what I could call mine. For there has come over me a feeling of possession about these woods. They belong to me, not simply by right of ownership, but by right of usage. This stretch of earth is mine because I am here upon it, and feed within it, and find my pleasure inside its natural boundaries. And so I proceeded to lope easily about this newfound corner of my realm.

Of course, to my human eye, any one part of Murcheston Woods has always looked much like any other part, and I must rely upon such distinguishing features as the stream to tell one square yard from another. But as a wolf I see in every leaf a distinct mark. I detect an unforgettable scent with every breeze and find an inexhaustible uniqueness in everything. There are times that I recall from my man's life, when I have entered some place or other for the first time and felt a familiarity about the rooms, when the furnishings and appointments seem to create in me a memory for things previously unknown. Such was the experience I now had, running across a landscape for the first time with all the comfortable ease of a long acquaintance.

I don't know how long I ran thus, nor for that matter where I ran to. I covered a great many miles that night and hadn't the slightest idea of a destination. All I know is that I ran without purpose or goal, solely for the pleasure to be had in running, until eventually I detected on the wind the intoxicating odor of men, mingled this time with a wealth of aromas so jumbled together that I couldn't identify them all. In the very instant that I caught the scent I turned my head toward it and made off in that direction.

I soon arrived at the far side of the woods, the natural boundary between my realm and that other world, where the fields of Darnley Well begin. It's a place I'd never been to, and I discovered there a modest cottage, a place of men, with their smell stronger and more deliciously intoxicating that I'd ever experienced before. It was, I later learned, the home of Old Grey, the place in which Liam was likely sleeping. A light burned in the window of that small, low structure, and some short distance off was a barn, dark and deserted, in which I assume the tools and cart are stored and the horses stabled. On the other side of the cottage, away from the trees, was a tiny plot of tilled earth, a humble coop for a few chickens and a pen in which a restless pig was pacing about, grunting softly.

The cottage was on the opposite side of a road that skirted the woods. This dry and unnatural bed kept me for a time from venturing closer. I'd never yet gone beyond the cover of the trees, except to cross the lawn surrounding the manor, but that's the very heart of my territory and so poses no possible threat to me. This open land, however, the grassless road and the treeless cottage, were redolent of man and his machines, and I was at first satisfied to lie in the brush by the road and quietly watch and sniff. Can't say that I wasn't attracted by the presence of men, but neither was I compelled by an irresistible desire. I simply lay there as I had lain by the stream so many times before, enjoying the perceptions that came to me of this new and strange locality. Aside from the occasional cry from the sty and the coop, and the soft whispering of the wind, there was no sound. The presence of man quieted the activity of nature, and this silence, coupled with the warmth of the night, lulled me into a light doze.

I didn't sleep long, and when I opened my eyes again, I saw in the threshold of the cottage, silhouetted by the faint glow of a single candle behind him, the figure of a man. As he stood there alone in the doorway, I was suddenly aware of the sharp pangs of my hunger. It isn't unusual for me to waken like this, stirred from slumber by the smell of prey. And I can't say that I was more attracted to the man than I would have been had a passing deer caused my waking. Yet I must admit that I suffered a rare disappointment when the fellow turned and entered the cottage again, closing the door behind him.

I didn't dwell on my ill luck, though I'm not accustomed to being crossed. Only turned my attention to the pig, whose sweet, fatty smell is not unlike man's. I darted across the road in three quick bounds and ran around to the far side of the coop. The openness of the barnyard deprived me of the cover I would have preferred, and despite being downwind I couldn't hide my presence from the unseen creatures surrounding me. The horses stamped anxiously. Hens cackled on their roosts. The pig was especially moved and squealed in futile protest at my intrusion, but as it was closely penned I didn't concern myself with its nervous appeal. I leapt at once into the sty and, capturing it easily in my jaws, killed it with a single shake.

I didn't have the leisure to enjoy my victim, though. No sooner had I slain the pig than I was startled by an explosive roar from the direction of the cottage, and the beast was torn asunder at my feet by no force I could detect. I didn't stand by to investigate. Quitting the sty in a single, powerful bound, I retraced my course around the coop and back across the road. As I reached the safety of the trees, another explosion erupted behind me, this time to no evident effect. I ran a short distance into the woods until I felt secure, then turned and looked back at the cottage. A man was walking about, the same who had just been in the doorway, I think. He was looking into the sty, and then glanced up and out into the woods. My safety was assured by the blackness of the night, and he thought better than to attempt to follow me. He was soon joined by two others, but as I saw no chance here for further prey, I turned and trotted back toward more familiar territory.

The excitement of the night had left me exhausted, and when I reached my usual resting place under the oak along the bank, with its cool grass and soothing sounds of water and woods, I soon drifted into a deep sleep that I didn't stir from until after the moon had set. Rising then, and glancing over my person quickly to assure myself that I hadn't sustained an injury in my daring raid on Grey's cottage, I walked back to the manor and cleaned and dressed for what I knew would be a full day.

I wasn't mistaken. Less than a half of an hour after I rang the bell outside the kitchen, Liam ran into the study to report excitedly that his father had shot at a wolf during the night, and that he was now organizing a party among the tenants to hunt the beast down. For a moment I was concerned, but a quick glance at the window showed me that a brisk drizzle was falling, and a more substantial storm threatened, so I'm reassured that no one will be able to track the course of my wanderings. Still, I think it best to mention this to Pike when he arrives, and see if he can discourage the fools from bothering too much over the incident. Doubtless, when the wolf fails to reappear in the weeks ahead, their interest will wane.

I find it curious, in recalling the events of last night, that at the height of my danger, when Grey had fired his shotgun at me and only just missed, hitting the dead pig instead, though I was much startled, I never felt fear. That a retreat from the sty was called for I understood instinctively. But that my own life was endangered? The thought never occurred to me. Why should it, I who exist only in the ephemeral Now, the wispy vapor of time that passes without leaving a trace. What's fear but the apprehension of future peril, and what do I care for a future I cannot see, cannot smell? How should it be possible that I fear anything if my very experience of life begins and ends with myself? Not even death seems real to me. The world exists, as it were, by my volition, and in every way that has any meaning for me, it shall cease to exist when I do.

8 July

I've just spoken with Pike. He tells me he's located Sterling and his missus, but there's no recalling them to their post, nor to any position this side of the grave. They're dead. The both of them died not a fortnight apart in a seaside village in Cornwall. A great distance for them to have traveled only to find their deaths. They were taken in by a niece of Mrs. Sterling's, the only family they had. That woman reports simply that Sterling died from want of life, and that his wife followed him soon after. Damn pity, but there's no sense shedding a tear over it now, I suppose. Still, they were both of them good servants and deserving of at least a mournful thought. I think it would be well to have Mr. Kirkland say a word about them at service.

11

Darnley Alone

15 July

A month now, and society seems as far removed as the days I spent before my lycanthropy. Every morning I awake better rested and more refreshed than I've ever done in London. This rustic climate is perfectly suited to my mutable spirits. The rains, though violent, are never so dreary as I've known them to be in town, and though the sun shines hotly, it lacks that dull pallor brought on by smoke and steam. And, of course, there isn't the stifling, wrenching stench given off by masses of humanity crowding the streets, the waste and the putrescence of their lives rendering life itself almost unlivable.

I'm involved every day in Pike's schemes for the improvement of the estate, and if I'm no longer as regular in keeping this notebook as I'd like to be, it's only because, by the time I'm finished inspecting seed and soils, supervising plans for construction, estimating costs and expenditures, overseeing labor, and generally making myself the most perfect yeoman, by the time all of this and more is seen to, I'm far better inclined to relax over supper with Liam and enjoy a quiet evening in the study than to continue my work into the night. Besides, one of the greatest pleasures of life in the country is that one day passes much like any other. Quite frankly, there hasn't been much to record of late. I only make this entry because Pike was called to Brixton overnight on some business concerning the delivery of rams he purchased recently. We're trying to bring a stronger strain of blood into the fold.

Liam is proving a marvel at managing my personal affairs for me. Taken command of the household like a general marshaling his troops. I did have to release one young whore who appreciated the lad's gifts rather too fondly, but I've since told Pike to employ only married women of sensible character.

My situation would be perfect, in fact, if only I weren't so bloody miserable. It's a damned frustrating paradox. On the one hand I feel quite alive in my new surroundings, occupied with business that leaves me little chance to mope about and pity myself. But I'm too keenly aware that the other hand still holds its grip upon me. The feelings of tortured loneliness that I suffered in London haven't abandoned me here. If anything, they're worse. I still yearn for some companion to act as my partner, if not in the true work I'm about, at least in my mundane life. I thought to have abandoned this sense of solitude, this longing for someone I cannot have, a desire that smolders yet won't extinguish. And who is there now besides Liam to fill this role? In all the world there's no one else, and I'm afraid he's still a boy in many ways. Superstition pervades his mind and I can't say when or even if it will ever release its influence on him. Just yesterday I had planned the most delightful escape for the lad, a summer's picnic in the woods, just the two of us. He protested, of course. The boy's too diligent by half. But in the end I had my way, and we soon were walking out across the park, me in the lead as guide, he in the rear as porter, looking like an expedition setting off for the darkest jungle reaches of Africa.

From sheer force of habit I led him directly to the oak tree by the stream where I've lain in quiet comfort so many times, listening to the sound of the woods and tasting the breezes. Never had I returned to this spot between my transformations, and I was pleased now at the lovely setting it afforded our little party. The sun filtered its way through the green of the leaves, and spots of brightness danced about on the cool turf at the foot of the tree like a tribe of fairy sprites. Shafts of light pierced the surface of the stream down to the very stones at the bottom, changing rocks and fishes into sparkling gems and naiads. The wind blew gently, set up a barely audible counterpoint to the trickling of the water, a symphony of nature that lulled us both into a state of easy repose on the grass.

We enjoyed a cold roast chicken, some of Cook's best sausages, an exceedingly sharp cheese, a loaf of hard black bread, and a fine old bottle of Oloroso sherry. At first, Liam was too preoccupied with the duties he'd left behind to enjoy himself. I didn't waste my breath arguing with the lad. I simply resorted to a more straightforward form of persuasion, which is to say that I kept his glass filled as often as he sipped from it. The result was more than satisfactory, and Liam was soon relaxing with his back against the oak, reading a book and nibbling idly at bread and cheese.

For my part, I lay down by the stream and constructed an armada of leaf boats, launching them to great fanfare, watching helplessly as they bounded and bobbed amid the rushing waters until all were scuttled against the rocks or drowned in the treacherous eddies below. Tiring of this nautical debacle, I rolled over to ask Liam what he was reading, for I've ceased to make recommendations to him, relying now on his own sound judgment and eclectic leanings to guide him through the library. A hell of a disappointment it was, then, to hear that he was reading Augustine's *Confessions*.

"Good Lord, you're not!" I exclaimed. "What attraction can you find in that old faker's pitiful moaning, especially on such a delicious afternoon as this? You've quite shattered the beauty of the day, Liam."

The boy laughed at my response, and innocently asked why I should object. "It might do me good, I think, to read of a man's struggle over the course his life should take. I know it's presumptuous, but I find his experiences not very unlike my own."

"You're just sounding ridiculous now," I told him, turning away and looking to the cover of limbs above. "What have you got in common with Augustine? With every advantage at your disposal, every benefit that a boy in your position could enjoy. A world of ideas from which to pick and choose at leisure. How on earth can you compare that to the simpering, sin-riddled crap of that old fool? Tell me the truth now, are you working so hard that you no longer have time to use your discrimination? I can easily draw up a list of more worthwhile material. But don't insult my reason by saying you enjoy Augustine. For God's sake, boy, *no one* enjoys Augustine."

Liam looked hurt by my comments, and perhaps I was too mocking, but this is exactly the sort of thing I've feared might happen with him. His moralistic bent is not yet smothered, is in fact strong enough to find expression in the philosophically fertile ground of my library. Still, the lad was bold enough to answer in his own defense. "I'm sorry if Augustine is no longer in favor with your society," he said, and stung me a little with the words, "but I can't help what I like."

"But you *can* help what you like, Liam. That's the whole point of my giving you the freedom of my house, of making you my secretary, of rescuing you from a life that was suffocating your natural abilities. So that you could learn what's best and most worthy to be appreciated in this dreary world. Or at least, I thought I was rescuing you. But now it appears you don't want to be rescued. You'd rather return to your father's way of living, having ideas of what's right and what's wrong served up to you without any effort on your part. Just set your mind up for sale on the easy market of popular opinion. You know, it doesn't matter if it's your own father or some dead nigger saint telling you how to think and what to believe. It amounts to the same thing."

Liam shook his head in confusion. "I suppose I'm still too dense to understand such things," he confessed, "but I thought you wanted me to expose myself to all sorts of new ideas."

"New ideas, yes. But not this," and I snatched the book from his hands. "Liam, there are no new ideas here. Just more of the same oppressive, malignant shit that passes for reason among the simple-minded and fearful. Well, just tell me, what sort of twisted intellect would take a simple lark, stealing a few bloody damned apples of all things, and turn it on its head until it becomes an abomination worthy of divine contempt? It's like watching a pig wallow in its own filth, and I won't have you polluting your mind with it." And so saying, I tossed the volume into the stream.

That was the end of our picnic. I admit I was harsh with the lad, but I had to act decisively. It's only to be expected, quite natural, that his more vulgar attitudes shouldn't be supplanted without a struggle. But I can't take any half-measures in the fight. I've done that once before, and lost the one thing in my entire life that might have saved me from this wretched loneliness. I won't let it happen again!

Liam sulked about for the rest of the day and avoided me at breakfast the next morning. But I know how to get around his moods by now, and made it up to him that evening with a beautiful copy of Lucretius' *De Rerum Natura*, which I hope will start him thinking in the right direction again. Until he does start down that path, becomes a true protégé of mine and not just a project, I fear my sense of solitude will stay with me, no matter how pretty my surroundings or my company might be.

20 July

Pike's just presented me with another project, this the grandest of all. I've been privileged to witness a demonstration of the latest in harvesting machinery. That is, a miniature of the latest in harvesting machinery, constructed by Pike himself to show me how this new threshing device allows three men to do the work of eight, and do it more than twice as fast. I believe those are the ratios he quoted. It's a remarkable piece of work, but I confess my enthusiasm for such things is checked by Pike's current estimate of how soon I'll see any return for all of his improvements. He's been so thorough in turning the entire operation of my lands upside down in the name of progress, that he now tells me I shouldn't expect to make a profit for at least four years, and more likely six if the price of corn continues down.

So it would seem that this scientific agriculture is designed to increase every yield except that of money. If it weren't for the mining in Brixton, I'm positive these projects would bankrupt me. Yet Pike continues in his tiresome way, indifferent to expenditure. As if I should consider myself fortunate to supervise the ruin of my finances for such a progressive cause. I must reconsider my unbridled support of these wild schemes.

And if these worries aren't distressing enough, I had a visit from Mr. Kirkland today. No real notion of how long our talk lasted. According to my watch it took only an hour, but such conventional measures of time are irrelevant when dealing with the vicar. Like Joshua of old, he stops the sun in its course. Wants me to attend Sunday services this week. Says he understands my reluctance to do so, and wouldn't even ask if it weren't for the fact that the tenants are adopting my own lax attitude toward such diversions. Kirkland seems convinced that my presence at one of his sermons, my endorsement if you will, might help to stem this flow of irreligion.

Notwithstanding the questionable soundness of his plan, I told him I'd do my best to make an appearance. I suppose I really should. Religion may be so much humbug, but it's just the sort of humbug the laboring classes need if they're to remain happy and productive in their lives. I might even bring Liam along with me. He's maintained a coolness in our relations lately, and an outing such as this could be the very remedy he needs to see the folly of his brooding disposition. And, of course, his company will certainly make the trial less trying.

22 July

How wonderful the day has been! I'm pleased to record that my show of support for the vicar has been a great success, if not for Mr. Kirkland then at least for me. The ugly truth is, the service wasn't so well attended as the vicar would have liked, even though he'd published it about widely that I'd be occupying the ancestral pew. I fear the announcement of my intentions might have produced a detrimental effect upon attendance, as there weren't enough of the devoted on hand to fill a quarter of the chapel. Still, I did what I could and can't be blamed if it didn't work out.

No, oddly enough the true success of this adventure lay in the matter of the sermon itself and what it portends for my relations with Liam. The topic of the sermon was one chosen expressly by the vicar to address the maternal development of a handful of young girls in the village. Some months ago Kirkland apprised me of this crisis at Darnley Well, and I'd set Pike onto the problem at once. But he's enjoyed only mixed success in finding which young rascals assisted the girls to their compromised conditions, and in the end he was forced to suggest quite emphatically that certain boys accept the responsibility, even though the evidence implicating them was slim at best. Kirkland hoped to ease the tensions created by this awkward situation with a reading taken from Genesis, the bit about Adam's loneliness in the garden and God's providing him with a wife from his own rib. He attempted to draw a comparison between poor Adam, who had little to choose from in a bride, and the present business.

Now, while I'm not the one to say whether this approach met with any reasonable success in placating the difficult feelings of either the arbitrary young husbands or their fertile wives, it proved a wonderful inspiration to my own problems. The gist of the message is that God, in His provident wisdom as Celestial Panderer, placed within Adam's reach a cure for his loneliness, and that it was up to him to make the best of it. This reading set me considering my own position, the loneliness that's plagued my every hour, that's dogged my heels even to this demiparadise. And then I thought about the pleasure I take in Liam's company, and the barrier between us that keeps that pleasure from being perfect. I have the inklings of a plan from all of this. It's yet so cloudy in my mind that I'm afraid even to write it down lest it prove too absurd when I actually see it before me. I must think very carefully on it. If it seems manageable, it could be my salvation from the solitary world in which I find myself trapped.

31 July

I am in London. Murcheston and all that damned mess are far, far behind me. And so is Liam. And yet more troubles follow me here. When I arrived at my flat not thirty minutes ago, I discovered a note from my man tendering his resignation, "owing," he writes, "to the irregular condition in which Your Grace maintains his household, a condition which often leaves me alone, unsure of my responsibilities and unready to act so completely on your behalf. I was hired, need I remind Your Grace, not as a steward or a secretary or a business partner, but as a valet. And so I have taken the liberty afforded by the vast quantity of time that I have found on my hands to procure more regular employment elsewhere."

Just as well be rid of the opportunistic bastard. Lucky for me, in fact. I require to be alone. I need time to consider myself, to learn to understand better what I am, or rather, what I've become. True, I fear solitude now more than ever. More than anything, except company. So I must stay apart for a time, to learn what sort of creature exists within me. I realize at last that, until these past few days, I haven't fathomed the depths of what I am, not fully. Even now I only know that I must find an answer, but how or where, I'm damned if I can say. I may find a way within this very text before me, this record of my life as a werewolf. I'll study its entries in every detail, looking for some explanation for myself, a clue that escaped my notice before but might now uncover some fact about my dual nature that I've been too blind to see, too dazzled by the novelty of my condition to comprehend. For that's how I feel, like I've been dancing with my eyes closed tight on the edge of a precipice, incapable or unwilling to know the danger I'm in. And now my eyes are opened and I can see clearly. But what is it I see? The height is too dizzying. I reel about in my thoughts, falling first one way, then another, until I don't know in which direction lies safety and which offers the oblivion of destruction.

Something has happened to reveal this to me. I can't call it horrible, not any longer. I can't deny that it's I who have done it. But why? What good can come of it? For there must be something, some lesson to learn. There are no setbacks, no failures. Every seeming failure is only a chance to understand myself more completely. That's what I must force myself to see.

I'll begin by putting down on paper the events that led me to this pass. Perhaps I can find here a way to reconcile myself to myself, discover the thread that runs through both my natures and thus reshape my being into a single whole again.

I knew that the only possible remedy for my pain lay with Liam Grey. I knew it, but I doubted. An apostate to my very nature, that's what I'd become, certain of my purpose, yet unwilling to introduce another to my secret. I'd felt an affection for the lad from the first. Offered him an exalted station in the little community I'd built around me. Promised him an even larger stage on which to act when we should journey to London. In return, I asked only that he stay by my side, that he heed my tutelage, above all that he accept the truths I elucidated for him. Was it so much, the things I demanded of him, the trust I required, the faith in my judgment?

For, in spite of all that I could give the boy, there remained a barrier between us, an insuperable wall that held us apart. Of course, the evident cause would be my lycanthropy, which has kept me separated from the world of men in spirit if not always in fact. But there was something else there, and I can't even now say with certainty what it was. Perhaps I misjudged the degree of gratitude Liam must have felt for all the favors I bestowed on him. Or he might have sensed the difference in me, and just as he was attracted to the spiritual sympathies we shared, held himself aloof from that element of my being that was more volatile and passionate, more threatening to his innocent nature. How can I guess now what the cause for this coldness might have been? But I felt a portion of my affection for the boy was not returned.

And now I see that part of the reason for the scheme I settled upon was the fear I had of losing the one tie still binding me to humanity. My solitude until that point wasn't so complete as I believed, and this single light of fellowship meant more to me almost than the secret of my lycanthropy. The dawning realization of this fact led me to my desperate plan. It was a dream that the possibility might exist, remote, almost unthinkable, but there nonetheless, the chance that I could bring a soul to me, usher someone into my world. To know what I know and not be afraid. To care for my cares and understand my nature. It seems madness now, true, but at the time I allowed my hopes to obscure the dangers involved. I determined that, if Liam were to continue by my side, then he should, he *must* be made aware of what I am. I decided to reveal to him that I am a werewolf.

Accuse me of taking less care in my preparations than I should have done. Undoubtedly I wouldn't be where I am now if only I'd been more careful. But what then? Would I have learned what I've learned? Would the deepest corners of my being be so wholly revealed to me as they now are? Isn't the doubt I've gained worth the cost? At the time, I hardly considered my course to be a plan of action at all. Nothing more than the telling of a tale.

On the day of the last full moon, when the servants were busying themselves with closing the house and preparing for their holiday, I called Liam to me and informed him that, after he'd seen off the last of the household, he should report to me in the study before departing. This wasn't so unusual, since he took it as among his many duties to supervise this domestic exodus. After he'd bidden farewell to the last of the staff, therefore, with instructions not to approach the estate until they should hear my call, he appeared promptly at my study door.

I guided him in and, without a word, led him through the open doors into the garden, where I'd arranged for a table with a bottle and two glasses. Sitting him down, I poured for both of us. He looked at the glass I placed before him, and then, rather conspicuously ignoring it, asked in a pleasant voice what it was I wanted.

"Liam," I began, remaining on my feet and looking down at him, "I'll be direct."

"If you will, sir," he answered in bland tones that couldn't fail to cut me with their detached politeness.

"I think, Liam, that after only a month in your new station, you no longer desire to be in my service."

He looked troubled as I said this. I remember distinctly the cloud that passed over his bright young countenance. But he didn't look shocked. He didn't protest his earnest desire to continue in my service. Didn't show me by involuntary actions his depth of gratitude for all I'd done. He only responded, "Not at all, Your Grace. I'm quite happy working here."

"Ah, working here, yes," I pursued, "but are you happy with me, Liam? That's the point. Are you happy living here with me?" At this he seemed confused for a moment, and, standing, he looked away. "What is it? What's troubling you, boy?" I continued, trying to find a way into his thoughts.

But suddenly Liam recovered himself and turned about to confront me. There was a strange look upon him, so that he appeared less like the charming lad I thought I knew and more like a young man. Glaring at me defiantly, he declared, "I'm not a child, Your Grace."

I wasn't prepared for such a display of temper, but I didn't show my surprise. I simply said as calmly as I could, "No one has implied that you were."

"I like that," he scoffed, with a freedom that was new to him.

"Who treats me like a child around here if you don't? I give orders to the entire staff and manage the running of your whole estate, and everyone gives me the respect I deserve but you. Christ, but you're as bad as Old Dad."

"When have I ever behaved badly toward you?" I exclaimed in my defense, feeling abused by the accusation.

"Pulling me away from my responsibilities to go on your silly picnics. Throwing my book into the stream. I suppose you thought I'd got it out of your damned library, but I didn't, you know. It was mine, bought and paid for with the wages I make in your hire. And even if it weren't, what right had you to tell me I couldn't read it if I had a mind to?" Liam had become thoroughly heated during this harangue, and I could tell that he'd been brooding over these supposed offenses for quite some time. "And having me to dinner every night and keeping me up till all hours in the study, as if I didn't have to get up early enough to get my work done for you."

"But we breakfast together. You never rise until I do."

He made a scornful noise. "A lot of good I'd be if I laid around until then. I'm three hours up by the time you stir. Not that you need to stir yourself. You're master right enough and shouldn't be troubled. But that doesn't give you the right to keep others from their duties." And with that he turned about and stormed off to a corner of the patio.

Good God, what a flood of anger I'd undammed. Liam's discontent ran far deeper than I'd thought, and was, I had to admit, not entirely unfounded. Until that moment I hadn't considered that he actually saw himself as my butler, and not, as I'd hoped he did, as my companion and protégé. I felt disappointed, hurt, almost betrayed, and for an instant I abandoned my judgment and allowed these feelings their free expression. Putting my glass down loudly for emphasis, I remarked in bitter tones, "I suppose this is what you'd call gratitude, then! After raising you up from the shit and filth of your life, holding you above the rotten whores who'd have your innocence for their sport and 'get little howling bastards for you, offering you the only way you'll ever know of escaping the miserable future you seem determined to embrace, I deserve your contempt after all of this, I suppose!"

Though spoken in anger, my words had a better effect upon him than a more calculated reproach might have done. He turned around again to face me, and I could see how his mood had softened. "I don't mean to be ungrateful. I only want to do my job, to handle your affairs so you needn't be bothered. But I can't understand why you gave me this position if you don't treat me with the same respect you afford Mr. Pike."

"Is that all you want from me, Liam? Employment? A damned job? Pike is nothing to me. I'd sack him tomorrow and not lose a second's sleep. I'd hire another as good as he is and never miss him. Is that what you want for yourself? I can offer you so much more than that, my boy, a whole world more than that, if only you'll let me."

He looked puzzled. "I don't understand, sir. What else do you want?"

I crossed to his side and placed my hands gently on his shoulders. "There's nothing I want from you but the pleasure of your company. You're an engaging lad. You have a quick, inquisitive mind and a ready desire to learn the niceties that life can offer. Yours isn't a nature suited for a life of servitude, and quite honestly I'm dismayed that you thought I held you in such low esteem."

"But if I'm not your servant, what am I?" Liam inquired in a voice that sounded more confused now than frustrated.

"What would you like to be?" I asked, placing an arm around his shoulder, looking down upon him tenderly. "Name your station. My confidante? My student? My assistant? My ward? All I require is that you will stay by me, enjoy the life I can offer you, and share in the comforts and privileges of my rank and my condition. I don't want you as a secretary, Liam, but as a dear and trusted friend."

He looked up at me, but couldn't for a long time say anything. So I brought him back to the table and sat him down. He took the glass now that I'd offered before and emptied it. Then, replacing it on the table, he shook his head and muttered to no one in particular, "I really don't know what to think. You have me so befuddled, sir. I'm afraid I still don't get it."

"Then think nothing for now," I advised him. "Just consider what I've told you, the advantages that can be yours, the pleasures and the position. The wealth and the knowledge. That especially, Liam. The secrets of a life above all the squalor and ugliness, a life beautiful and sublime, more wonderful than anything you've ever imagined, or ever read of in your books. But don't give me an answer until you're ready. It won't be long before you'll know what to say. In the meantime, I have a surprise for you. I want you to stay with me here tonight, to assist me in my work." Liam's mood quickly brightened at this, for I knew he'd been as curious as a cat to discover what work I did in such seclusion every month. "I want you to know, Liam," I went on gravely, more to still my own nervous spirits than his enthusiasm, "that it's very important work, very serious and, yes, even dangerous. What you see this evening will doubtless frighten you. But I know you're an intelligent lad, and you won't allow your fears to get the better of you. There's no room for superstition in science, is there?"

"I won't disappoint you, sir," he assured me excitedly. "What is it we're to do?"

"You'll know that soon enough. Now it's still early, and there's nothing we can accomplish until the moon is up."

"The moon, sir? Is it astronomy, then?" he asked, sounding a little disappointed.

"No questions yet, Liam. You'll have time to ask all the questions you like tomorrow, but for now let's go out to the stream for a quick bathe, and then consider how we should prepare you for the work ahead."

There is a place in the stream, some two hundred yards from the oak, where the opposing banks go off in their separate directions, the bed drops down several feet, and a little pond is formed. It was a favorite retreat of mine when I was a boy here, and its waters are unusually cool and refreshing. I'd chosen it as a likely spot for my plan because of the freedom the place afforded. There we would both be, without clothes, stripped of the symbols of our civilized conventions, where I couldn't shock Liam by casting my garments aside once the transformation had begun. As to the potential dangers for him, I didn't even consider them seriously. I loved the lad, after all, and should my affection for him alter with my shape? Was it possible I should feel less for him at a time when my whole consciousness was nothing more than feeling? What protection could Liam possibly need from that side of my nature?

Once we reached the pond, we put aside our clothing and leapt, yelping, into the chill water. We splashed about and cavorted like a couple of schoolboys, playing at who could throw the other farther across the pool, wrestling and straining strength against strength to keep from being plunged beneath the surface, laughing and screaming and as often as not ending up the both of us half drowned and spluttering for air. It was an exuberant, forgetful sort of game we played, and by the time we pulled ourselves gasping back up onto the soft turf it was but a quarter of an hour before moonrise.

Now the difficulty of my situation began to present itself to me in unmistakable terms. The closer the time for my metamorphosis came, the more anxious and unsure I was as to how I should explain myself to Liam. To simply blurt out that I am a werewolf seemed lunacy, but to delay the revelation until the last minute would be cruel and likely frighten the lad out of his senses. As Liam lay beside me, however, breathing deeply the cool air of twilight, he offered the chance I'd been looking for to introduce the topic.

"What is it that we'll be doing once the moon rises?" he inquired anxiously. "Shouldn't we be making preparations, sir? It can't be long now before it's up."

But even then I balked at the opportunity to state the truth directly. Instead, I rolled over to face Liam and said, "We just have to wait here. That's all." I could think of nothing more to add. Was it cowardice not to have said more? But what words are there for such a moment?

"I don't mind telling you, sir, I'm a bit fearful," he went on, sitting up and reaching for his clothes. "I wish you'd let me know what I'm in for. You said it might be dangerous, and I can't help but suppose that we could protect ourselves better if we weren't lying here so open and unclothed like this."

"I was wrong, Liam," I told him, desperately searching for the words that would prepare him. "There's nothing for you to fear. Remember that. Nothing at all to be afraid of. I'll not allow you to be harmed. But Liam, there is, not a danger, but a peril, more to your mind than to your person. A peril that you must be ready for." I looked deeply into his eyes as I said this, and saw there the innocence and expectancy and youth that I'd come to love so much these past months, a look so like that other I remembered from years past, whose memory gives me such pain to recall. "Liam," I went on, "what are you prepared to believe about what you witness here tonight?"

But my question came too late, for at that moment I felt my body stirring with the warmth of my transformation. Liam said something to answer me, but I can't recall what it was. My mind became distracted, occupied with the change coming over me. I remember for a moment wanting to tell Liam again not to be afraid, but I don't know if I ever spoke the words. I looked about to find the moon, but couldn't see it through the trees. I was oblivious to Liam, unaware that there was anyone with me, my consciousness filled only with the sensations of each second as my body underwent the metamorphosis so familiar, yet always so new.

I was alone in the woods. But even before my transformation was complete, I was drawn by the scent in the air. It wasn't the usual scent of man that I've found so compelling before. This was a stronger smell, more pungent yet more enticing, a smell of sweat and humanity, unmixed and pure, without the odor of metal or clothing. It was heady and intoxicating, and my heart pounded more rapidly as I followed the irresistible trail in the air. It was the smell of fear that drew me on, the scent of terror, and it acted as a drug upon my senses, causing all else to fade away in my mind until only the scent existed for me, the scent and the man.

A few moments and I saw the object of my pursuit, rushing frantically, awkwardly ahead of me, pushing away branches, stumbling and crawling and rising only to stumble and crawl again. There was no question of stalking my prey. The fear made him mine just as surely as if I'd laid a trap for him. I rushed headlong through the trees and in an instant had caught the naked youth in my embrace. I pulled him to the ground with me, and the smell of fear filled my whole being. I didn't kill at once. No, that would have put too quick an end to my pleasure. I let the smell grow and grow as I played with my catch, rolling him about beneath me, toying with his terror. Did he make a sound? I can't recall. There was only the scent for me, nothing more, and that I have with me even now. The strong, lovely smell of human fear.

When finally he was dead, I lay down beside him and satisfied myself. I ate calmly, and tasted the fear in his meat, in his blood. Its flavor was rich and luscious, and for the remainder of the night I returned time and again to enjoy it.

The next morning I awoke beside the corpse of Liam Grey. I lay there for a long time, looking at that beautiful face that had somehow escaped mutilation. The eyes were open and expressionless, and all the color had gone from the lips. His ivory cheeks were begrimed, and mud and dirt matted his hair. I reached out and stroked the icy softness of his skin, now rigid in death. The touch opened the stream of my tears. I grasped the lad in my embrace, moaning and wailing, rocking gently back and forth in the soft earth with the boy's bloodied breast pressed to my own. My heart aches still at the loss, and I feel a greater emptiness in my life than I have yet known. Damned weakness, I know, the stupid weakness of sentiment, but my tears call out for the boy even now as I write, spill upon the page before me! Why? Is my new self a curse? Am I doomed to be two parts of a man, never whole? Must there always be this emptiness at the heart of me, never filled?

No. I will be strong in this, too. Strength alone is my salvation. Liam is dead, slain by my own hand in the most savage manner. His final moments of life were a nightmare of pain and horror, yet I carry no more responsibility than if I'd witnessed the attack from a distance. Impossible to generate a sense of guilt over such an act. I know with a certainty that I'm innocent of all evil intent in Liam's death. It was my nature that caused me to pursue him, my nature that was seduced by the smell of his fear. The same nature that led me to kill Cabrini. The same nature that would kill again if given the opportunity.

Brave words. These arguments fail to soothe me. They can't dry the flow of my grief. Though guiltless, I fear the nature within me that's capable of such an act. The killing of Cabrini was an easy thing, almost accidental. My two halves were in close sympathy, and there was a justice to his death, brought about as it was by his own greed and his criminal acts. But I loved Liam, loved him dearly, almost as completely as I ever loved her. I love him still, and it's that love which I was confident would protect him.

Love. What is it but a phantom, a gossamer tie that binds like iron coils? Invention of a civil world frightened by its own deepest longings, not daring to admit that the love it's created is little more than a wisp of mist passing through the jungle. Men use their affections and morality to hide from the violence everywhere around them, and so men are convinced that they live in an ethereal realm far above the jungle floor. But they're in the very heart of it, and when it suits their purposes, when they've caught some poor imbecile stealing a loaf of bread to feed his family, or when one civilized nation eyes another with a bestial hunger, then the mist clears for an instant. Love vanishes, and man is once again a creature of the wild, more cruel and savage than any animal. We live in an Age of Blood.

And so it isn't merely the loss of Liam Grey I mourn, but foolishly, the loss of my own last remnants of humanity. I'll wipe my tears away myself, for I can see the truth about my nature at last, the truth I've set behind me time and again, avoiding it, blinding myself to it. It is this: I am not a man. I am no more human than a wolf is. That is what I've dreaded knowing. The change that was effected in me that morning in Transylvania is far more than just a physical metamorphosis. My very nature has been refined, purified, and returned to the state it held before society came along to pervert men from their true selves. The affectations of civilization—remorse, love, fear, hatred, above all guilt—these I've stripped off, and must leave them now behind me with no regrets. What's left is my true, essential self. Though inexpressible, it's more clearly my self than I've ever had the courage to admit. I am not a man, but an animal, and in that profession is more freedom and honesty than all the morality ever written.

I eventually overcame my grief, got up, and returned to the house to wash off the blood and mire, and then went back and buried Liam. That done, I rang the bell and waited until the servants began to troop back to the estate. Pike came promptly, armed with some drawings of a new contraption, the operation of which he wanted to explain to me. Before he could start, however, I let him know that I was suddenly called to London, that I should be leaving within the hour and that he should find Liam and tell him to prepare for my departure. As to the household, I informed Pike that as I didn't know when I'd be able to return, he should organize things as they'd been before my arrival. He was to release the staff until further notice and close up the house. I was sure to inform him that Liam would be going with me to the city, so that he'd have to look into the house occasionally himself. Other than that, however, things are to return to the way they were before this little interlude in my history.

Pike asked about the preparations he'd been making for improvements, and I told him that those he was willing to implement immediately he might proceed with. No future plans should be made. He left the study crestfallen, but I have no desire for him to go puttering about the place too eagerly while I'm away. Of course, news quickly reached me that Liam wasn't to be found anywhere, so I made a show of putting a few things together myself and had one of the other servants drive me to Brixton.

And now I sit alone in London, my plans to be a country squire as empty and ruined as my efforts to return to a life in society. All such plans are futile. I can't deny what I am any longer. I've treated my lycanthropy as something I put off and put on every month, like a suit of clothes to play in. Now I must face it for what it truly is. My being. My future. The thing that I am, whether the moon hangs full and fat in the sky or is hidden in the shadow of the earth. At all hours, at all times, I am a werewolf. It's the skin I wear, the air I breathe, the very light that illumines my life. No, not the light. Say rather, the darkness, for that is my life now. Darkness will make clear my way. It's the only life open to me.

12

The Village

A note from Pike. Old Grey is making impertinent accusations.
Dares to say I'm involved in the boy's disappearance, that I'd lured
Liam into a wicked life and now the lad has succumbed to the
black arts I've practiced on him. The old bastard actually has the
nerve to say so openly! Pike assures me his story is being ignored,
attributed to the grieving fancies of the man's distracted imagination. That's still no excuse. I don't care why this withered old
relic is maligning me. He'll hurt for it or I'll be damned!

I wrote back that I last saw Liam after the staff had departed,
that we simply arranged accounts for the month and he walked
off in the direction of his father's cottage. That should put the
ball back into the old man's court. I can profess the same bafflement as everyone else, protecting my interests through ignorance.
There's not a whisper of suspicion to implicate me. Liam will soon
be given up for lost, the unfortunate victim of cutthroats or his
own melancholy nature. The staff can attest to the fact that he
was disaffected with me, and aside from Grey, who distrusted me

already, no one can suspect anything. Besides, even if it were possible to connect me to the boy's disappearance, where would anyone go with the information? I'm magistrate on my own lands, after all, and jury, and I daresay that's security enough. Still, I find that I think often of Liam, not with guilt, but simply as a recurrent memory. Like E.

I think too much. That's why I've taken to the streets again, to dispel my choler. I walk far and without any destination through the byways of London. The night—the dark, luscious blackness of the night—God, but it's balm to me! In its soothing embrace, I come desperately close to finding that peace that's eluded me so long. It's only now, while moving like a phantom without a will of my own, uncaring and uncared for, that I see with certainty what I've become, and what I was and what I now must be. True, I'm alone without Liam and miss his company, but I'm now more content in my double nature. No! Not double! I am a single thing, whole and complete. I'm coming to understand, but more than that actually to know that there's nothing I can do that's wrong, not if I heed my desires and keep that singleness of purpose always before me, that sublime perfection which governs my werewolf's being. I've heard it said that, before a man can be truly free, he must kill the thing he loves. I see the truth in that. In killing Liam I've discovered myself. In devouring him— my weakness—I've uncaged my strength. My judgment, my power, my sense of what's right for me, these are the sole allies I require, the only justifications I need. So I must come to embrace my solitude, to accept my nature for what it is and not try to mold it one way or another to fit the society about me. I am alone the means and the ends of my own destiny.

14 August

I wander aimlessly through the city, every night ranging farther afield. Find myself now amid the squalor of the river, now among the sterile gardens of Regency Park, then staring out across the black, seaside wastes of Gravesend, hardly aware of how I get from one to the other. There's no purpose to these marches. I don't muse while I walk. I'm not seeking further insight into the mysteries of my nature, a brighter enlightenment with which to delve the depths of my soul. I require only solitude and oblivion. To empty my thoughts, recapture in my human form the werewolf's peace that I know is truly mine, the unreasoning life that's more than life as men know it, that so envelopes and liberates my senses every month. Of course, my solitude is never complete, not even in the most desolate landscape. The night has its own inhabitants, creatures no less social than their daytime brethren, but whose dispositions, like mine, are more suited to the shadows. In general they keep to themselves on the streets, and only congregate in the dung-ridden taverns where they pursue their perverse desires. They're good company for my tastes, and I don't begrudge them their bit of darkness.

I was accosted only once, three nights ago. A pair of rascals with but a single knife between them, wielded inexpertly by the larger of the two. Our commerce was brief, yet satisfying. They emerged from two doorways, one before and one behind me. The fellow in front, a beefy oaf, the one with the knife, asked where I might be going along their stretch of road. I didn't even pause to consider the question. Pointing off to my left as though to answer him, I lunged forward bravely and lashed out with the heavy knob of my walking stick. The blow caught him full upon the temple, dropping him instantly, braining the poor bitch's son before he even had the chance to utter a moan. I then spun about and crouched low, ready to pounce upon his companion, but all I saw of that fellow was his heels. So I continued on my journey, leaving the knife upon the ground where it lay, although from the evidence of the blood and hair I later found on my stick I doubt the rogue will have further use for it.

I saw her the other night as well. Was it a week ago? Climbing into a carriage. Her husband must have gone in before, taking her hand and pulling her inside while I watched from the shadows.

They drove off and I followed, clinging to the darkness as they made their way through muddy, ill-lit streets. Ran on behind them, trailing them in the night. They stopped at last in the quiet retreat of their lane, such a perfect nest of respectability. Saw her descend and wait for him to alight, but I ran off again before he appeared. Couldn't see them together, the domestic idyll. I returned later. A light burned within, from her room I imagined. Does she sleep alone? I sat on the curb and watched until the light went out, and then watched a while longer in the near perfect darkness of the city.

16 August

A package arrived from Mrs. Wattles today. It's a tiny volume, in Latin, with the cumbersome title of *The Memoirs of Severus Portinus, Governor for Forty Years Over a Remote Corner of Gaul Under the Authority of the Emperors Philip, Decius, Gallus, Valerianus, Gallienus, Claudius II, Aurelian, Tacitus, Probus, Carus, Carinus, Numerianus and Diocletion, Containing Such Remarkable Observations Concerning the Habits and Practices of this Savage Gallic Race as I Observed During the Length of My Governance*. Judging from the size of the thing, Portinus' rule was uneventful, but Mrs. Wattles has included a note that I should find a marked passage particularly instructive.

A quick glance at Portinus' prologue reveals that he managed to hold onto his post for so many years and through such a turbulent political climate owing to the relative insignificance of his portion of the globe, which left him completely overlooked by Rome. The passage itself will require little effort to translate, though Portinus was rather idiomatic in his Latin. I can begin tonight.

24 August

Here is the tale of Severus Portinus in my own rough and hurried translation. The poor fellow was posted at the very ends of the earth and instructed by the Emperor to perform a census upon the Gallic population—households, servants, livestock, and all. So he laid out a grid and established a date for each sector during which the census should take place. When Portinus was finished he called in the headman of these Gauls, one Vinctorix, that he might see the plan and advise his people of it.

"Vinctorix arrived and gladly consented to look at the finished map. He glanced perfunctorily over the whole, muttering his approval that all seemed quite reasonable and commending me on my tactical skills. Suddenly, the old man took a sharp breath, and for a bare moment his demeanor changed dramatically from callous attention to dreadful care. But almost as soon as I marked the transformation, it had passed, and the aged priest was looking up at me again with his usual benign familiarity. He regretted, he informed me, that it would be quite impossible to allow my troops into one of the squares on the assigned date. I was incredulous. This square was an almost empty little seaside area with a single village, from all reports little more than a rough collection of huts. I asked why there was a need to delay.

" 'You needn't delay,' Vinctorix said. 'You may take your census this very moment if you like. But you would be advised not to attempt it on that date.'

"Again I asked why, and got the mysterious answer that the date indicated was the night of the full moon. My officers, who had been stationed in the region longer than I, looked knowingly at one another and laughed. I seemed to be the only person in the room unaware of the jest, and I turned to my aide and demanded an explanation.

" 'It's nothing, sir,' he replied, still chuckling. 'Just one of their superstitions.'

" 'Not a superstition at all, my friend,' responded Vinctorix earnestly. 'I have seen the event with my own eyes and can attest that it occurs just as you have heard.'

"I was really beside myself with indignation now. 'Will someone please tell me what in the gods' names we're talking about!'

" 'Allow me, governor,' Vinctorix offered. 'There is, in our region, a certain malady, an affliction unknown in other parts of the world so far as I am aware. It goes by a Gallic name that I think is not translatable in your Roman tongue, but you might call it the Mark of the Wolf.'

" 'The Mark of the Wolf?' I repeated.

" 'Just so, Your Eminence. The man suffering from this disease seems to all outward appearances a normal man, and indeed is so, for the majority of his days. But at the time of the full moon, he . . . changes.' Vinctorix stared at me with the black-eyed, lifeless stare so common among those people. It never failed in all my years among them to cause the nape of my neck to tingle. 'He transforms, if you will, into a wolf, a monstrous creature, ravenous and bloodthirsty. He roams the countryside searching for whatever prey is so misfortunate as to cross his path. He devours anything, but prefers the meat of humans, and will often traverse great lengths to acquire this delicacy.' "

(Ignorance and superstition! If a man is stupid enough to serve himself up like a trussed hen, then of course he must expect to be eaten! But to think that I would go out of my way for human flesh is abominable!)

" 'Are you quite serious?' I asked. I'd thought the old man the most sober member of a drunken race, but I began to doubt.

" 'Would that I were not,' he remarked with a deep sigh. 'But I assure you, I have witnessed these things with my own eyes, and will hold to the truth of them even under torture. There is no cure for this terrible condition. For this reason, those who are afflicted are viewed by our people as specially touched by the gods, and we dare not harm them. Instead, we send them off to live apart, to a village by the sea,' and he indicated with a passing gesture the village on the map. 'Their needs are attended to regularly, and their monthly lusts are sated with a supply of sheep and hogs. No man is allowed to venture near the place within forty-eight hours of the full moon. This is why I tell you, Your Eminence, that you must not send your troops into that village on the date you plan, or they shall surely die. That, or worse.'

"To say that I was dumbfounded by what I heard would be putting things delicately. I was speechless, more so because I knew Vinctorix to be a sane, honest man than because of the lunacy of his tale. Still, I was determined to learn more, and sent my officers from the room while I personally questioned the fellow on the matter. I learned that, because of the divine nature of the disease, its sufferers could not simply be executed, as I suggested be done with them if the story were true."

(Of course! Typical human kindness!)

"Only if these people refused their voluntary exile or attempted ever to escape the vicinity of the village, were they 'returned to the gods,' with the highest honors, naturally. Furthermore, before Vinctorix had been allowed to assume his office of high priest, he was required to witness the transformation of the beasts firsthand, so that he should know for himself the truth of it.

"The way this was accomplished was quite simple. In the village was an ingenious double cage, with inner walls spacious enough for a man to spend the night in, and outer walls sturdy enough to keep the claws of the wolfmen away from his throat. This was most important, Vinctorix assured me, for the least scratch from one of these was sufficient to pass the contagion. From the safety of this sanctuary, Vinctorix saw what he said he shall never forget and could not even bring himself to describe.

"I doubt that any new governor was ever presented a stranger circumstance to deal with. I did not want to offend the locals, or the census would be that much more impossible than it already was. But I couldn't bring myself to believe what I had just heard. I decided, therefore, to put Vinctorix to a test. I told him that I desired to see this spectacle for myself. At first the color rushed from his wrinkled face, and he appeared to suffer from distraction at the very suggestion. But he remained silent, and I could tell that he was considering my proposal seriously. Finally he said yes.

" 'I am no longer the ruler of this place. You are,' he admitted. 'And it is now your charge to see what I have seen.' "

(So, these Gauls make at least an effort to live, if not with lycanthropes, then beside them. It seems a noble experiment. Yet what does it amount to really but exile? And are we not already in exile, our very nature held separate from their world by fear? They do fear us. Even this Gallic truce is based on fear, their fear of something greater than they are, something stronger, more favored by nature.)

"The journey was easy, through thick, well-traveled forests that gave way to flat coastal plains. It did not seem long on the second day out before we heard the roar of the surf and saw the tiny collection of huts spread out facing the sea. As we approached the village, we were met by a youngish man, perhaps no more than twenty, although with these Gauls it's not always easy to tell how old they are. He greeted Vinctorix in their Gallic tongue, and then asked the obvious question about his unusual escort. The priest explained the situation in a few words, and although the fellow appeared troubled at the news, he did not object.

"We camped outside the village that night, and the next day the preparations for the event were quickly made. Sheep and hogs were let loose and allowed to wander freely. The cage was pulled out and examined carefully to make certain that it was still sturdy and secure. When Vinctorix and the young man were satisfied, my soldiers dragged it to a place near the center of the village just where the brown grass of the dunes gave way to the brown sand of the beach. It was very large, this double cage. The inner walls were at least ten feet on a side while the outer measured about twenty, leaving some five feet between the two sets of bars, enough space, I was assured, to keep me safe. Inside this cage I placed a bed roll, a lantern, some reading matter with which to pass the time, and food. Then, although there were still hours before the full moon, I entered and Vinctorix locked the doors behind me.

"My centurion refused at first to leave me in this helpless situation, abandon me, as he saw it, to these Gallic madmen, but I ordered him to go, to travel as far away as Vinctorix should instruct, and not to return until the full moon had set. I did not particularly enjoy the sight of my troops marching away in the distance. I was quite frankly scared out of my wits. I could speak only a few words of Gallic yet, and these people had no Latin at all, so there was nothing I could do but read a little, eat a little, and watch them as they watched me. There were no more than a score or so inhabiting this village. I could not tell much about their living arrangements, but the men and the women didn't seem to be paired off in marriage, and there were no children about at all. They were curious about me, naturally, and friendly enough, offering me some of their own food, which consisted mainly of fish."

(A village of lycanthropes! A city of werewolves! My God, what a dream! But why do they allow themselves to be quarantined in this way, when with a concerted effort they might live freely? Yet how free can they live in a world of men, where one's very nature must lie hidden, disguised in a form and face so foreign to the true core of one's being? The world is my prison. I am locked in this human shell, striving ever to escape!)

"The time passed slowly. The full moon seemed to be a very long time coming, but eventually it came. As the moment approached a great anxiety filled the village. At first, the people wandered about in the shadows of the early twilight, nervously, without any apparent aim, avoiding sight of each other and of me. Soon they disappeared completely, keeping themselves either secreted inside their huts or hidden behind the low dunes that separated the beach from the plains. These dunes kept the moon hidden from me as it rose over the horizon, but I could tell without a doubt when that moment arrived, for a low moaning went up from all around me, a chorus of soft noise that at first was clearly human but rapidly changed, until it was unmistakably the sound of a pack of animals. I strained my eyes, trying to pierce the deepening gloom, to see what was occurring there in the darkness. I caught a brief glimpse of a figure, I think it was a woman, darting out of the shadows and back again. Although I saw it just for an instant, only a momentary image, this shape, this damned thing not man and not beast has haunted my dreams ever since.

"The night grew darker, and as the moon was still not over the dunes, I had only my little lantern for illumination. Its sad light scarcely sufficed for my cage, and so I was unprepared for the sudden rush made upon me by the first of the monsters. All I heard was a low growl from behind, and I turned quickly to see the beast fling itself against the bars of the cage, clawing the air in an effort to reach me. I screamed, screamed like a terrified child at the sight of the thing, larger and more terrible than any wolf. It pressed itself against the bars, but the cage did not tremble. If it had I probably would have fainted. The thing's mouth snapped futilely and its tongue appeared to be lapping up the very air between us. Its howls of frustration brought a second creature to the cage, and then a third and a fourth until I was surrounded by these monsters, howling and roaring. I had nowhere to turn to escape their attacks. All I could do was to sit on the ground as close to the very center of the cage as I could get and close my eyes to the sight. Still, the sound almost drove me insane. I have been in many battles in my life, both before that night and since, but never have I felt Death sitting more closely at my side, seen his evil grin and smelled his foul stench more plainly than I did at that moment.

"How long this went on I cannot say. Eventually the beasts tired of the game and ventured out in search of surer meat than mine. When I opened my eyes again the moon was high and I could see several of the wolves feasting on the carcasses of the prey that had been provided for them. Some few still prowled closely about my cage, unwilling to admit defeat. One in particular paced around and around, relentlessly glaring at me, staring hungrily, greedily upon me, unmanning me with his eyes. For I could not have been mistaken. I have seen those eyes too often in my sleep since then to have been wrong. There was an intelligence there. Something diabolical beneath the brute power of the creature, some vestige of its other life. Those eyes consumed my soul, devoured my spirit with their fevered intensity, and left me less than the man I was before that night began. Occasionally one or another would throw itself up against the bars, but for the most part I was left alone. Gradually I calmed my nerves, although I never was relaxed enough to feel at ease, and as the majority of the creatures went off into the night, I managed to rest a little, keeping my eyes open nonetheless.

"So the night passed, and before sunrise the moon had set. By then all of the monsters had lost interest in me and deserted the village, and I had no chance to see them trans-form back into their human shapes, not that I much wanted to. They straggled back, naked and covered in mud and gore, and washed themselves in the sea. None of them approached me, or even looked at me. They seemed, in fact, to be em-barrassed. I sat patiently, ate the rations I had, and waited for Vinctorix to return with the key. This he did somewhat ear-lier than was expected, mainly at the insistence of my cen-turion. I was released from the cage and wasted no time in putting that mad place behind me. My soldiers could not help but notice the half-eaten animals lying about, but none of them dared to ask what I had seen, and I never mentioned what passed that night to anyone until now, not even to Vinctorix, who was discrete enough not to inquire.

"When I returned to my headquarters I immediately is-sued the necessary orders. I dispatched a strong force to go to the village, surround it completely so that none could escape, and kill everyone they found there."

There it is. Such is the compassion of men. To destroy my kind, to kill regardless of the threat. And are these Gauls really any better than the Romans? They managed to live in peace with werewolves, true, but it was the peace of a prison! Sympathetic jailers! Can there never be peace between us, then? Is it as im-possible as this tale suggests? Am I doomed to my solitude? Well, if I am, so be it. A werewolf alone in a world of men. There's something great in that, isn't there? To know what I know, and still travel among the weak who would be my prey under more intimate circumstances? Yes, that's my life now. That, and my life at Murcheston, that better life of mine, truer, more pure. The very distillation of strength. All men are fools who wouldn't see the superiority of such a life. But then, is it a surprise to learn that all men are fools?

27 August

My stay at Murcheston has got off to a wretched beginning. Pike met me at Brixton himself and as we drove out to the estate he informed me that the search for Liam Grey has been fruitless. Yet he still hasn't given up all hope of unraveling the mystery.

"The boy seems to have gone out of the earth like a puff of smoke, and devil a man can say why, unless Your Grace knows of some cause," he added, somewhat too pointedly to be an after-thought.

I looked hotly at the man but kept my composure. "And why do you suppose that I might know some special reason for the boy's running off?"

"I'm afraid he just wasn't the running-off sort," Pike retorted. "I've know Liam since he was a baby, and that doesn't fit him at all. And if he didn't run off, what then? That's what I keep asking myself," he muttered, tapping his skull. "What then?"

"And have you answered yourself, Pike?" I asked wearily.

He nodded. "Aye, Your Grace. That I have done. If he didn't run off, then I'm afraid I've only one way to settle the thing to my satisfaction."

"And that is?"

"He was done away with." And Pike clicked his tongue with finality.

"You mean spirited away?"

"That, or murdered."

"Murdered?" I exclaimed. "Is there any evidence to suggest that he was killed?"

"None but a feeling I've got about it, sir. And the boy's father, he seems convinced that it's so, too."

"Old Grey?" I asked, amazed that Pike should voice any sup-port for the man's wild claims. "Has he admitted as much to you, that he believes it was murder? Have you questioned him on this?"

"No need for that," Pike replied with a shake of his head. "He tells me regularly what he thinks."

"And what precisely does he think, Pike? What exactly is he telling you?"

"That some beast did it."

"A beast," I said, perhaps sounding too disinterested. I hadn't expected the man to hit so near the truth.

"Aye, probably a wolf, though Grey says it's too big for that. He tells me the signs are all over the woods that some creature has been prowling about there for months now. It even killed his hog some time back."

"And then returned to have the boy for his dessert? Do you believe this tale?"

"What I believe, sir, is that no one knows those woods like Old Grey does, and if something's there, it wouldn't escape his eyes for long. But," Pike continued nervously, "I fear that's not the end of it."

"What else?" I asked, for the first time actually worried at what I might hear.

"Old Grey thinks that, whatever is out there, you know of it yourself, and you let Liam be killed by it."

I was silent for a moment, not really knowing how to respond. The case had never been stated to me so directly before. "I don't quite follow," I said at last, feigning disbelief. "He thinks I was the beast's accomplice?"

"Not an accomplice, sir. More like a master. He says the thing only seems to come out when you're here, so you must control it somehow."

This was too much. I couldn't have such things being intimated, not by anyone. "And you allow him to make these accusations?" I yelled, no longer reining in my fury. "You let him spread his beshitted theories about the county for any fool to hear? Is that how you manage my affairs, Mr. Pike?"

"Me?" Pike defended himself. "I've told him often enough that he'd better stop his talk, or he'd have to answer for it. But the old man is sick with grief over his boy, sir, and no one is taking him very seriously anyway."

"*Very* seriously? Please tell me how seriously that is! Sack the bastard, Pike! Sack him now, this very day, or by God, I'll sack you tomorrow!"

"I'm not surprised you feel so, sir," responded Pike calmly. "It's a grave thing the old man is claiming, grave and mad. But he's only a tired old fellow after all, and losing his boy like this, it's enough to wear down the wits of anybody. But it'll pass, Your Grace. I'm sure of it. Maybe we could let him stay on in the cottage for a bit, in retirement, you might say. Jemmy could handle the grounds by himself, and I'm sure nobody will listen to Old Grey's crazy ravings."

"Pike," I commanded, more in control of myself now, though still furious, "I want him off the estate. *Now*, Pike. Him and his son. I won't put up with such insolence. Not for another hour."

"Aye, sir," he sighed, and that was all I expected to hear of the matter.

But it wasn't all, not yet, for as the cart neared the drive leading up to Murcheston, a figure stepped out from the cover of the trees and stood in the middle of the road. It was Grey, looking as immovable as Time itself. As we approached, he began to shout, croaking in a voice weary with life. "Where's my boy? Where's my Liam? What have you done with him you bloody monster, you and that creature of yours? It's a beast of hell you're in league with, and it's taken my boy's soul away with it! But there will be a reckoning! There will be judgment on your damned soul!" I confess it, I was shaken by this unholy apparition. Pike halted the cart and called for Grey to clear the road. The fool wouldn't listen, but continued to rant like Elijah.

Pike descended from the box and told me not to be angry, that he'd move the old man off. But I wouldn't wait. I took the reins up and lashed the horse, plunging the cart headlong toward Grey. The old man kept up his harangue, and for a fleeting moment it looked as though I might end this business for good. At the last instant, however, he jumped from the path with a surprising agility and I sped on to Murcheston.

When I reached the house I was positively shaking with rage and frustration. To be confronted *that* boldly, in my own home, on *my* land. It was too much, and I wailed through the house like a banshee, hurling chairs and tables and whatever I could grasp about the rooms in a frenzy of madness until I collapsed in exhaustion in the study. Pike showed himself shortly thereafter to say that Grey had only been bruised a bit. I expressed the opinion that if he appeared before me again he might hope to escape with a few bruises. I dismissed Pike with a further exhortation to sack the hateful lunatic at once. I'm incapable, it would appear, of putting this whole affair of Liam Grey behind me. I wish to God I'd never looked on the young simpleton.

29 August

God damn all these people to hell! They're making it impossible for me to enjoy the least security on my own lands. I can't live near them anymore. Not while they're so close as Darnley Well. I'll evict them all, the entire tenantry. I can't risk discovery any longer. I'm going wild at the constant apprehension of it, the nightmare of having my true nature divulged. Of course, to turn out so many people, displacing some forty or fifty households, the scandal would be enormous. It might even echo so far away as London. Still, it's something I should have considered long before now, and for the most sensible of reasons. The agricultural end of my affairs has been a constant drag upon my income, and I know I'd benefit substantially from letting these people go and relying exclusively on the mining.

Last evening I transformed and went out again into the depths of the woods, roaming widely, exploring the farthest reaches of my domain. The night was strangely silent, with no breeze and few scents to entice me in any particular direction. I varied my pace to suit my temper, sometimes racing headlong through the trees, sometimes crouching low and creeping along, sometimes just trotting about easily, but always in a straight line. Always dead on. And so I invariably reached the edge of the woods and looked out over a sea of blackness that even my eyes could hardly penetrate. In the distance were the pale lights of Darnley Well.

I was standing along a fallow field that lay between me and the village. I'm not used to crossing so much open land. I would probably have turned back if the sky hadn't been cast over with clouds, and had I not detected the scent of humanity, so strong that it carried over the field without the breeze, rich and varied, mixed together with all the wonderful scents of men. Lured by the smell, I moved slowly along one of the overgrown furrows, inching my way toward the lights on the other side of the field. I stopped when I'd got about fifty yards from the first hut, although I can't say exactly why I did. I knew instinctively that I mustn't enter the close circle of buildings. Instead, I rounded slowly about the outer edge of the village, sniffing the air, waiting for something to move out of the safety of the glowing hearths and into the darkness of my realm, the night realm.

I prowled for hours, patiently, never growing careless or eager, never troubled by the thought that I might or might not find the prey I sought, only prepared to act should the opportunity arise. And it did arise. It always does. I was moving slowly past a barn when a scent reached me that was distinctly human yet somehow different, pure and full like the smell of fear but not so delicious, saltier and wilder. I knew the meaning of this scent, although I hadn't encountered it before, and it sharpened my hunger to a fine point.

I crouched low and listened. The barn before me was filled with the gentle noises of the livestock as they rested, but there was another sound coming from nearby, outside the walls, on the far side of the barn facing away from the village, a violent rustling and grunting, like a struggle. I moved silently, circling wide in the direction of the sound. As I came around a corner I saw two shapes, human, lying one atop the other on a pile of hay shoved carelessly up against the side of the barn. The sight of these two fucking beasts, their sounds and smells, the heaving of their sweaty exercise sent me into a frenzy of desire. But still I didn't lose myself. I crept forward cautiously, biding my time, knowing that the right moment would come and that I would know it when it did.

Did I make a noise that gave my presence away? Or were they more nervous, more aware than might well have been expected? For whatever reason, they suddenly stopped their fucking and began whispering to one another. Right or not, the time had arrived when I must act. With a low growl I rushed them. I can't be sure what happened next. I saw them clearly, standing, huddled together. The boy held some frail stick in his hands. I leapt at the last possible moment only to feel a sharp pain in my left foreleg as I was pushed forcibly against the wall of the barn, carried there by my own momentum. I wasn't stunned by the violence of the impact, only surprised to be so thwarted, and I turned at once snarling at my prey. The boy was holding a pitchfork, waving it menacingly in my face, one of its long tines already stained with my blood. I crouched low again as if to leap, but the lad kept the sharp points inches from my eyes and so held me at bay.

The air was now filled with the smell of their fear and their rutting, and it took all the concentration of my will to remain steady and alert. Had he only lunged at me, I could have ducked aside and gotten at them easily. But he kept the pitchfork steady and level, and his defensive attitude presented no chance for attack. Still their fear grew and enflamed my awful desire. The girl hung close behind the lad, and as I tried to circle slowly about, they maneuvered around as well. Every step I made sent pain shooting through my shoulder and leg, but I held my position, snarling and snapping at the pitchfork in mad hatred. So we remained for a time, maybe a few minutes, maybe much longer. Finally the girl had the sense to yell for help. At first her cries merely fired my passion the more, but soon I heard a stir in the village as men answered her call. I turned and raced as fast as I could back across the field and toward the woods.

I didn't stop until I reached the trees. Under the protection of their cover I lay down and licked my wound. It wasn't deep, and healed itself when I transformed again. No party came after me through the dark, and I wandered back to the oak beside the stream where I slept until morning, the excitement of my adventure having left me exhausted. Of course, when I awoke I knew that I'd have to prepare for a trying day, so I ran as fast as I could back to the house, and, ringing the bell for Pike, awaited his news.

It didn't take him long to arrive. Before I'd finished with breakfast he was at the door and didn't hesitate to tell me that there was indeed a wolf at large in the woods. "A monstrous animal it appears, Your Grace," he informed me almost gleefully. "From the tracks we found this morning it must be at least twelve or thirteen stone. We've got the dogs ready to go after it, and I thought you'd like a chance to join the hunt, seeing as the beast is sure to make a magnificent trophy."

How could I refuse? To do so would have implicated me in the affair, confirming Old Grey's wild stories. I honestly can't say that I wanted to refuse. There was something so ridiculous about the situation. It was positively delicious. Going on a hunt for the mysterious wolf. Armed and ready to brave its fearsome fangs. What a tale it would be to tell, if there were anyone to tell it to. I told Pike to wait for me outside while I readied myself, and then took my time as I dressed and selected a weapon. I finally joined him and young Jemmy Grey after half an hour and we walked to Darnley Well, taking very nearly the same path I'd taken just hours before.

We arrived at the village and proceeded at once to the barn, where a group of perhaps a dozen men and hounds had already assembled. One of the number was the boy I'd attacked. As we approached he was relating the tale of his adventure, obviously not for the first time, for the young liar had already managed to embellish it with fantastic bravado and imagination. I took an immediate loathing to him as he displayed the pitchfork still stained with my blood. Pike, Jemmy, and I completed the party, and so we set off across the field. The hounds strained frantically at their leashes and set up a hellish baying while we all darted straight back toward Murcheston.

A cold feeling sank into the hollow of my stomach when I listened to the hounds. My scent! I hadn't thought of that. These cursed whelps, they could follow my scent, perhaps right up to the very walls of the estate. I fell back to the rear of the party as we moved along. What could I do? Find some way to disrupt the search? Order them all home? That would simply draw attention to myself. What then? Nothing. I could only carry on and hope that the dogs might fail.

They were damnably well trained for their work, and took us directly to the woods and into the trees, following the same path I'd taken last night. I held back, just keeping pace, wondering whether my scent were not somehow altered along with my form, and whether the dogs might be incapable of connecting me with their quarry. The rest of the men were silent as we picked our way through the undergrowth in pursuit of a monster that only I knew was already among them.

It took us over an hour to get to the stream, to the oak where I had lain and nursed my wound, and here the dogs fell thankfully into a great confusion, milling about after the scent but unable to locate it, or so it seemed. They were taken off their leashes and paced all around the oak with their muzzles to the ground, quietly snuffling the grass. The men surrounded them, waiting expectantly for one or another to pick up the trail again and so set off baying after their game. I alone stood apart, for fear that one of the beasts might catch my smell and start howling triumphantly that the chase was on. So we stayed for three-quarters of an hour, watching the animals as they attempted to discover me, until at last the men grew frustrated and gave up.

I experienced one final moment of fear as the hounds were trooped past me to return to their kennels. One of them turned and began snorting at my feet, intrigued by something he detected. But a sharp pull from his master ended this inquiry, and while the rest of the group went back again toward the village, I proceeded to the house with Pike to discuss what was next to be done. I agreed that traps should be set. Otherwise, little could be accomplished until the wolf showed itself again. Notwithstanding the general alarm, I stipulated that, as before, no traps should remain upon my arrival. The woods were my private sanctuary, I reminded him, and I would not have them violated.

Pike hemmed and hawed at this for a bit, before asking me bluntly, "Do you think, sir, that it's wise for you to be so free about the grounds with this creature prowling around? If it's one wolf, then it's as certain to be a dozen."

"Only the one has been sighted," I answered with confidence. "And by the time I return I doubt that it will still be a problem. Either it will have been killed or gone on to some other place."

"That would be true enough, Your Grace, were it not for the fact that we've had this trouble before. You recall that mare that was killed these month's past? And then there's Old Grey. He was bothered by a wolf not two months ago, and I daresay it was the same beast. Likely it made away with poor Liam, too, so that it seems the old man was right after all."

I turned upon Pike fiercely at this mention of Grey. "Are you saying you agree with that madman's accusations? You think I had something to do with all of this?"

"No sir, not a bit," he recanted quickly. "I don't say anything of the sort. I only think that the old fellow was right about the one thing. A wolf he saw and a wolf there is, no doubt. And it's my fear that the wolf has staked out these woods here as his home, and won't leave until we drive him out or kill him."

"You do what you want," I said with annoyance. "But if there are no further sightings within a week I want you to give up this hunt. Any man found in the woods after that time with a gun in his hands is to be considered a poacher and dealt with accordingly. Am I understood?"

"Aye, sir," he answered resignedly, "you are that."

I must find a way now of halting this panic over wolves before I'm endangered any further. Should I really evict the entire population of the village? I admit, that appears drastic. But perhaps that's just what's needed, some drastic solution that will give me the peace I seem always to want, never to have. My greatest concern is that, having tasted the nearness of Darnley Well, I'll be hard-pressed to stay away the next time. I'll try myself next month, and if I can't control the urge to return, I think I must turn out the entire community. It's for their own safety, after all. Thank God, Brixton is too far away to be a real temptation to me, or who knows what problems I'd have.

13

To the Death

8 September

Why do I go on writing like this? Nothing changes. My life is now the same from one day to the next, one night to the next. I only write to pass the time until the world is dark again, and I go back out into the streets. Solitude remains my sole salvation and my singular curse. My life is a round of desire and revulsion, longing for the company of others and finding that I can't partake of society without endangering my secret self. Neither the country nor the city has provided me the solace I need. Only the night soothes me, stills my tortured spirit. Again and again I return to my nocturnal wanderings. Swept up into the sordid, silent current that moves about the alleys and shadows of the city after sunset, anonymous yet pervasive, a dark population, an accidental brotherhood. We walk our divergent ways in single file, always alone, avoiding all communion. I go among these people, yet not among them—sharing their world, but all the while separated by a gulf that can't be spanned. I drift through a vast archipelago set in the black ocean of night, never reaching shore.

But the sun must rise again, and I must return to my flat at last. And the question will come to haunt me as it always does. What am I? Not human. But I was human once. If I cared a whit for my lost humanity, could I so carelessly live with the knowledge that I have killed twice now, and would have killed a third time had luck been with me? The worst thing I feel is a slight annoyance at these acts of violence, how they've complicated my life. I would almost rather not have committed them. But it's a foolish wish. As likely wish not to breathe, not to live.

And so to stop these questions and the pain of my loneliness, I sleep, or if I cannot, then I drink until I can, or if I can't drink enough, then I walk. I suffer through the lonely hours of light, waiting for darkness to come again and ease my pain. To live this way, neither here nor there but always somewhere else, is a hell no Dante ever dreamed.

18 September

Good Lord, I've had a visitor today! I was roused from my afternoon slumber by a persistent knocking and for a second I had the devil's own time figuring out what the noise was—it's *that* long since anyone came to my door. It was Merry. What is it about the fellow that makes me like him? His stupid simplicity is too unaffected to despise. He's like a great panting hound that comes around wagging its tail no matter how often you beat it. Truth is, I made no effort to be civil to the man, my mood being what it is of late. Still, he remained for a full quarter of an hour and left with as good a grace as he came with. He extended an invitation for dinner before he went. At his club, of course. Not at his home; not with her. I refused. It's too grotesque, to consider dining *with* someone whom I might otherwise be dining *on*.

Have I become so callous? To see in some poor oaf nothing but so much red meat? All the stories I've read of the vicious cruelty of werewolves, mad creatures lusting after the blood and flesh of men, those tales I'd always believed to be the products of prejudice against my kind, can they be true? I rail against them as gross fictions, and yet, haven't I offered proof enough of their veracity? To kill twice, so coldly. And yet not without provocation! Cabrini! And if only Liam hadn't run! But what of this last time, at Darnley Well? I would have killed, done it carelessly, heartlessly, with no reason or need!

Questions, questions, questions! All these God-damn uncertainties that cloud my mind and make my every hour a cipher! Where will I ever dredge up the answers to quell these miserable riddles and gain some little bit of ground on which to build my new life?

But why should I even make the effort? It's not explanations I'm seeking, but excuses! Like some besotted wretch rummaging through the corners of a wasted life searching for a reason to keep from cutting his own throat, I'm still carrying this last vestige of my human weakness about with me, this need to satisfy my intellect. To hell with intellect! I don't need answers to justify my actions, my nature, the one thing about me that's permanent, that tastes of eternity. As likely change the color of my skin or the sound of my voice. Hunting, killing, these have always been a part of what I am, of what all men are, down deep where there are no answers, where reason dare not look for fear of being blasted by the truth. So what if my rapacity is directed against the very creatures that once were my brothers? I'm no longer one of them. It can't be wrong to kill when killing comes so naturally. I won't be afraid of what I am. I can't be frightened of myself. Won't have my actions dictated by the weak morality of men. Let every man, every *thing* look after itself. That's the way to get through life. Not with answers, but with actions.

21 September

I've discovered a world within reach of the world I know, and yet more alien than if it lay on the far side of the moon. In my walks through the city I've begun to stray from the usual paths by which

I've always gone, from the common thoroughfares that always de-fined the boundaries of London for me. Now I learn of another life, a squalid, ugly world, sick beyond imagining, that sits within and about the streets I've known, like some parasitic vine encir-cling an ancient and dying oak.

It takes very little to find these places. You have only to possess the intent to uncover them, and you'll stumble upon them as easily as you find your way home. It happened for the first time by accident, just the other night. I was wandering after my aimless fashion, taking my direction from the random meanderings of my mood. The last landmark I remember distinctly was St. Paul's, rising pale and bulbous over the night. I had left that pretty pic-ture behind me when I suddenly realized I was in a quarter of the city I'd never seen before. Nor have I ever known its like. I hadn't traveled far, and yet the transformation in my surroundings was so complete I might have covered several leagues in but a few paces, like the lad in the fairy tale with the djinn's magic boots.

The buildings I'd just been among were stately and proud, those enveloping me now squat, grotesque, twisted, with walls crumbling away to expose the spaces behind like a whore display-ing her wares. The streets I'd known were relatively clean and well-lit. This I now surveyed was dark and rotten with shit and filth, the stench of which first roused me from myself. The odd passersby I had encountered along my usual paths were cloaked and secretive, but at least they'd walked like men. These passing now about me skulked in doorways and scurried around more like animals, bent, misshapen wraiths with eyes cast down, their gazes diverted from the stars, resting always on the mud and the refuse of their sorry lives. Whether these human beasts were preyed upon or preying, I couldn't tell. The scene before me was altogether as foreign from the places I know as any place could be, more akin to the horrific bazaars of the Orient than any British lane. I was fascinated by it all.

My walk continued. Along the street were storefronts, and I stopped frequently to stare through the broken, dirty panes to see what might be worthy of commerce in such a decaying market. From what I could make out in the dark, the chief product of the district seemed to be empty bottles and old rags. I doubt that any of the shops I peered into could have made a single sale in the past ten years, so dreary and abandoned they appeared within. They might have done better business charging rent against their doorsteps, for I was perpetually trodding upon some sleeping figure or other cowering in the shelter afforded by such partial lodgings.

It continued, this panorama, block after block, street upon street, offering no respite from the contagion of such indescribable poverty, covering more area with its squalor than I would have thought was available in the crowded city. Still, I had no desire to escape, to return to the placid safety of the world I'd known. The degradation represented here, the abject beggary of the inhabitants, everything I saw and everything I felt spoke to me of mankind stripped of his unnatural advantages, his intelligence and mastery, and reduced to that primal state I so longed for. Here was man as I knew him to be, really, under his skin. The same sort of thing that I am. Only, while I've discovered strength in the jungle of nature, here was man reduced by nature to a state of utter hopelessness. The odor of shit and offal, and viler stuff too miserable to speak of; the starvation and disease I confronted at every turn, in every alley and along every street; mothers with hungry children clutched vainly to their withered breasts; the aged and infirm sucking air through black mouths, gasping to remain in a world that did not want them; the sounds of men and women in fierce embrace, satisfying their ugly desires, fucking with more violence than affection, removing for an instant one ounce of the total pain they felt, only to add later the quantity of a single heartbeat to the suffering of the whole; the cries and whimpers piercing the night's calm, impotent appeals against an unfeeling world; everything I heard and everything I saw spoke to me of man as he truly is, a weak, greedy, mean little animal, erecting his cities as vain protection against the merciless onslaught of nature, subjecting his fellows to greater misery than nature herself ever devised. Yet some would call this *in*humanity!

I was suddenly sickened by the scene and began to search for a way out. I looked about for some lane that might take me back to the streets I thought I knew, but nothing offered the least promise of escape. In every direction I spied greater and greater despondency, all ways equally immersed in despair. So I chose a street close by and strode boldly down the center of it, or as close to the center as I could place myself, for a stream of sewage flowed down the middle. I thought that if I could but stick to a direction, I must inevitably come out at some place familiar to me. But the way I had selected, after twisting along for a space, turned out to be a blind alley, and I had to retreat and start anew. I tried again, but once more came upon a dead end, a high fence hammered haphazardly together, intended to keep something in or something out.

I turned a second time, and would have gone back, but I was startled to discover a figure lying prone atop a rubbish heap. I couldn't tell in the darkness whether it was a man or a woman, but only that it was emaciated, reclining there in such a careless attitude that it struck me as the very monarch of this depraved arena, resting in state over its proud domain. What a spell it cast over me, this person, not so much an animal as merely a thing, a bit of the spirit of the place ripped off of the whole and tossed aside. I wanted to see more of it, to know it, perhaps even to rouse it and address it. Why? I don't know why! It called to me, this ghoul, without a voice, without a noise it called to me, and I responded. I stepped carefully up to it, slowly made my way along the dust and filth of the street, up the side of the pile of refuse to kneel at last beside the figure in dumb homage. Reaching into the inner folds of my cloak, I removed a match and struck it.

It was a man. Yet not so much a man as a skeleton. I must have known all the while that it was dead, for the revelation carried no surprise for me. It seemed correct that it should be dead. Death was the rightful ruler of this hell. The white eyes, floating in the cavernous sockets, stared directly at me. The mouth drew back in an open and toothless grin. And from those eyes, and from that mouth, and from the nostrils and from every part of the thing the dried remains of a black bile, the liquor of life, oozed out in a sick stream. Any foul odor it may have given off went unnoticed in the general stench. It was proper in this place that a corpse be lying discarded like this, so much useless bone and meat. I passed the match over the remainder of the carcass. It wore only shreds of rags through which more of its yellow skin might have been exposed had not the rats and the cats and the stray dogs already gotten to the thing and laid it open. A sound behind me recalled me to myself. I turned, but saw nothing. Only the shadow of a phantom, doubtless the wild beasts of the streets, impatient with my presence, returning to their meal.

I left the place at once by as direct means as I could fashion. I scaled the wall obstructing my way, only to find myself at the end of another alley. This led to another street as like that which I had left as if it were its twin. I chose another alley, and this one took me to another street down which I thought I heard the lapping of waves. I turned toward the sound and soon came to the river and within sight of the few landmarks I needed to make my way back to healthier air. But I noticed as I walked that the destitution I'd left was not so much supplanted by a pleasanter aspect as it seemed to be covered over. And so the images I saw last night have remained with me, and wherever I go now I see the squalor that exists just beneath the pretty surface of the city. A thin coat of varnish that can be stripped away, exposing the wretchedness beneath. It's right that I should know this, should carry this secret of the civilized world about with me, I who have my own secret self to hide.

27 September

It's happened again. I'm beset at every turn by circumstance. My victims seem eager to throw themselves in my way. Why should I cavil at obliging them anymore? To hell with all excuses. Simply act, that's my philosophy. Feel. Do. Don't stop to think and doubt. I'm only the agent of nature, performing in accordance with her precept that the strong live off the weak.

Naturally I did all that was conceivable within my power to avoid another such incident. When I met Pike at the station, I asked him whether his hunt for the wolf had met with any success, but he admitted that no sign of any wolf had been discovered and the search was called off as I'd instructed. Satisfied, I asked offhandedly if there were any other news. Pike replied that, yes, indeed there was further news. My postponement of all future agricultural projects (and it didn't escape my notice for an instant that Pike termed the projects merely "postponed") hadn't been well received in the village. With harvest approaching, Pike feared that any ill will the workers held against me might surface just when a cooperative effort was most needed.

Moreover, my summary eviction of Grey had caused some problems. The old man had lived in the cottage for almost as long as anyone at Darnley Well could remember and didn't have any other family to whom he could appeal for shelter. Jemmy had tried to get his father to accompany him south, where work is plentiful. But the old fool insisted on remaining nearby in the senseless hope that Liam might yet turn up, and so Jemmy had gone off alone, first setting his father up in Brixton with an easy job at the mines. Nothing hazardous for the old man, just making himself available for errands and such, and tidying up the grounds generally. Just enough to pay for his keep.

But I wasn't happy to hear it. I wasn't going to allow Old Grey so much as a foothold on my lands, not after the things he'd been saying. I ordered Pike to go to the mining office at his first opportunity and see to it that Grey was sacked. Pike looked astonished, but I ignored him, and as he voiced no objection, I considered the matter resolved. Still, when I descended from the cart at the door of Murcheston, he muttered, more for his own benefit than for mine, "It's a hard life for an old man."

"Not so hard as it might be made for those who don't recall

their place!" I snapped. "Now you do what I've told you to do, or Old Grey's lot will look like soft butter compared to yours!" Perhaps I shouldn't have been so short with Pike, but he knows where I stand on this matter, and how firmly I stand. It makes no difference to me whether the old fool's rumors were heeded. It's enough that he breathed them. Even if he were but to whisper them into an empty tree trunk I'd have done the same. Already too much has been revealed, and with his errant tongue and his art for striking so near the truth, Grey could easily have developed from a nuisance into a genuine threat.

What happened later, then, after my transformation, was an act of fate, the final closing of a door left ajar too long for either my safety or my sanity. It's as if nature puts these things in my way, to show me the path that I must follow, whether I will or no.

The night was black and thick, with a howling wind that sent the heavy clouds tumbling across the sky and filled the air with a wild melange of scents, a mixture that seemed to come from everywhere at once. I'd been lolling about the stream for over an hour, breathing deeply the life of the night, the lush decay of autumn, wet and full, when I sensed that something was amiss far into the woods. The cause of my alarm, the strange jumble of scents spilling forth from the breeze, was at first hard to separate from the common odors of the night. But once I became aware of them— the pungent smell of man colored by the faintest hint of fear, the oily sweet aroma of hare, the stale smell of green wood fresh cut, and some new scent, sharp and smoky—once I detected them on the wind, I couldn't easily lose them again. I checked the breeze once more and then proceeded rapidly toward the source of this wonderful adventure.

I was led to a small clearing. It was in a part of the woods I knew well, or at least well enough to know that there'd been no such clearing there before, but a small stand of saplings. The saplings had been felled, creating a circle of open space in the center of which lay a pile of bloodied, eviscerated hares. I stayed for a long while silently looking on at the sight, unwilling to move forward into the clearing but curious and hungry to investigate. The hares themselves were an indifferent lure and I could easily have walked away from them, but I couldn't so readily leave the mystery of their presence there, nor the growing smell of man that suffused the scene, nor the uncertain smokiness in the air. The fear that I'd detected faintly before was heightened now, made more pure by its nearness. I knew there was a man close by, and that he knew I was there, but the wildly blowing wind made it impossible to locate him exactly.

I waited for a time because waiting seemed the thing to do, to see what might happen with this mysterious clearing, this invisible man, this unknown scent. As no such revelation was forthcoming, however, I crept slowly away and began a wide circuit about the place.

As I moved, the breezes were calmed and the smells now fixed themselves in the night, no longer tossed about by the wind, but flowing strong and certain from their source. The whole scene was now made clear to me. The man was on the far side of the clearing close to the edge of the trees. I moved forward barely a step and peered across the open space. I saw him, a shadow within shadows, sitting patiently, motionless, the gun raised to his shoulder giving off the sharp, smoky smell that had confused me at first, the scent of gunpowder.

That the man hadn't seen me was obvious. He knew I was nearby, but he faced just off to my right, and so I circled to the left, traveling far out from the clearing so as to come up from behind him. I must have covered only eighty or a hundred yards, but I spent the better part of an hour doing it, inching forward and lying still, hardly breathing, scarcely moving. The wind again picked up, so that the rough swaying of the trees helped to mask what faint sounds I made, and I was perhaps only ten yards away from him at last when I crouched and prepared to spring. I could see him clearly in the darkness, still facing the clearing, still holding the gun up to his shoulder. I felt the hunger within me grow.

But it wasn't enough, the inevitability of this moment, the certainty of the kill. Alone it couldn't satisfy me. No, I wanted fear. I wanted the taste of fear in him, wanted to feast on his terror as I killed him. So I growled softly, and I leapt.

A single second passed as I launched myself into the air, and yet in that brief span the man flung himself aside and fell hard to the ground. I couldn't alter my progress now, but sailed through the empty space he had just occupied, lashing out impotently with a broad swipe, only just brushing the barrel of his weapon. There was a flash, a sharp report, and an explosion. Fire and powder filled my senses, stung my nose and tongue with their acrid odor, burned my eyes with their sulfurous flames. My paw hurt fiercely and I howled in pain and mad frustration, but I didn't wait about to continue the fight. I fled. Not out of fear. Only startled by the awful force of the gun's blast.

I ran to the stream where I could relax and nurse my paw for a moment. There was no doubt the man would be after me. Still, there'd be time to rest and gather my strength, for in the dark he wouldn't be able to move quickly. I made no effort to devise a plan of defense. My very nature was all the plan I'd need. My sense of myself, the instincts I'd so often relied on, would instruct me when the time came. I had only to lie on the bank of the stream and bide my time. The only concern I had, if concern you can call it, was for my injury. I sniffed it. There was no blood, but the fur over a large part of the paw had been burned away. I licked the wound and tasted the bitterness of the powder, then dipped the paw into the sweet coolness of the stream. The water stung at first, but soon the pain subsided and the joint stiffened. I lay down on the muddy bank and allowed myself the brief luxury, not of sleep, but of rest, of easy repose with my eyes open, aware but not expectant, willing to let my adversary approach, confident that he could not draw near me without my knowing of it well in advance.

But he was clever and in no great hurry himself. An hour went by, a quiet time that bred complacency and carelessness.

When I detected him at last, through the sound of the wind and the smell of the oncoming rain, he was almost upon me. He'd circled around and advanced toward me now from downstream along the top of the bank. The smell of fear was now all over him. It hung on him as mist wraps an island in a shroud. He moved as one already doomed to death, and my heart beat faster at the taste of him in my nostrils and across my tongue. I found a thicket close to the bank, where the man was certain to pass, and I crouched under it and waited. I could still hear nothing over the rush of the wind, but his scent came stronger to my senses and I knew he was very close. My muscles tensed and I lapped the air trying to taste him on the breeze. But something was wrong. He'd halted, so near to me that I was made frantic for his smell, but he didn't appear yet. I waited, felt my muscles quiver convulsively, aching for release. Slowly, how painfully slowly I stuck my head out from the thicket and looked back along my path to see where he was.

He was perhaps twenty yards distant, crouched low and ex- amining the ground before him, somehow able to see even in the thick black of the night. The gun he held idly in his hand, resting his weight on it like a cane. The very sight made my hunger flame inside me, and I broke cover and lunged at him. But again, his quickness surprised me. Even off balance he was able to dodge to one side, though not before my claws raked across his arm. I felt his clothing rip and his flesh tear in my grasp. Still, I'd failed to deal him a telling wound, and I knew I must flee or face the muzzle of his gun once more. I leapt down into the bed of the stream and raced along its banks. A great eruption rent the earth at my heels. I darted across to the other side, but another explosion met me there, and I leapt back again. I ran along the stream, my paw aching at every stride, my tongue hanging limply from my jaws, running with no thought of slowing or straying from my course. A flash of lightning and a crash of thunder overhead sent me scurrying across the stream again, as a heavy rain began to fall.

And yet, in spite of all, still I felt no fear, only a sublime exhilaration. In the face of death, against an adversary my equal in cunning, I was filled with the excitement of the chase. My strength, my vitality drove me forward more forcibly than my pursuer could, compelling me along the banks of the stream, putting distance between me and the man, but luring him on as well. What I felt more than anything was the brilliant ecstasy of control. The situation belonged to me now, not to him. I don't know how or why I should have felt this, but it was true, true because I believed it. My very hunger made it so. I slowed my pace and looked about me, up at the top of the bank, to see what advantage I could find to turn this pursuer into my prey.

And so I didn't notice the mantrap until it snapped shut on my left hind leg, holding me fast. I'd been flushed like a pheasant, my sense of power belied by such a simple ruse, and I roared in anger and despair. The toothless jaws of the trap neither broke the skin nor hurt the bone, but I was just as surely helpless as though they had. For a long time I chewed madly at the iron bands and the chain, but all to no purpose. I tried to pull myself free. Useless. The harder I fought against it the tighter it seemed to grip me. I was caught, without hope. I knew the man would have heard my howl of rage, would know what it meant, would be upon me before long, finding me a ready target.

And yet in spite of all I never felt afraid, and this more than anything is what saved me. Gnawing at the chain proved futile, so I began to follow it, to see what held me paralyzed. The stake to which the damned contraption was affixed was iron like the rest, but I nevertheless tried gnawing it away. As I set my teeth about it, I had the notion to dig up around the thing to get a better grip. I began to claw frantically about it, exposing more and more of it with every sweep of my paw. The pelting rain had softened the earth about the stake and made my work easier. Suddenly I caught the man's scent through the smell of the storm and I knew he was approaching fast. I gripped the stake again in my teeth, and this time it moved slightly as I shook it. I started digging again, turning up large clods of earth, when I heard the man coming up behind me. I turned and crouched low, determined to take whatever opportunity I could to kill the bastard.

He came through the trees cautiously, almost gingerly, and I could see at once that his wounded arm was hanging limp at his side and his vision in this darkness was obscured by the rain driving against his face. I lay motionless, mud and dirt begriming my coat, making me invisible on the earth. He crept nearer to me, leaning forward as if to peer between the raindrops. I didn't know the length of the chain or how close he had to come before I could have him, but my muscles tightened in preparation for the moment. It came with a blaze of lightning that illuminated all for an instant, freezing the two of us. Our eyes met in the single fraction of a second, and as he brought his gun up awkwardly to his shoulder, my legs exploded in a burst of strength. He was standing just beyond my reach, and I felt the anguishing tug of the restraint upon my leg, impeding my flight—but not halting it. For as I reached the full length of the chain, the stake pulled free of its muddy grave, and I flew on and crashed against my foe, flailing him with my claws and teeth, ripping the flesh from him, gorging myself on him in the thrill of my conquest. I knocked the gun from his hand and sent him reeling backwards. With a final swipe of my claws, I cut him wide open across the chest. And then I felt the familiar burning in my own body, and I knew that the moon was setting.

I almost fainted from fatigue, the inhuman exertions of the struggle compounded by the physical demands of my transformation. I breathed in great bursts of air and fell down against the earth. Lay prone in the mud, feeling the rain drum hard, cold drops against my hot skin. The man lay beside me, some way off, but I cared little for him at the moment. I only closed my eyes and allowed myself the luxury of a rest as the rain cooled my nerves and soothed the pain of my hand and my smarting leg. When I opened my eyes again the transformation was complete. The rain was falling easier now, though still incessantly, and a dismal light, the rumor of a new dawn, filtered into the woods. I sat up and released my leg from the trap. There was some blood, caused from the jolt I took as I pulled the stake free, but the cut was already healed. My hand likewise was tender from the severe burn I'd suffered when the man's gun went off, but it would be right enough in a few days. Satisfied with my own condition, I turned to confront my adversary.

It was Old Grey, of course. He lay some few feet away, still alive, though dying, his breath little more than fitful gasps. His crumpled form was tossed up against the muddy bank, his chest torn and blood-soaked, his eyes wide and staring in horror at me. I stood, and there was yet some soreness in my ankle. Grey didn't move, didn't utter a sound. But his eyes followed me. I crossed over and sat down next to him, leaning against the bank of earth behind him, bending into him confidentially. I don't know why I wanted so desperately to speak with him before he died. I'd felt no animosity toward him all the while we were battling each other, and now that the struggle was over I experienced a certain compassion for him I hadn't known before, a sort of defiant sympathy for this poor deluded relic, gambling his all on this wild scheme.

"You were a fool to come after me, old man," I said, not tauntingly, but sadly, as a matter of fact. "I gave you the chance to leave, to get away and put all this behind you, but you wouldn't have it. You had to come back here. Why? To avenge your dead son? Liam is dead, you know. Of course you know. That's why you're here, why you're dying now." As I watched, he shut his eyes in pain, whether from the words or the wounds, I couldn't tell. I know only that this confrontation acted as a catalyst for my own suffering. All my feelings of solitude, my longings for a soul to share my life, my need for Liam, the love I felt for him, the anguish at his betrayal of me, all of this rose within me, spilling forth, flooding my spirit with confusion and grief.

"Yes," I went on, "you know he's dead and you know what killed him, don't you? But you're wrong there, Old Grey. You think I murdered him, the werewolf, the monster, that I stalked him, hunted him down and devoured him in my bloodlust. But I didn't. His fear killed him, not I." I was conscious of tears falling from my eyes, mixing with the rain as it poured down my face. "How could I have murdered a boy I loved as dearly as you did yourself? He died at my hands, yes, but I'm as innocent of the crime as nature herself. Fear and superstition, the things you taught him, the legacy of hate you bequeathed to him in your common ignorance, those are his murderers. If only he hadn't fled, he'd still be alive, would be sharing my destiny with me. I would have made him like me, if only he hadn't run! What power he would have known! What a glorious existence we would have shared together!"

Old Grey looked upon me again, but this time his fierce eyes cursed me. "No, you're not about to accept that explanation, are you," I continued, feeling the hatred seething within him, seeing his dying spirit compose itself in a mute cry of rage. "You came back to kill the thing that killed your boy. But tell me, old man," and I brought my face up against his own, almost kissing him with my words, "in all the while you knew something was out here, some beast prowling the night in these woods, did the truth never occur to you? Did you never remember those tales you must have heard as a child, and didn't you consider, even for the briefest moment, that *I* was the beast?" I put my lips against his ear and whispered, "Shall I tell you something else, just a little something to take with you to your grave? You are now as I am, Grey. *You* are a werewolf, too, marked by the beast. Do you hear me? That's what I give you in exchange for your son's life. *You* are as I am, a creature of the night. So live, old man. Call up your strength and live through this, and the next full moon will prove to you how innocent I must be of Liam's death. Live, damn you! Or die and go to hell!"

I looked once more into his eyes, but there was no longer anyone there to listen to me. He'd died silently, and I don't know if he ever heard the truth I told him, that he did indeed leave this world a werewolf. I stayed there for a few minutes longer, restoring myself against the coolness of the rain-washed bank, allowing nature herself to cleanse away the last vestige of guilt I experienced for Liam's death. With a heart more pure than I've possessed in many months, I rose from the bank and proceeded to the house, where I readied myself for the task of burying Grey. The work was difficult enough, and made the more unpleasant by the caprice of the weather, which alternately stormed and steamed all afternoon. When at last I'd finished, and patted down the earth over the old man with a satisfying finality, it was well into evening, and I've decided to wait one more day before summoning Pike.

28 September

This morning I called for Pike as soon as I rose and brought him into the study. I gave him the news bluntly, saying that I've determined to abandon my agricultural interests completely. "They've become a drain upon my purse, Pike," I informed him. "They're digging too damned deeply into my pockets. The only profits I show on the books are all from Brixton, and lately even those aren't growing as quickly as they have done. I just can't keep it up any longer, you understand. It's got to stop. I want Darnley Well cleared out."

I waited for a response, but the idiot only stood there for a bit, looking about the room as if he'd misplaced something and was trying to recall where he'd left it. "Pike," I said at last. "Did you hear me, Pike? It's finished."

"Aye, sir," he muttered softly. "Heard you clearly. Quite clearly."

"And have you nothing to say?"

"Say, Your Grace?" And he turned a pale face toward me, shaking in his struggle to control himself, moving anxiously around the room. "Say, sir? After all this while, after watching you play with this place, with the people here like they was just chits on a game board. What have I to say? I've said enough, thank you, sir. I've said to these poor families more times than you know, 'Don't you worry about the duke. He's kindly disposed to this land. It's land he's grown up on, land that's part of his name. He knows what this land is. And he knows what they are that keep this land. So don't you worry. Just till the land, care for it, and the duke, he'll care for you.' "

"Now look here, Pike," but there was no stopping him.

"What have I got to say?" he went on, circling around and around the room, speaking to himself, never looking at me, never moving nearer to me. "What have I got to say to these people now? That it's all up? That I've been as much a fool as they? A blind man leading them over a cliff to their ruin? 'Where are we to go now, Mr. Pike?' they'll ask me. 'What's to be done with our children now? What of our homes and our crops and our animals now? What will you say to that, Mr. Pike, I'd like to know!'" And he turned on me suddenly. "What's a man to say to questions like that!"

"A man can say what he'd like," I returned coldly, "but he'll keep a civil tongue before his master, or he'll find his brains dashed out on the floor."

That brought the fellow up short, and he soon recalled himself. Still the remainder of our talk wasn't pleasant. I assured Pike that the inhabitants of Darnley Well would be looked to. Employment would be found for them in Brixton, in the mines. He himself could be confident of a position suitable to his station. I'm sure I can arrange something with a degree of responsibility but no real authority. Even Mr. Kirkland will be tended to, and a fine pension made available to him. My only stipulation to all of this is that it be carried out at once, without delay. I want no one in Darnley Well this time next month.

Pike would have been resigned to anything I commanded. There was little left that he could fight for, I think. He only made one comment as he left, a pathetic coda to his career. "I'll make it all as you say, sir. Not a soul will there be for miles about when you return. I think it might just be Christian charity to remove all these people from your lands, and out of harm's way. All this time, I've just been a simple man trying hard *not* to understand what's going on about me. Thank God Almighty, I still can't figure it out. I only know that I'll not be part of it after this last business. I'll leave everything fallow and foul here, sir, and then I'll be off myself. I've lived here too long to see such things come to pass, and it's best I lived here no longer. God's luck be with you, whatever it is you're doing."

I won't wait about to supervise the job. I have no desire to explain myself to anyone, much less to everyone. And yet, I'm certain of the justice of this move, as severe as it might seem to one not possessed of the facts as I am. I've known what it is these many months, the secret of my being, that I'm a thing apart from men and their world, something alien and separate, and therefore not answerable to their understanding. I've fought the knowledge, denied it, lied to myself every step of the way. No longer! I'm through with such weakness. I am endowed with a nascent freedom, and at last it's time to learn what it truly means to be a werewolf.

14

Captive

2 October

Back in London, and another note from Mrs. Wattles. God, but that woman is persistent! Something more than just intrusive this time. Regrets that she missed me before my last trip to Brixton. Says she's run across a singular manuscript, the most significant piece of lycanthropic literature ever to come her way. Tells me it's a shame to have let it slip through her fingers. There's the rub. I wasn't in, so it was impossible to get the funds to buy the damned thing. The seller evidently knows what he's got and isn't likely to let it pass out of his grasp for tuppence. Still, though the opportunity was lost this one time, she feels certain the fellow might be persuaded to renew his offer.

    The whole business strikes me as suspect. If I didn't know the lady better, I'd swear she were trying to tease me. In the entire note there's not a single word about what makes this bloody manuscript so special. Just effusive crap about what a marvel it is and how privileged I am to have this chance. And then her impertinent tone. She has the gall to lay this missed opportunity right at my feet. Says that if I hope to gain the thing, I must be more responsive to her call. As if I were her fat lap dog!

Of course, I'm intrigued by her appeal, ill-mannered as it is. Though I must confess, notwithstanding past successes, my ardor for these things has cooled. My desire for the dry bones of scholarship has been sated by these last rounds at Murcheston, such isolated moments of violence that have left me feeling exuberantly alive. After all, the only things I've learned of any true importance have come to me not by reading, but by acting. The books were useful at first, when I knew nothing. But I'm so much wiser now than I was then. I share such harmony with nature that knowing and being are almost synonymous within me. My merest instinct is superior to all the knowledge of men, infinitely superior. I can't think what useful information there could yet be for me to learn from books.

Still, I don't suppose a few sentences expressing interest in this manuscript will cost me anything, and if the second opportunity does materialize, I'll decide then how I wish to deal with it. Likely my curiosity will get the better of me in the end.

12 October

Again out into the streets of London. Again, with renewed vigor, out to stroll with the goddess Night, among those whose lives are engulfed within her shadowy coils. The dark is their element, as it is mine, and I breathe easier, walk freer amid them, sharing, not a sense of belonging, but of mutual alienation among such company. Their lives in many ways parallel my own existence. They gather in public houses and Cheapside taverns seeking the camaraderie of their kind, and yet remain aloof, never inquiring of another what his business might be, what the tale of his life is. It's an unhealthy climate for the curious. We all carry about in our demeanor, in our garments and bearing, the sum of our lives, and it should be all that's ever asked of us to reveal. That's the way to live, just to the ends of our fingertips and no farther.

20 October

At her house, keeping a pathetic vigil in the shadows, watching the lamps come off and on, shadows sliding by the windows. Just to be near. Just to wait for . . . what? For something. What part of me longs for her so? Where does this desire take root in me? If I knew then I could rip it out! But it's twined itself about my soul again, suddenly, sending shoots into every corner of my darkness! How can it live where there is no light? How can I live without her?

No! Better to run from her, to escape her! I am sufficient to myself. I must be. For what alternative is there now than solitude? What solace is open to me but strength, my own strength exercised as I will? For what companionship am I fit for now? I who am neither this nor that!

26 October

I'm at Murcheston, and for five miles around there's not another soul alive. I feel soothed by the very knowledge that I enjoy such solitude, for I've been too much in company the past few days. Indeed, I've passed this last transformation in the heart of London and been entertained almost to death.

This most recent adventure began three days ago, rather late in the afternoon at my flat in the city. I was still asleep when an insistent knocking roused me from my slumber and summoned me to the door. It was a message from Mrs. Wattles, sent by her usual courier with instructions that it be placed in my hands and opened in the boy's presence. Presumptuous, I thought, but I was yet too bleary to take issue with a manner I knew to be more emphatic than polite. So I opened the paper and read the following:

"Your Grace, shall I offer yet another chance to obtain the thing which, if you only knew its contents, would be the dearest treasure you could ever hope to possess? Or shall I let pass again this most remarkable volume, the only copy I have ever seen of a work quite as legendary as its subject? I have before me now the treatise *On Lycanthropes and Lycanthropy* by Malachi Browne. Are you familiar with the work? Do you know the reputation it holds among the *cognoscenti*? This astonishing study, the only work of serious scholarship to record the medical basis of lycanthropy, in fact, a miracle of devoted research that presents not only the apparent manifestations of the condition, the physical machinations, but explains the causes and interior workings of the metamorphosis as well. No, even beyond all of that (if more were wanting), this textbook written, so it is rumored, by one who was himself stricken with the disease. Stricken and saved! One who discovered, if such a thing is to be believed, the only certain cure, the only available remedy for lycanthropy! If this volume might prove of interest to you, I suggest that you come at once, for the owner has only lent me the book for a short while, and only on the assurance that an offer will be forthcoming. To disappoint him a second time would be to lose the book forever. Hurry! Hurry as if all depended upon it, as I am convinced it does."

I stood unmoving for several moments as the words danced before my imagination. "A cure for lycanthropy!" I rolled the idea about in my mind for a bit. "A cure!" The notion that it could exist had never occurred to me, never once entered my thoughts. And yet, if it should be true, would I take advantage of it? For an instant I was presented with a choice I hadn't dared to dream were possible The chance to change the thing I was, to return to what I had been, a man like other men! Shall I admit the idea caused my heart to leap in my breast? Was I really so quick to quit my present state? Was it a sign of innate weakness, or simply fatigue at the precarious existence I had molded for myself? For whatever reason, I wasted little time in making my final journey to the bookshop in Black Abbots Yard.

The sun had already set when I arrived, and the Yard was deserted. I strode quickly to the store and gazed through the window before entering. As usual Mrs. Wattles was nowhere in sight. The only light was the faint glow of the same, solitary candle. No sooner was I past the threshold, however, than she materialized at her desk, black and huge, as though she were sitting there invisibly all along, like a spider hidden within the lacy strands of her web.

"Have you decided to come at last, my love?" she asked, and she sounded relieved, as though she'd been waiting a very long time.

"As quickly as I could," I replied testily, my nose filling with the odd scents of her exotic perfumes. "Your message was interesting. You should have told me before what the damned thing was about. I'd have come at once and been spared this mad rush."

"Would you have?" she asked, almost contritely, lowering herself into her chair. "We are fortunate then to have this renewed offer presented to us. But the owner, he originally placed certain restrictions upon my freedom, forbade me to communicate the contents of the book or place anything in writing. Was most emphatic upon this point. It was primarily to overcome this severe handicap that I spent the past month bargaining for just this opportunity, the chance to tell you what I have found, to conjure you here with the tempting truth."

"You might have simply come to me yourself before now, or entrusted your boy with the message verbally," I observed.

"Ah, yes," she nodded, "that I might. But again, the owner insisted that knowledge of the offer be limited to but the two of us. No other was allowed to enter into the secret. These collectors, so often an eccentric lot. And as for bringing the offer myself," she demurred, "I am not often seen about the streets of London these days." And she smiled a particularly dark and thick-lipped smile.

Had I not had my mind upon the book, her answers would have struck me as oddly inadequate, but at the moment I was scrutinizing her cluttered shelves to see if I could catch a glimpse of this treasure of all treasures that she'd gone to such lengths to acquire. When I asked if the book were available for my inspection, however, or if the owner had disallowed my actually seeing the thing before I purchased it, Mrs. Wattles replied that it was sequestered in a special cupboard at the back of her shop.

"One should always have a secret place where prying eyes cannot delve. Or do you not have such a chamber yourself, my pet? A *sanctum sanctorum*, as it were, in which to bury away that part of yourself you wish to keep private and secure?"

I acknowledged that such a cell would be a great comfort at times, and asked, rather shortly, if I could see her own little sanctuary. Taking the candle from her desk she rose without a further word and, by its weak illumination, led me on a twisting path far back into the recesses of her private forest of books. I followed silently behind her large yet gracefully gliding form for a greater distance than I'd thought the shop could contain. Back and forth, around bookcases and along passageways redolent of yellowing paper and decaying bookpaste, we journeyed through the darkness. The infernal sameness of the place, as one tall, heavy case gave way to another identical to it, made our way seem even more confusing and sinister. A sudden conceit came over me that we were some devilish Hansel and blackamoor Gretel, wandering helplessly through the woods, without a trail of bread crumbs to leave behind us. Or perhaps I was Theseus on his labyrinthine journey, following my destiny to a fatal appointment without the aid of Ariadne's thread.

As my mind toyed with such phantasms, the figure before me moved on inexorably, like a disembodied shadow. She drifted through the maze with the confidence of a black cat at home in its lair, never hesitating or pausing to glance left or right as she turned first down one path and then up another, but always looking straight on. Our pace neither slowed nor quickened. We walked rather more rapidly than I'd thought Mrs. Wattles capable of going, but she showed no strain and moved steadily forward, like the spirit of a righteous intent. We traveled this way for what seemed several minutes, when without warning our path opened up to a sort of natural clearing. To our right, a stairway led up into the darkness. Before us, stretching to the edges of our circle of candlelight, was a continuous wall of books. Set into this was a heavy wooden door, opened and exposing an inky hole.

For a time we stood before this portal, Mrs. Wattles to one side of the door with her back to me, holding the candle in one hand and fumbling for something inside her capacious black dress with the other. After perhaps half a minute spent idling there while she searched her pockets, my patience wore away and I demanded, "Might we at least proceed into the cupboard and be seated? Whatever it is you're searching for, you're as likely to find it within as without."

"How horribly thoughtless of me to keep you waiting about out here, my love," she responded. And removing her hand from her dress she rapidly spun around to face me. "Please go right in and close the door behind you." In her grasp she held a pistol pointed at my breast. A blind, monstrous rage came over me. I didn't think, didn't consider what course of action I should follow. I saw my danger and acted with an animal's cunning. Leapt at her, lunging for the weapon with one hand and her throat with the other. But Mrs. Wattles wasn't unprepared for such violence. Before I could reach her she raised the pistol up and brought it down forcibly upon my skull.

The blow stunned me, left me dazed and impotent, but failed to render me quite unconscious. I felt her huge, soft hands take hold of me and drag me into the room. She left me there, on the floor, and bolted me in. In the darkness, like a child, I lay breathing prone on the ground where she had deposited me. Slowly I recovered my strength and pulled myself up to explore my prison. A cell, little more than eight feet from side to side, the only furnishing a straw pallet in one corner. The door, solid and heavy, reinforced with iron strips. Set within it, just below the level of my chest, a hinged partition, large enough to allow a plate of food to pass through. Madness engulfed me. I clawed at this window, trying desperately to pry it open, but to no avail. Then, suddenly, the partition shot aside and candlelight streamed in. In an instant I thrust my arm through the hole, a vain attempt to grab hold of my captor, but I only flailed about in the empty air before I heard Mrs. Wattles speak.

"I would put that arm back, my dear, or I may be forced to take a coal shovel to it." The sound of her voice unleashed within me a venomous stream of invective. I shrieked every manner of threat and curse at the nigger bitch, the fat, sooty whore, swore infinite violence upon her bloated carcass if she didn't let me out at once, demanded to know what lunacy had possessed her to dare use me this way.

"My lunacy is of a very ancient and infectious sort," she explained with all the mild detachment of a physician describing the symptoms of some common ailment. "To put it succinctly, as I know you would care to have it, I fully suspect your grace of being a werewolf, and am determined to prove the truth of this to myself, with my own eyes, and then to kill you."

God, how I raged! Roaring within the black inevitability of my cage, my temper cast a shadow over my reason. I beat against the door with both fists, but my blows fell ineffectually against its sturdy mass. Had I kept my wits about me better, I might have thought to deny the charge as insane, the product of her too long confinement in this world of weird, diabolical books. But what does my beast's nature know of such guile? All I knew at the time was that I'd been found out at last. How this woman should have discovered the truth from the remoteness of her London bookshop didn't concern me. Indeed, my freedom wasn't even foremost in my mind. I'd have gladly suffered lifetime internment if only she might be placed in the cell with me. I wanted her dark throat within my grasp, to cut off the life from her lungs, to beat her to a bloody death, to eat her black heart, this was the one desire that possessed me. I continued my futile assault upon the door, weighty symbol of her temporary triumph, kept on beating at it until my hands throbbed and ached at every blow, until I could no longer stand from exhaustion but dropped to my knees, and even then I continued to pound upon the thing again and again.

I don't know when I fell insensible to the floor. I only know

that I awoke the next morning to the sound of Mrs. Wattles calling me through the window in the door. My night's sleep (if it
were in fact morning) had done little to refresh me. But my temper was much improved, and with a supreme effort I controlled
my anger. I attempted to rise, but a sharp pain coursed through
both arms, and I fell back to the ground. Managing to get up, I
held my hands before me in the faint light. They were bloodied
and swollen, a proper payment for my insanity. Mrs. Wattles offered me a plate of bread and cheese, but I let her know I couldn't
take it from her, and pushed my hands through the opening to
show the damage I'd wrought.

"I thought you might do yourself some sort of injury," she
mused as she examined them warily, cautious lest I attempt again
to grab her. "I have some medicines and bandages nearby. Keep
still while I retrieve them and I shall dress your wounds."

While she was gone I cleared my head and considered my
position. I was trapped, completely helpless, locked away and at
her mercy. Any physical confrontation was impossible. Even if I
could tear the life from her throat through that tiny opening, I'd
merely starve to death inside while her corpse rotted without. No,
I must find some way to escape my dungeon. But that would take
time, and I knew that time was something I didn't have in indefinite supply. The full moon was only two nights away, and if I
failed to effect my release before then, my transformation would
bring, not liberation, but doom.

When she returned I asked her, with a tremble of fear in my
throat, what she had planned for me.

"As I mentioned last night," she replied, "I shall keep you
here until I am convinced that you are indeed a werewolf."

"But how will you know for certain? Am I to be locked in
here with no hope of defending myself?" I asked pathetically.
What a woeful noise I tried to make!

She chuckled. "Come now, my love. Shall we abandon the
pretense that you are surprised by my accusation? Might we not

begin from the proposition that you know perfectly well why I suppose you to be a werewolf?"

"I confess that I have an interest in the subject, but it's only a childish pastime. My God, it's all superstition and myth! The literature you've provided me with is ample proof of that. Nursery tales to frighten children with, most of it. How can you for a minute suppose that werewolves exist, much less that I am one?"

She answered with a sigh, "I see we must play this game out. Very well. I shall put the evidence before you, and you tell me yourself whether my suspicions are unwarranted. One," she announced, sounding like a barrister in court, "your interest in the topic. Nothing incriminating there, but the beginning of the trail, nonetheless."

"It's nonsense," I interjected frantically, but Mrs. Wattles chose that moment to pour some astringent liquid over my hands and the stinging pain silenced me instantly.

"Two, your regular trips to Brixton and your estate. I have kept close record of your travels, Your Grace. I believe I mentioned to you once before that I have acquaintances in your country, and they have been most helpful in my investigations. Your trips coincide perfectly with the full of the moon. Now for a man to visit his ancestral home on a monthly basis is not unusual, but to do so according to a lunar calendar, that is something significant. Of course, no one else could have suspected the relationship, for no one else knew about your interest in lycanthropy. But I have made the connection, and I think it a telling one."

"That proves nothing. I'm a hunter, and the full moon allows . . ." But again she stopped my tongue, this time by grasping my right hand in a painful grip and wrapping it tightly in a bandage.

"Three, your remarkable and erratic behavior. Really, my dear, for a man in need of the most severe privacy, you seem to have gone to great lengths to attract attention. Dismissing the entire household, only to staff the manor from your tenants a few months later. Speculative ventures into experimental farming, followed after several weeks by forswearing agricultural production altogether. And now I understand that you have evicted every soul from the estate. Only the population of Brixton remains on your holdings. Did you truly believe that such actions would go unnoticed, uncommented upon? Did you feel so secure in your secret that you'd allow yourself to be made the subject of every loose tongue in the country? And that does not even include your interesting behavior in London. You have drawn the light of scrutiny upon yourself here as well, alternating as you have done the roles of recluse and rakehell. Of course, in itself that is nothing. Many a man's mood runs such extremes. Great is the number of lords who act the tyrant in private and the humanitarian in public. But as part of a larger pattern, it is revealing. It speaks of a man with a secret, something so awful to consider that he cannot even allow other men near him, lest the truth be revealed."

I was fascinated now by the fullness of her understanding, the way she was able to dissect my life and reassemble it before my eyes this neatly, showing me things that had been invisible to me before. I thought I'd been devilishly clever all along, and here, this woman so many miles from Murcheston had little trouble in following my every step as though she were beside me the entire time.

"Four, the inexplicable disappearance of that young boy. Of course, until then I did not take my fears seriously. I excused them as the wild imaginings of an old and lonely woman, but when news reached me that a boy had been missed, that you had shut down the estate and left the county even before the mystery was made known, I could not afford to blind myself any longer to the truth."

"What truth is that? That I am a monster? A devil?" I allowed a note of wildness to shrill my voice, the desperate cry of a sane man at the mercy of dementia. "How can you think that I am a werewolf? Such things aren't real! They don't exist!"

"But they do exist, my love. You know they do, and so do I."

"How can you know such things?" I shouted. "How can you know what cannot be?"

She gripped my hands firmly, painfully. "My entire life has been a merry dance with things that cannot be, my dear. I was raised in the streets and villages of Haiti. Have you never been there? It is a land where the eternal spirits of the earth live alongside the sons and daughters of time. There I learned many strange things, and saw many stranger still. When I was brought to London as a bride, I made the most of my unique understanding of the world. That is how I came to open this bookshop and cater to those who toy with a realm of mysteries that I know to be very real, very true. Witchcraft, spirits, gods, voodoo. It is all as genuine, my dear, as madness. This universe of ours is a terrible place, filled with terrible things. It is a universe with which I communicate freely. For me, to accept that you are a werewolf is as easy as to accept that you are the Duke of Darnley."

"I don't know," I said plaintively. "Perhaps such things can be. Maybe you have seen them. But that's still no explanation of why you think I'm one of these monsters? What have I done to deserve this wild speculation?"

"As I said, it was the disappearance of the boy that first alerted me to the danger. Naturally, you are believed to know more of this affair than you admit. In this as well you have been reckless, my love," she admonished, tending now to my left hand, "careless and overconfident. Like any man tempted by the power of that other world, you were seduced by your own cleverness. Having fallen prey to this monstrous curse, you found a way to convince yourself that what is wrong is right, that what is evil is natural and just. And so, caught in the embrace of delusion, you have left a track behind you which is wide and clear, for those who know the signs."

"Signs?" I screamed. "How dare you speak to me of signs! Innuendo, suspicion, hearsay, these aren't facts upon which a sane man would justify kidnapping and murder."

"But I am not finished, Your Grace. There is one fact more,

the fifth and most damaging of all, and yet the one which you have failed to take into account. Perhaps because it is so obvious. You have been seen. You know that you have. A couple you terrorized at Darnley Well, they saw you, observed you more closely than you realize. The boy is a good hand with a bit of charcoal or a pencil. He's been busy entertaining the curious, making sketches of you, the wolf larger and fiercer than anything ever known in the county. He relishes the chance to relate his adventure, recreating your features for any who will ask him, proving his bravery with every sketch, but proving more than that. Much more. Here, here is a sketch he made, my dear, procured for me by my acquaintance in Brixton."

She released my hands and held up in front of the opening a large sheet of brown paper. I peered through the door and saw for the first time myself, my teeth bared and snarling, my eyes filled with lustful desire, my ears pointed and bristling in anger. It was a werewolf, there could be no question to a knowing eye. I felt all hope of shaking her faith ebb swiftly away as I stared into my own ravenous image.

"When I saw this," she continued, "I knew beyond any doubt that you were the beast. And I began in earnest to devise a plan to lure you here. It was not easy. I had to find a way to pique your interest, so that you would rush here quickly, with no chance to tell anyone, so I might detain you in this way."

"And the book by Browne? The cure for lycanthropy?"

"You must forgive me. A ruse, my love, a fabrication."

Mrs. Wattles folded up the sketch again. Her case was impressive, I might even say conclusive, except for one point. "If you are so well convinced that I'm the creature in that sketch," I asked her, "why preserve my life in this way? Why didn't you kill me when you had the opportunity?"

She was silent, but I could tell that the question was echoing in her mind. Why hadn't she killed me? Why this elaborate trap? I knew it! In spite of her wealth of evidence and carefully constructed arguments, she didn't believe, not entirely, didn't perfectly believe the truth. She doubted, and so long as she doubted, I had hope.

"Your hands should feel better soon," she said, not offering an answer. "The medicine I applied will still the pain. You must not exert yourself in that way again, my dear. Such futile demonstrations can do you no good. You cannot escape, and only further harm will come of such actions."

"Tell me one last thing," I begged her. "How will you know, how will you be convinced that I'm not what you say I am? What can I do to clear myself of this insane charge?"

"Do?" she replied, surprised at my question. "Do? I will tell you. On the night of the next full moon, I will remove you from this place and take you to a special chamber where we may sit across from each other, where I can watch you closely. On that night, if you will save yourself, you must simply do nothing." And she handed in the plate of bread and cheese again.

I was able to take it this time, and as I did so the window shut and I was once more thrust into darkness. Still, in spite of all, my spirits were buoyed up by our talk. My two needs had been answered. She doubted, I could count on that. She wouldn't kill me until the last possible minute, and so I knew what time I had. And I also had a way out of my cell. *She* would bring me out. It was certainly her sense of curiosity, her desire to see me transform that compelled her to this fatal error. All I required now was patience. That, and a reliance on the instincts that had saved me so often before.

That day and the next passed in relative quiet. Twice each day Mrs. Wattles arrived with a plate of food, and twice each day I pled my innocence to her. But she said as little as possible, and I felt confident that, until she saw with her own eyes the transformation begin, I was perfectly safe. In the meantime, I passed the dark hours readying myself, sitting calmly, listening to my inner nature, feeling the peace that only the beast feels. And I thought long and hard about what she had told me, how careless I'd been in hiding my secret from the world. Of course she was right. My confinement was proof enough of that. But where had I erred? What was my mistake?

It was, I finally decided, in keeping the scope of my precautions so small. Attempting to live in two worlds at once, I had at first secured my solitude only during my transformations. But this was too shortsighted, and soon I was forced to extend my measures to the entire household throughout the month. Even this proved inadequate, and I had to eliminate Old Grey and his family, and then all of Darnley Well itself. But by then it was too late. My secret was out. Not the secret itself, of course, but the fact that I possessed a secret, which in the end proved just as damning. As Cabrini had predicted it would. And so it was only through timidity that I'd failed, and now my human weakness was returned to betray me. I cursed my former self and the half-measures I'd taken, and I vowed, should I escape this trap, this snare I'd set for myself, that I'd never be weak again. Whatever I have to do in the future, I will do. Nothing and no one in all the world is as important as my own safety, that much is paramount. It must always be so.

It was near the end of the second day, as I was sitting on the floor just finishing the meal of cold beef and spinach that she had left, that I heard the bolt of the door draw back and Mrs. Wattles order me out of my cell. I rose at once and slowly opened the door. I don't think I was anxious about the test before me, but I was eager, and had to calm myself lest I appear too calculating.

She greeted me with a candle in one hand and the pistol in the other. Motioning, she politely ordered me to climb the stairs leading up to my left. I ascended. The second story of the bookshop was identical to the first, and she directed me through the forest of bookcases until we arrived at what I can only describe as a little room. Actually, it was nothing more than an open space from which the shelves had been pushed back to create a clearing some ten or twelve feet on a side. But the impression was definitely of a private chamber with books for walls, complete with a bed, a table and chair, a large chest and a desk similar to the one in the front room below.

"I am sorry," she said as she placed the candle on the table, "that I have not two chairs, but I rarely entertain, and space is at such a premium here that I have never owned but the one. Still, if you would be so good as to pull over that chest, I feel we can make do." This I did, placing it opposite to the chair, all the while with the muzzle of the gun fixed upon me. "You may take the chair," she offered graciously, and I sat down as the lady rested herself upon the chest. We sat for a moment in silence, she watching me closely, I looking about, measuring my surroundings, judging my chances.

I began after a time, speaking in as weak a voice as I could muster, "What are you going to do with me?"

"Is it not obvious, Your Grace?" she said, sounding rather irritable and preoccupied. "We shall sit here until the moon begins to rise, at which time you shall start to transform. I shall then kill you."

"No, no," I cried, "I mean when I fail to transform, what shall you do with me?"

A deep crease appeared on her brow, and I silently triumphed that my suspicion was correct. She doubted. "If that occurs," Mrs. Wattles said softly, "and I do not think that it is likely, but if it does, I shall show you the door."

"You won't shoot me, then?" I asked excitedly.

"My love, if I am mistaken in this, then you are free to report me to the authorities as a public menace and have me brought before the magistrate."

"If I do you will surely be hanged," I let her know.

"I am aware of that," she replied coldly. "Let it be a testament to my conviction."

"That I am a werewolf? I still can't comprehend how a woman of your intelligence can suppose such a thing possible. I admit the evidence you've cited is suggestive, but, good God, this is the nineteenth century! Surely you don't admit that werewolves exist, not really."

"I believe what the facts lead me to believe, Your Grace," and she sounded positively annoyed now. "I learned long ago never to discount what the old tales teach. There is more truth in them than modern men give credit for. I do confess that the idea was a long time brewing within me before I acknowledged it, but believe it I do. There is no better explanation for the evidence."

"I don't know about that. I hadn't thought of myself as requiring an explanation until recently, and I'm unprepared to offer one. But let's suppose you're right, that this wild fantasy of yours is true and I'm a werewolf. What of that?" I begged, leaning forward across the table. "Why must I be killed? Mightn't I be allowed to live my life in peace?"

"Peace?" she cried, waving her pistol carelessly about to emphasize her words. "Can you honestly speak of peace? Your Grace, you are now by your very nature a murderer. You have killed once that I know of, and would have done so again, and will continue to do so unless you are stopped. The werewolf is a monster that feeds on blood and death, a savage, unholy thing that has no place in creation. Other predators shun man if they can, but the werewolf seeks him out, makes him the single object of his lust. You have felt this yourself, the irresistible desire for human flesh. Admit that you have! Peace? What peace have you given your tenants? What peace did you give that boy? Here is the only peace that you afforded them, and it is the only peace you shall receive from me." She lifted the pistol before me as the symbol of the eternal peace she promised. And in doing so, she turned the muzzle away from me.

On the instant I sprang forward, upsetting the table and extinguishing the candle. A shot rang out and I felt the heat of the bullet as it ripped through an empty fold in my coat. The last thing I saw in the flash of the powder was Mrs. Wattles, a look of shock and horror in her white eyes, as she fell backwards off the chest and onto the floor. I was in the dark now, darkness complete and utter, and I knew what to do. I leapt over the woman's prone figure, strong and confident now in my element, able to see while she was blind, free to act while she was trapped. I wrenched the pistol from her grasp and cast it aside in a single, fluid move. Then, snatching the pillow from her bed and strad-dling her thrashing figure with my knees, I lowered it onto her face. With all my weight I pressed down as she fought for air, and her strength was such that she almost threw me off. But I pushed down even harder, felt her nose crack under the pressure, heard her muffled screams. It took only a few moments for her to die. Once her struggles were finished, I gave a final push against the pillow and then raised it from her face. I placed my hand against her mouth, felt the wetness of the blood from her crushed nose. But there was no breath. I threw myself back against the bed in exhaustion, and then the heat began to swell inside me, and I knew the moon had risen.

I spent the night in the forest of her bookshop, gorging myself on her fat flesh. I'd almost expected it to taste different than white man's meat, gamier and wilder. It was the same, though. Delicate. Luscious. I wandered far through the deep, varied darkness of the shelves. Her smell permeated the place, and I never lost my sense of where I was no matter how far back I explored in that maze. I was unnerved by the unnatural stillness, but after a time I caught the sounds of mice scurrying about within the walls, and heard the birds nesting under the eaves and in the attic, and I was soothed by their presence.

The moon finally set and I rose, naked, in that weird, book-lined chamber. My clothes lay scattered about the floor, and her half-eaten corpse was spread out beside them. I was now faced with the problem of disguising my handiwork. No chance of burial here in the city, as I was accustomed to do with my victims. I didn't take long to decide upon a course of action, though. The obvious solution suggested itself almost at once.

First, I had to work my way back to the front of her store. It wouldn't do to get lost among her books, not now. It took me some time. I removed a volume from a nearby shelf to start with and proceeded on my way about and around the bookcases, leaving crumpled pages behind me as a guide, picking them up again as I followed dead ends and crossed and recrossed my path. Within half an hour I emerged into the front room, sunlight streaming through its window. Then, retracing my steps by following the paper path I'd left, I returned to Mrs. Wattles and began to hunt about her chamber in search of a match.

I finally located one in the chest by the table and lit the candle that I'd extinguished the night before. By its light I took a final look at the lady. She stared back at me, eyes wide, with a placid countenance. The foolish bitch. She had no reason to do what she did. She was in no danger from me. What possessed her? Why did she feel such a passionate hatred for me, for my kind? Is it inbred in men to loathe a being so much like them in appearance, so superior in cunning and instinct? I knelt down beside her, stared deeply into those unfathomable eyes. Is that what man hates about werewolves? The fact that we, in our sympathy with nature, feel the world more wholly than man can ever hope to do? For I am the lost soul of men, that abandoned, forgotten part that feels and does not reason, that knows and doesn't think. I am man as he was meant to be. I'm Adam, living at one with nature. This inescapable hatred, it's the power of envy, the desire of the imprisoned human self to see all creation fettered and chained to insensitivity. Man has lived away from Eden for so long that he secretly wishes to destroy the only path that can ever return him to paradise. I stared at Mrs. Wattles. "Is that the reason you hate me?" I asked silently. "Is that the cause? Can you no longer live with the knowledge that someone has discovered the way back to nature?"

Her empty eyes offered their response: a blank.

I rose from beside her. Then, beginning from her bedside and working carefully toward the stairway, down the stairs and back to the front of the store, I removed a single volume from each bookcase I passed and, laying it open in some airy spot on a nearby shelf, I lit it. By the time I reached the front room, I could hear the fire blazing lustily overhead. There would be little enough to find of Mrs. Wattles, and doubtless the authorities would be satisfied with the obvious explanation.

I was for an instant struck by my own folly at not having considered how to leave the shop without being detected by other residents of the yard, but luck was my accomplice in this. It was Sunday, and since few people actually lived in Black Abbots, there was no one about to see a cloaked figure hurry away from the building as the first flames began to lick from the upper windows.

I walked cautiously to my flat, taking a roundabout way merely out of prudence. I didn't rest when I arrived home, but packed a quick bag and left at once. I had to return here, get back to my real home, Murcheston and the woods. I feel so alive now, so gloriously, deliriously real. I relished the act, taking her life, not out of some sense of vengeance or justice enacted against my captor, but for the killing itself, the feeling of her strength as it ebbed away beneath me, of her frantic struggles as her death drew near, and the sound of her final muffled screams as her breath emptied itself from her lungs. The exuberant sense of power at the moment of my victory, it's still about me like a scent, as intensely satisfying as any sensation I've known. What sweet power I feel, the power of one in command of himself, of his world! No one, nothing can take from me this sense of rightness in everything I do!

I'm sitting now in my private study. The darkness lies thick about me, and the weak candlelight only makes the black seem deeply lush, velvety and beautiful. Somewhere, some miles away out there, men are huddled together about their fires, shivering in dread of the world surrounding them, closing in upon them, taking away their light, their life. But I? I piss on the light of men, and revel in the darkness that follows. I think I shall run tonight, go out into the woods and romp naked through the trees. And if some wayward fool comes skulking across my path, I might try if I can tear him to pieces with my bare hands. That would be something worth doing, I think.

15

The Final Entry

4 November

Alone.

I went to Darnley Well today. Don't know what drew me to the place. I've spent my days wandering about the woods mostly, visiting familiar spots. The houses are boarded. Straw and hay blow idly through the lanes and drift up against walls and fences, accumulating in rotting piles. The only life is a tribe of cats that's taken up residence in the smaller cottages. They seem like prosperous tenants and I didn't disturb them. Doubtless the abandoned corn and fallow fields produce a fat crop of mice, and such industry should hardly be interfered with.

As I walked through this ghostly landscape, images came to haunt me, Wattles and Liam, and even Old Grey, dying with a silent curse upon his lips. I relive the moments I shared with them at the end, like a hunter recalling his most rewarding kill. I remember them, and enjoy the feeling of strength, that experience of force exerted against force, until only *my* will exists, *my* desire. I fulfill myself each time I take a life, replenishing the power within me, making myself that much more my own. God, what a thrill it is, to test one's life against another's! I come out of each contest more alive than before. More certain of the rightness of my being. More secure in my oneness with nature.

Some marks of the former life of the place were left behind. A chair resting outside a door. Tattered curtains blowing through shattered windowpanes. I passed by these signs of decaying domesticity and wondered whether, in another world, a separate reality, some form of such simple pleasures might have been mine. Might I have shared my life with another? Would I have found peace there, in the marriage bed, the father of some sprawling brood? Is there some secret to that existence that escapes me, a love I do not understand? Where is she now, and what is she doing?

And where am I now? Huddled here, alone, bereft of all companionship, in hiding, smothering my light, almost extinguishing it. I, who am so much stronger than those fools who throw away their nights in weakness and despair. Only their numbers keep me where I am. I know what would happen if I presented myself to them, tried to explain the truths I've discovered. They'd hunt me down and destroy me. Like ants swarming over a lion and devouring him with ten million stinging bites. Detestable vermin crawling across the face of nature, obscuring the beauty of her handiwork, the sweet violence of her world, where all is simple, all perfect. Strength is rewarded with strength. Weakness is the only sin. There must be a way, some chance for me to live the life I know I'm destined to live. But how? How when I'm surrounded by hatred and stupidity? How?

6 November

I went into Brixton today, for food and drink. There are only myself and the horse at Murcheston, twin creatures living apart from our kind. Not even in my imagination can I conjure up an idyllic world of lycanthropes, some community peopled by werewolves, stocked with men. Predator and prey, living together during the month so that you can't tell one from the other. Until the full moon.

But look how far I live from such an Eden. Brixton is a trap for me. I wandered about for a while after placing my order with the grocer. All eyes turned in my direction, wherever I went, ever under scrutiny. "The mad duke." I know that's what they call me. I've heard the bastards whispering it when they thought I was too far away to hear. Too far for *me* to hear, with the ears of a werewolf? They'd be amazed at all I've heard!

I got away from that place as quickly as I was able. But I could only return here. There is no middle ground. Not yet. Not yet. No safe, happy place where I can enjoy the peace of being my true self. Is it weakness for me to hide like this, or prudence? I must concoct a plan, some way to put an end to this netherlife I live.

9 November

I had a visitor today. I was wandering about the grounds idly, contemplating the sky, dark and penetrating, when I heard a voice hallooing. Without thinking I leapt into the nearest shadow and crouched down low against the wall. Instinct, of course. In a moment I calmed myself and stepped forward, though for all my isolation I felt intruded upon by this interruption to my aimless routine. My mood was not brightened when, turning the corner of the manor and striding out into the main drive, I beheld the bemused countenance of Mr. Kirkland standing beside a withered old horse.

"What is it, vicar?" I said, greeting him perhaps too brusquely, for he seemed uncomfortable at my rough manner.

"How do you do, Your Grace," he stammered. Maybe his meekness softened my heart, for I led him inside to the study and offered to put a kettle on. This he accepted, I think more from a desire to be left alone to gather his wits than through any need for refreshment. I busied myself in the kitchen, and when I returned he seemed more at ease.

"A pleasure to see you, vicar," I lied. "What brings you out so far from Brixton?"

"Oh, the weather, the weather I should say," answering lie for lie, since it had been threatening rain all morning. "Just knocking about the countryside, you know, enjoying the day and thought to look in and see how Your Grace is faring."

Every nervous gesture and furtive glance from the man told me that he'd come with a purpose, one he was obviously embarrassed to introduce, for he had yet to look me in the eye. Something in this situation appealed to me at last, and I thought I might toy with him a bit. I determined to let the conversation run along whatever course he wished to take it, throwing in his way as many obstacles as I could.

But trying to confuse Kirkland is rather like putting a blindfold on a blind man, and soon the mouse had the cat running about in frustrating circles. We talked about agriculture, though neither of us has any practical interest in it; about coal mining, though together we know somewhat less than the average schoolboy concerning it; about the schedule of trains through Brixton, though we each have little use for the information; about the next elections, though they're too far in the future to be of any importance; about the public morality, concerning which we already knew the other's opinion; in short, about every topic the vicar could think of except the one on his mind. We went on in this way for at least an hour, and I began to feel my enthusiasm for our game cool, when he at last screwed up his courage and launched into the real reason for his visit.

"I suppose Your Grace wonders what has brought me to your door," he began.

"I'd thought it was the weather," I answered.

"The weather?" he repeated, startled. "Oh dear me, no. The weather is most inclement for such a journey. I have come to inquire after your health," he confessed at last, addressing the fire.

As the health of the fire was of little consequence, I could only assume that he meant *my* health. Of course, whether he meant the one or the other, they seemed equally out of the way of the old boy's business, and poor enough cause to venture so far on such an oppressive morning. I asked him bluntly, "Why should my health be of interest to you?"

He didn't seem prepared to answer the question, however, for he looked at me as if I'd just posed an incomprehensible paradox. Kirkland knitted his brow for an instant, folded his hands together as if he were about to pray, and said, "Your Grace, the old duke, your grandfather, was more than just a kind benefactor to me. I considered him a friend, and always did my utmost to serve him well, even though that meant at times reminding him of his position when he was somewhat too free in his manner. He was a good man, though not a perfect one."

"I remember the Governor, Mr. Kirkland," I replied, feeling uncomfortably like I was about to hear a sermon.

"He was not, as I say, a perfect man, and yet he always was attentive to my guidance, poor though it must have been. He was rather like the young Saint Augustine, wanting to be good, but not too good and not all the time. A gracious man, who was not above allowing himself to be reprimanded by a humble cleric such as myself."

"And doubtless your reproofs were sufficient to show him the true and narrow path, vicar. But what has this to do with me?" Yet I knew what it had to do with me, and so steeled myself for the accusations of cruelty towards my dependents, neglect of the public welfare, unnatural seclusion, and whatever other sins he was prepared to name to my credit.

But he offered no reproof against any of these. "I only mention this," he went on, looking directly at me now, "because I know the great respect you hold for the old duke, and so you might not think me presumptuous in what I have to say. Your Grace, you are a very young man, and I am a very old one. I am aware that we share little enough in our tastes or experience that might establish the basis of a communion. I only wish to observe that you are deeply troubled. I do not know from whence your difficulties stem, nor even what they are, but they are evident to me, so very evident that I felt, as a Christian gentleman, I could no longer stand idly to one side and witness your suffering. I do not ask your confidence. I cannot ask so much from a man of the world. I only want you to know that I pray for you, and that if I can do anything tangible to help you find solace, please, please, never hesitate to ask me."

That was all he had to say, and he soon left. I offered him a carriage, for the sky was by now looking fierce, but he preferred to try his luck with only his poor nag for company. It was the most extraordinary interview. For my part, I still can't make out what it means. Fool that he is, why should he have traveled all that distance, with thunderclouds threatening the whole way, merely to say that he was concerned for me? If he were suddenly overcome with the desire to perform good works, I think there must have been some more likely candidate within his new sphere at Brixton, someone closer to salvation, who might have benefited from his ministering attentions more than I.

Doubtless there's some motive in his madness. Likely he fears for the security of his new parish. Thinks he might just show himself to me, play at being interested, and so keep his benefice sure with as little bother as necessary. Or he could be, even at this moment, telling his new congregation all the strange and insane things that he witnessed here. There might even be some past indiscretion to be atoned for, an ancient trespass against the Old Governor, and now he does penance by looking in on the old boy's crazy heir. Whatever his real reason for coming here, I'm certain he feels holier for his pains.

There's the difference between us. I'm at one with my desires. I can't hide what I truly want from myself, the way men do. My actions are all of a piece, all derived from the same self-interest that directs all creatures. While men blunder about in the day-light, blinded by the delusion that their souls are somehow untouched by Providence, that they're superior to other animals in degree and not merely in kind, I acknowledge my debt to the beast within me. I embrace it. Lie with it. That's where I find my peace, if only men will leave me to it. But no, I'll never know peace in a world of men. I must battle them for every restful moment I enjoy. True freedom can never be mine so long as I'm alone in this world.

10 November

This is my final entry. I'm returning to London tomorrow. I'll stay there until the time of my next transformation. There's no reason not to go. Living out here, so far from anyone, it's simply too difficult. I can't keep food from spoiling, and I must go into Brixton now at least three times a week. I'm becoming ridiculous. Rather live in London during the month and come back here at the full moon. The way I've been doing. The way I'll do every month for the rest of my life. Damn all men! Damn them to a hell of bestial tortures! I, who am so much more than they, trapped in a life I must keep hidden. No way out for me. No escape. Helpless with all my strength and cunning, as surely as I was held captive by Mrs. Wattles in her cell.

And the incessant pain of my solitude overflows the stops I've erected against it! Where is she? What is her life like, so quiet and peaceful, so much the domestic nightmare? I know her soul far better than he can, better than she knows it herself! How can she live in such a world that he can offer her? Yet what have I to offer in exchange? What can I give but terror and suffering? My deepest soul I must keep from the one thing, the only thing I love or ever shall! There are no tears that can wash this hurt away. Elizabeth! I see you damned to a mundane hell, a pale earth too cold to ignite the flame that smolders in your soul! And I am captive, chained in a place where I cannot reach you, cannot rescue you!

I should stay away, but I can't. I'm returning to London because she is there. I'll leave this journal behind. There's no sense anymore in taking it with me. It affords me nothing but pain now. It's all a wild game, writing for no one to read. My hopes of someday revealing myself to the world are lost. What rubbish it all was! What crap, to think I could ever safely say to the world, "I am Darnley, the werewolf!" I'm through with it all.

I am the mute prophet of self-awareness, the modern Cassandra, doomed to know the truth that no man will believe. Destined to a life above the mob, high above the sprawling, stupid, fucking hordes of humanity. Yet, should I once reveal myself, I'd be brought crashing down among them and be devoured by their damned, bloody, rotten weakness. I could kill them all, rip their steaming guts out for their blindness that makes me suffer so! Damn them! Damn them, every last one!

Book Three

16

Meredith's Return

The fire had long gone out. Whitby leaned forward in his chair, just infringing upon the pale, unhealthy light cast by the sputtering gas lamp as Meredith turned over the final leaf of the manuscript. For a long moment there was perfect silence between the two men, one spent and exhausted by the labor of reading endless pages, the other frozen in his chair, incapable or unwilling to break the spell cast by this unreal narrative. Meredith rose at last and proceeded to the small table, where he poured a glass of wine. "Thirsty work," he muttered.

Whitby started at the observation. "You're not finished, are you?" he demanded, a desperate note sneaking into his voice.

Meredith remained standing, but shook his head slowly. "No, not yet." And he took another drink of wine. "What's left of the tale is mine to tell. No other human has ever heard it, save one. And she is gone now these many years." He looked into Whitby's eyes as he said this, found there the hunger and anticipation that had been building in the man, growing until he could not mask it anymore. He must have the story. Meredith smiled his grim smile and turned briefly away. For this had been hard, to relive those events he had tried so vainly to forget. And what lay ahead was harder still, to tell his own story, not Darnley's anymore. Yet, it must be done.

"Well?" Whitby coaxed.

Meredith closed his eyes and made himself return to that night, the horror and the lunacy that engulfed him on that long journey back to London. The train had screamed through the dark, hurtling Meredith deeper into the madness of Darnley's nightmare. For what else could it be, he had reasoned. For hours he fell into that pit of utter madness, shocked by the enormity of Darnley's dementia, but also awestruck and fascinated, like the visitors to the asylums who come as to a theater, seeking entertainment in the weird antics of the madmen, passive onlookers to a wild pageant of tortured humanity, comforted to know that they can leave when they will while the actors are doomed forever to tread the stage.

What other explanation was there than madness? The thing was too insupportable! A werewolf! He had supposed that Darnley was living under a shadow of some kind, a scandal forcing his odd behavior upon him. He had assumed these problems were tangible and that help might be affected somehow. As he read this cursed document, however, and peered into the recesses of a mind laid waste, Meredith felt undone by the prospect of even facing Darnley again. They had been friends once, companions, almost brothers, and yet, as the one's life had passed in a haze of commonplace cares and worries, the other had descended into this lunacy, this werewolf's dream. How could it be other than a dream? It was so much easier to believe that Darnley was a madman than to suppose even for a moment that what was scrawled across those pages were true.

He was equally troubled by the catalogue of slayings. What did these delusions of murder and blood portend? Meredith had left Darnley resting fitfully in his valet's bed, in the very heart of his home, but totally incapacitated, his leg shattered, unable to move without suffering the most horrendous pain. Surely it was impossible that he could prove somehow dangerous, wasn't it?

And pervading all, what of Elizabeth? She had never mentioned those two furtive meetings with Darnley. Of course, Meredith knew that they had for a time been lovers, in their youth, before there could be any question of infidelity. He had entered into his marriage with open eyes about his wife's past with Darnley, and had trusted that such things might be forgotten. Forgotten by her, yes, but he had never counted on Darnley's fierce passion. And now the least intimation of an understanding between the two of them, and the question erupted within him, "Why had she chosen me? What could there be about me to hold onto a creature so brilliant?" He felt no anger towards her, hardly suspected her constancy. But what hope was there for him to keep such love as hers, so passionate and fierce at times, and he, a simple man leading a boring life? These thoughts finally pushed all others out of his mind as the train sped along its inexorable path, the fiery machine unable to turn aside from its road, like Meredith himself, forced to advance toward a dark and dreadful appointment.

The train pulled into Waterloo Station and Meredith leapt into a cab, a dark fear rising within him, an anxiety he had been trying to deny for love of his friend and sympathy with his pathetic condition. It plagued him all the long, winding way back through London and grew steadily as he approached his return. As the hansom brought him nearer to his door, a presentiment of disaster crept over him. And when the cab at last turned the corner into the familiar lane and Meredith saw an odd collection of carriages sitting about on the street, he suddenly knew a cold dread in the very center of his heart. He jumped from the cab before it had stopped, threw some coppers to the cabby, bounded up the steps, raced inside. He burst into a scene that at first helped to steady his nerves, so calm it appeared to his fevered mind. Gathered in the front parlor were several men, all strangers, and Meredith's first response, as heartless as it later seemed, was one of studied politeness, the immediate recourse of the civilized man.

"Gentlemen," he said without thinking, "I am Charles Meredith. How may I help you?"

One of the company stepped forward, a heavily whiskered man of formidable build, wearing a dark, dusty suit and possessing a haggard and weary appearance. He took a deep breath, expanding his already expansive breast, and, as gently as he could, stated, "Mr. Meredith, I'm afraid I must report an incident to you."

With a great rush the whole situation unfolded itself to Meredith's eyes—a murderous fiend sleeping in his home, Elizabeth and the baby nearby. At once he heard the screams, the hellish cries, the anguished pleas. The horrific vision played itself out before him on the instant, for it took but an instant more to recall the one fact that he should have considered from the beginning. The moon had been full last night. Without waiting to hear more, Meredith darted up the staircase—flying, not running—only to be stopped in horror at the top of the stairs. The picture before him was enough to justify all his wild fears. Furniture was overturned and shattered. Great gashes had been cut in the rugs, and the floorboards beneath were gouged and scored. He staggered down the hall. When he came to the guest room, where Prowell had been put up since Darnley's convalescence, the sight sucked all the life from his lungs. A cold sweat burst across his brow and the fluid in his veins ran cold and thick through a still, frozen heart, as the shriek echoed silently in his brain, "All true! Dear God, it's all true!"

About the room, on the floor, on the walls, even on the ceiling, blood, dried and black, was congealed, so thickly in spots that it clotted. Not a soul was there. The bed looked oddly tidy, with one corner neatly turned down as if ready for a night of slumber. But lying just within the threshold was a large mass, like a bundle of soiled linens, draped with a blanket. Meredith reached down to this pile at his feet and drew back the cover.

It was Prowell. Or it had been Prowell, for only with an effort of imagination could one reconstruct that collection of meat and clothing into a human shape. What was left of his entrails lay splayed out on the carpet. His face had been mostly torn away from the bone. His arms and legs looked unharmed, however, and it was by an unusual mole on his right wrist that Meredith recognized the man. The gentlemen he had left in the parlor now came up to him. One of them took him roughly by the shoulders, pulling him away from that grotesque figure. Meredith turned and was violently sick.

He didn't allow himself time to recover fully, for his worst fears were still not answered. Wiping his mouth clean with his sleeve, he looked upon the fellow assisting him and whispered only, "Elizabeth?"

"She is well, sir," the young man said, and Meredith felt again a cold emptiness in his vitals.

"Your wife has sustained some minor injury," the weary fellow added from behind him. "A scratch. You have a brave lady there, sir. A very courageous lady, indeed."

Meredith's world congealed about him as he heard the words. Was there anything these men might have told him more terrible than this, that Elizabeth had been hurt? But hurt how? Hurt by whom, by what? He pulled himself up and bolted back out into the hall, raced wildly to his bedchamber. As he neared the door, he could see that it was damaged severely, mauled and mutilated. There was a gaping hole in one of the panels, as though something had dug its way through. He rushed to be at his wife's side, but when he reached the room, he was met by a large man who detained him. Meredith struggled with him, tried to break free and get past, but was held easily in the man's tight grip, as if he were nothing more than a child.

"My wife!" he cried, over and over. "My Elizabeth! God, let me see her!"

"She's fine, sir," the man said, never loosening his hold. "The doctor's with her now and he says she's fine. It's just a cut along her arm. It's not even very deep, sir. Just a couple of stitches was all, sir. Five or six. She put up a game fight against the beast, but she's fine now."

Every effort these fools made to console him only fueled Meredith's madness, for the evidence he saw no longer allowed of any interpretation but the one, the single, impossible, deranged fact that everything he had read was true, all of it, the murders, the transformations. The monstrous wickedness of the whole nightmare was as real as the man lying dead and devoured in his home, as the hole in the door, as Elizabeth resting in the grip of what unthinkable fate he dared not imagine. And so the news that his wife had been brave, that she had fought valiantly, that she had been only slightly hurt, took on a terrifying significance that only he in the whole world could appreciate. He and one other, who was gone. Meredith collapsed in tears of despair.

"Llewelyn," he heard the weary man say sternly from behind him once again.

The fellow restraining him answered as though giving a report. "The doctor says she needs sleep now, sir. He's given the lady a sedative, and she should rest comfortably for several hours."

"Very well," the other returned. "I'll take over from here." Meredith felt large hands grasp him gently. "We'll just have a peek in, all right?" whispered the weary man. "Just look in so you can see for yourself that she's well."

They tortured him with these petty reassurances, but Meredith had neither strength nor courage enough to tell them why he feared that she was not well, that she was in fact more desperately cursed than they could ever comprehend. Instead, he allowed himself to be led to her side like a confused infant. He didn't notice the doctor, nor did he see anything but his beloved lying peacefully, her left arm bandaged from the wrist to the elbow. He couldn't cry, not even now, could only stare and imagine what might lie ahead. A voice, he did not know whose, whispered in his ear, "The baby is well, too, sir."

After a minute, he was taken out of the room and practically carried down to the parlor, where the men he had seen earlier, municipal constables and a few detectives from Scotland Yard, had reassembled. They related all of the story that they knew, but it was not much. Elizabeth had as yet been unable to say anything, and the only report of events came from Blaine, the butler, who had hidden in a wardrobe most of the night while the maid and cook cowered in their rooms. The baby's nanny was evidently a material witness as well, but had been terrified into mute insensibility and had yet to utter a word.

The police report held that early in the morning, before the lamplighters were about, the constable, while making his final rounds of the night, was accosted by Blaine running down the middle of the street in his nightshirt. The man was frantic, claiming that a lion had got into the house and was at that moment murdering the mistress.

While the constable stated that he didn't believe the story at first, owing to Blaine's reputation in the neighborhood as a drinker, he naturally felt that he should look into the matter, if for no other purpose than to put Blaine safely to bed. The front door was locked, and as no one answered the constable's knocks, he had to force an entry through the back way by the kitchen—alone, for Blaine refused to return with him inside.

The house was quiet except for the sound of a child's cries coming from somewhere upstairs. The man took a quick look about. It was apparent that there had been some disturbance in the back by the servant's quarters, for a door down that hall had been quite thrown off its hinges. The constable took a knife from the pantry and, holding up his lantern, proceeded down to where the splintered door lay athwart the passage.

He found Prowell's lodgings a shambles, shredded from one corner to the other, and the door to Blaine's room across the way ripped and cracked top to bottom, though still standing as if by some magic. The man then turned and made his way to the front of the house, the baby's whimpers urging him forward all the while. He moved through the kitchen and out into the foyer, up the stairs and cautiously towards the end of the hall, where the cries seemed to be coming from. As he passed the guest room he glanced in. His mouth went dry at the ghastly spectacle of Prowell eviscerated at his feet. The constable fell back against the balustrade in horror, but he instantly recovered himself, more urgently resolved than ever to find the crying child and to rescue it from whatever ungodly terror lurked within the house. Or so he reported.

Proceeding down the hallway, he found the door of the bedchamber closed, but with a gaping hole in the panel as if someone had tried to rip the boards physically asunder with an ax. He reached in and unlatched it. Elizabeth, pale and unconscious, with a small pool of blood glistening at her side, lay on the floor just within. The nanny was sitting bolt upright in a corner of the room, shocked into immobility. The infant, wailing, was clutched tightly to her bosom. There was no clue as to who or what had so devastated the place.

Blaine's version of what happened prior to this discovery had been difficult to come by, for the man was in such an excited state that he could not tell the thing coherently for many hours. The police had prompted him, however, with alternating doses of gentleness and severity, until at last they could piece together a satisfactory narrative. Shortly after retiring for the night, Blaine had heard a loud commotion coming from Prowell's room, where the Duke of Darnley was convalescing. The only way the fellow could describe the sounds was by howling and roaring himself in a hideous and comical fashion, and he swore that he hoped never again to hear such noises this side of hell. These growls were followed by a great eruption that shook the very foundation of the house. Blaine bolted from his bed at once to see what could cause such a riot.

As he opened the door of his room there was another trembling shock. Peering into the hall, he saw Prowell's door buckle outward and splinter in a terrible explosion. There emerged from this confusion of wood and plaster a lion. The police report stated the fact coldly, almost bloodlessly: a lion. Screaming, Blaine slammed his door shut, with just enough time to draw the bolt before the creature rushed against it, clawing at it, trying hungrily to rip a way through. Blaine glanced frantically about for a refuge from this nightmare and then jumped into his armoire, cowering there, his hands clasped over his ears, unable to keep out the noise of the beast raging just beyond. He had no conception of time as he sat waiting for a certain and grisly death. The monster might have been just a few seconds or several minutes at the door, crashing repeatedly against it. Almost it seemed that it was willing to devour the door itself as a substitute for the man within. Blaine reported that he was on the verge of renewing his lapsed faith when, without any warning and for no apparent reason, the murderous assault ceased. Still, he was not prepared to leave his sanctuary. Not until hours had passed did he find the courage to quit the wardrobe, squeeze out the small window in his room and run to fetch the constable.

Much of this was explained to Meredith as he sat awaiting the doctor, but the man paid little attention to any of it at the time. His mind was too full of wild apprehensions about his wife, insane dread at the unimaginable trials that lay before them, before her. He recalled that abomination he had seen at Murcheston, that head mounted on Darnley's wall. Was it really only a few hours since then? The monster roared again and again into his thoughts, pouncing upon his fancy with a ferocity that left him beyond the aid of reason. He sat paralyzed under a weight of terror he could not dispel, a panic so numbing that his very breath seemed stilled in fright. And through it all, the immutable source of his despair, the black truth that cast all color from his mind: the monster was out there. That beast was somewhere out past the reach of humanity, crouching in a realm where no soul dared to wander, but where even now Elizabeth was crossing over, infected by the vile contagion, lapsing into something terrible, some dreadful, cursed thing. His tears froze at the thought of it.

And so he sat, silent, oblivious, unapproachable. He was aware that several times the weary man came up to him. He heard the fellow introduce himself as Inspector Ash. But nothing that he said could break through the host of fears besieging Meredith's consciousness. Nothing reached him until the doctor entered the parlor. At once Meredith jumped to his feet and called to him, "How is my wife? How was she hurt?"

Ash held up a hand to calm him, but he brushed it aside and rushed to the doctor excitedly. "How was Elizabeth injured? I must know how she was hurt!"

The doctor was the same who had dressed Darnley's wounds only a few days before, and Meredith's mad appearance and wild demeanor at first startled him so that he could not answer, but only looked about at the assembled constabulary for protection. One of the men leaned over to him and whispered something, however, and the physician squinted and muttered, "Oh yes, I recall now. Mr. Meredith, is it not?"

Meredith ignored the old man's calm demeanor and asked again, more insistently, "How was my wife injured?"

"Be easy, sir," he said in a soothing tone that made Meredith want to throttle him. "Your wife's injury is only superficial. Nothing, I assure you. A cut along the left forearm."

"But how was it delivered?" Meredith tried again. "Did the monster inflict it, or did she sustain it some other way?"

The doctor looked about distractedly and said, "The monster?"

Meredith glanced imploringly to Ash, who smiled at the doctor and said, "Would you please repeat for Mr. Meredith what you told us concerning the cause of his wife's injury?"

"Oh, as to that," the old man replied, "she cut herself with one of your hunting knives, sir. Quite cleanly, I think. No secondary damage to the skin. Undoubtedly a very sharp instrument. Defended herself bravely with it. Found it still grasped in her hand, I understand. Yes, the hunting knife, most definitely. Either that or the animal, but a clean wound, either way." And with this he departed.

"We've sworn the doctor to secrecy concerning the details of this disturbance, Mr. Meredith," the inspector said. "News of a wild animal at large in the city—well, the panic it would cause we just couldn't handle. People can behave worse than beasts themselves at such times. The safety of the public demands that no word of this be allowed to escape from your house."

Meredith did not listen, did not care. His mind was busy grasping this single fact, the only slender thread he had to cling to. The hunting knife! There was a chance that the thing had not harmed Elizabeth! "The hunting knife," he murmured aloud, to reassure himself. "It must be that! It must be!"

Ash pulled a notebook from his coat pocket and flipped through it. "Yes, it would appear so. Blessed good thing it was there. We think the lady managed to hurt the creature with it, and how she did that without being more seriously injured herself is a miracle."

The legion of agonies that had tormented Meredith so savagely these minutes past, the whole infernal lot of them abated somewhat, only slightly, but enough to foster the seed of hope. Yet, the threat was still there, still real. And the question came instantly back to him the stronger he tried to assert otherwise. "Was it the knife?" The conflict within soon overwhelmed him, and Meredith fell back into a chair and covered his eyes. The inspector kindly ordered the room cleared, and only the two men remained to discuss the events of the past night.

Ash waited in polite silence for a bit, then removed a pencil from his coat and began the interrogation. "Have you any idea, sir, where the beast may have come from?"

"Yes," Meredith said. "Yes, Inspector, I do know, but I'm certain you won't believe what I have to tell you."

"There isn't very much in this whole business that I would have believed before coming here," Ash assured him. "I don't think anything you can say will strain my credulity farther than it's been strained already."

Meredith looked about the room quickly, until his eyes lit upon the manuscript. He had dropped it upon a table when he entered, and it sat there forgotten in the meantime. Walking over to it, he picked it up and handed it to Ash. "Here you are, Inspector. This will explain everything far better than I could do."

The man flipped through the pages idly, but Meredith could tell he had no intention of reading the thing. "If you don't mind, sir," he went on impatiently, putting the journal aside, "minutes are rather at a premium now. I haven't time to read books, so if you'd just tell me the story as simply as you can, I'll be about my work. I have a lion roaming the streets as we sit here. And I think you should know," he added pointedly, "you are very deeply implicated in the affair."

"I?"

Ash's manner turned gruff now as he listed the causes for suspicion. "Where did the lion come from, sir? From your house. Where was it first seen? Emerging from a windowless room. How did it get in there? That is the point I think should concern you now, Mr. Meredith. How did the beast get into your house in the first place? Who brought it in?"

"And you believe that I allowed all of this to happen," Meredith stated flatly.

"What I believe is that a man-eater is wandering through London, and if you don't cooperate with this investigation, then the blood of more victims will have to be paid for. It's killed twice and likely will kill again."

"Twice?"

"Your man Prowell," Ash ticked off, referring to his notes, "and the Duke of Darnley. Of course, we haven't located the duke's remains. The beast probably carried them off somewhere, to hide them in the crotch of a tree. Lions do that, I understand."

Perhaps it was the duress under which Meredith had been acting for most of the day and the preceding night, but there was something in this latest revelation, the notion that Darnley was now to be considered his own murderer, that struck him as marvelously comical. He laughed. He laughed until the tears rolled down his cheeks, until his sides convulsed.

Ash stood by, thoroughly confounded now. Failing to appreciate this sudden display of mirth, he called for one of his men to watch Meredith until he could compose himself and went out to confer with the others. The constables were currently scouring the streets and alleys all about the vicinity searching for some trail to follow. The creature had escaped by crashing through the large French windows of the guest room that led to a balcony, and then leapt down into the garden, soared over the wall and ran off in the direction of the river. But after this its trail was hard to follow, and soon all of the inspector's men returned lucklessly.

Once Meredith had quite regained his composure, Ash reentered the room, this time with the police reporter and several constables present. "Now then," he began with an officious bearing, "you were about to tell me what you knew concerning this lion."

"It is not a lion, Inspector."

"What's that?" he asked excitedly. "How do you know that? What in heaven's name is it, then? By God, sir, if I find you've been willfully withholding information that might prove valuable, I will personally see to it that you're hauled before a magistrate this very afternoon!"

Meredith paused. He didn't much like the idea of telling Ash all that he knew. There was no doubt that he would sound perfectly insane doing so, but he had no alternative, not anymore. The inspector wouldn't read the truth for himself. He was convinced of Meredith's complicity already. There was no choice but to commit everything at last to the man's official notebook. Besides, Meredith didn't care a damn if they all thought him mad. The creature had invaded his home, his family, and he wanted time to gather himself, to see Elizabeth, to prepare her for the awful truth. He therefore took a deep breath and just put the case bluntly.

"It is not a lion. It's a werewolf. More specifically, it's Darnley you're after. He is out there somewhere now, lying naked and injured. Find him, Inspector, and you have your monster."

Meredith considered the silence which followed to be about the lengthiest and most awkward he had ever been a party to. Ash looked at him with a pained and abused expression, as though he suspected the man of imagining such nonsense solely to torment him. The rest merely shuffled in embarrassment, deferring their opinions until their superior had a chance to pass his own judgment. "Do you mean to say, Mr. Meredith, that the Duke of Darnley somehow brought the animal into your home and is controlling it?"

"I mean to say precisely that the Duke of Darnley *is* the animal. He is a werewolf, a monster in the shape of a man, or maybe the other way around. I mean to tell you that he transforms at the full moon into a beast resembling a wolf. If you require corroboration, you will find it in the manuscript I offered you. Take it. Read it. It's in Darnley's own hand. Consider it a confession, if you will. Only stop wasting your time looking for the beast. The moon is down now and the beast is gone. Only Darnley remains. Now go out and find him."

Ash turned away for a moment, trying to understand this sudden dementia. With his back to the room, he muttered, "Am I to believe . . ."

"Believe anything, Inspector," Meredith begged, throwing himself back in the chair, tired of it all, this mad game, wanting only to be left alone by the world. "Read the manuscript and believe any part of it you like. I don't care. I'm beyond caring. I won't try to convince you that any of this is true. You go out there and fight this thing. You hunt it down and kill the creature. Only let me wash my hands of it." And he folded his arms petulantly and was silent.

Ash walked over to the manuscript where it lay discarded on the sofa. He picked it up, turned to the first page and read for a moment. Meredith saw an eyebrow go up, but that was all. "Mr. Meredith," the inspector said with a pained smile, "you've been under a tremendous strain these past hours, and I think we've imposed upon your good nature long enough. Gentlemen," he ordered, turning to his men, "we can continue our investigation from the Yard."

And so they left. Ash took the manuscript with him, perhaps to read it later, but Meredith doubted now that it would do much good. The only benefit to come from the thing seemed to be that it exonerated him from suspicion. "Now I'm only a fool," he thought wearily, "at worst an insane eccentric, but no longer an accessory to murder."

Elizabeth remained in a narcotic doze for the remainder of that day, and Meredith slept fitfully in a chair by her side the whole time. His sleep was plagued by wild dreams of monstrous creatures stalking through the shadows of his home, lying in wait for him while he was compelled by some force he could neither resist nor comprehend to wander aimlessly down endless dark corridors.

He awoke to find Elizabeth sitting up in bed calling his name gently, and in the flood of his emotion Meredith clumsily upset the nightstand when he embraced her. She wept softly on his shoulder and he did his awkward best to comfort her. Elizabeth possessed a strong spirit, he knew, and it took only a little to soothe her, to tell her that Eugenie was safe and the immediate peril past. He wanted desperately to ask her about the ordeal, to hear from her own lips that the creature had not touched her, but just at that moment the doctor arrived and Meredith had to put off his questions until after the examination. This was quickly done, for as the doctor had mentioned, the wound was not severe. The greatest danger had been from shock and loss of blood, and the old physician acknowledged that Elizabeth was recovering her strength quite regularly.

When Meredith and Elizabeth were at last alone again, she turned to him and, clutching his arm, said, "I must tell you, Charles, tell you everything, now, before I lose courage."

He sat beside her on the bed and took her hand. She told her story in a clear voice that never wavered but once, when she spoke of Eugenie. Elizabeth had not been able to sleep that night, owing to his absence from their bed. She lay awake reading when the noises started. At first she couldn't make them out at all and considered that they might be coming from the street. But then she heard the savage roar of the beast and Blaine's scream, and she knew at once that something was inside the house.

She leapt from the bed and ran to the nursery where she quickly scooped up the baby. Then, with the child's nanny close behind her, she went back out into the hall and met Prowell just coming out of the guest room. He stood between the women and the staircase and, turning to Elizabeth, told them to go back into her bedchamber while he looked into things. Her eyes glazed with tears as she recalled the suddenness of what happened next, the great, dark shape flying up the stairs in a single leap, falling upon Prowell, carrying him back into the guest room by the force of its onslaught. Elizabeth did not hesitate. Her only thought was for Eugenie. With the baby grasped fiercely to her and pushing the nanny ahead, she retreated into the bedroom without looking back and locked themselves in.

She didn't consider at the time where this mad devil might have come from. She only knew that their lives were in danger. Elizabeth held Eugenie out to the nanny, who took the baby, clutching it as though the infant might somehow protect her from the horror howling without. Then, looking about for a weapon, Elizabeth's eyes fell upon Meredith's hunting knife. Why it should have been there neither one of them could recall. Meredith knew he must have brought it up from his study for some reason, but when and for what purpose he didn't remember. It was an act of Providence that it was there, that's all, for no sooner did Elizabeth take it in her hand than the door of the room trembled violently, and the monster raged in anger and frustration as it tried again and again to burst its way through to its prey.

The hinges proved sturdy, but the door was weak, and the creature soon cracked the panel and began clawing viciously, wildly trying to get at its terrorized victims. A hole appeared, and now Elizabeth could see the fangs of the beast as it chewed at the wood and ripped away great splinters in its maw. The door was quivering, and the creature would quickly have gotten in had not Elizabeth acted. With the animal snarling and clawing before her, she held the knife firmly in her hand and slashed at the thing. She missed, and it answered the attack with a massive paw thrust through the hole in the door panel, tearing the air between them. What followed was a crazed duel as both Elizabeth and the beast flailed blindly at each other, claw against steel, trying with every pass to rip an opponent that neither could reach. In the furor of their sweeping attacks a gash appeared on her left arm and the pain almost undid her, but with a burst of frantic strength, she quickened her blows and at last brought the edge of the blade deeply across the monster's outstretched leg. It yelped in pain like a wounded pup, turned and fled. She fell to the floor, the blood seeping from her wound, lay there fearful of another assault, until her eyes closed and she fainted.

Meredith now knew all there was of the occurrences of that night, yet the most difficult task lay ahead. Having relived those awful minutes of combat with the monster, Elizabeth looked up into his face with tired, confused eyes and said, "I don't understand it, Charles. Where could the animal have come from? How did it get into the house, into Prowell's room? There's no window there. And where is Darnley?"

Of course he had to tell her the truth. There was no alternative, no easy fiction he could create to hide the horror from her. Still he was afraid. What if she didn't believe him? Ash and the others, what mattered if they thought him mad, but Elizabeth must believe him. For her own soul's sake, she must believe him! He held her tightly, trying to draw his resolve from her, unwilling to look into her eyes. "I know how it all happened, my love. I know the awful secret of it. But promise me something before I tell you. Promise that you will say nothing, not a word until I'm finished. It's insane, I know, but you must believe that everything I am about to say is true. At least, I believe it to be true."

Elizabeth pulled herself away and held his face in her cool hands. "Tell me, Charles," she said softly.

Meredith told the story as best he could remember, every bloody detail of it, and Elizabeth was attentive from beginning to end. When he had done, after more than two hours, she merely reached out to him and held him in her still weak but comforting embrace. He marveled that something so gentle should have so much strength to offer.

And then, another thought slowly began to rear its shape within her, a dreadful thought, stronger in its terror than her strength could withstand at once. She looked at the bandaged arm and gasped, and turned her eyes to her husband, eyes filled with fear and confusion, imploring him not to say what she knew he thought, what they both now thought.

"It's not certain," he tried to reassure her. "The doctor says it's far more likely that you did the thing yourself, with the knife. He's quite positive, actually. I'm sure there's no cause for alarm."

"No cause, Charles?" she asked incredulously, passionately, tears welling up and pouring down her face. "No cause to fear that I am now the same as that thing out there? No cause to believe that he has made me a monster? No cause but this!" she hissed, raising her arm up between them. "Oh dear God!" she cried again. "He wasn't trying to kill me last night! He wanted to do this to me! He wanted to make me like him!"

"What are you saying?" Meredith asked. "How do you know that?"

"He called me into his room after you left, begged me to sit by him through the night. Charles, you know how he invited me to go with him before, to Murcheston. I see now, he wants me, Charles! Wants to infect me, make me his partner in this madness!" She turned her head away, her face pale with shame and anger and fear.

Meredith took her hands gently in his own. "He's gone now, and we must not lose sight of our hope, my love," he said, looking fondly at her. "There is cause to prepare ourselves, yes, it's true. But there is as yet no cause to despair utterly. We don't know, do we, not for sure that he has succeeded, that he inflicted that wound. Let us begin to steady our souls with that. And whatever comes, let us be ready for it together."

They clutched in a desperate embrace, trying to redouble their store of strength in each others' arms. "And whatever is past between you and Darnley, let us not stop loving each other," he added silently to himself. Yet, even as they clung there, alone with only themselves for solace, and even as he loved her all the more for her suffering, Meredith's doubts returned to plague him, and he wondered in the deepest pit of his mind, "Has he claimed her for his own? Shall he yet wrench her from my grasp?"

"I don't know how such a thing can be?" she whispered to him later, when the shock was subsided and they had quietly agreed not to mention the dark possibilities ahead of them. "But if such malevolence is allowed to exist in the world, Charles, then we must determine how to stop it."

"We? But what can we do?" he protested. "The authorities have discounted the thing completely, and what can we two do alone? Why should we even bother now that it has left us?"

She grasped him roughly by the shoulder and gave him a firm shake, though it must have pained her arm to do so. "Charles!" she reproached him severely. "He has made an attempt upon me once. He will try again if he has the opportunity. It's up to us to deny him that. Before he returns, we must find him."

"But isn't that the job of Scotland Yard?"

"You said yourself they refuse to believe you," she answered, too readily for his peace of mind.

"Then we can easily avoid him. It's only the full moon we need fear. Let's go away until he's discovered and destroyed. Let's go where we will be in no danger from him."

"But other people *are*, Charles, in frightful danger. Other women and other men. Other children, prey to Darnley. We must at least try to stop him, to find him out and destroy him." Her eyes were afire with a ferocity he had never seen in her before, and Meredith believed she could do it herself, kill the thing by her own hand.

"But how shall we find him, one man with the whole city to hide in?"

"You have the memory of his journal to guide you, the record of his wanderings through the streets and alleys. He's likely to keep to his habitual haunts. Find them. Locate this Black Abbots Yard to begin with. The police said he was moving toward the river and you mentioned how he often frequented the docks. Look there. But Charles, we can't give him the freedom to rest secure while he waits to terrorize us again. Before the next full moon we must find him. You must, my dear." She paused, and glanced at her bandages. "This other thing, we shall deal with in time. But Darnley we must deal with now. Shall you be strong and do it?"

Of course she was right, for she was always right. She was ready herself to rise from her sickbed and begin the search if he would not. Meredith's only regret was that he should be the one weak vessel available to carry out this campaign. Still, he put a bold face on, though it failed to fool her. "I'll do what can be done to find this thing," he said bravely.

"It's not a *thing* you're after, Charles," she reminded him. "It's Darnley."

"Of course it's Darnley," he answered, surprised.

"Are you aware of it, my love? Are you truly aware of what you must do?" She looked at him, her gaze full of ominous portent, and suddenly her meaning and her urgency became clear. Until that moment, Meredith had managed to keep them separate in his thoughts, Darnley and the beast. But Elizabeth had seen at once what he had avoided seeing. To destroy the beast he would have to destroy Darnley. He would be forced to kill him as he was, a man, before he had the chance to transform. That was what Meredith was called to do, to put an end to this nightmare. He bent down and kissed Elizabeth gently and told her that he understood. "But can I do it?" he asked himself silently. "Can I kill Darnley?"

He walked out of the room to let Elizabeth rest, though something of her strength stayed with him. Still, as his feet carried him through the house, it was hard to remember a time that seemed sane and certain, when reality was not suspended in a glass, hovering in some viscous agar of madness, when the world was right and it was Darnley who was mad. Now the world seemed to have gone insane and Meredith could not find where sanity lay anymore.

17

The Age of Blood

*T*he world owes no debt to even the bravest intentions, and Meredith's days and nights now passed in a haze of frustration and failure. Inspector Ash returned, but only to take Elizabeth's statement and leave again. No word was mentioned of the journal. Meredith searched for the places mentioned by Darnley, but his own poor recollection of the manuscript and its veiled references proved slight assistance in his hunt. It occurred to him that Darnley might even return to his flat, that he could have the brass to do as much, and so he hid himself nearby over the course of some few afternoons, but nothing came of this.

Every evening, Meredith would retreat to his study, Elizabeth by his side silently stroking his brow, the gathering dark filling him with a dread he had not known since childhood. His sleep was visited by visions it was almost a sin to conceive. Yet each morning he would wake to a reality more terrible than any dream he could create, lost in the unreal landscape of a real nightmare. What sort of monstrous world was this, he wondered, where werewolves stalk the shadows and demons haunt the daylight? Where was God in such a place? How could He allow such hells to be? What had become of the guiding hand of His creation, when everywhere was blood and death and horror? Meredith prayed, who had not prayed in years, for God to soothe these doubts mastering him, fears that He had abandoned men, abandoned him.

The search continued, day upon endless, lightless day, until Meredith was forced to admit that his efforts to locate Darnley were hopeless. To find a single man in London with only the barest flicker of a clue to light the way was daunting enough, but when the man kept so closely to the dark, when he moved about the blackest regions as effortlessly as a shadow, when the devil himself guided his every step, shielded him from detection, the task felt impossible. And then, the faintest breath of success, a glimmer to carry Meredith through these dismal days. He found Black Abbots Yard. He went there, saw the place with his own eyes. All was rubble, a black pit upon the face of the city, thoroughly razed by the fire Darnley had set to disguise the murder of Mrs. Wattles. Only a few ebony beams jutted up from the ashes, fingers reaching toward the sky from out of the earth. Meredith briefly contemplated the magnitude of this devastation, wrought as it was by a single man, and he prayed that Darnley was not thus the cause of some other, anonymous death in this. But such a quick flash of proof only made the surrounding darkness appear that much more impenetrable, and Meredith remained lost, without any idea of where to turn next. He even traveled to Brixton, went up one day at Elizabeth's insistence, only to find Murcheston dark and deserted. He left instructions with the stationmaster to wire him at once should Darnley appear, but with no real expectation of hearing anything. Darnley would remain in the city. Of that, Meredith felt certain. And there was something else he was sure of. Why he could not say, but he became convinced that Darnley was nearby, watching, waiting to be discovered. Darnley had always been the better hunter, and Meredith began to fear his superior skill.

Elizabeth urged him on, although her encouragement only fanned the fire of his doubts. Though he tried to be worthy of her unquenchable faith in him, he knew himself to be weak. It was such a temptation to pretend that none of this was real, that it never happened.

It was easier for her to be resolute. She'd seen the monster, fought against it, had her own terrible reminder of its reality, while all Meredith knew was what he'd read and heard. Every hour, he was forced to exert his will simply to sustain some belief in this lunacy.

Yet, he knew Elizabeth was right. Despair was a luxury for others to indulge in. He must make no room for it. He resolved that she would be his faith, that he would abandon his will to her goodness and strength. For if nothing were done, he reasoned, if he were to throw it all up, what would happen next month, and the month after?

In truth, one final ember of hope kept smoldering deep within Meredith's soul. He knew in his heart that Darnley was not so purely evil, despite this disease not so monstrous that he could spread his terror throughout the city. Meredith would trust to the Darnley of his youth, the man he had known to be good, to continue for his sake, if for no other's. Else how could he find the courage to go on? Yet bound with this, he hid one secret doubt. That somehow his wife was tied to Darnley by fate, that some power of destiny was drawing them together, and he was only the supporting player in another man's story.

One evening, when he wandered home after a wasted day, Elizabeth greeted him as he stepped through the door.

"He's been here," was all she said. Elizabeth had been sitting in the parlor with the baby, dandling it upon her knee, making little Eugenie coo and giggle, sounds of joy too seldom heard about their lives of late, when she glanced up through the window, out across the street. There he was, just standing. Dressed in some outlandish rags, half hidden in shadow, but it was him. "I ran for one of your guns, Charles, in the case in your study," she told him, "but when I returned he was gone."

"My love," Meredith tried to say soothingly, "you mustn't attempt anything rash."

"They weren't loaded!" she exclaimed, not hearing him. "Not a one of them was loaded!"

"And no reason they should be."

"No reason? Charles, we're besieged! He's out there waiting for his chance! Can't you feel it?" Of course, he could. He felt it every day as he wandered the city streets, but he had not wanted to alarm Elizabeth. Now such gallantry was useless, perhaps even dangerous.

He promised her he would load the weapons, but he insisted on keeping the cabinet locked. "I'll give you a key, my dear. But please, be careful. You're not used to firearms."

The thought of Darnley hovering about their lives caused Meredith to make one final appeal to the authorities. He went to Scotland Yard, ostensibly to inquire of Inspector Ash what luck he had enjoyed in finding the lion, more specifically to tell him again why he had failed and how he might succeed. Meredith found the man looking as weary and beleaguered as he had appeared before, able to spare but a few minutes.

"We have not found the creature," he informed Meredith, not even looking up from the piles of papers spread haphazardly across his desk, "and I will tell you in all honesty that we are not actively searching for it."

"Good heavens, why not?" Meredith exclaimed. "You better than anyone should understand how dangerous he is. The thing has already killed five times!"

"Twice," the inspector corrected.

"Two times or a hundred, it doesn't matter! Even if you don't believe that Darnley is a werewolf, that's no cause to give up the hunt. Lion or monster, there's still a man-eater out there! You can't debate that."

"What would you have us do, Mr. Meredith?" Ash demanded coolly. "Send dogs sniffing about the streets? Put out a squad of men to stroll the thoroughfares with guns and rifles? I told you before, a general panic is far deadlier than your lion. And besides, the beast has been quiet for over a fortnight, and so I hope we've seen the last of it."

"But you haven't, you know. It will kill again, Inspector. Depend upon it. When the moon is full it will kill, and then what will you do?"

He heaved a labored sigh. "I don't think I should waste my time worrying about that until it happens. The painful fact is, I don't believe you need to worry about it at all, Mr. Meredith. It's not your concern any longer. It's mine. In the meantime, as I told you, I am quite busy. If you will excuse me now."

"But the journal, Inspector," Meredith persisted, one last, half-hearted effort to enlist the man in the truth. "How do you explain that?"

"A mad fantasy, sir. If the Duke of Darnley were alive today, I should recommend that he be confined to Bedlam. Forgive my callousness, but that is what I should do." And rummaging through the jungle of his desk, Ash pulled out the manuscript and handed it to Meredith. "Here," the man ordered. "Take this back again. I won't be needing it." So saying, he returned to his official papers and bid a laconic good afternoon.

Meredith wasn't particularly disappointed at the outcome. He hadn't expected any success, but he had to try, especially as all his other efforts had proven futile. The illusion of doing something helped him to sleep at night.

Then, one afternoon, Darnley returned. Not Darnley himself, but a young boy knocking insistently upon Meredith's front door. At first the new butler refused to admit him, but the lad slipped past and dashed through the house, laughing and taunting the servants, until finally Meredith appeared to learn what the row was about. As soon as he saw the child, a ragged, dirty street urchin, no more than twelve or thirteen, with sullen, hungry eyes and sunken cheeks, Meredith knew who had sent him and his heart beat wildly.

"I got a message for you, Merry," the child announced with an air of self-importance almost laughable in one so frail. "It's about the dog you lost and have been searchin' for."

Meredith dismissed the servants and ushered the boy into his study where they could speak in private. "No tricks, son," he said severely, trying to take command of the situation. "Where is he? You can take me to him at once, I suppose?"

"I'll take you to him, don't be afraid I won't," he answered defiantly, "but only after dark. That's my charge and I'll follow it if it please you or if it don't. After the sun goes down we're to set out and not a second afore."

It was clear the lad was not impartial in this business, was already seduced by Darnley to act on his behalf. What unholy promises had been made, Meredith wondered, to ensure this poor boy's willful co-operation? He instructed him to sit by the fire while he prepared for the journey. "Is it far?" he asked, giving away his nervous excitement.

"As far as it needs to be and not a step farther," replied the imp. "But if you was to walk straight there and come straight back, you'd be home before midnight." As it was then only four o'clock, this cryp-tic response said little. So Meredith put on a large cloak, gathered together a few necessaries, and went to tell Elizabeth the news.

She was triumphant at first to hear that Darnley had been flushed, but when she learned that her husband was about to confront him alone, her enthusiasm withered. "Hadn't you better go to the police first, Charles?" she asked with the slightest tremble in her voice. "They might believe you now there's a message from Darnley himself."

"We have tried that route before, my love," he reminded her, "and found it closed to us. I have nothing tangible to show them, and even if I did they would refuse to believe me. They have had his journal, and look how they ignored it. No, I must try this alone. Besides, I have the lad to deal with. If I attempt to communicate with the authorities, he will bolt, I'm sure of it."

Elizabeth conceded that he was right, and she embraced him tightly. "Be careful of him," she warned. "Remember that Darnley is a fiend and I know he wants to harm you."

"I'll be careful," was all the comfort Meredith could think to offer. So saying he tore himself from her arms and, after some last few prep-arations, returned to the boy in the study.

In Meredith's absence, this child had poured himself a glass of brandy and was sitting well back in a deep, green baize chair by the fire so that his legs just missed touching the floor. They sat together for perhaps a quarter of an hour longer, waiting for the last rays of the sun to vanish from the sky, and as they did, Meredith questioned his companion about Darnley. The boy was proud, despite his humble appearance, and it didn't take much to loosen his tongue.

"The Grace is a great man," he crowed, admiration glowing from his cavernous eyes. "The way he talks of things, the plans he makes like his brain ain't never asleep. Lor', but it's a wonder! A'course, he needs me to be his legs just yet, for he don't get around too good."

"I should think not," Meredith offered. "The last I saw of him his body was quite broken. He couldn't move without pain."

"He ain't crippled," the boy asserted in his master's defense. "If his leg was broke afore, it ain't so broke now. Ain't nothing could stop the Grace for long. It's only he do limp a bit. But soon that'll change." He leaned forward and Meredith heard a taint of Darnley's madness seep into the lad's voice. "His leg'll heal itself, good as ever it was. He tells me he ain't never got to be hurt for long. Only till the next full moon. That's when it happens," and the urchin gave a wink, as one worldly man to another. "That ain't all, neither," he continued slyly. "He's promised me that I should be a great one like him sometime. He can do it, too. Think on that for a bit, will ya? That's something for a chap to think on."

It took Meredith a moment to comprehend what this pathetic creature was telling him, but once the full import of the words became clear, a sudden horror seized his very soul. "Dear God, lad! Do you know what you're saying? Don't you realize what he is, what he means to do to you?"

"Do you think I'm daft?" he shot back ferociously, spilling his glass to the floor. "I know what he is, all right. Ain't it me what found him sleepin' so sound like a great mongrel, so peaceful? Didn't I watch how he changed, the glory of it, the miracle it is, till he was only lyin' there naked? And weren't it me what saved his life, bein' his legs where he couldn't yet go and his eyes where he couldn't yet see. I found him clothes and I brought him food. I done for him, and now he's near healed and movin' about. And that ain't the half, neither! I done for him, so in a few nights he'll do for me. That shows you whether I'm such a fool as you think."

Meredith prayed that his ears were deceiving him. "You don't know what you're wishing for, son! Darnley isn't a great man. He's a beast, a monster! How can you want that kind of existence for yourself?"

But the child only threw himself back in the chair, kicking his heels gleefully and laughing a sick, weak laugh. "You think I don't know what monsters is?" he asked with his dirty grin, his eyes flaming hard and inhuman in that fragile skull. "Me, livin' in the streets since I was old enough to suck a tit. Me, with nothin' to call my own but my arse, and not even that most of the time. Beat on and shit on by any stinkin' scum what wants the little I got. And toffs like you wouldn't piss on me to stop me from burnin'. I been drownin' in monsters my whole life. But now, I'll be able to get some of my own back. I've been longin' to be a monster like the rest of you. I'll be the biggest monster you ever seen." And he laughed again, cackling from the depths of Darnley's insane influence.

What could Meredith say? Words would be wasted, and ultimately it didn't matter. Here was only one more life to be saved, that was all, one more among thousands, an entire city's population to be delivered from Darnley's thrall.

The time had come for them to depart. Meredith took the butler aside and instructed him to wait up, saying that if he were not back by sunrise, to go to the authorities and tell them what little he knew. Then, with the boy in the lead and the man behind, they went out into the darkening night.

The air was cold and Meredith pulled the collar of his cloak tight about him, but the boy, in his few tattered garments, seemed indifferent to the chill and walked as openly as if it had been May, not December. An odd picture they made, incompatible companions, trudging along relentlessly, never speaking, never slowing their pace. They began in the direction of the river, staying on familiar roads for a time, but soon left these and descended into a labyrinth through the heart of the city's foulest regions. It was as though London underwent a transformation as Meredith marched on. Gradually, the streets became dirtier, the lamps burned less clearly, the shadows grew deeper and blacker. The people likewise seemed to wither and shrink before his eyes, until they seemed more simian than human.

The boy, of course, was oblivious to this. It was his world, after all, and doubtless everything in it seemed as right to him as a village green to a country lad. Still, such ready acceptance of filth and disease struck Meredith as more unnatural even than the decay closing them in.

They proceeded without comment for an hour or more until, taking a sharp turn down a depressed street, their road abruptly vanished, ending in a sudden descent to the foul, foaming waters of the Thames. On their left, rising among the general depredation, stood a building that appeared even more unstable than its neighbors, as though it were kept standing only to make the rest of the place look safe and secure by comparison. It was to this bare hole that their way led. No door graced the entrance, and they passed in silently, stepping over the refuse of former residents, all fled now, gone on to more humane lodgings. Just as they were crossing the threshold, Meredith heard the celestial sound of the bells of Westminster chiming the hour hard by, and realized to his amazement that they could not be more than a quarter mile from the Houses of Parliament.

The boy led him quickly through the blackness of that house, and would, in fact, have left him behind had Meredith not called for him to wait, straggling after, in danger at any moment of ripping himself open upon some splintered framework or jagged fragment of a shattered window. He asked for a light, but the child answered insolently that he didn't need a light, and there wasn't much farther to go anyway, so shut up. Meredith carried on as best he was able. They ascended a staircase, and from the groans it made perhaps it were better that they wandered blindly, else he couldn't have found the courage to venture so far into such a palace of corruption.

At last they emerged into a large upper room, illuminated only by the light of the moon through the paneless windows. The place appeared to have been rapidly deserted, and boxes and packing materials lay spread out from one end of the floor to the other. The boy turned to Meredith upon entering and said only, "Here." Then he left him alone. Meredith looked about, frightened to be abandoned in this place, and his hand reached instinctively into his pocket.

But he was not alone for long. A voice soon boomed from out of the shadows at the far end of the chamber. "Merry! Damn your bones, it's good of you to come so quickly!"

It was Darnley. He hobbled forward into the pale light and Meredith could see at once that what the boy had said was true. His leg was not completely healed, yet here he was walking, he who just days before had been unable to move.

"Yes," he remarked, giving his leg a gentle pat. "Don't be surprised that it isn't better than it is. You know the thigh was quite pulverized by that fucking cab. Still, another transformation should make me whole and perfect again, wouldn't you think?" And he chuckled easily, as if he had been showing off a war wound of which he was particularly fond. "And this," he went on, holding up his left arm and displaying a small scar, a mere scratch, "this I owe to your charming wife. She cut me damn clear to the bone with that toothpick of hers."

Darnley moved forward, and Meredith saw that he had the use of a cane, a beautiful thing with a massive gold knob. His dress was otherwise made up of bits and pieces from all corners of society: a threadbare shirt under a richly brocaded waistcoat; a cheap woolen cravat around his throat stuck through with a diamond pin; heavy laborer's boots on his feet and trousers that had been stylish once, but now were a mere patchwork; and on his fingers, a gross display of jewelry that sparkled vaingloriously in the moonlight. Darnley sat on a small packing crate in the center of the room, with a larger crate before it as a table. "Come on, Merry," he said pleasantly, almost affectionately, inviting his guest to an adjacent box. "Sit down. You've had a long go of it, I think. Relax, man. I'm not going to eat you." And he smiled a wicked smile.

These words failed to put Meredith at his ease, but he accepted the offer and placed himself opposite, taking the precaution of moving his seat back a foot or two as he sat down, so as to be just out of Darnley's reach. The action didn't go unnoticed.

"That's rather unkind of you, Meredith," his host said in a hurt voice, but not without a touch of glee in it. "You're my guest, after all. Am I so profligate as to threaten the life of a man I've gone to such lengths to entertain? Or do you fear this poor old cripple so much?"

"What I fear," Meredith answered hotly, "is the thing this cripple has become! What I fear is the monster that tried to deprive me of my wife and child!"

"Yes," Darnley replied, nodding gravely, "I thought you'd feel that way. But come now, Merry, look at it from my perspective. What I did was only in accord with my nature. You can't blame me for what happened any more than you can blame a cat when it kills a mouse. The creature must act in sympathy with its instincts. Isn't that fair?"

"Perhaps I cannot blame the cat, but I can destroy it to protect the mice! I could destroy you now for what you've done," he shouted, rising to his feet enraged, working himself into a sudden fury to aid him in what he had to do. "You are a mortal menace to every human being who comes near you, and it would be a service to mankind for me to kill you here!"

In the pallid moonlight, Darnley's eyes narrowed into icy slits, calculating the depth of the other man's anger. A thin smile broke across his face. "Please, Merry, let's be honest with each other," he admonished in the old, patronizing tone Meredith had heard so often before. "You might want to see me dead, not that you wouldn't suffer for it yourself. Your conscience, I mean. But you're not the man for such a job, not now. You'd have to wait until I transformed, until you could kill me cleanly and guiltlessly, like a real huntsman. Then maybe you could do it, if you could forget that the beast in your sights was me. But not now, so stop this pretense and take your hand away from that revolver in your pocket."

For an instant Meredith's eyes flared like coals, but then the fire went out. His shoulders slumped visibly, and he let go of the small pistol he had taken from his home. He sat down again, beaten.

"That's better," Darnley said soothingly. "Put the candle there, Dick, and go get me something to drink." The boy! Meredith had forgotten about him. He would easily have foiled any attempt on his master's life. The child materialized now at Meredith's elbow and placed a candle on the table. "A marvelous lad," Darnley went on. "Does any number of things for me. Has kept a close eye on you these past weeks, while I've been about on other business. One or the other of us has kept close to you all this time, you realize. There's not a move you've made I haven't known about."

"Yes," Meredith confessed. "I thought as much."

"Now," Darnley began enthusiastically once the two men were alone, lighting the candle as he spoke, "perhaps we can talk some sense, you and I. Merry, you've no idea the things I've been thinking since I came here, the plans I've made and the way things will change. Christ, but I'm filled with so many desires! My every thought is a revelation! My very breath is life itself! Tell me, did you read my journal?"

"Yes, and was sickened by what I found there."

"Must you always be so fucking parochial?" he jeered. "Try to think of the larger picture and not just the unpleasant little details for once. These are modern times, Merry, and the old ways of thinking just won't work anymore. Do you understand? Can your mind grasp something glorious that just might be dressed out in unpleasant truths? Or are you only able to see backwards, to dead times, dead histories? And dead notions of right and wrong, Merry. All the old morality is dead. Right and wrong are dead. The only thing that remains is strength. *That's* alive. Whoever is the strongest decides what's right. Nobody else deserves to."

Darnley's eyes sparkled as he spoke, yet Meredith thought the light within them was not a true flame, but the false brilliance of dementia. "Don't talk to me of right and wrong," he answered. "You only want to twist morality around so that it fits your murderous hunger. But it can't be done, Darnley. Some things won't bend that way, not for any man's whim. They're solid and true. They have to be, or else what's to become of society?"

"Fuck society!" Darnley screamed madly. "I tell you, right and wrong don't exist! History is a pageant of depraved acts that seemed perfectly right centuries ago. Human sacrifice, mass suicide, infanticide—they've all been practiced and called 'moral' at one time or another. What malignant horrors do you indulge in daily that a hundred years from now will seem like barbarism?" He almost frothed in his fury. This sudden burst of venom blew over as quickly as it came on, however. Darnley passed his hand before his eyes and wiped away his black temper. "But I'm getting ahead of myself now, Merry. You've got me excited with your talk of morality. Promise that you'll shut up and hear me out, and then you can tell me what you think."

Meredith didn't want to listen. Yet, he felt that by giving Darnley a hearing he might uncover the flaw in his mental armor, make him see the impossibility of leading this insane existence. He might even get Darnley to agree to a voluntary confinement during the times of his transformations, help him to a normal life, or as much of one as were possible for him. Perhaps it was a foolish hope, but it was the only hope left. So Meredith sat passively and let Darnley speak.

"It was a basic mistake I made, you see, that led to this anguish I've suffered, this terrible pain, being half-human, half-beast, belonging to both worlds and neither. But why shouldn't I have been deceived? The truth, when I finally saw it, when it flashed through the fiber of my being like an electric shock, it seemed almost too tremendous to be real. But it *is* real, Merry. And my work is only just beginning. That's why I've sent for you. Do you understand?"

"I can't follow you at all."

"God, but you're dense, Meredith," he exclaimed, but then shook his head in confusion. "Or maybe it's me. I overflow with such energies I can't make out when I'm rambling anymore. Let me tell you how I arrived at these marvelous insights and then perhaps you'll understand better. It was while I was at Murcheston the last time, after I made the final entry in my journal. I walked out upon the moors that evening in a dejected mood, and the dreariness of that vast waste was a balm to my dispirited thoughts. Night was falling, and the air turned cold before I realized how far I'd traveled, that I was actually within sight of Brixton.

"I looked about at the town and found something unusual. A collection of tents and colorful wagons assembled along the road. It was a troupe of traveling performers, a nasty shit-hole of a carnival, and I wandered about the tents and signs, looking at the homely attractions, the dog-and-pony acts, the fire-eaters and Indian fakirs and African cannibals, all the usual assortment of filthy cheats that one finds in such places.

"Then I came across a remarkable looking handbill. It advertised a rare medical marvel, the bafflement of doctor's throughout Europe and Asia, the Celebrated Dog-Boy. Painted on the poster was a sort of rendering of a hairy young man with a long tail he was holding between his legs. I confess, I caught my breath at the sight. Nothing very lycanthropic in the rendering, but for all I knew here might be a fellow creature. At any rate, it would cost me only a penny to find out. I handed the coin to a dirty, toothless man at the entrance and stepped inside.

"The place was bare and cold, and a crowd of men, all looking like they wanted to avoid being seen, stood milling about. Lanterns hung from poles suspended over our heads, and sawdust was strewn across the dirt and grass of the floor. The lights smoked slightly, sending a thick scent of oil through the air that mingled with the sweat and fat of humanity. In one corner stood an Oriental screen, and not far from this was a table set with soap, razor, water basin, towel and the like. A gentleman's toilet. Shortly after I entered, the toothless man followed and closed the flap behind him. He proceeded to the center of the stage, nothing more than an empty area before the screen, and began an aimless narrative that I can hardly recall and that I won't bore you with here, before at last presenting the specimen himself.

"The Dog-Boy appeared from behind the screen. He looked to be no more than fourteen or fifteen, tall and gaunt for his age. Dressed in the most fantastic costume. I don't know what I expected. Some coarse piece of fur sewn together to represent a dog's coat, I suppose. But I wasn't ready to see a lad march out before the audience dressed in the cavalry uniform of a Prussian hussar, hanging about the boy's malnourished frame like a shroud draped over a skeleton.

"As soon as the boy came forward, the old man produced a fiddle and played a military air. The Dog-Boy commenced his act, marching up and down before us in fine imitation of the Prussian gait. Strode about like a scarecrow in all his regalia. Drew an invisible sword with which he cleaved the air like a madman. Next the boy stepped up to the table and, still in time to the music, began to preen and wash himself like a scabby peacock. I was beginning to find the stuff too low even for my tastes, and I looked for the exit, only to find that I couldn't possibly leave without displacing a good many men and drawing considerable attention to myself.

"When I glanced back, the boy had ceased his pantomime and was beginning to undress, taking special care with his uniform and hanging it delicately upon a peg in the center pole. Then, with his back to the audience, in a single swift motion the lad threw off his filthy undergarments and proudly put on display, for every one of us to see, a tail at the base of his spine.

"A tail, Merry! A vestigial cord of flesh some ten inches or more in length, completely inanimate, with no musculature at all. The boy just stood there, hands on hips, rocking back and forth at the waist, allowing the thing to sway gently. As the old man kept up his accompaniment on the fiddle, he invited each of us to step forward and test the tail for ourselves, prove that it was authentic and not some fleshy rope affixed to the lad's ass. At first no one was willing to approach, but finally a rough-looking character pushed his way to the front and, grasping the tail firmly, gave such a strong pull that the boy yelped and fell into the dirt. He quickly got back to his feet, however, and assumed the same stance as before, inviting inspection by all.

"I looked on but didn't try the thing myself. It proved to be genuine, though, a useless lump of flesh protruding at the very tip of the spine where the vertebrae trail off into the bony coccyx, the useless tail we all carry about beneath our skins. And it was the thought of this universal human tail, a reminder of our animal ancestry, that caused the truth of my condition to flood my mind in a sudden, brilliant rush, like a dark ocean overflowing my thoughts. All along I'd been keeping separate from humanity, you see, holding myself apart as something different. And yet, at the same instant I longed for companionship. But it's all been so needless. This lad's deformity made me realize that I'm no different than you or any man, not really. We both carry our tails, only yours is kept under the skin. Inside I'm just as human as I ever was, only more so. Do you see? I'm the physical manifestation of what we all are, beasts at heart, animals in a jungle of our own making. We are all werewolves in the making! Me, that boy, you, all of us werewolves! Only I am the first to see it! I'm not alone in this and never was!"

As Meredith watched Darnley relate this story, saw his eyes burn fiercely in the flickering candlelight, he knew that the lunacy which gripped him was far more potent than any arguments that could be brought against it. Darnley's mind was now fixed on this single idea and nothing could dislodge it. But still Meredith would not relinquish his hope. "Are you saying that you are prepared to come forward and reveal your true nature to the authorities?" he inquired.

"Reveal myself?" Darnley responded, looking at Meredith as if he had forgotten he was there. "Yes, I'll reveal myself to the authorities. I'll make myself bloody well known to everyone presently."

This answer filled Meredith with a sudden delight that all might yet be well, that Darnley might not be beyond the reach of reason. "But how will you do it?" he asked. "Can I assist you in any way to come out of your hiding?"

For an instant Darnley stood transfixed, his eye bulging as he stared at his friend. Then he jumped to his feet and rushed him, threw his hands about his shoulders and pulled him close. Meredith momentarily feared for his life, but Darnley was only embracing him in an excess of feeling. "Yes, Merry, yes!" he shouted exuberantly. "Yes, you *will* help me! I knew you would! That's what I wanted to hear from you. That you understand and will be at my side, assisting me in the difficult work ahead."

"But what must be done other than telling all to Scotland Yard?" Meredith exclaimed, catching Darnley's fervent energy. "I'm certain that, once your medical condition is confirmed, no charges will be held against you." This last remark was more hopeful than accurate. Still, Meredith was willing to believe anything if only Darnley would come to his senses.

But the words cast an unexpected pall over Darnley's enthusiasm. He pushed Meredith out at arms length and his brow furrowed deeply as he stared into the other's eyes, wrenching from him the truth of this misunderstanding. Darnley released him and turned away in disgust. "You don't see it at all, do you?"

"I see that you must be helped, that you must return to the world of men."

Darnley swung around violently and the fat knob of his cane came crashing down on the crate between them, sending the candle flying across the room and plunging all into the pale, white moonlight again. "No!" he screamed in frustration. "That's not it! It's not the world of men I'm speaking about! Can't you see? It's the world of werewolves, right here, in London! At the next full moon I'll begin, roaming the streets and spreading my lycanthropy wherever I can. Doubtless many will die in the first few months, but many will also survive, and these are the ones who will be the new men, like me! The world will be changed forever, can't you see that?" He looked at Meredith with longing in his eyes. "And I want you to be there when it happens, Merry. To share it with me. To be at my side."

For the first moment after hearing this, Meredith couldn't make out the meaning behind the words, the enormity of the plan being described to him. To prowl the city, not merely to feed upon the populace, but to multiply the horror, to create an epidemic of this disease, this monstrous sickness, it was a more evil scheme than he was willing to think any man capable of. "How can you mean to do such a thing?" Meredith asked in stunned disbelief. "How can you bring such a horror about?"

"It won't be easy and that's why I need your help," Darnley answered eagerly, oblivious to Meredith's revulsion. "Of course, once I transform, I won't be able to control myself, not completely. It will be up to you to see that the thing is done logically, methodically, so our opportunities aren't squandered. I don't want to waste my initial attack on just anyone, you know. There must be a crowd, a gathering of the most prominent people in the nation. But don't worry about that, I've already determined the wheres and hows. I just want you there, to join me in the first glorious conversion of mankind to our new way of being. The introduction of a new age, Merry! God, what a magical thought!"

Meredith's heart went numb as he listened. "How in God's name can you stand here and tell me that you want to make the whole world like yourself?"

"And why not? Look about you, Merry!" and with a grand gesture Darnley took in the entire dark expanse of his nighttime realm. "Look at this world of murder and rape and disease! The nineteenth century is dying in its own filth! I've seen it! The city chokes the life out of these people, caking their bodies with soot and grime, caking their souls with blind rage! Violence is seeping into your civilized world, in a thousand dirty alleyways like this one, a million hungry souls ready to be revenged upon your kind! The twentieth century is rising like a dark cloud climbing into the sky to swallow it all up, to devour the old morality! New horrors await! New wars with new ways to die! A new age, Meredith, the Age of Blood, and I will lead the world to it!"

What arguments were there in the face of this? How explain to a madman his madness? "Your plan is evil, Darnley," Meredith said softly, from the depths of everything he believed in, every faith he held true. "It must not happen. This Age of Blood you want is a nightmare, and I will not allow you to carry out this insanity."

Darnley looked strangely hurt at first, like a little boy thwarted in his game, his mouth hanging open in surprise that his vision was not shared. Then, a thin smile spread across his face. "How's Elizabeth?" he asked calmly, coldly. Meredith's blood froze, and Darnley laughed quietly. "You see," he continued, "I've already started. I saw her blood before I left. How is she? Did she recover quickly? With only, perhaps, a little fever at first? And then strength and energy returning quickly, miraculously? That's how it happens, you know."

Meredith glanced about, suddenly adrift in the room, helpless. "My God, Elizabeth was right. You did it on purpose," he gasped, stunned. "You might have killed her, but you didn't. It's not just me you want. It's her! All along, it's been her, to make her like you!" Darnley hung his head, looking darkly forbidding at the floor. "How could you do this thing to her?" pleaded Meredith. "My God, Darnley, you love her."

"Love?" Darnley muttered. "What's love?" The two men stood staring at each other for a long moment, defining the gulf spread out between them, the feelings they shared, though so different, so horribly different. "Elizabeth is already with me," Darnley hissed, cutting through the silence like a gash. "Now it's your turn! Join me, Merry! Join *us!*"

The image of Elizabeth came before Meredith's eyes, Elizabeth changing, transforming, and for a moment, he could not imagine a world without her. He must be with her, whatever happened, whatever she became! He *would* be with her, no matter what! And if Darnley's was the only way . . .

Then he saw her as she was, proud and beautiful, and he knew she would not live, they would not live in the world of Darnley's making. "No!" he exclaimed, "she isn't yours to have! We'll find our own way through this if we must, but we won't give in to your madness!"

"Bravely put, old man," Darnley replied, moving toward Meredith with a grin. "But you can't stop me, you know. You can't kill me now, and you won't be able to find me later. You might as well come with me, Merry. I'm the destiny of mankind. There's no other future. You must either be a part of it or be devoured by it. There's no middle ground." And moving like quicksilver, he lashed out with his hand, his nails cutting a red swath in Meredith's neck.

Meredith staggered backwards, out of reach, but Darnley limped towards him, lunged at him again. Suddenly the boy was behind trying to tackle Meredith, to detain him until Darnley could come up. There was no time to think. Striking the lad a heavy blow that sent his poor, skeleton's frame sprawling across the floor, Meredith ran to the door, stumbling over boxes as he went. Darnley's leg left him unable to follow, but from behind Meredith could hear his voice, laughing at him, calling out insanely, "Merry? Did I hurt you, Merry? Did I draw blood from you? Did I break the skin? Did I, Merry?"

He raced blindly through that lunatic asylum, fearful that he would lose his bearings, would not be able to find his way out and so be trapped there with the monster that Darnley had become. But he escaped, fell down the staircase and burst out of the corridor back onto the street. He ran from the place and did not stop until the chimes of Westminster called him to his senses. Following their sound, he emerged back into the world he knew, out of that impossible fantasy, that blood-drenched nightmare.

But the nightmare was not over for him. When he returned home, he related the events to Elizabeth, only making them somewhat less horrific than they were. And when he told her of Darnley's attack, of the scratch the madman inflicted, he felt almost calm, as though his fears for her were easier now that he had joined her in uncertainty. For Darnley could have had no other purpose. To pass his lunacy on. To make Meredith like him, that was the sole reason for their meeting. Yet there was no telling if the curse could be communicated while Darnley was a man, before the moon was full. So they each clung to their hope, husband and wife, and together faced a future they could not imagine.

And on top of this there loomed for Meredith the one unanswerable question: How could he stop Darnley? How was he to manage anything, pitted against such evil? As he lay his head upon his pillow that night, vainly courting a sleep that would not come, he searched for a plan. But all that came to him was the startling revelation, "I don't even know when the full moon is."

18

The Hunt

eredith would not make another attempt upon Darnley's life. He explained to Elizabeth that Darnley would be expecting something, that he was too secure in his lodgings, guarded by that boy and his own preternatural cunning. She refused to understand at first, insisted that she would go herself if he would not, would find the place alone and kill him—impossible plan for a woman who had rarely held a gun in her hands before. In the end, it was clear that there was nothing either of them could do for now. Meredith would not shoot Darnley while he was a man, and Elizabeth realized as much. She knew, in fact, that had he been such a man she might not have loved him as she did. So they were forced to wait out the long days until the full moon.

They spent the time speaking little about this business, knowing only too well what lay ahead, the lonely pass that fate had brought them to. Each clung to a separate hope for escape. If Elizabeth released a stifled sigh, Meredith would stroke the red scar along her arm and whisper, "It is the hunting knife, my love. I have seen such wounds a score of times. The hunting knife, I am certain of it."

And if he, in his turn, sat in a brooding cloud before the fire, she would come up behind him and play her fingers through his hair, saying, "There's nothing to it, Charles. Only a beast can make a beast. Only then can the thing be passed on. You're safe, my pet, perfectly safe."

So they waited. But when the day arrived, no word of comfort could lift the oppressive spirit that hovered about the house. They sent the servants away, had the new nanny take Eugenie off for a visit to Elizabeth's family. In silence and in solitude they took every precaution for . . . what? Too many terrible options opened up before them whenever they considered the future. They could only hope together, side by side, each drawing on the other's strength to see this thing through.

Meredith made his preparations as dusk descended, trying not to consider anything but the hunt. From the gun cabinet he took a pair of pieces, a rifle that had always shot true and a dreadful shotgun, double-barreled and stunningly powerful. He proceeded to clean them both, Elizabeth sitting at his side all the while. He tested the cartridges, the powder, made certain of every detail, and still the time limped by. He next took a pair of pistols and inspected them thoroughly, showing Elizabeth how they loaded, how they fired. At last, putting the pistols in his pockets, Meredith rose, and taking Elizabeth by the hand, and giving her fingers a squeeze as he looked into her eyes for a moment, they proceeded to the cellar.

They had already made certain that the place was quite secure. Locking the door at the top of the stairs, Meredith descended with his wife and together they sat at a small table, a single lamp resting between them. He removed the pistols from his pockets and placed them before Elizabeth. "Should I change, my dear," he told her with false calm, though with a catch in his throat, "after you have saved me from my fate, you will have to go to the authorities with what little hope we have left. Ask to see Inspector Ash. Here are the directions you will need to give him. It's the way to the empty house where I last saw Darnley," and Meredith produced from his pocket a folded scrap of paper on which he had scribbled a map, detailing the way he had taken to escape from Darnley's lair, as near as he could remember it.

Elizabeth nodded that she understood and took the map from him. Their hands touched, and they clasped them together again, their arms encircling the weapons upon the table. They rose and embraced, and Meredith felt the warm, silent tears slowly trailing down Elizabeth's cheeks. The two stood there, holding onto each other against the encroaching dusk, the approaching moon. Then, each taking a pistol from the table, they sat where they were, upon the floor, and reclined, and waited.

"Are you all right, love?" Elizabeth asked in a gentle whisper.

"I feel quite well," he answered, sounding absurdly at ease. "What time is it?"

She studied a large watch she had brought with her into the cellar. "We're still a quarter of an hour till moonrise."

"Are you sure of that?" he insisted, sitting up in alarm, for it suddenly occurred to him that there was no possibility of seeing the moon as it broke over the horizon.

"I have your good chronometer, Charles, the one you use when you travel. And the lunar tables in your almanac are quite explicit."

He lay back again in her arms. "Very good, my dear," he responded, as casually as though they were discussing the railway time-tables. And so they passed the time, chatting idly about one thing and another, the odd sort of short-handed speech that married couples grow into. Every so often one would inquire, "How are you feeling, love? Quite well?" And each time the other would answer as honestly as may be, "Yes, quite well."

As they spoke, they heard the bells of a hundred churches chime half past the hour, brilliant pinpricks in the fabric of silence that surrounded them. When the night was again still, Meredith considered how he longed to hear them ring again, a quarter-hour hence, to know that this trial had passed and that their lives were to be renewed on terms more equitable than they had lived before. For a second life, he had heard, was always a better one, more valued and more valuable. He thought to himself how these same bells had been ringing like that every quarter hour of his life, yet familiarity had left him deaf to their call. He asked Elizabeth how much time they had left.

"Hardly any time at all now, pet."

"But how much exactly?"

She hesitated before answering. "Don't, Charles, or every second will be hell." She laid a delicate hand upon his brow, and he looked up into her eyes. They appeared calm, almost serene, hiding no sign of the torment that might have been there had she been alone to face this ordeal. For he realized that there was a sort of odd blessing in their joined fates. In solitude, such an evening would have been madness to endure. Together, they could face even this.

"I love you, my sweet," she told him. "I shall always, always love you." They shared a kiss, long and full, conveying all the love they might squeeze into the moment. Then they lay back again, and were silent.

A few moments passed and Charles said, "Elizabeth, if this thing should happen to me . . ."

"Hush, my dear," she told him.

"No, but if it should, be sure that I am well along in my transformation before you shoot. Otherwise, there might be awkward questions for you to answer." She did not reply, but only held him tighter in her arms.

Now he could sense the sweat trickling down his sides, and the warm clamminess of his skin. "This is what it is like," he considered, "the metamorphosis. This is how it happens," and the thought caused him to sweat all the more. His whole life seemed dammed up now within this dreadful moment, and in a near despair he clutched the only thing he had to keep him from insanity. His arms convulsed about Elizabeth and he gasped, as a man drawing breath to keep from drowning, "I love you! Dear God, I do love you, Bess!" He looked deeply at her, trying to freeze her features, hold them unchanged and steady. It was almost as if he were in a timeless time, and she the only mark to frame the world with. How long ago had he heard the chimes ring? Two minutes? Twelve? He couldn't say. He was being held in an eternal now from which only a great shock could free him, and set time on its right course again.

And then the shock came. Meredith heard the chimes of the church steeples ring again, ring the three-quarters, and they knew that the danger was behind them, that they were not damned. Not yet. Now Elizabeth wept, wept fully and gratefully. "The knife!" she sobbed as she leaned against his chest. "The knife, Charles! Thank God, the knife!" Yet there was no time for them to rejoice, for now his work began.

As slowly as time had passed before, so it seemed to race headlong at last, like a reckless current carrying them bobbing in its wake. They burst up the stairs and through the door, and Elizabeth took the pistols while Charles grabbed the shotgun and slung the rifle upon his back, concealing both under a great cloak. There was time only to share a last look. No words could have held a truer farewell than that which passed quietly between them in that one, swift second. Then he was gone.

The streets were deserted, it being late on Christmas Eve and most people safely tucked away at home or in church. A light snow was falling, barely dusting the ground with whiteness. At the first opportunity Meredith hailed a hansom. The driver gave a queer look as he deposited his arsenal in the cab, but an extra shilling deflected the man's curiosity, so that Meredith was soon dropped off within sight of Westminster, from which landmark he hoped to retrace his steps to the decaying house by the river, Darnley's den. His hunter's instincts served him well, and he walked directly to that unholy quarter and found the place, as sinister and forbidding as he remembered it. Shouldering the shotgun and taking the opposite side of the street so as to possess a broad field of fire, he moved slowly toward the house. There was no certainty that Darnley was even nearby so long after moonrise, but this was where the search must begin, and so Meredith crept quietly up to the gaping doorway.

The moon was masked behind a light cover of clouds and drifting snowflakes, and a soft, milky whiteness suffused the entire scene with an ethereal air. Meredith passed over the threshold cautiously, almost tenderly, and walked around and about the scattered refuse of the passage, moving with the light, steady tread of a man in the woods, choosing each step carefully, conscious of every noise and cognizant of the slightest breeze blowing through the halls. He arrived at the stairs, and here he had his first truly anxious moments, for it was impossible to ascend that ancient stairway without causing the floorboards to scream with every footfall. It seemed that surprise was not a luxury he could rely upon. With a sharp breath to steady his legs, he raced upwards, two and three steps at a time, burst into the upper room panting heavily, his gun raised, and scanned to left and right for any sign of life.

The room was still. Meredith quickly placed his back to a wall and began to scrape his way about the perimeter of the place. The light was not so good as it had been that previous night, and he found himself relying more on his sense of hearing to guide him as he inched along, when his foot stepped into something wet and slippery. He crouched down and touched a hot, soft, sticky mass that he recognized at once. Meredith's stomach churned violently at the discovery. He took a match from the pocket of his coat and struck it against the rough sole of his shoe. The flame flared brightly for a second, shocking his eyes, and then subsided into a steady glow. What it illuminated was a figure, a youthful face with a look of pristine peace, and a torso that had been mangled and devoured until it was a misshapen clod of flesh, bone and blood. Meredith's breath came in short pants as he tried to keep himself from retching. It was the boy, of course, the one who had brought him there.

Dipping his hand into one of the scores of wounds that covered what was left of the lad's body, he detected only a slight warmth, enough to assure him that Darnley had slain the boy almost the instant the moon was up. He rose and looked in the flickering matchlight at the abandoned room. Meredith heaved a great, relieved sigh at the thought that he was alone in that house. Yet he knew that he had lost his first, best chance.

It was out now. The monster was roaming the streets of the city.

Darnley's dream of a world of his own kind had begun. Meredith made his way back down the stairs, moving as safely as he could through the dangerous passage. When he reached the street at last, he turned and began a methodical inspection of the ground surrounding the outer walls. The snow was still dusting the earth, and before long he saw what he hoped and dreaded to see: the prints of the beast outside a shattered window. They led off beside the river, toward the thickest part of the city. Meredith knew that the hunt must continue now without cease until it was resolved. He broke away onto Darnley's trail and into the ghostly pallor of the night, with the snow falling in wild flurries and windblown eddies. He didn't pause to consider his best course of action. There, in the new-fallen snow, Meredith followed the huge footprints of the creature. He was oblivious to everything but this one sign, proof that he had the scent of the monster. He ran like a madman, armed for destruction, dashing through the streets of London, stooping occasionally to inspect the ground before him. All of his senses were immersed in these tracks and the thing to which they led.

Darnley had set out on a path that took him along the river, but in a zigzagging course that stayed away from the lighted streets, and edged along the shadowy alleys, the close walks between the houses, and even over fences and through gardens and yards. Meredith quickly saw that he couldn't keep up with Darnley's mad pace, that he had to dart about, off and on the trail, but he continued as long as he could, until the falling snow that blessed his first pursuit now thwarted him by falling more heavily still, and obscuring the signs of the monster's passing. He came at last to a place near the river where an alley opened up onto a small courtyard from which two other streets exited, and he watched as the final footprint blew away before his eyes. There was no means of knowing which way Darnley had taken, and he was forced to admit the chase could not go on.

Meredith stood looking like a fool, bereft of any hope, paralyzed by despair. "What can I do now?" he groaned to himself, anguished by the thought of what might lie ahead for the world. "It's out there, prowling in the darkness, but where? The city is so vast and time so dear." He looked overhead at the clouds as they rushed past the lu-minescent moon, and he prayed.

If there were an answer to this riddle, if Darnley could be found, the solution lay in the journal, Darnley's journal. Meredith knew as much, but what of it? What had Darnley done before that might lead him to understand his intention now? But he had no intention. He was always so adamant about that—no premeditated plan, only the desire of the moment. And then an idea came to him. "What does he desire at this moment?" Meredith wondered. Of course, Darnley had told him what it was, to transform the entire city of London into a city of werewolves. And to do that, he had wanted a crowd, some important gathering into which he could carry his curse. Not just any crowd, either, but the most highly placed people in society. "People of prominence," Meredith recalled the words. But where could Darnley hope to find anything like that at this late hour?

And once more in this mad night's adventure, the chimes gave him their answer. The myriad bells of the city rang the three-quarters in their sing-song melody, but underneath these and close by came the less regular sound of the bells of Westminster Abbey, calling the faithful to Christmas mass at midnight, the congregation promising to include the most aristocratic and powerful men in the empire. Meredith set off again, faster now and more frantic, for he knew that seconds could not be spared.

He was forced to stop once he came within sight of the towers of Westminster, however. It wouldn't do to approach such a singular company with gun in hand. The scene before him looked blissfully calm. A parade of carriages was pulling up to the curb and discharging its gaily attired occupants in their furs and finery. The bells continued their sweetly raucous pealing, festive carolers to the Yuletide celebra-tion. All seemed as peaceful as any Christmas morning could hope to be. And yet, somewhere nearby, the werewolf was stalking the night, perhaps was even there already, looking on from the depths of some dismal alcove. At least, Meredith hoped it was, for that was his only chance to put an end to this horror.

He had an expansive space to cover in the street before Westminster Abbey, was standing now at the open end of a dark lane across from and just to one side of the north tower. He glanced about to find a more propitious vantage point from which to conduct his watch, and decided upon a wide storefront about another twenty yards farther along the street. It sat back slightly in shadow, elevated some three feet above the pavement with a walkway in front and a railing which afforded good cover, providing a more dominating view of the square. Staying close to the walls and concealing his weapons as best he could in the folds of his cloak, Meredith moved cautiously along until he was settled within the security of this shallow recess.

Now there was only the waiting to be done. The snow had ceased to fall so thickly, drifting down in tiny flakes that stung like freezing rain where they struck his face. He pulled his collar more tightly up about his ears and, laying the gun beside him and bringing his rifle to a ready, comfortable position, he scanned back and forth over the street and the pavement before the Abbey. From where he crouched, he could see both the west facade and the entire north face. It had to be only a few minutes until midnight, for the crowd was growing thicker and he could hear the choir within as it entertained the assemblage with a Christmas chorale.

The music and the chimes and the roll of the passing wheels as they displaced the mud of the streets and the steady, snow-muffled hoofbeats of the animals as they trooped past presented the very image of tranquillity, and Meredith began to feel almost ludicrous sitting where he was, rifle poised amid the serenity of this scene. He was lulled into a sense of soothing normalcy, as if the events of the past month had all been a terrible dream, and the bells in the belfry above were only now rousing him from his troubled sleep. Overhead, the clouds continued their hurried race across the face of the moon, and for a moment Meredith actually convinced himself that he was the lunatic, and this was his own mad fantasy as he waited in the cold and wet for something that did not really exist.

And then he saw it. Close to him, far closer than he expected. Some sixty yards away, coming out of an alley farther down the street, he caught the glimpse of something, perhaps the glint of an eye as it reflected the flickering streetlamps nearby, or a shining snout as it moved out of the shadows for an instant and then disappeared again. Meredith raised his rifle quickly and took aim, but he could make out nothing else in the blackness of the spot. He held still, waited for some motion that would confirm what he thought he had seen. Nothing followed, and yet he could not be sure that he had been deceived, the alley was so dark. He feared to glance away, but he knew that he couldn't let himself become preoccupied with phantom targets when so much was at stake. Just as he was about to relax his aim, the clouds parted and the moon shined down, illuminating the entire scene in a pale, ghostly light. The shadows were dispersed, and there it was, visible now in the alley, not crouched as if ready to spring, but standing boldly, glancing up and down the street, looking for some likely victim amid the sumptuous choices offered to it.

It had not seen him, did not know it was being stalked as it stalked its own prey. The time was right. The moment had come. Yet Meredith could take but a single shot, only one chance to finish this insane affair, and it was not there, not yet. A lamppost, the shadows, the blowing snow, a thousand little things caused his judgment to question the certainty of the thing, and he lowered the rifle, moving out from his cover to find a better shot. His eyes never left the creature as it stood, defiant against the night. Meredith moved toward the cathedral, placed himself almost directly between Darnley and the crowds of the faithful, full out in the open. It was as if he were invisible there, kneeling now, raising the rifle once more.

He leaned forward and took aim. But as he brought his sight upon its head, the creature turned and looked on him. Across the distance their eyes met, and Meredith's finger faltered on the trigger. What did he see there, in the gaze of the beast? It was Darnley himself, staring out at Meredith as from a great, deep hole, observing him across an inhuman gulf, looking at him with the same disdainful look he'd given him so often. They were transfixed, one by the other, frozen in a second of time that was an eternity. Then slowly, his hungry eyes never releasing Meredith from their gaze, Darnley moved out of his hiding place, crept forward, slowly, stealthily, directly towards him.

Without a thought Meredith heard a rifle shot erupt through the ringing of the chimes, and a corner of brick exploded in the wall inches above Darnley's ears. He had fired, and he had missed. With a snarl Darnley leapt to the attack. Meredith tried to place another bullet in the chamber, but his numbed fingers fumbled with the cartridge and the rifle fell to the ground. He spun around and looked back, back to the niche where he had left the shotgun. He heard the soft padding of Darnley's pursuit behind him as he raced for the weapon, his feet slipping in the wet snow, stumbling, running now with his arms, his hands, clawing the air to reach the gun, there on the walk before the storefront. He could hear the slathering pant of Darnley's breath, just as his fingers reached around the almost frozen barrel of the piece. Meredith spun about again and slipped on the icy street, falling with a grunt to the ground, and he felt the breeze of Darnley's massive form as it sailed over his head to land beyond him.

The monster turned and snarled at him as he lay there, the muzzle of the gun poised idly to one side. They confronted each other in that instant, the werewolf's tongue tasting Meredith's fear in the air. In his eyes, those cunning, human eyes, Meredith saw all the madness and hatred that had consumed his friend.

But now the crowd was alerted, and Meredith heard cries and shouts of alarm coming up behind them. Darnley was distracted, for the briefest moment glanced away over his shoulder, allowing Meredith to bring the shotgun to bear. The glint of a light off the barrel caught Darnley's eye, and before another instant passed he was gone, bolting off into the shadows, to wait for another opportunity.

Meredith had no time to consider what to do. The crowd would soon be upon him, standing alone in the snow, no monster to prove his story, only the recently fired rifle in the street and the gun in his arms. He ran. To save himself he followed Darnley's tracks, printed anew in the snow, weaving this way and that, about streets and alleyways, leaving the sounds of the people far behind him. Before long the snow hid the trail once more, and Meredith was left alone in earnest, with only his failure for company. Darnley had been thwarted, yes, but he was still alive, still stalking the night, and there was no telling where he might turn up next. All chance was gone at last.

Still, it was hours before Meredith allowed himself to give up all hope. He wandered the streets in the darkness searching for any sign of Darnley's passing, the least scrap of a clue that might set him on the scent again. There was nothing. The snow obliterated all. The hunt was over, and now the nightmare was renewed.

He staggered home at last in the gray light of an overcast dawn. The streets were yet silent and empty, muffled in a quilt of white. The only footprints in the snow belonged to the lamplighters as they made their rounds, extinguishing the streetlamps one by one, proclaiming the night at an end. Meredith walked through the door of his home and rested his gun in a corner of the foyer. Elizabeth had not slept all that night, and she rushed out now from the parlor, without speaking a word clasped Meredith in her arms as though she might never let him go again.

"Thank God!" she whispered over and over. "Thank God, you're all right!" Meredith stood there, his arms draped limply about her, too tired and crushed to return much of her love just yet. At last, her cheek still pressed against his, she asked, "Is he dead?"

Meredith could not answer, could not even shake his head to acknowledge his failure. Elizabeth pulled away from him and looked into his face, and there she saw it written as clearly as upon a blank page. Darnley was alive.

She drew him into the parlor, sat him down and made him tell the whole, awful tale. The scant consolation they were able to take from it was that no one was hurt, save that pathetic boy. Darnley's plans had been thwarted. Yet he was still out there, still plotting and scheming, still ready to spread his madness throughout the world.

"Don't worry, my love," she said to him, taking his head in her arms and smoothing his brow. "We shall try again next month."

"Next month?" Meredith cried in despair, sitting upright and burying his head in his hands. "How can we hope to do anything next month? We don't know where to begin looking now. He might be anywhere. Holed up in some alley or living among the poor creatures down by the river. The city's too large and he's too cunning to allow us a second chance."

"We can't give up, Charles," she said sternly. "We've got to keep trying."

"But there's no hope! None! Do you understand that?" At last, the cloud of despair that had been creeping slowly through his soul overwhelmed Meredith. All seemed black about him, without a single, flickering spark that might dispel the shadows. Darnley had won and was only waiting now to enjoy his victory.

Suddenly, the two were startled by a crash from inside the house, glass shattering and spraying somewhere hard by. Elizabeth cried in surprise, but Meredith somehow knew what it meant, and he rushed into the foyer.

For a moment, he stood there alone. No one else was in the house that might come to his aid. Then, slowly, the study door opened across from him and Darnley stepped through. He moved almost casually, as though he were an invited guest, and a slight smile played across his lips. He was dressed in rags, filthy workman's clothes shredded and stained with blood that told a fearful tale, and his face was smeared with the gore of his last victim. In his hands, he held the hunting knife, the one Elizabeth had used before to drive him off.

"Hello, Merry," he said, balancing the knife in his hands, testing its weight. "What lovely toys you leave lying about." Meredith looked quickly into the corner where his gun lay propped. Darnley saw the glance and shook his head. "No, I shouldn't try it if I were you. I'm faster than you, and stronger. You see," he continued, patting his leg, the one that had been shattered, "I'm all better."

"What do you want?" Meredith demanded, trying to keep his voice steady.

"What do I want?" Darnley repeated in disbelief. "I want to kill you, of course."

"But why, Darnley?" Meredith pleaded, less for himself than for the man who had been his friend. "You don't have to do this terrible thing. We can still try to help you. Why go on with this nightmare?"

Darnley's eyes narrowed to mere slivers of darkness. "*Why?*" he spat out. "Because I can. Because reasons don't matter and you've been in my way long enough. I tried, Merry, to make you see, to get you to join me. But you wouldn't have it. You failed the test."

Meredith saw his entire world going out, being extinguished in a blackness too deep for any light to penetrate, an insanity too profound for reason ever to reach. "You're a monster," he declared simply, firmly, as a final statement upon these last mad moments. "You're more of a monster now in the daylight than you ever were at the full of the moon. It's not the wolf that's caused this. There's some madness in you."

"A monster, am I?" Darnley laughed. "My God, we're all of us monsters, Merry! The world is peopled with monsters! Are you just now getting that? Millions of monsters creeping across the face of the earth every day and every night! And what would you do? Would you rid the world of us? Would you kill all the monsters?"

"No," came a voice from out of the shadows of the parlor. "Just you." Elizabeth stepped forward, the pistol she had kept near her all night raised in both her hands, and she fired. But she had never fired a weapon before, and her first two shots missed, striking the wall behind Darnley. He crouched low and dove off to the right. She fired a third time, and the bullet caught him in the side. Darnley slid along the floor and clutched the wound, but it seemed to only fuel his madness. "God-damned bitch!" he howled as he got to his feet. She fired again and again, and one of the shots grazed past his shoulder, sending him to the ground once more. But his eyes never left her, and the hatred there burned more fiercely than ever.

Meredith awoke now as from a doze. He saw Darnley readying himself to strike, knew that Elizabeth had but a single bullet left. He leapt for the shotgun in the corner, grasped the barrel in his hand, spun about, frantically fumbling for the triggers. Darnley's entire body was coiled to spring, the knife set to be buried in Elizabeth's side.

"No!" Meredith shouted, and Darnley looked at him now, staring into the implacable blackness of the gun barrels. For a moment, the certainty of the outcome could be read upon his face. Then, with a horrible scream, he leapt through the air at Meredith. Elizabeth fired, but the report of the pistol was buried in the explosion of the shotgun as Meredith emptied both barrels full in Darnley's face. The sudden recoil sent Meredith into the wall behind him, and halted Darnley's flight in midair. He slumped to the ground, a faceless creature spilling hot blood over the cold marble floor.

Elizabeth stood motionless for an instant, then raced to Meredith's side and threw herself upon him, giving vent at last to a flood of tears. Meredith only stood there, hugging tenaciously to his wife, letting her tears melt into him.

Not until later, after the body had been taken away and Inspector Ash appeared with his officers and constables, did Meredith feel any strong emotion well up inside him. And then, it was just anger that the business should take so long to conclude.

"Now, as I understand it," the inspector repeated, referring to his notebook, "this fellow in rags here burst through the French doors of your study and found that knife lying there."

"Yes," Meredith answered wearily, "whatever sounds right to you, Inspector."

Ash looked askance at this, but let it pass. "He next attacked you and the lady, and the two of you defended yourselves in the only way you could. Lucky to have such an arsenal at hand," he added wryly.

"Inspector," Meredith said, eager for the whole thing to end, but equally eager, just once, to speak the truth, "we both know what happened here, don't we?"

Ash sighed and flipped through his notebook again. "What happened here is what I enter on these pages, Mr. Meredith."

"Of course," Meredith answered, but as the inspector was finishing his investigation and ushering his men out the door, Meredith stopped him with a final question. "Tell me, Inspector, are you going to search for the beast again? I understand it was sighted last night."

The inspector made no reference to his notebook this time. "No, sir. I believe that business is finally over." And with that, he left.

It was Christmas day, and a hazy light lay over the city. Elizabeth had already gone off to sleep, a thankful rest after days of uneasy slumber. With the servants safely returned now, and Eugenie back in the nursery, Meredith joined his wife in their bed. Yet, in spite of his profound weariness, he found that he could not rest. Perhaps it was the light filtering in through the bed curtains, or the still lingering excitement of what had passed. But whenever Meredith tied to sleep, the image of Darnley stared into him with his animal cunning, haunted his dreams, his thoughts. It prowled about the edges of his consciousness and stalked him whenever he would close his eyes.

And in the nights that followed, Darnley would return to glare at him still, with the dark, sinister look that recognized in Meredith— what? The man he appeared to be? Or the beast buried deep within, kept always at bay, waiting only for release, that release which Darnley had found, to wreak calamity upon the world?

Epilogue

hitby sat across from Meredith silently as the older gentleman finished his tale and lowered his head. He could not tell whether this appearance of fatigue was from exhaustion or simply resignation, the accomplishment of an act held in abeyance for so long and which now could be left behind as a thing finished. They remained that way for many minutes, until at last Meredith looked up and spoke in an emotionless voice.

"I don't care, I think, whether you believe what I have told you or not. It's only important to me that I have told it. The story is now yours to do with as you like." So saying, he slid the pages of the manuscript once again into the ornate box and, locking it shut with the key, placed it on the little table beside Whitby. Then he rose, stretching himself, in some pain from having sat for so long, and walked across the room to where his coat hung on a peg. Taking it down, Meredith prepared to leave.

"What am I to do with this?" Whitby asked in dismay as he stared at the box, his voice cracking from the dryness in his throat.

Meredith did not answer at once, but crossed over to the hearth where a few embers still glowed and made a move as if to take the box and throw it on the fire.

"No!" Whitby exclaimed, grasping it to him to protect it.

"Whatever you think best," Meredith said. "It matters little to me now. I have done what I came to do. The thing is over for me, and you can make whatever use of it that you see fit. Burn it or publish it. Tell it to your friends at the club. It's yours, after all." Then, after a pause, he added, "I only make one request. Don't reveal anything that I have told you until I'm dead. That, I think, will not be long now. I am dying and am not likely to live to see this next summer arrive." He spoke this death sentence upon himself calmly, as if he were quite accustomed to the idea and it was now only old news. "After that, you're free to dispose of the story to anyone you care to. All of the principals will then be gone."

Meredith turned to leave, but before he did so, Whitby called him back. "What shall you do?" he asked.

Meredith stood silently looking at the young man for a time. "I have no one left in the world," he said at last. "My Elizabeth is gone, and little Eugenie passed on many years ago. I am an old man alone in the world, and I am dying. That gives me something you can't grasp. I have freedom. There is no one now to whom I owe anything, not even myself." He motioned toward the box held in the younger man's arms. "I don't even owe myself that anymore. Still I'm weary of this world, weary of its darkness and despair. I think I'll likely go on as I have done these many years, and await my welcome sentence of reprieve."

Meredith turned again to leave, but paused and, with his back to Whitby, said, "By the way. I have not congratulated you. I heard earlier that your father had passed away. I know how dearly you looked forward to the news. Farewell, Darnley." And with that, he went out the door, leaving the young lord behind him with the tale.